Beneath Hallowed Ground

A Modern Novel

Steven P. Locklin

grey gecko press

Published by Grey Gecko Press, Katy, Texas.

www.greygeckopress.com

Printed in the United States of America

Design by Grey Gecko Press

Illustration / cover art by Nathan Morimitsu & Staci Reed

Library of Congress Cataloging-in-Publication Data
Locklin, Steven P.
Beneath hallowed ground / Steven P. Locklin
Library of Congress Control Number: 2012950916
ISBN 978-1-9388211-8-9
10 9 8 7 6 5 4 3 2 1
First Edition

For Mari,

*For all the usual reasons, but also
because your words tell beautiful stories*

"…in a larger sense, we cannot dedicate — we cannot consecrate — we cannot hallow — this ground. The brave men, living and dead, who struggled here, have consecrated it far above our poor power to add or detract."

Chapter One

Present Day
July 21

T he rain hurled down in a blinding sheet, reminding Jason Sparks what a weathered Conch fisherman had once told him—a tropical rain drenches a body down to the soul. At the time, Sparks had thought that the man's wisdom had welled from a rum bottle, but now he began to understand.

Cursing his circumstances, he made his way along the poorly lit pathway from the parking lot to the beach condominium, trying not to stumble into the intruding palmetto bushes. The walk had lasted only a few minutes, but he already felt like he had fallen into his hotel pool back in Fort Myers. The officer ahead of him paused for a moment and pointed to the darkened mass that had to be the condo. The officer said not a word and hurried back to the dry patrol car.

It must normally be a nice job for a police officer, working on Sanibel Island. Lying a couple miles off the southwest coast of Florida, connected by a causeway, the island was a curious blend of expensive bungalows, hotels, houses, and tourist shops, all carefully blended into a landscape of beaches and wildlife marshlands. This exotic piece of the deep Caribbean was just a short drive from the T-shirt/bathing-suit culture of Fort Myers Beach. It was a great place to visit and do some shelling, sit in the sand, and dream away an afternoon.

Not a place you'd expect to be viewing a dead body during a thunderstorm.

Sparks circled the condo—this unit was a separate building, more like a little bungalow—toward the Gulf side and came upon three men working around the body, covered in a tarp, in a patio area illuminated by temporary lights. The rain, caught in the light, sparkled like ice.

"Someone here named Johnson?" Sparks had to half-shout his question over the roar of the rain.

"That'd be me." Johnson was a slight man, despite the rain gear he wore. "Are you Sparks?"

Sparks nodded.

Johnson motioned to the tarp and the two men walked over. Sparks lifted the corner.

The body belonged to a man in his forties, slightly balding, with a mustache. He looked to have been in pretty good shape, but his face was swollen and bruised. It wasn't difficult to figure out the cause of death. The knife slash stretched from one ear to the other and had cut clear through the windpipe and esophagus, nearly severing the head. There was little blood on the body—a good downpour had washed away the gore.

"You know him?" Johnson asked. The officer studied Sparks's face as they squatted over the body.

Sparks didn't answer the question. "Can we go inside and get out of the rain?"

Inside the bungalow, they shook off the water, and Johnson directed Sparks to an area the crew had already gone over. The rain was stronger now, the thunder more disconcerting.

"I'm Lieutenant Barry Johnson, Lee County Sheriff's Special Crime Unit." Johnson put aside his raincoat and then managed to extract a dry cigarette. "You have ID for me? And do you know who the guy out there is?"

"I had an appointment with a Mr. Drury for tomorrow," Sparks said, pausing as he showed Johnson his identification. "If that's him out there, I wouldn't know . . . never met him."

"The bureau places you out of Washington. What's your business in Southwest Florida?"

Sparks ran his hand through his hair. He suddenly felt tired. "I don't even know if it was official business or not," he replied. "I got a call yesterday from a guy identifying himself as Frank Drury. He knew who I was, knew I was an agent working as a special liaison with Treasury. He said he had information that could be worth millions of dollars to the government. Said he would only talk to me and would only talk here on Sanibel Island."

"That was enough to get you on a plane?" Half statement, half question.

"I went to college in Miami and still have friends and family there. I was going to swing down to see them and take a week of vacation."

Lightning flashed, followed immediately by a concussion blast of thunder from above the bungalow. The crew members crowded at the door, cursing and yelling that they weren't going to stay out there in the storm. Johnson waved them in. Then he turned back to Sparks. "Millions of dollars? He wasn't any more specific than that?"

"I would have said so if he was. He refused to be specific, insisted I meet him here tomorrow. I flew in this afternoon, checked into the hotel I told him I'd be at, and figured I would hear from him in the morning. Then I got your call . . . . how did you find out about me?"

Johnson moved to a handsome mahogany table against the window. It stood out in the bungalow's teal décor and looked like a favorite piece brought from somewhere else. "Your name and room number at the hotel were prominently displayed here on the top page of his appointment book. At least, I assume it was Drury's."

"You've got a positive ID on him?" Sparks asked.

"His driver's license, credit cards, and passport, as well as other incidental things in here, suggest that this place was his. We're still early in the investigation. Hell, we've only been here for an hour." Johnson held out Drury's address book for Sparks to see. "But whoever killed him was very neat about it, other than the method. The room was searched—very methodically. The only things you can tell might be missing are some pages from this book. Drury evidently kept it as a notebook as well. No smartphone or laptop around."

Johnson was right on that assessment. Many of the book's other pages had been taken. In fact, aside from the page with Sparks's name on it, there were only three other pages with writing on them at all.

"Any valuables taken?" Sparks asked.

"Not that we can tell so far," Johnson said. "Wallet is empty, but the bungalow wasn't ransacked."

"Professionals. They were after something," Sparks said. "Who found the body?"

"A couple on their honeymoon came walking by on the beach and decided to cut through the property. They found the body around dusk. Can't tell for sure yet until we have an autopsy, but I don't think he was dead too long. The rain started in heavy right at dusk."

One of the officers approached Johnson, giving Sparks an opportunity to walk around the bungalow. The three-room unit sat by itself, away from the other ones, separated by heavy vegetation.

Inside, except for the mahogany desk he had already seen, the bungalow was furnished in the typical light-colored, cool material so often seen in these vacation places.

Against the far wall in the bedroom was a work desk of modern design with a computer screen and a keyboard, and a bookcase. The books were exclusively historical. Sparks sat down at the desk and suddenly realized that there was no computer to turn on.

"You could have asked permission." Johnson was in the doorway and his tone was clearly one of annoyance. "You're lucky this was the first room we worked, or I'd be kicking your ass."

"Sorry. You notice something out of place here?"

"Uh, yeah . . .. . . you think?" Johnson said.

"Someone took all his files and then decided to be safe and took the whole damn computer for good measure," Sparks said under his breath.

"And there's something else . . ." Johnson added as he glanced pointedly at the desk.

"I've already noticed it," Sparks said. "There are no disks or memory sticks, either. Someone took everything he had backed up."

Johnson was done with Sparks after another half hour of questions. Still, he asked for Sparks's vacation itinerary and phone numbers. The storm had moved onshore, so the rain and wind had died down by the time Sparks got back to his car, parked on the main road. The deputy who had showed him the way to the bungalow was still in his cruiser with the interior light on. Most of the drive back from the island, across the causeway, and into Fort Myers found Sparks wondering about the circumstances of the murder.

Why would Drury—apparently some kind of historian—pick him out of the entire U.S. Treasury Department to call about some information? Someone must have given him Sparks's name, since he had asked for him specifically. Drury's urgency and his statement that the information was worth a large amount of money to the federal government were intriguing.

Approaching Fort Myers on San Carlos Boulevard, Sparks caught up to the lightning, rain, and wind of the storm cell that had just left Sanibel. With the lateness of the hour, there wouldn't be much parking close to the hotel, which meant a long, wet walk from his car.

His thoughts turned to his family in Miami. He looked forward to seeing them.

A few minutes later, he reached the hotel near the Southwest Florida International Airport. The rain had reached the same intensity he had experienced on the island, and just as he had expected, he had to park on the outskirts of the lot.

With his raincoat collar turned up, Sparks headed along the path that ran next to the lot and through elaborately landscaped grounds, branching off to the pool area one way, the tennis courts another, and a third way to the hotel. The entrance at the end of the path, accessed by room key card, was closer than the hotel's main lobby.

The rain was deafening and Sparks walked briskly. A flash of movement out of the corner of his eye caught his attention as he came around a bend in the tree line. Moments later, a splash broke through the din of the rain. In an instant—the millisecond it takes for an image to flash through a mind—Sparks thought of Drury, his throat cut from ear to ear. Sparks's body tensed ahead of his conscious thought as an arm wrapped around his throat.

I'm not gonna let him slit my *throat! Back right, under the rib cage! Move now!*

The figure pressed against Sparks's side and wrapped a leg around his. Sparks threw his arm back with all the force he could muster and was met halfway by the striking arm of the figure. He snapped his head back into the face of his attacker.

They staggered apart, and Sparks swung around to face his assailant. The black shape was covered in shadow, but made no effort to run or hide his presence. He crouched low with the knife still in his right hand, turned up.

A single profane word came from the dark, and the shape lunged at Sparks. The knife swung up from below.

Hand to the arm! Block!

Sparks could tell he had the advantage in strength and quickness as he gripped the killer's arm. *Killer.* His mind raced. He had little doubt that this was the man responsible for Drury's death. The two of them were locked arm-in-arm, muscles straining against each other. Though the other man's face was inches from his own, Sparks didn't look at it, instead concentrating on turning the knife arm out and away from his body.

Turn it away . . . he's concentrating on the knife . . . a little longer . . . now!

With all the effort his adrenaline-charged body could muster, Sparks shifted his weight to his left leg and thrust his knee into the area of the killer's groin. The knife arm immediately relaxed as the attacker gasped in pain and fell back onto the grassy slope.

Sparks staggered from the sudden loss of force against him. He readied himself for another assault. The man struggled to his feet, far from incapacitated. Sparks pulled his wet coat off and risked a quick glance both ways down the path.

They were alone.

Did the killer still have the knife?

The answer came as the man assumed a stalking stance with the knife again in his right hand. Sparks figured that the killer had realized that his target was more dangerous than he'd first thought. Suddenly, the other man lunged—not with the knife, but instead going straight for Sparks's legs.

The force of the blow was lessened by a quick side step, but Sparks still took enough of a hit to throw him back into the mud beside the path. The man threw his shoulder into Sparks and brought his arm up, preparing to strike. On his back, with the man's arm against his throat, Sparks knew the blow was coming and with every bit of strength he could find, he lifted the man up as the blow came down.

The man fell to the side.

Sharp pain . . . burning.

"Hey! What the hell's going on?" The shout came from the direction of the hotel.

Despite the pain, Sparks turned toward the four shapes standing about a hundred feet away and then moved to face his attacker. "I'm a federal agent, call the police now," he yelled.

The killer slipped into the shadows in the direction of the parking lot.

"Hey, are you all right?" asked a youthful man, who was now standing over Sparks, along with his three companions. Two were women. "Come on, let's go after that guy, Travis."

"No . . . don't," Sparks said. "Help me up."

Once on his feet, Sparks ran along the path to the hotel, but veered left as it closed in on the parking lot. Cutting through the tree line, Sparks reached the lot in time to see a dark sedan accelerate through the area.

His attacker was gone.

The kids approached cautiously from behind. "No way to get a plate?" asked the first one.

Rainwater streaming down his face, Sparks's thoughts screamed through his head as he fought to catch his breath. The burning along his left side remained.

There was a sharp intake of breath from one of the women. "God, you're bleeding."

Sparks looked down to see his shirt saturated in red along the entire left side. Nausea swept through him.

Johnson pulled apart the crumpled, bloody shirt, discarded on the hospital gurney, and looked at the slash in its side. "He was trying to go up underneath your rib cage," Johnson said. "Fortunately for you, it was more of a glancing slash."

He turned to face Sparks, who sat on the edge of a nearby bed in the emergency ward. A resident and a nurse were applying tape to the bandage while Sparks held up his left arm, but the action didn't come without considerable pain. "You want to tell me now what this is all about, or am I going to have to call Washington and get your boss to give you a lesson on federal-local relations and how you should help the sheriff's deputies of Lee County?"

Sparks shook his head and sucked in his breath as another layer of tape was placed on his side. "He was a pro, and it's obvious he's the same guy who did Drury. I believe in coincidences, but this is more than a stretch."

"A pro that uses a knife instead of a gun?" Johnson said.

"You would think a knife wouldn't be the weapon of choice. It's not one hundred percent effective—I'm living proof of that. It's messy and requires close contact." Sparks paused. "This guy uses a knife because he likes it."

"All the more reason to help me," Johnson said. "What's going on here?"

"This isn't about need-to-know crap or anything like that, Johnson. I simply don't know what Drury was all about. But it's obvious someone thinks that Drury and I were a lot better acquainted than we were."

"Or that you have or knew about something he had at the bungalow."

"That's clear," Sparks said as he gingerly put on a new shirt Johnson had brought. "Have you got a safe house I could stay at for tonight? I'll go back for my things in the morning. I didn't come prepared to fight off evildoers."

"No gun?" Johnson asked.

"I *was* going on a vacation after this little detour."

Johnson tossed the bloody shirt to Sparks. "Vacation's over. Something weird is going on here. Watch your back."

Chapter Two

September 23, 1862

Jackson Prescott eased his solid frame into the black coach and sat facing forward. The horseman started the animal off smartly from in front of the hotel and moved into the flow of traffic. The ride to the Executive Mansion would only take a few minutes, and Prescott needed every second to collect his thoughts.

He didn't know the reason for his summons, which had come in the early morning, barely fourteen hours ago. A messenger from Secretary of State Seward's office had brought word of a meeting that would be held at 3 p.m. between Prescott, Seward, and the president. The messenger had been plain in his delivery—Prescott was to speak to no one before the meeting. A carriage would pick him up from in front of the hotel half an hour beforehand.

Why was he being brought to Lincoln? Could it have something to do with his personal heritage? Born in Boston, Prescott's father had moved the family to Charleston, South Carolina, in 1840 and worked as an import-exporter. His late uncle had built up the business, but had had no other heirs to leave it to, so in the end, Prescott's father had inherited it. Rather than sell the business, Prescott's father had worked to expand its influence in Charleston, specializing in cotton exports and manufactured goods coming in from Europe.

Prescott, though raised in the South, had been taught firmly from the beginning not to forget his New England heritage and to be proud of it, despite the taunts of other schoolchildren as he'd grown up. He'd been sent home to Cambridge—across the Charles River from Boston—to attend Harvard, and afterward, he had returned to South Carolina.

It was when he had returned home that the conflict with his father had begun. Prescott had found that his father had hardened. The business had grown ever more prosperous, and greed had festered in his father. The rift between the two became unbridgeable seven years ago when his father announced to the family over dinner that the business would be expanding yet again with a new venture—brokering trade for Negro slaves.

"You would turn the family's business into the very filth you used to disdain?" Prescott had said.

"I have decided this is an excellent opportunity, Jack," his father had said, his voice edged in ice. "There's much money to be made with our associations. It's a dirty business, but competition is forcing me to make this decision. The pressure is too great not to expand our interests."

"Our interests?" Prescott's words slashed at his father. "The importation has been illegal for years, and you'll bring shame to us all. With a simple statement, you declare to the world what our family stands for, and I, for one"—he glanced at his two sisters—"will not become a part of it. You've brought an outdated, disgusting, vile institution to our doorstep."

"A doorstep that you still benefit from, Jackson," the elder Prescott said. "The matter isn't up for further discussion, and I'll not have you upsetting the family."

Prescott rose from his seat and threw his napkin into his chair. "That situation will presently be remedied."

Prescott left the house that night for the final time. He did speak to his father on one more occasion, but the discussion followed the same path. Prescott's final reply to his father's financial reasoning was as simple as it was direct: his father would have to add the loss of a son to his financial ledger.

Now, seven years later, Prescott was traveling in a Washington carriage on his way to meet the president on a subject he knew nothing about, except that the original courier who had contacted him in Maryland had used the words "a matter of extreme importance to the Union."

The city was alive with the movements of the day as the carriage passed by the unfinished Capitol building. Prescott had overheard many people speaking at breakfast in the hotel's dining room about the startling news that had been announced the day before: the president intended to free the slaves now held in the Confederacy.

A bold political move, Prescott thought, but one that wouldn't hold weight unless the Union won the war, which now seemed in great doubt. George McClellan's troubles at the hands of Robert E. Lee in Sharpsburg just days ago provided Prescott with all the proof he needed that this was going to be a long war, and a long war meant the South might gain a permanent separation if Northern citizens didn't have the belly for a long fight. And Prescott was certain that they didn't.

That thought brought sadness, for his full title was Lieutenant Jackson Prescott, of the 12th Massachusetts, Army of the Potomac. And he had been there at Sharpsburg for the bloodiest day man had ever seen, near a creek called Antietam.

The carriage brought Prescott up to the mansion's main entrance. He stepped from it with his customary firmness. It was his way to keep his balance within—always show decisiveness. The Negro doorman gave a small smile to Prescott and motioned quietly for the lieutenant to follow.

"Are you sure you know where I'm supposed to go?" Prescott asked. "I haven't been introduced. I have no papers."

"Are you not Lieutenant Prescott?" the doorman asked in return.

"Of course, but . . ."

"That's all the information that's necessary, sir."

"Lead on."

There was singular lack of activity as they walked into the building. Prescott took special care to glance at the paintings and the fine furnishings.

As they turned a corner, they were met by a man of average height, dressed in a tailored suit of dark blue with a rumpled white shirt and a black cummerbund and matching tie. His longish hair hung over his ears, his face dominated by a pair of heavy eyebrows and a pronounced, authoritative nose.

Upon assessing the pair, he shuffled his papers and immediately took charge. "Ah, Lieutenant Prescott. You're just about as I imagined you would be from the descriptions I've heard of you. Came through the battle without injury?" The man extended his hand. "I'm William H. Seward."

"Mr. Secretary, I'm honored to meet you, sir," Prescott said, taking the man's hand. "As you might guess, this is my first visit here, and while the experience is worth the anxiety over the past fifteen hours, the reason for my being here still escapes me."

"All in good time, Lieutenant," Seward said, motioning for the doorman to leave. "The president is ready to see you now, and I'll join the two of you in a few minutes. He's up the stairs, down the hall on the right."

"Just go down on the right and walk in, no introduction?" Prescott asked.

"You'll find the president detests the formality of official meetings and relishes personal discussions best. He's preoccupied today, as you might expect. You have heard the news of his proclamation?"

"I have, indeed, sir."

"Fine, fine. Well, go ahead, then. I'll return in a few moments."

Prescott climbed the stairs and made his way down the corridor. There were sentries stationed in the hallway, but they let him pass without challenge. He stopped just short of the doorway to straighten his sleeves and refasten a button. Holding his hat before him—and thankful he had something to do with his hands—he walked into the room.

The office was furnished simply, with a table and seven chairs in the middle, and a separate desk facing the room with a high-backed chair. The walls were covered with maps and newspapers stacked high on the tables and desk. There were two large wicker baskets half-filled with debris, though there was much about that deserved similar placement.

A lone figure stood at the half-opened window, looking out over the grounds. His hands were behind his back. President Lincoln was tall, with chin whiskers and a darkness about the eyes. His clothes cried out for proper tailoring.

A creak in the floorboard announced Prescott's entrance.

"Lieutenant Jackson Prescott, 12th Massachusetts, reporting as ordered, sir." Prescott was surprised and pleased with the firmness of his voice.

"Lieutenant." Lincoln walked from the window and around the desk to Prescott. "Thank you for coming to see me immediately. But I think you'll understand the urgency once it has been made clear." He shook Prescott's hand with a strong grip and motioned for him to sit down. He then sat behind the desk.

"First, I'll let you know that I have a special duty the Union needs to have filled and your name came up specifically because of who you are, Lieutenant. These are dire times for our country, young man, and I hope what I'll be asking you to do is within your abilities and desires."

"As to my abilities, Mr. President, I am just as any man, but as to my desires, I have always felt that it was my duty to serve my country."

"I'm pleased to hear that, son, but I must ask you about your family and your ties to the South. The Prescott name is prominent in Mr. Davis's government. Your father was mentioned as a possible cabinet choice, and your family's ships have—I believe I'm being fair here—been associated with blockade runners this past summer. I would like to hear in your own words your feelings on this. From your commander, I heard that you have distinguished yourself more than once on the battlefield, but I would like to know your manner of mind about your place in the war."

"My father and I disagree on many things, sir, and I haven't spoken with him in more than six years," Prescott said. "He's spent the last six years as, among other ventures, a slave broker. When he entered that business, I chose to leave the family. I correspond with my mother and sisters alone."

"It requires a determined man to contradict his father on such an issue," Lincoln said. "I grieve for this country every day that this war continues. And I fear that it will continue for a very long time. But the end result, whether it comes next month, next year, or beyond, must be the preservation of the Union . . . no matter the cost."

"We shall win the war, sir, with willpower and courage," Prescott said, crossing his legs as he began to feel more comfortable.

Lincoln studied Prescott's face for a few seconds. "Yes . . . well, I do, indeed, hope you're correct, Lieutenant. Tell me about your background."

For the next few minutes, Prescott talked about growing up in South Carolina, but he was sure to point out that his family always stressed its New England roots. He talked about his love of the outdoors, his family that still lived in Charleston, and his military service. Finally, he touched on the horror of Antietam.

Lincoln stood and walked around the desk, pulling up a chair next to Prescott, who was surprised by the gesture but appreciative. He could understand now why Lincoln could charm common folk as well as people in power. He had a relaxed way about him, and Prescott, who always felt he was a good judge of men, could see there was much more to this man than the country bumpkin he had been portrayed as in newspaper editorials.

"Tell me, Lieutenant, do you feel General McClellan should have pursued Lee these past days? Do you feel there have been mistakes made during this campaign?"

"It's not my place to criticize my commanding officer, sir," Prescott replied.

"I respect your loyalty, but you didn't answer my question," Lincoln said, "but, then again, perhaps you did."

Seward entered the room and closed the door behind him. "Forgive me, Mr. President, Lieutenant—I had to send some notices off with the afternoon courier," he said, taking a chair on the other side of Prescott. "Have you started with the business at hand?"

"I was learning more about the lieutenant, though I believe Secretary Stanton's evaluation was very thorough," Lincoln said. "He's intelligent, appears resourceful, and his loyalty to the Union is strong."

"Evaluation? Secretary Stanton?" Prescott edged up in his seat. "Gentleman, I do feel privileged to meet you, but I desire to know why I've been brought here. Fifteen hours ago, I was with my unit. A courier comes in the middle of the night with a message from General McClellan's command ordering me to report to Washington. I'm taken by armed escort on a wild ride to a railroad depot and put on a lone train car behind a single engine, implying it was arranged entirely for me. Upon my arrival, I receive another order this morning to be brought here without an explanation as to why."

Lincoln motioned for Seward to explain.

"This is a perilous time for the Union," Seward said. "The Rebels are putting together a formidable resistance, and the war could become one where simple attrition will win the day. The blockade we have in place has been effective, but I'm sure you read the newspapers and hear the talk. The politics of war are often the most treacherous. As we speak, the Confederacy has two representatives in England and France working to garner favor with political or, possibly, material support. For the sake of our discussion, we'll concern ourselves only with the Confederate representative in England, James Mason."

"I read about him and the other in the newspapers," Prescott said. "They were detained off an English steamer . . ."

"The *Trent*," Lincoln said quietly.

"Yes, that's the ship. If I remember, they were released back in the winter."

"After careful negotiation," Seward replied. "Our own representatives in England have sent word of rumblings in the halls of Parliament. Continued Rebel success on the battlefield, a more drawn-out conflict, and we may fall prey to foreign intervention."

"Is this true? Could we be facing a fresh threat from Europe, sir?" Prescott asked.

"Even with General McClellan's tremendous victory last week notwithstanding." Lincoln's gaze was measured. Prescott thought he was still waiting for a response from the lieutenant on the question when they were alone.

"It's difficult to estimate the true danger, but we do know this . . ." Seward made sure he had Prescott's full attention. "We cannot afford for other influences to come to bear."

"And that's why you've come to me?" Prescott asked.

"You've heard of the gold strikes in the Colorado and Montana territories in the last years and months?" Seward said.

"Just what has been in the newspapers. There have been some discoveries, and there are the beginnings of a gold rush. Many prospectors are on the way to Western Montana territory."

Seward leaned forward in his chair. "We have some well-placed information that some Southern interests are determined to use gold from that area to finance their war effort, or at least give it away in return for military support. Do you know a man named Jameson Stallard?"

"Patriarch of the Stallard family," Prescott said. "They're a prominent family in South Carolina and Georgia. They've done business with my father, though I've met neither Mr. Stallard nor any of his family."

"The Stallard family has been involved with sympathizers out west in bringing a large shipment of gold to garner favor in Parliament. We don't know how much, how, or where they intend to ship it. They could take it down the Mississippi, unload it short of New Orleans, and try to go through Texas, or they could go through Canada—many sympathizers there—or they could try to get it through a northern port as contraband cargo." Seward stood and walked slowly around the room as he continued. "We had a man—a spy, if you like, though I hate the use of that word—who got us this information, but unfortunately, he has been lost."

"Lost?"

"He was killed in a skirmish outside Sharpsburg a few weeks ago," Lincoln said.

"We believe it was unrelated to his work on this gold-smuggling group," Seward added. "It was an accident of war. But it leaves us with little information to use. His last wire said he was going to Philadelphia to see a Mr. Cassias Fitzroy, a rather unusual name."

"'Fitzy'?" Prescott was stunned by the revelation.

"You know this man?" Lincoln didn't seem surprised.

"He was a business associate of my father's. He may live in Philadelphia, but his heart is with South Carolina. He was born and raised there. He and my father did business together for years before the war. He'd be the perfect man to help the Stallard organization."

"Well . . ." Lincoln paused. "It seems we have an opportunity here. Would you be willing to try to contact this organization and learn for us where and when they plan the first shipment, and give us the names of the people involved here in the North?"

"I'm flattered, sir, and honored, but I'm a simple soldier. I'm not trained in the manner of methods I believe would be necessary."

"Your colonel was quite complimentary," Seward said. "You have an enviable knack for staying alive in dangerous circumstances. We would be relying on that ability. The work in this business is dirty, even devilish, Lieutenant. Many men are being asked to go through hell every day to fight for something as simple as an idea. You yourself have done so. You've been through it, seen the elephant. Your tasks will be just as deceitful as is necessary. And you'll have to think quickly and make decisions on your own." Seward's voice rose with urgency. "We can't go in with regular personnel and arrest people. We won't get everyone involved, and more importantly, the gold might still leave the country. We need a complete list of the names, both here in the East and wherever the gold is out west."

"I still don't fully understand this," Prescott said. "At twenty dollars an ounce, how could they possibly move that much unprocessed gold out of the country to make it worth the interest of England or France?"

"Two things make it possible," Lincoln said. "Your predecessor's last wire said that the gold would be not gold ore, but processed gold. Close to pure and more easily transported, though that still must be a large problem for them to overcome. Railroad traffic is too unpredictable for a quiet operation and traveling by wagon would put them at the mercy of the winter snows and spring rains."

"And the second item?" Prescott asked.

"The final wire also said the source of the gold was the largest strike ever found. It's a mother lode. The inference there is that the source could be unlimited."

"Then take a brigade and find the strike and close it down," Prescott said.

"Without knowing the location, it could take months, and diverting resources out there would be difficult," Seward said.

"And in that time, the Union as we know it could cease to exist," Lincoln added quietly.

Seward sat down next to Prescott and looked at Lincoln, then at the lieutenant. "You could be ordered to do this, but the president and I feel you should have the choice. If you refuse, you'll be returned to your unit, no further questions asked. You'll be sworn to secrecy under the threat of court-martial. But there will be no record of this conversation, and there will be no official hindrance to your career because of your decision."

And with that, he finished. The two men stared at Prescott.

"And you must have a response at this time?" Prescott asked.

"Life's important paths are often chosen with little notice," Lincoln said.

Prescott nodded. He understood and was convinced of their need. "I accept."

Both men smiled and Seward slapped Prescott's knee. "That's my boy," he said. "That good New England stock. I'll take your leave for a moment and begin creaking the old wheel into motion."

He hurried from the room and left Prescott alone with Lincoln, who now leaned forward to make their discussion more intimate.

"There's an additional matter." Lincoln rose stiffly and moved to the open door. He glanced outside, then returned to his chair. "I must speak quickly to you. What we spoke of, about this group of men, was all true. But I must apologize, for there's another truth of which I didn't speak. And even the good secretary doesn't know this. The final message from our operative said the group was in communication with someone within this administration . . . a very important someone."

"Certainly not, sir!"

"One thing you would learn living here in Washington: the politics are as foul and fetid as the summer city. It seems I cannot rely on even my own cabinet, if I'm to believe the cryptic words of a dead man. The only men I truly trust are my own Mr. Nicolay and a gentleman you'll come to meet in a short while."

"Can there not be an official investigation, arrest the traitors?"

"Moving against them without clear proof would doom this administration politically." Lincoln shook his head. "And as much as I'll enjoy returning to practice law in Illinois, my country calls for my service as long as I'm able." He reached over and placed his hand on Prescott's shoulder. "Give me the name of the man, more if there are more than one, so we can cut out the sickness . . . or I fear the Union will be imperiled."

"I'll do my best, sir, but . . . there's one problem. Fitzroy knows my family, and he knows about my father and myself. I cannot go to him and expect him to believe I'm interested in helping the Confederacy. I'm sure he's aware of my rank and position."

Lincoln's face faded to melancholy. "We do have a remedy."

"And that would be . . . ?"

"To do a traitor's work, one must wear the coat of a traitor."

Chapter Three

Present Day
July 22

Sparks stepped from the sheriff's sedan, squinting at the sun's reflection off the hotel's vast glass exterior. July in South Florida was oppressive. A single step from an air-conditioned car or building and the humidity sucked one's breath away. Sparks immediately felt the perspiration on his forehead as he pulled his raincoat from the back seat. He thanked the driver and headed through the main entrance back into the main lobby's cooler surroundings.

Wearing his own sport coat, but with a shirt borrowed from Johnson, Sparks went to the front desk and inquired about any messages. There were two, one from the bureau—something about misplaced paperwork—and one from a rather forceful young woman in Cambridge, Massachusetts. In a demanding tone, she was asking why the hell—the hotel clerk had actually used the word—Sparks hadn't called to tell her he was stopping in Fort Myers on his way to Miami.

"Jennifer . . . Jennifer." Sparks smiled as he turned toward the elevators.

"Mr. Sparks," the clerk said. "There's another message. The concierge left a note saying he has something for you." She pointed over to the right front corner of the lobby.

The concierge's desk held a prominent position in the lobby. The man at the desk instantly drew respect from Sparks, for he was smartly dressed and groomed and carried a sophisticated air of competence. Just the sort of person one expected to hold this position at a four-star. Sparks approached the desk, wincing in pain from the slash wound in his side as he sidestepped a three-year-old running past him.

"Good morning, sir, can I help you?" asked the concierge with a cultured British accent. The picture was complete.

"The front desk said you had something for me. Jason Sparks."

"Yes, I do. I have a package that was dropped off for you yesterday morning. I apologize that you didn't receive it when you arrived, but the gentleman gave me explicit instructions to give it to you this afternoon . . . not when you checked in yesterday. May I see some identification, please?"

"That's strange."

"The identification?"

"No, the instructions," Sparks said, showing his driver's license.

"I thought so as well."

The package was a standard manila envelope sealed with tape. On the outside was Sparks's name, but nothing else. "Can you describe the man?"

"Late forties, I'd say . . . balding. He had wire-rimmed glasses. He did seem preoccupied and somewhat nervous."

"Nervous?"

"Yes. He looked around quite a bit." The concierge stopped for a moment to direct a bellhop in the direction of a large family trying to maneuver an overloaded luggage rack, then returned to Sparks. "I almost thought for a moment that he was asking me to hold on to something illegal, but he said he was afraid he would miss an appointment with you and that this was just a precaution. Everything's fine, I hope."

"Sure, thanks."

Everything wasn't fine. The concierge had just described Frank Drury.

Taking the elevator, Sparks scanned the people, then the hallway after he reached his floor. At his room, he pulled out the .38 caliber service-issued handgun that Johnson had loaned him and slid the card into the slot. A quick perusal of the room revealed nothing missing, and the room didn't appear to have been searched. The maids had not yet been there, and Sparks could tell that everything was where he had left it before his drive out to Sanibel Island.

Double-locking the door, Sparks sat on the edge of the bed and opened the envelope from Drury. The letter was typed, single-spaced, with narrower than normal margins—much like a college term paper would be set up.

Mr. Sparks,

I do so hate melodrama, but if you are reading this letter, then either I am dead or incapacitated. What seemed to me like a simple inquiry has become something sinister. You do not know me, but I am not one for exaggeration.

My full name is Professor Frank Drury, and I am on sabbatical from the history department of the University of Pennsylvania. My specialty is the Civil War. My bungalow on Sanibel Island is my working home away from home, and while it has usually been a getaway place during the winter recesses from Penn, I have been here throughout the summer, working on a project unrelated to the circumstances that caused me to contact you.

About ten days ago, I received a phone call from a man who identified himself as Peter Coleman. He said he represented a New England family that had come into some information pertaining to an incident during the Civil War. He asked if I would be willing to meet with him and see if my expertise could help.

I was intrigued, of course, and I met with this Coleman last Monday. The story was interesting, because while the information they had was new to me, I had heard about something similar from another source.

Drury may have been worried about his safety and the confidentiality of his information, but he didn't seem rushed when he wrote *this note*, Sparks thought. The FBI agent took off his jacket and gun holster and propped up the pillows on his bed. He continued reading.

This "New England family" said they had come across a letter that had been written in 1863 and delivered to a law firm in Boston with instructions that it be forwarded to a certain Florida family at the end of the war. It seems the law firm dutifully held on to the sealed letter, but just as the war was coming to an end, the firm fell upon hard times and one of the partners died in a fire at their offices.

Apparently, he died while setting the fire so as to collect insurance on the building, according to a newspaper account from back then. Much of the official papers handled by the dead partner were destroyed, but the lone other partner in the firm did have access to some documents. Still, it appears the letter in question was among the surviving documents, but it was never delivered to the Florida family and instead got misfiled and eventually stored permanently.

The letter was eventually found and opened. The letter was handwritten from a Southern gentleman by the name of Parker Stallard, and it was addressed to his brother, Lawrence Stallard. Parker Stallard wrote that he knew the location of a large stash of gold and that if Lawrence received this letter, it meant that Parker had not survived the war. Parker meant for Lawrence and his family to have the gold.

The letter doesn't give the gold's location, but only specific directions from a starting point. Evidently, there was a second person with whom Stallard hid the gold. Their theory was that the second person, and hopefully his decedents, would have the missing information.

I had heard of a family that goes back a number of generations in Florida. I didn't remember the name off hand, but I went back through old research and found they were, indeed, named Stallard, and they had been around northern

Florida since before the Civil War. I never got in touch with them directly, but I checked the Internet yesterday. The family doesn't have a Web site, nor is it mentioned in any others that I could reach. You should check into families in that part of Florida.

At first, I was quite intrigued by the thought of trying to locate this gold, but I have come to feel uncomfortable with the man with whom I am dealing. He seems quite unsavory, and when I hesitated to mention the family, he became threatening. I have felt like I am being followed, and I do fear for my safety, but I really have no proof there is anything wrong.

Apparently, my feelings have been correct if you are reading this. I finally acquiesced and told Coleman about the Florida family. I feel I have done them a great disservice. As I said on the phone, I have a friend who has had some dealings with the Treasury Department, and he sent me your name as sort of a department trouble shooter. I hope you can rectify any wrong I may have caused by dealing with this Coleman fellow. I have no phone numbers or addresses to help you along with your investigation.

Sparks sat for a few minutes to digest what he had just read. This Coleman, or one of his agents, was responsible for Drury's death and the attempt on his own life. This unnamed family in New England certainly believed there was lost gold somewhere. And they had already shown a willingness to use lethal methods to get their hands on it.

Sparks swung his legs around and reached for the phone between the two double beds. First, a call to the office, then one to Miami, and then one to Cambridge and a certain young lady who left demanding messages.

"Dad, it's about time you called me." Jennifer's tone was one of scolding with a twist of teasing. "Uncle Terry said you changed your plans and hadn't arrived in Miami yet. What's going on?"

"Nothing, Jen," Sparks said. "Just a short diversion on business, but it appears I'll be delaying my vacation for a few weeks or so. I've got something that has come up at work."

"And, of course, it's really, really top-secret, need-to-know, for-your-eyes-only-type stuff," Jennifer said with a little laugh, just like her mother used to tease him with. "Nothing dangerous, right?"

"Nothing dangerous." Sparks picked at the bandage along his left side. "I might get a nasty paper cut if I'm not careful."

"Well, if you delay it a couple of more weeks, I might join you and Uncle Terry and Aunt Joan. I'll be finished with summer school work, and I'll have eighteen days before the fall semester begins."

"Great. Tell me how it's been going," Sparks said. He listened intently for another ten minutes while Jennifer, his daughter and the light of his life, gave a dissertation on the subtleties of contract law. He left with a plan to call her in the next week or so to firm up an itinerary for a vacation. Still, Sparks knew it would probably have to be scrapped, but there was no use disappointing her until later.

Next up was a short phone call to West Kendall in Miami-Dade County and Terry and Joan. Sparks would give his apologies. Fishing in the Keys would have to wait.

Chapter Four

September 24, 1862

Prescott shuffled to the cell window in the Old Capitol Prison. His lieutenant's uniform had been replaced with a gray prisoner coat and pants. A somewhat ironic choice of colors on the commandant's part, Prescott thought as he glanced around the prison's interior wall.

Prescott knew about this place. The Federal government had met in this building for years after the British had burned down the old capitol during the War of 1812. Then, if he remembered correctly, it had been a boardinghouse. Its simple design reminded Prescott of many of the houses in Philadelphia, where, if everything worked out soon, he would be knocking on the door of one Cassias Fitzroy.

Since the building was downtown and near the still-under-construction Capitol building itself, it seemed out of place. But there was no mistaking its purpose and effectiveness, a chilling reminder of what was happening in the country.

He had been in the cell only a day, but he was already claustrophobic. The colonel who had taken custody of Prescott, after he had left the president's residence yesterday, had immediately placed the lieutenant under arrest. Lincoln and Seward had explained that for security considerations, Prescott was alone.

The two of them, plus Secretary Stanton and the colonel who had just processed him, would alone know his true position. When the time arrived for reinforcements, when he had enough information to hang the entire group, he was to send a wire to Lincoln or Seward. When contacting either, Prescott was to begin the wire with two words: "North Star."

How to explain his change back to his Southern roots called for a most radical plan. And it bothered him. Lieutenant Jackson Prescott, a solid and resourceful soldier, his colonel had called him, was being branded a traitor by the War Department, and a convincing amount of evidence was being distributed to the press even now, with a detailed record of his attempting to lend secrets to the South. Now he was awaiting, not a trial, but a transfer to a prison farther north—just where, had not been revealed. A trial was to be scheduled sometime in the future.

"You, away from the window! It's against the rules." The guard stood at the door to the small room. Behind him was a stern-looking man with a colonel's uniform. Prescott left the window and moved toward the door but stopped at the room's middle.

"This is outrageous! I demand to be allowed to contact my colonel with the 12th Massachusetts," Prescott said. "There has been a grave error here. I've been accused of something I know nothing about. I want to see the commandant."

"I'm Colonel Wood, Lieutenant Prescott." The man moved in front of the guard. "And you'll demand nothing of me or this command. My instructions are to hold you until tomorrow, then release you into the custody of Colonel Brison, on orders from Secretary of War Stanton himself."

"Where am I to be taken?"

"Fort Delaware. From there, I don't know, nor do I care," Wood said. "I take no satisfaction out of being in charge of you. If the charges against you are true, then you're everything I despise. You're a traitor, which is worse than being a Rebel, and I will await word of your execution. And then I'll have a drink to honor it."

"I'm innocent of these charges. I must be allowed to prove my innocence."

"I'm sure counsel will be provided." Wood turned and stepped away.

The guard, grinning, pulled on the door. "Now don't be trying anything while you're here, or I'll just have to make it unnecessary for there to be a trial."

Prescott was awakened from his cot by the sudden opening of the door. A road-beaten cavalry officer, his blue uniform covered with caked-on mud and dust, strode into the room. The guard followed close behind, but was stopped short as the officer turned into his face.

"I will see the prisoner, alone." The officer closed the door in the guard's face.

"Damn, it's about time you got here." Prescott walked with urgency up to the officer.

Colonel Andrew Brison put his finger to his lips, his eyes telling Prescott to keep quiet. Then, in a loud voice, he said, "Prescott, there are some questions the Secretary of War would like you to answer before we transfer you to Fort Delaware. It will go easier on you if you give us information now." He cracked the door and peered down the hall. When he appeared satisfied the guard was gone, he eased the door shut.

Brison was a good-sized man, an inch more than six feet, with a sturdy solidness about him. His dark brown hair and eyes turned black in the room's dim light and framed his square face, which was accented by a prominent nose. "I just spent nearly two days in the saddle. It's not like I was attending a presidential reception with a fine young lady from Washington society," Brison said. "We don't have much time, and I want to get some sleep."

"I didn't mean . . ."

"Not another word. After we rest up a bit today, I'll be back to transfer you at seven tonight. We'll go by wagon with a single team and one other guard besides me. You'll be in leg irons, but you'll complain about your ankle swelling up, and I'll take them off once we're out of the city. The driver won't be in on this because we need him to help establish the details of your escape. When we reach the outskirts of Baltimore, I'll make up an excuse to go in the back with you, and you'll then overpower me and shove the driver off the wagon. We'll take the wagon a good ways up the road to where we'll give you one of the horses, and you'll be on your way with money and my uniform."

"And you?"

"I'll wait long enough, then double back to pick up the driver and begin my theatrical debut."

"The rest is up to me."

"I don't even know what your assignment is, but the president seemed damn certain it was very important."

"And I haven't a clue about how I'm going to go about it, either."

Brison smiled. "Well, keep an eye out for trouble and a good cigar in your breast pocket. That's my motto."

The sun was touching the horizon as Prescott, in leg chains and with his hands tied with rope and sitting in the back of the covered backboard, was taken away from the Old Capitol Prison. Wearing a clean uniform, a refreshed Brison sat in the right front. He carried a rifle and his personal sidearm, while the driver sitting to his left carried a sidearm. They left the prison and took a road heading north-northeast out of Washington for the long ride up to Fort Delaware.

Brison would occasionally look back at Prescott, but other than that, there was no recognition of their plan for the staged escape. The details were straightforward, but Prescott was still worried. The driver was armed, and he was a decidedly reckless variable.

The early evening brought with it a chill, as cool air moved through without rain, but the stars were beginning to appear and a clear night with a new moon was settling in. The wagon continued west at a moderate pace. They were to stop on the southeast side of Baltimore, about forty miles away, for fresh horses and food—at least, that was what Prescott had made out from the driver and Brison's conversation. Lanterns tied to the horses led the way, but the trip still called for alertness.

Prescott was too nervous to fake sleeping, so he sat pensively in the back. About ten miles out of Washington, he complained to Brison about his leg irons, and Brison released him in good order with a few choice words about trying anything. Now it was closing in on midnight and the time had arrived.

Brison glanced back to Prescott and nodded.

"These ropes are cutting into my hands," Prescott barked over the wagon noise. "Can you loosen the rope a bit? Then I can lie down. My back is stiff as hell."

"The ropes looked fine to me earlier," Brison shot back. "As far as your back is concerned, you can go to hell."

The driver laughed, but then steadied himself as they came to a difficult bend in the road.

"Look, Colonel," Prescott yelled with more urgency, "these ropes were wet when I was tied up, and they're tightening up. I don't give a damn about how you feel about me. I'm still an innocent man until I'm proven guilty by a military court."

Brison glanced at the driver, who shrugged and continued concentrating on the team and the road. Brison leaned his rifle against the seat and jammed the butt into the corner of the floorboard and climbed into the back. He pulled a knife from his belt and made his way to Prescott, trying to steady himself as the wagon rumbled on.

"You ready?" Brison said as quietly as he could above the noise. He cut the ropes.

Prescott nodded and rubbed his wrists.

"Take my gun. Now, I'll make a noise like you hit me over the head."

At that instant came a muted thud, but for a second, neither Brison nor Prescott recognized what had happened. The both turned to the front as the driver went limp. Then wood splintered from the seat area and flew back to where they stood swaying.

"Gunshots!" Prescott cried.

"Get down!" Brison yelled.

Bullets darted past them and more hit the wagon's side. The horses, without a steady hand, cried out and increased their speed in panic.

"What the hell's going on?" Prescott said, now on his knees and crawling along toward the front and the now-dead driver.

"Robbers, I don't know," Brison said, barely able to keep his balance while on his knees as well. "First thing, we've got to get control of the team."

"I'll go for the team—you get your rifle and see if they're behind us."

The wagon lurched to the right as the wheels dropped into a rut, throwing both men onto their faces against the right panel. The left side wheels came off the road, hung in the air an agonizingly long second, then dropped back to the packed-down surface. Prescott reached over the driver to get the reins. He didn't worry about shielding himself from the sharpshooters because there was no way to do it.

The reins were gone, having dropped down in front of the wagon and behind the two-horse team. If anything, the horses seemed to be running faster.

Prescott checked the driver. The shot had caught him cleanly in the chest near the heart. Prescott pulled him from the seat and dropped him into the back as Brison came up from behind.

"I can't see if anyone is following us, but you've got to believe they're there," Brison said.

"The shot came from the front," Prescott said. "It's a hell of a shot no matter how far away they were. I can't reach the reins. Come on."

The two made it back to the bench. Another large kick threw them both forward into the seat. Brison caught the edge with his jaw.

Prescott looked up as they both regained their balance and what he saw made his stomach turn. The long stretch of straight road was about to end in seconds with a sharp bend to the right. He looked to the left and could see nothing but the outline of trees.

"We'll never make the turn!" he shouted to Brison.

"Better to jump now than get caught up in a rolling wagon," Brison said.

"I can try the team."

"No time, it's got to be now."

"The right side looks like it might be grassy and soft."

"Let's do it."

Brison grabbed his rifle and satchel and ripped back the cover on the wagon far enough that they both had a chance to jump at the same time. They had only seconds now. The turn was almost upon them. They both jumped from the wagon at a backward angle. It seemed like the jump itself was slow and for a moment, they were suspended in air.

But the ground came rushing up and both men met it with their feet, only to roll over onto their hips, backs, and shoulders. They had landed, with no small amount of luck, on a slight incline away from the road, and it served to cushion their fall. They still tumbled down the incline, gasping and crying out as they went out of control.

Just as they stopped and were regaining their senses, they heard the crash of the wagon and the panicked cries of the horses as they failed to make the corner.

"You all right?" Prescott surveyed himself as best he could in the dark. He was scraped up but nothing was sprained or broken.

Brison wasn't so lucky. "My ankle's pretty bad. It hurts like hell."

Prescott checked it and was relieved to see that it was probably not broken. Nonetheless, Brison was in no shape to defend himself, and that was foremost in Prescott's mind as he heard the approach of horses from down the road where the shooting had occurred. "It's not broken, Colonel, but I'll bet you won't be dancing at any of those Washington balls," Prescott said. "Here they come. Damn! I didn't take the sidearm from the driver. Where's your rifle?"

"It's got to be around here close to us. I lost it while we were tumbling."

A quick search on his hands and knees, and Prescott found the rifle. He felt it and realized that it was a new rifle he wasn't familiar with. It was a breech loader, not a muzzle loader. He pulled the lever back as he reached Brison. "You've got the cartridges for this?"

"Here in the satchel." Brison was working on his ankle. He looked up at the road. "They're almost here. If we stay here, they won't see us."

"Unless they saw us jump from the wagon."

A group of horses came galloping by them and pulled up at the road's turn.

"The wagon rolled over," a voice said. "Check the back for any survivors and see where the payroll box is. Pat, you check on the horses. See if they're usable."

Prescott and Brison could see a light coming from the road. One of the bandits had lit a lantern. Prescott motioned for Brison to remain, and he crawled parallel to the road into the area inside the elbow of the turn. Protected by the woods, he could see the accident scene. There were four of them, but just three remained with the shattered wagon. They quickly checked the area.

"Damn it, Tom," said the apparent leader. "You said this had to be the payroll shipment, and you pulled the trigger before I could stop you. Would they ship a payroll without some kind of armed detail? You stupid idiot!"

"I could have sworn I saw another man up front, but when the wagon went by us, there was just the driver," Tom replied.

If Brison had been able to move, Prescott would have taken the thieves right then and waited for the fourth to return. But one man against three wasn't good odds, so he quietly made his way back to Brison in less than two minutes.

"They're simple road bandits," he whispered to Brison, who was trying to stand with difficulty. He slipped back down against the bank.

"I would advise against trying to take them. They're murderers," Brison said. "How many?"

"Four."

"I'm in no condition to help you."

"But we need the horses, or we're going to have to stage this stupid escape all over again."

"All right, take me up to the tree line opposite the crash, and I'll cover you."

"I'll swing around, cross the road out of sight, and come up from behind them," Prescott said. "You'll know when I need help."

It took a few minutes for Prescott to move Brison into position. It wasn't necessary to be quiet because the three men on the road were engaged in a loud argument over whose fault it was that they had attacked the wrong wagon. Leaving Brison with the rifle, Prescott made his way back down the road to where they had jumped. He crossed the road and worked his way up the left side, Brison's sidearm in his hand. He reached the point about opposite from where he had left Brison.

"As soon as Petey gets back with the horses, we're leaving, and that's it," the leader said. "I don't even believe we're on the right road."

"No, I can be pretty certain when I tell you that you made a bad decision," Prescott said, stepping out from the shadows. "Up with the hands."

The startled men raised their hands slowly.

"The only damn thing you got right, Tom, was that there was another man up front," the leader said, shaking his head. "And he's a goddamn prisoner. Listen, we don't have a quarrel with you. We thought this here was a payroll wagon from Washington. We'll let you have one of the horses from the team and be on our way."

"I'm afraid there's more to it than that," Prescott said. "You killed the driver, and I don't plan on hanging for it. Guns . . . on the ground . . . and move away from the wagon."

The leader glanced down at the pile of wood and metal that had once been the wagon and saw a rifle leaning up against it. The other two men stepped back.

"Look, boys, he can't get all three of us at the same time, and Petey will be back soon," the leader said, then directed his words to Prescott. "We scatter, mister, and it will be two against one, maybe three against one."

"You don't understand . . . what's your name?"

"My name is Stump."

"Stump?"

"Shut up. My mama gave me that nickname."

"Well . . . Stump. You make a move, you'll be the first to die." Prescott leveled the gun on Stump, then moved it over to the one called Tom. "Or you."

Stump dove for the rifle as the other two started to run in separate directions toward the darkness. Stump reached the rifle and got behind the wagon, brought up the rifle and was swinging it around to Prescott when he died, the bullet from Brison's rifle exploding his head. Prescott took careful aim and fired at one of the running figures, who suddenly grabbed the back of his leg and stumbled onto the road. The third man, Tom, stopped and held his arms in the air, his head twisted to look back at his two companions.

Brison hobbled from the shadows just as both he and Prescott caught sight of the fourth man, the one called Petey, reining in his horse and turning around to head down the road toward Baltimore, leaving the two team horses behind.

"He arrived just in time to show he had no stomach for this kind of work," Brison said. "Over here and lie facedown on the road. You, too." The wounded man half-crawled, half-walked back into the circle of light to lay down.

Prescott leaned over Stump's body. "A shot to the head," he said, directing his words to Brison. "You were pretty damn sure of yourself."

"I'm good."

The two robbers were tied securely to the horses. Brison, though still hampered, was beginning to put a little more weight on the ankle. Prescott exchanged clothes with one of the robbers, then took two of the saddles and prepared the horses from the wagon. It was around 1:30 a.m. when they were ready to move out.

"This is a nice rifle you've got, Colonel," said Prescott, gently running his fingers along the stock and hammer. "I haven't seen a rifle like this."

"A Spencer Carbine—it's new. Hasn't been issued yet. I've got a friend in procurement."

"My unit only has the Enfields. My men can rip off sometimes four shots a minute when they put their minds to it. Though I wouldn't say much for the accuracy when they do that, though."

"This Spencer can fire seven rounds without taking the stock off my shoulder," Brison said. "It's much better than even the Sharps repeater. This increases each cavalry soldier's firepower twofold."

"Great," Prescott said sarcastically. "We've been able to pro-duce sufficient carnage with just muskets and artillery."

"It will help us win the war, Lieutenant."

Prescott nodded and offered his hand. "I appreciate your help, Colonel," he said. "I'll ride as far as the outskirts of the city, then I'm going to swing out to the west and head for Philadelphia."

"Right. Actually, these men helped us along quite a bit. I get to keep my uniform, and you get to escape after uncharacteristically helping a Union soldier capture two murderous thieves. It will be a little bit of good newspaper attention for you."

A few hours later, the pair began to come up on signs for the city of Baltimore. They stopped long enough to shake hands again.

"Good luck to you, Lieutenant."

"Thank you, sir. Tell the president I'll do my best. Though I be-lieve this is the craziest scheme I've ever heard of." Prescott shook his head.

"Men can do great things when providence declares they must," Brison said.

Chapter Five

Present Day
July 22

Sparks navigated through the Dulles concourse, heading for baggage claim. He enjoyed traveling, yet the hassle of tussling with the crowd for position around the conveyor annoyed him. He found his bag quickly and was headed for the exit when two dark suits approached him and identified themselves as being with the bureau. Sparks recognized one, agreed to go with them, and was guided outside to a waiting limousine. Sparks wasn't surprised by who he found in the backseat.

FBI Director Clark Griffin had been a professional friend for twenty years, and Sparks had watched with interest as his coworker had risen steadily through the agency. Sparks thought of him as brilliant, outgoing, and caring about the rank and file—yet unafraid to be ruthless. Sparks had always managed to avoid that side of Griffin's personality, but it had always festered in the back of his mind that maybe his friendship with Griffin was as much responsible for his selection for his present position as his skills were.

He had broached the subject once over a beer at a picnic, and Griffin had spat back at him, "I'm amazed that for a man of your intelligence, you would come up with such an inane notion. I can't afford to put friends into positions where they would prove a liability to me." Sparks never mentioned the subject again. He was pleased at the vote of confidence, no matter if it came with a right cross.

"Jason, thank God I'm not having to call Jen and make funeral arrangements," Griffin said, extending his hand. Griffin was in his mid-fifties with hair more gray than the original brown. A health enthusiast, he worked out five times a week and kept the routine up no matter what crisis he faced—always saying it helped him keep his mental sharpness. His expressive green eyes faded from delight to consternation. "I also want to know why the hell you didn't have your standard issue."

Sparks closed the door and glanced back as one of the agents put his bag in the trunk.

"It sounds a lot worse than the actual injury, Clark." Sparks kept it informal, knowing it was acceptable when they were alone. "As for not having my sidearm, I really didn't think my trip to Fort Myers was going to be anything more than an initial contact on some bit of information I could pass along to the office and forget about while I was fishing in the Keys."

"Sometimes the most benign of situations can prove to be the most deadly. You also know my regulation that agents remain armed while on official business, no exceptions."

"I was going to Miami to visit my stepbrother, Terry, and his wife, Joan, and I didn't want to risk having a gun in the house."

"Yes, that's right. They lost a son. I remember. It was a terrible tragedy to lose a boy like that."

"And they've never allowed a weapon in their house since. I didn't want to go against their wishes."

"I understand, but I'm unhappy nonetheless. Anyway, there's a much more important reason I came out here to pick you up. That message you sent about missing gold from around the time of the Civil War—well, I briefed Adrian Torrez, the president's chief of staff, and he surprised the hell out of me by coming back at me with this file. It's the first time the file has been distributed outside of the White House in a hundred and fifty years." Griffin pulled the file from his briefcase. "It was filed away as a forgotten part of history."

"Before I read this, can you give me a quick synopsis?"

"I've read it cover to cover twice, and I still don't believe we can necessarily link what happened in Fort Myers to a secret cache of gold lost more than six generations ago. But if the gold is out there, someone would be well motivated to find it before we do."

"What are the details?"

"First, a little history lesson." Griffin pulled a bottled water from the limo's compact refrigerator, then offered one to Sparks, who waved it off and grabbed a Diet Coke instead. "In late September and early October of 1862, the nation had been at war for more than a year and a half. There had been some major engagements already with casualty numbers never before seen in the Western world. Then at the Battle of Antietam—"

"General Lee's Army of Northern Virginia and General Mc-Clelland's Army of the Potomac fought the bloodiest single day in American history," Sparks interrupted. "Sorry, I had a distant relative who fought in the battle and is buried there."

"You've studied Civil War history?"

"A little. I've done some reading, but I haven't had time to make it a full-time hobby. I just found it interesting."

"You'll need to become something of an expert in the next few weeks. Because the Union troops held the field at the end of the day, September 17, it was considered a Union victory. But the numbers were staggering, Jason. Twenty thousand men were killed or injured in one day. That's five times the number of Americans killed or wounded on D-Day. On the heels of this, days later, Lincoln announced he would be signing the Emancipation Proclamation on January 1. And any interference from any of the European powers on the side of the Confederacy was lost."

"Drury's letter to me—by the way, here's a look at it," Sparks said, passing it to Griffin. "His letter said the message kept at the Boston law office was written in 1863."

"The story of that gold goes back to the summer of 1862 and probably before that," Griffin said. "Lincoln's operative, probably through George McClelland's Secret Service, run by Allan Pinkerton, had uncovered some evidence of a plot to help the Confederacy's cause by shipping gold to Europe in exchange for material or political help from the European powers."

"Allan Pinkerton?"

"Yes, the founder of the Pinkerton Detective Agency." Griffin nodded. "His group uncovered a plot to assassinate Lincoln before he was inaugurated in 1861, before the war."

"I didn't know."

"That was how he found favor with Lincoln and helped established his company's reputation. That first operative was killed in a skirmish near Sharpsburg, Maryland, around the time of the battle. Lincoln felt it was a separate incident from the man's work of seeking out the Southern sympathizers in the North who were putting together this operation. So, Lincoln handpicked a man by the name of Lieutenant Jackson Prescott from a Massachusetts regiment.

"Prescott had made a name for himself with his superiors for his intelligence and ability to handle difficult circumstances on and off the battlefield. He was picked because his family knew the one man who was tagged as a link to the conspirators. They set up Prescott as a traitor with some trumped-up information and set up a false escape. Prescott disappeared for a couple of months, and Lincoln, Secretary of War Stanton, and Secretary of State Seward all feared for his life, but then he contacted them around Christmastime, 1862, from Chicago.

"His wire, preceded with the code words 'North Star,' alluded to a factory in Chicago that was producing war materials for the Union cause, but was also processing and melting down gold to be formed into ingots and some coinage. The wire said the first shipment was to be sent in the near future."

"From where?"

"The wire didn't say, but the blockade was still in place. In one way, Lincoln thought floating it down the Mississippi River might have been their first choice. Even with the blockade, the gold could have been unloaded well above the city and taken by wagon through Louisiana and Texas and into Mexico, then shipped out that way. But then the Union gained control of the Mississippi when Grant laid in a siege at Vicksburg."

"If they could move it through the north undetected," Sparks said, "then they could smuggle it out on a northern trade ship and not worry about the blockade."

"Very astute, because apparently that's what they decided—once the siege of Vicksburg began that spring," Griffin said. "The report says Prescott contacted them again in February, saying that no real change in plans had been made, but that he was working his way into the confidence of the main operational initiator. The action man. Prescott didn't get too specific, but he at least implied he was gathering a wealth of material to bring down the conspiracy."

"Speaking of wealth, how much gold are we talking about?"

"I'll get to that in a moment," Griffin said, pausing to push a button and bring down the opaque screen that separated the limo's front seat from them. "Dan, I can see the traffic's bad. We'll forgo the side trip and head straight to the bureau."

"Side trip?"

"Bobby's soccer game. I thought you could read the file while I watched the last half of the game, but we'll never make it. I'm going to catch hell from Maggie."

Sparks smiled knowingly. He had spent a number of holidays at the Griffin house since his wife had died, and no army general in the world had Maggie Griffin's desire for precision timing when it came to dinner parties, backyard barbecues, or even the daily schedule. Clark himself both marveled at and lamented her attention to detail.

Griffin continued, "Prescott sent what turned out to be a final message from Harrisburg, Pennsylvania, in late June of 1863. His wire set up a date and a place in Philadelphia where the gold would be stored before being smuggled out. He made it clear he would need troops and officials at that location. Lincoln and Seward believed this meant Prescott would close out his charade and the conspirators would be brought down with the evidence he had accumulated. Then"—Griffin held out the last word and paused—"*nothing.*"

"No contact?"

"None. The date came. The warehouse was searched with no results. Outgoing ships in Philadelphia were checked and double-checked. Nothing. The file has remained open and every president since has been briefed on the lost shipment, more now as a curiosity than anything else."

"That was supposed to be the first shipment," Sparks said. "Did they ever find out about any other subsequent attempts?"

"No. The entire network collapsed somehow. They're pretty sure the gold never made it out of Philadelphia. And they're sure the gold never made it south to Richmond or Charleston or anywhere in the South. There just isn't any record of it anywhere, which made the White House believe it was either lost or ended up in someone's personal possession."

"How much gold are we talking about?" Sparks asked.

"The file says almost five tons."

"Five tons!"

"If the gold is very pure and intact, that shipment was worth over three million in 1863. Its worth today would be in the neighborhood of one hundred and fifty million."

Sparks rounded his lips together and exhaled. "A hell of a motive for murder."

"Murder many times over, Jason," Griffin said. "You'll need to watch yourself on this one. I imagine whoever is behind the inquiry is well financed and willing to hire dangerous people. You can expect them to be ruthless. There's one other unrelated item . . . I'm going into the hospital for some tests. I've had headaches and some minor motor function problems."

"Jesus, Clark."

"We'll see what's up. God, I hate hospitals. Haven't been in one, except for my physicals."

"Let me know what's going on, all right?"

"Sure. Anyway, Goldberg will be your contact as of now."

Sparks wasn't pleased with this development. By his estimate, Marshall Goldberg was a good administrator and handled the bureaucracy well, but he hadn't had much field work. He was also known as a manipulator. Griffin had been selected over Goldberg to the director's position and the word was Goldberg was furious. Sparks didn't know him personally, having only met him briefly twice.

"I know Goldberg pisses people off," Griffin said, as if to ward off the expected objection, "but he has good organizational skills, and he believes in the bureau's goals. He'll give you the support you need."

"Don't worry about me—you just concentrate on getting better, whatever it turns out to be. Am I to talk to him today, and is that part of the reason you picked me up?"

"Knowing your tendency to disappear without following regs, I thought it best I give you the news in person." Griffin offered a sly smile.

"That hurts."

"The truth sometimes does."

Now it was time for Sparks to smile. "I could just fax in my preliminary report and be gone."

"You do, and you'll never get a taste of Maggie's apple or blueberry pie again."

"That's not fair," Sparks said in mock horror.

Tap . . . tap . . . tap.

Marshall Goldberg waited with little patience in Griffin's office. He detested being held up by someone else. He had fired people before who were chronically late. His tapping with the pen on the arm of his chair grew in urgency.

The office was competently furnished in Goldberg's eyes, but if it had been his office, as it should have become two years ago, it would have had a markedly different décor. Gone would be the sports motif on the far wall, with its signed photos of baseball players posing with Griffin. In would be Goldberg's authentic Picasso sketches, which his mother had passed down to him when he turned twenty-one.

He wasn't fond of Picasso, he just liked the air of sophistication the sketches brought. He had used his superior organizational and interpersonal skills to help streamline the bureau. It would be those same skills that would land him this office—sooner rather than later, if the rumor about Griffin going into the hospital was accurate.

Griffin swept into the office and headed for his desk. "Sorry I'm late. The traffic from Dulles was awful."

"Things were slow today because I finished reworking the budget projections. You have a copy on your desk there."

"Good. There's something else I need to brief you on," Griffin said. "I'm going to be heading into the hospital for tests . . ."

"Nothing serious, I hope."

"They need to check it out, so I'll be out of the office for a while. Obviously, you'll be handling affairs as you have in the past."

"Of course."

"But before we go into the usual, I want to show you this file and brief you on an operation that will be going on."

Griffin then went into a lengthy briefing on the possible lost gold and the murder in Florida and the attempt on Sparks's life. Goldberg listened with attentiveness, trying to comprehend the millions of dollars being discussed.

"Why is Sparks the point man on this?" Goldberg asked. "I know he's done liaison work with Treasury, but . . ."

"Sparks's duties are a little more refined than that. He reports to me alone—you for the duration of my hospital stay—and he has broad discretionary powers. He operates alone until he feels he needs bureau support. He'll be instructed to communicate with you regularly."

"I really don't know him that well. Can I pull his file?"

"Saved you the trouble, though I can tell you as much about him as that file can."

"You two close?"

"Yes, but my evaluation of him for this position is without prejudice. I had a three-man advisory panel pick the person for this position from the final list of ten. They chose wisely for me." Griffin leaned back in his chair as Goldberg opened up the file.

"Jason Patrick Sparks. Forty years old. Former University of Miami baseball player, an outfielder, good hitter with a great arm. Played a little minor league ball before applying to the bureau. Widower. Lost his high school sweetheart, Casey, in a car crash about ten years ago. I was with him the night it happened. It was around Thanksgiving—just before. It crushed him and hampered his effectiveness for quite a while. She was a beautiful, brilliant woman. Since her death, there has been no one serious. Their daughter, Jennifer, who was about twelve at the time, has been especially close to him ever since."

"This would make her college age now," Goldberg said.

"Yes—actually, she's a first-year law student at Harvard. Jason is extremely protective of her. Not that he doesn't let her live her life as she's become an adult, but he always makes time for her. Professionally, he's one of the finest operatives you'll see. He's intelligent and reacts swiftly to situations. He can be utterly cold. If you're in a dangerous situation, you would be well served to have him at your side—which is hard to do because he prefers to work alone. He bends . . . hell, he *breaks* rules, Marshall, but his judgment is without repute."

"You know I'm a stickler for adherence to regulations," Goldberg said, "but I won't step on the relationship and methods you've established with him. Dangerous to have someone on his own like that, though, isn't it?"

"I would agree, but Jason is a special case. Treat him as such."

"You promised I'd get a chance to see you before the fall term," Jennifer Sparks lectured. "I don't have to give you a first-year law student's explanation of contract law, do I?"

Talking on his cell phone, Sparks was driving back to Dulles with a fresh suitcase. "I'm sorry, Jen—you know I'd rather spend time with you than go tramping through swamps in Florida in July. But that thing I told you about just grew into a full-fledged assignment. That's all there's to it."

"All right, but you owe me big-time, Dad. I expect a full two weeks with you during semester break, and I expect you to visit me on a couple of weekends as soon as you're done with this case."

"I promise."

"Besides, there's someone I want you to meet."

Sparks's eyes widened. Jennifer had had boyfriends in the past, but she had never given him much information on them, much less brought them together. Sparks had always thought she avoided introducing them because she knew they weren't the real thing. "Male or female?"

Jennifer laughed. "Male. His name is Bret Thomas and we've been spending quite a bit of time together. I think you'll think he's a good guy."

"Well, this is a first. OK, you've got me motivated to get my work done."

"My mission is accomplished."

"I'll talk to you soon."

"I love you, Dad."

"In triplicate, Jen."

Chapter Six

September 25, 1862

The night was alive with movement. Gusts of wind enveloped the empty street and swept trash along the business fronts. Prescott walked with his head down. There was no thunder, but the wind lent an uneasy feeling of rough weather approaching.

Under his arm, Prescott carried a newspaper dated that afternoon. A small story on the front page in the bottom left-hand corner told the brief tale of a suspected Southern sympathizer, a Union soldier, who had escaped after helping his captors defend themselves against road bandits. Though the article termed the action honorable, it still deemed the soldier dangerous and a fugitive.

After separating from Brison, Prescott had given Baltimore a wide berth and headed north to Philadelphia. Once the nation's capital and now a vibrant shipping port, the city was familiar to Prescott. He had socialized with a group from Harvard that was from the city, and he had come to visit them on two holidays. He longed for those joyous times. Now he couldn't help but believe that those times would never return.

Prescott occasionally glanced at the address in his hand. He walked past a patrolling city policeman, who eyed him with caution but didn't stop him. Turning onto the correct street, he found the house on the left side, three down from the cross street.

Cassias Fitzroy's house was elegant and well maintained. Prescott could see fresh paint even under the dim light of the gas lamps. The remnants of a flower garden adorned both sides of the walkway up to the steps. Prescott looked both ways and saw just one carriage headed away from him—no other traffic, the officer gone. He heard midnight's distant chimes as he climbed the steps. He knocked firmly on the door, and, from inside, he heard someone approaching. The door lock clicked, and a small, round man with a balding head and wire-rimmed glasses, still dressed in his day clothes, stepped into the gap between the door and the frame. "Yes?"

"Uncle Fitzy?"

Fitzroy studied Prescott's face, his eyes widened in recognition, and he gasped before quickly stepping out and looking down the street from his doorway. "Get in here quickly," Fitzroy said, letting Prescott in and closing the door. Only after he had locked the door did he welcome the traveler. "Oh, Jack, my boy! I can't believe it's you! What are you doing in Philadelphia? Are you well?"

The questions came fast without time for response, and Prescott laughed as Fitzroy grabbed him by both cheeks and pulled his head down to kiss his forehead. "It's good to see you, Fitzy," Prescott said. "Though I wish the circumstances were different."

"I saw the paper, my boy. Come in, come in, we have much to discuss."

"I'm sorry about the lateness of the hour, but . . .

"Don't give it a minute's thought, Jack. Some tea to warm you up from the blow starting out there, or perhaps something a bit stronger?"

"Please. Tea is fine for now."

"I'll get it, and you come on in here and sit down. I have a small fire burning tonight . . . probably could have made do without one."

Prescott sat down in one of the chairs facing the fireplace. The room was appointed with various sailing mementos and items from around the world. Just from where he was sitting, he could see ivory carvings, probably from the African continent, and more carvings and a mask in the corner he couldn't identify. Fitzroy had told stories to the family about his travels abroad, many times with his arms flailing as he roared his tales of adventure. Prescott remembered sitting on the floor as a boy, listening. Another time to remember with a smile tinged with sadness.

Fitzroy brought the tea service and chatted on about having to do everything himself because the servants had the day off for some special family occasion. After some chatter about how his business was going well, especially with the war on, Fitzroy let the small talk fade away for a moment. "I saw the newspaper today, the same one you have in your hand. Do you want to talk about it?"

"The article had the usual embellishment. I suppose I'm to be lynched as soon as I'm found."

"Knowing your feelings about your father and the Southern cause, I find it hard to believe you suddenly decided to lend aid to the Confederacy, Jack. I thought it had to be a mistake."

"I know you count my father as one of your best friends, and I know he and I have been estranged for years, but what I'm being accused of has little bearing on my issues with him. I still oppose slavery. I'm still shamed by my father's business. And I still believe his greed turned him into something with which I cannot associate myself."

"It has always saddened me to see that you two could never settle matters. Don't you miss your family?"

"Of course. I just couldn't reconcile his actions."

"You're a lieutenant in the Union Army. Why help the South?"

"You wouldn't have to ask me if you'd seen what I've seen in the past year," Prescott said. He put down his tea and rubbed his face with his hands. "I was at Antietam. It was the most god-awful hell any man could witness. My regiment was among those moving down from the north along a road heading into Sharpsburg. We struck in the early morning—there was still fog hanging along the ground in some places. We attacked through a cornfield . . . back and forth we fought . . . some minutes we would drive them back . . . then they would surge at us. All the while, there were men screaming, barking orders. Others were cussing every foul word known . . . others cried out to the Lord. All the while, we were shredded by bullets and canister."

Fitzroy sat without reaction, the fire's embers hissing the only sound besides Prescott's voice.

"We lost two-thirds of my company," he continued. "I saw one of my friends die as his head exploded. I saw another take the full brunt of canister fire from a Rebel artillery piece. There wasn't enough of him left that you would have known it was a man."

Prescott rested his chin on his hands with his arms on his knees. "I saw a drummer boy of sixteen run ahead to grab the colors when the flag-bearer went down. He used to be the one to go get a stray ball when we would play baseball by the camp. He loved to earn his keep by helping out with odd jobs. He was really adopted by the men. The boy was an orphan, made so by the war, and he had joined the company somewhere along the line. No one remembers where or when—he was just there. So he charged past many of the older soldiers and went up to the line in that cornfield. He reached the colors and raised them up high, as far as he could with his arms outstretched . . . and the men rallied behind him.

"He took a bullet in the chest just as I reached him. I drew him behind some dead men so that we were somewhat shielded from the fire. I could see right away that the wound was mortal . . . but all he was concerned about were the colors. A boy, Fitzy . . . a boy whose only concern in life should have been where he was going fishing that day after school . . . died in my arms with more courage than any ten men I could find around me." Prescott, his eyes moist and throat swollen, stared into the fire. "I've never seen death the way we saw it that day."

"There's nothing I could say that would comfort you, son," Fitzroy said.

"My reasons for doing what I did are simple," Prescott said, his voice strong again. "We were paroling a small group of prisoners after the fight. I told a captain to relay to his commanding general the best way to avoid another entanglement during their withdrawal. I was finished with incompetent generals who use up good men like cattle. I was finished with the butchering, and I didn't want to see any more. I'll do whatever one man can do to shorten the war. If that means helping the Rebels have their country, then so be it." Prescott looked directly at Fitzroy. "I'll not take part in their slaughter again."

Fitzroy let the silence settle for a minute and finished his tea. He got up from his chair and took a copy of the newspaper from the table and sat back down. He read the article on Prescott again.

Prescott realized how much the battle had affected him. He knew recent history, and he knew that John Brown, the half-crazed abolitionist who had died on the gallows just a few short years ago, had been right. The country was paying for its sins. And there was only one acceptable conclusion.

"You look exhausted. I can offer you a bed in the basement," Fitzroy said. "It really isn't too bad. I stay down there myself during some summer evenings."

"I appreciate the offer. You've always helped out my family. You have my thanks."

"Come, let's get you some things and you can sleep. Then, we'll see about tomorrow and the days that follow."

Downstairs in Fitzroy's house, Prescott awoke the next morning to light filtering through a grimy window. He had never seen a home with a basement window and thought it peculiar. He didn't know what time it was, since he had lost his pocket watch when he was processed back at Old Capitol, but he knew it must be late for how rested he felt.

As he sat on the bed, gathering himself, his thoughts turned to his father. "I wonder what he would say to my face right now," Prescott said softly.

"Son, words cannot express my gratitude upon the receiving the word of your heroic actions for the South. I know whatever influences help mold your opinion that the South's cause is a just, true one were a godsend. Your mother and your sisters have received nothing but positive remarks from friends concerning your gallant efforts."

Whatever the reaction, chances are the end result will be something I can't possibly imagine, Prescott thought. He stretched and walked up the stairs to the first floor and peeked through the crack left by the partially opened door.

"Fitzy?"

"Ah, my boy. Come on up. I've got some food prepared for you."

"I am hungry."

"Of course, and this is real food. Not that hardtack and fat-fried corn meal the army calls food." Fitzroy laughed. "I'll wager your stomach won't know what you're sending down." He brought Prescott into the kitchen in the back of the house. "You can start with an apple, and I've got some fresh baked bread, and this is the best butter in Philadelphia. Widow Reverson has a small dairy farm that her sons run for her. Somehow, she comes up with the best tasting butter I've ever had."

Prescott sat down and began to eat, relishing the food. Fitzroy didn't need to know he'd had a fine meal just a few days ago at the hotel in Washington. Still, he hadn't eaten much since then, so this meal was welcomed just the same.

"I appreciate your help," Prescott said between bites. "I don't want to be a burden for you. You're in danger as long as I stay here, so I'll need to move along soon."

Fitzroy handed a sheet of paper to Prescott. It was a notice announcing a one-thousand-dollar reward for information leading to the capture of the traitor Jackson Prescott.

"They don't waste very much time, do they?" Prescott said.

"Yes. Actually, this was brought by the house not an hour ago, which means they had to have been printed up just last night. Seems strange to me." Fitzroy looked at Prescott.

"I gather I'm high priority," Prescott said. "The colonel I got away from seemed competent. I'm sure as soon as he got to Baltimore, he sent word back to Washington and got permission to get the notices printed up here immediately. I imagine his future career advancement would depend on him taking charge."

Fitzroy nodded gently. "I suppose you're correct. I need to go out for a while this afternoon on some business. I'll show you a small storage closet in the back that's pretty well hidden. If someone should come to the door and if, by chance, however unlikely, they perform a house-to-house search, you can hide back there. Then, tonight, I'm having someone to dinner."

"Is that wise?" Prescott asked.

"This gentleman is someone you need to meet. He's from a well-known Southern family, and he has the means to help you leave Philadelphia safely, either help you get back to the South or somewhere up north—whatever your desire."

"Who is he?"

"You probably know the family name," Fitzroy said. "Stallard. Parker Stallard."

Prescott found that Stallard presented an interesting appearance—tailored in a finely cut suit with an obviously expensive overcoat. He was slightly shorter than Prescott but carried himself as someone quick on his feet. Fair-haired with a kept mustache, his most prominent feature was a scar that carried from his left ear down to just short of his chin.

The dinner consisted of chicken, corn, and a special breaded stuffing Prescott found quite good. Upon meeting Stallard, there was a brief reference to Prescott's situation, but then the discussion became centered on the export business out of Philadelphia that Fitzroy owned and that, it appeared, Stallard had an interest in. The meal ended, and the three of them moved to the sitting room. The room faced west, and the sun was low on the horizon, splashing the sky and clouds with orange fire. Fitzroy offered cigars all around, and they settled into chairs.

"I consider myself a blessed individual," Fitzroy said. "I'm too old to fight, and my life has not been greatly affected by the tragedy upon us."

"But you must know people who have lost sons?" Prescott said.

"Yes. I guess I wasn't entirely accurate. I have known many families that have suffered a loss. I meant personally."

"So did I. It doesn't affect you that thousands of men, on both sides, are dying for an idea as vague as states' rights?"

"Your Mr. Lincoln has upped the ante there, Jackson. He's stated that he intends to abolish slavery with the new year. As if he holds the right to shape the determination of states that have long since left the Union."

"Men in the North will now be fighting to put an end to slavery, not solely to keep the Union together," Stallard said, blowing a generous amount of cigar smoke out into the middle of the room. He held the cigar away from his face and studied it for a moment. "Isn't it noble that a country that has established its foothold on this continent and seems ordained to cover its expanse from ocean to ocean owes much to the institution of slavery? The very people crying out for its demise are the very people who are wearing clothes and sleeping on bedding made out of its bounty."

"Past failure as a culture doesn't mean you cannot grow and mature," Prescott said.

"I'm a southerner, Mr. Prescott," Stallard said. "Our family has done business with yours, some of it involving the marketing of slaves. I detest the institution, though not, mind you, for the same reasons you do. I care not about moral implications or the growth of society's maturity. I only care that the South be allowed to develop its own government and establish new relationships with other countries so its people can thrive and prosper. I believe the institution itself is flawed beyond the moral—I believe it's ultimately flawed from a social-economic reasoning. The South will have to change, whether it wins this war or not. I would hope the European powers will intervene. The Confederacy has much to offer."

"It does, sir, in cotton," Fitzroy said, "but the blockade has effectively restricted free exports from the South."

"Yes, it has," Stallard said, glancing at Prescott. "Cassias here told me he had someone interesting for me to meet this evening. I didn't know that someone would be a fugitive from the Union Army."

"I would expect you would be glad to meet a person like myself," Prescott said. "Someone who has seen the errors of his ways."

"Any assistance you would give to the South would be based on saving lives, not taking them. That much I can see just from talking with you this evening. We both want an end to the war. I'm just more pragmatic about it—both in reasons for and how to go about accomplishing it."

"I wonder why a southerner, who wants to see his country free, would choose to spend his time in business in the North instead of fighting for South Carolina."

"As I said, sir, I am pragmatic. Oftentimes, the best solution to a problem comes from non-direct means. Many positive avenues can be explored in the North." Stallard sat forward in his chair. "We must all make our decisions and live with them. You're facing that now. Have you thought about what you're planning to do? Are you going to head south? I'm sure your family would welcome you back."

"No. You know my father, however briefly. He and I will not have a change of heart. And my ties to the South are only through family. No, I'll not go home. I may try Canada, but I actually may head to California. The gold rush may be over, but a man can make a living doing a number of worthy tasks out there."

Stallard and Fitzroy exchanged glances. Fitzroy got up from his chair.

"I've got some cleaning up to do," Fitzroy lamented. "You two continue. I won't be long."

Stallard waited for Fitzroy to leave, then got up and moved over to where Prescott sat.

"You and I would both like to see the war end soon," Stallard emphasized. "We may feel differently about why, but the result is the same. I can help you on your way if you would like. I have people up here who would be of service."

"I would appreciate anything you could do."

"Fitzroy said you can stay here for now. He doesn't have many visitors, though I have told him the neighbors are too nosy. Let me make inquiries, and maybe we can get you along soon. And if you're serious about heading west—well, I have associates out there as well."

The White Horse Tavern was an upper-scale drinking establishment where gentlemen of Philadelphia society were able to discuss politics and business away from their wives and families. Located just five blocks from Fitzroy's house, it made an ideal meeting place for the two transplanted South Carolinians. It was the middle of the afternoon, so the two men were practically alone.

"I received a wire from Chicago yesterday. The news disturbs me. Smythe says the final shipment for this season is delayed." Stallard took a deep drink from his mug and motioned for the barmaid to bring one over for Fitzroy, who had just sat down.

"Worried because of the snows?"

"No, I wanted to have the shipment melted down before I traveled there next week so I could take inventory. I wanted to see if a spring ore shipment was really necessary to complete our first shipment east. I was hoping we might be able to get that shipment out of the country before the end of the year."

"We haven't even decided on the best way to accomplish that, or even which port to use," Fitzroy said.

"I thought the southern route into Texas and out through Mexico might be the best way, but my contacts in that region are weak, and the probability of losing the shipment entirely would be high. Also, the Mississippi is becoming a higher risk because of all the Union activity around it. If I were a Union commander, gaining control of the river would be a high priority, so I would expect there will be activity there come spring."

"I believe you've already decided how you want to proceed." Fitzroy accepted the mug from the barmaid and took notice of her obvious attributes with a smile. "You know I'm wary of using my influences in Philadelphia. My Southern sympathies are known and only tolerated because I have acquired many business and political ties."

"I understand your concern, but my contacts are strongest in the North. Getting the gold from Chicago to Philadelphia will be enough of an undertaking, but, I think, a manageable one. I'm owed many favors, and I'll use them effectively."

"We'll have more time to discuss this when I travel out to Chicago in the winter."

"Do you believe you can have the deal with the interested parties in England by the time you come out?" Stallard asked, rubbing the upper part of the scar on his face. It appeared to bother him.

"I expect the gentleman will be arriving soon, and we'll begin discussions. I'm confident we'll be able to broker a contract where we provide the gold and he and his associates provide the influence to bring England over to the side of the Confederacy."

"Time is essential, Cassias. That's why I was hoping to bring a shipment east this year. A promise of great riches is not nearly as persuasive as a gold ingot in your hand. Could you convince them to wait for the first shipment next spring?"

"I'm hopeful."

"And, remember, every month we delay brings the South into further peril. Sharpsburg was not a good outcome for us. Lee nearly lost the war there," Stallard said.

"And could have won it as well. The way to Washington would have been clear."

"Nevertheless, McClelland may even now be pursuing and pressing Lee."

"Parker, my boy, we never said we wouldn't have to change our strategy as the fortunes of the war changed." Fitzroy's voice held a calming tone. "We have spent a good deal of money on this cause. The South will reap the rewards. I have confidence Lee can force a peace eventually, and when he does, we'll become the richest men on the continent while helping the South establish a stronger economy. Someday, I see free trade with the North opening up again."

"The North has so many advantages . . ."

"But they don't have the heart for it, Parker. Look at Prescott, even he knows the tragedy of this war is the loss of life because men don't want others to have determination over their lives."

"And what about the Negroes, Cassias, what about their rights?"

Fitzroy's face darkened. "Don't throw that at me, sir. It's not the same with Negroes, and you know it. There are abuses, I admit, but the majority are well treated and live in better conditions than if they were on their own. That's all they're capable of."

Stallard, not wanting to continue the argument, changed the subject. "What do you think of Prescott?"

"I've tried to figure that boy out for years," Fitzroy said. "The break with his father wasn't unexpected. I could see it coming for years. He was always headstrong. But I've talked to other people who have been involved in battle, and they have told stories that would sicken you. Seeing events like that could change any man."

"Do you think he would be useful to me out in Chicago and on the way back with the shipment?"

"You mean, do I think you can trust him?"

Stallard nodded, and Fitzroy took a deep breath, exhaled, and swallowed another dose of ale. "I don't know. He detests slavery above anything else. I wouldn't be surprised if he changed his mind midway through the trip."

"But he's a wanted man. I can help him, and . . . perhaps he has found something he hates worse than slavery."

"That's what he spoke about, to be sure," Fitzroy said. "The decision is, of course, yours, Parker. I would just tell you to be careful. I have a feeling that if you make the wrong decision about him . . ."

Stallard looked directly into the older man's eyes. They were clear and vibrant, but without compassion. There was something missing, perhaps the delight of youth, he didn't know. He only knew it wasn't there, and the knowledge left him melancholy—for he worried whether perhaps his own eyes looked the same.

Chapter Seven

Present Day
July 23

Sparks threw his suitcase on one of the double beds in his room and set his briefcase on the writing table next to the fifth-floor window of his Jacksonville hotel. After calling for room service, he washed up, opened his briefcase, and pulled out his laptop. He accessed the bureau's Web site for field agents and set up a search for "Stallard," cross-referenced with criminal files from across the United States. He got the street addresses for nearly one hundred Stallards living in north Florida.

He took out Drury's letter from his case.

My full name is Professor Frank Drury, and I am on sabbatical from the history department of the University of Pennsylvania . . .

"Damn, it's 5:10." Sparks grabbed the phone, quickly got the number for the Penn history department, and dialed. It rang eight times. A secretary named Crystal answered and after a short conversation, left Sparks waiting for a call back from Drew Corning, a former grad assistant for Drury.

Sparks's food arrived, and then Corning's call came just minutes later. Corning was wary at first, but after Sparks identified himself and explained he was working on the case and had been in contact with the professor before the murder, Corning seemed to warm up to him.

"I just don't get it," Corning said. "The professor was a stand-up guy. A bit of a history nut, but you kind of expect that. I worked with him on a lot of research, much of it to do with the Civil War."

"He mentioned to me that he was doing research about Civil War legends and such, and he came in contact with a family in Florida that had a family story about missing gold. He never talked to the family directly, but he remembered their name as Stallard. Do you remember any names like that?"

"Stallard?" There was a pause on the other end. "I don't recall for sure. Hold on a second. Part of my work involved putting down names, addresses, and brief descriptions and then cross-referencing them in a database." It took Corning a few minutes of moving around inside the computer system.

"Hey, I remember now! Here it is! We came across a small article in a weekly newspaper outside of Jacksonville. It was a profile of a local businesswoman. They didn't have a Web site at the time, so that's why Internet searches never hit on a story. The article said her family went back in northern Florida, southern Georgia, and South Carolina for eight generations, and one of the family stories passed down was that her great-great-grandfather knew about some hidden gold somewhere in the eastern United States. It was an interesting story, and we were going to interview her, but the professor got sidetracked, and it got put on the back burner."

"So you don't have an address or phone number for this woman?"

"Well, yeah, I do, because I talked to her," Corning said, sounding annoyed.

"You talked to her?" Sparks stopped taking notes.

"Hey, listen, I know how to do an efficient job."

"Her name?"

"You won't find her under Stallard. She was married, and her name is Tracy Stallard Coulthard. She works in the Jacksonville area. I've got her business phone number. She's a real estate agent."

Sparks thanked the grad assistant, hung up, and went right to the phone book. Within a minute, he was looking at an advertisement in the "Real Estate" section. It was for Tracy Coulthard. She had her own agency and was tied to one of the nationwide chains. A call got an answering machine, and he left a message about wanting to purchase a house.

Tracy Coulthard called back at 9 p.m. as Sparks was watching a movie while putting a clean dressing on his side. He said he was looking into buying a house in the area and asked if he could set up an appointment for tomorrow. Coulthard said she didn't have an opening for the next day, but when Sparks said he was looking to buy in the one-million- to two-million-dollar range, she quickly made time. The appointment was set for 10 a.m.

July 24

The Coulthard Agency was located in a large office building on the west side of the city, an impressive glass design with each floor recessed back from the one below it. The effect was not unlike a pyramid, except this structure stopped after five floors, with a flat roof. The Coulthard offices were on the second floor, facing west. Sparks met with the receptionist and sat down with his back to the tinted glass window that faced the parking lot below.

"Mr. Sparks, I'm Tracy Coulthard." Sparks looked up into a most stunning face, with light brown eyes with a wisp of something else he couldn't think of right away. Her face was delicate, without heavy makeup, and her brown hair framed her face with elegant detail. She was bending over from the waist and had her hand extended.

"I'm sorry, I was lost in thought," he said with some embarrassment. "I'm Jason Sparks."

"Welcome to Jacksonville. Come with me and we'll talk in my office."

As they walked down a hallway, Sparks couldn't help but notice Coulthard walking in front of him. She was wearing a business suit and skirt that was tight enough and finished well enough above the knee that he could see she kept herself in shape. She turned left at the far wall and walked with authority to the entrance of her office. *Walk* was too simple of a word, Sparks thought. She moved with firm athleticism.

Her office was the largest in the agency's and was masterfully decorated, with an impressive dark wood desk with a matching wall unit filled with real estate books, binders, and awards. There was a table and six chairs off to the left side, and the entire far wall was the same tinted glass. The blinds were turned just enough to keep the sun out on that side, but not enough to obscure the view.

"Please sit down, Mr. Sparks," she said.

"Call me Jason. My father was Mr. Sparks."

"Of course, please, call me Tracy. Well, so, you're moving into the area. Where are you coming from?"

"Washington, D.C. I'm moving from a government job to the private sector, and I need to look for a house."

"Do you have a family?"

"I have a daughter, but she's away at college. I'm a widower."

Coulthard looked up from the paperwork she had been organizing. "I'm sorry."

"No problem. It has been a number of years."

Coulthard smiled.

Sparks continued after a slight pause. "I would like to learn a little more about the agency and how you do business. It's important to me that my real estate agent goes all-out to get me the property I want for the best price."

"I built this agency from scratch myself," Coulthard said, folding her hands on her desk. "I hire and keep the best people I can find, and I'm a pretty good judge of character. We work hard, but the rewards are high. This agency has been among the top three in sales for the past seven years—in all of north Florida. We also take the same aggressiveness when representing someone who is purchasing."

"That's what I like to hear."

Coulthard presented her agency's standard plan. For the twenty minutes this took, Sparks listened intently. As they wrapped up their preliminary meeting, Sparks made an excuse about having to attend to some other matters. He stopped as he was at the door. "Forgive me, but I'm alone on my trip here. I was wondering if you have dinner plans?" Sparks asked.

Coulthard hesitated.

"We can make it business-related if you prefer," he added.

"That would be fine," she said. "I'd love to. But let me pick you up at your hotel. I know a good place to go, but I have a showing that goes until about six-thirty, and I'll need to swing by my house on the way."

"You do like to take charge."

"You asked first."

Tracy Coulthard picked up Sparks at his hotel at 7:15 p.m., and they drove to a restaurant along the shore just south of the city. It was a quiet place that, unlike a lot of places along the beach, required a certain mode of dress of its patrons. Gone were the T-shirts, sandals, and shorts that dominated many restaurants.

Coulthard had said she needed to stop at her place, and it must have been some stop. Replacing the business suit and skirt was the classic little black dress, which, in Sparks's estimation, needed the accent on the word *little*. For a woman in her late thirties—no, even for a woman in her twenties—Tracy Coulthard was spectacular. And what made Sparks all the more uncomfortable was that she clearly noticed the effect she had on him.

"I need to stop right now and let you know something," Sparks said once they had settled in and ordered drinks. He looked directly into her eyes. "I lied to you."

"You're married," she said, a statement, not a question.

"No, the personal information I told you was all true. I lied about my profession."

"I have clients who do that all the time." She smiled cautiously.

"I also don't need to buy a house. Well, actually, I do sometime here in the near future, but not in Jacksonville and not now."

Eyebrows raised, Coulthard put her elbows on the table. Rather than being angry about being misled, she seemed intrigued. "This is all very mysterious. Tell me more, Mr. Sparks."

"Actually, Special Agent Sparks. I'm with the FBI as a special liaison officer with the Treasury Department." He slid his identification across the table.

"You're kidding."

"No, and I need your help with a case I'm working on."

"A case? Well, at least you're not with the IRS. I was audited three years ago, and I don't ever want to go through that hell again." She smiled. "I can't say I'm happy about being lied to. Why didn't you just present yourself at the office?"

"I wanted to get a sense of you as a professional person."

"And this dinner is to get a sense of me as a private person?"

It was Sparks's turn to smile. "Something like that. It was for my personal benefit as well."

"A little self-confident, are we?"

"I don't normally mix business and pleasure, but I thought an exception to that rule was warranted."

"I'm glad. Now, what could I possibly help the FBI with?"

Sparks gave her all the details outside of the history lesson contained in the special report he had received from Griffin two days before. He included the murder in Fort Myers and the attempt on his life, plus gave the details that the family from New England would probably be contacting her soon. "Unless, of course, they've already contacted you," Sparks said.

"No. I can't believe that this is all true. That story was passed down through the family and we all thought of it as just a neat Civil War mystery story to tell friends at cocktail parties. I had some friends who told me we should do some research on it and see if it was possibly true. I thought about it, but work always seemed to get in the way. I really haven't had time."

"Does your family have any written documentation about the gold or anything having to do with the Civil War?"

"Sure. I've got some letters, a few old photos, and such. They're in a safe deposit box at my bank. I had a small house fire a number of years ago, and it kind of scared me into moving them into safe-keeping."

"Do you remember anything pertaining to a gold shipment?"

"Not specifically. The family legend was never written down. It was passed down by word of mouth." The drinks arrived, and they both paused to check the menu and quickly decided on their meal. He ordered salmon, and she chose chicken with angel-hair pasta. After the waiter left, Coulthard continued where she'd left off.

"My great-great-great—I don't know how many greats—grandfather was Lawrence Stallard, a farmer who lived northwest of here with his family beginning around the time the Confederates fired on Fort Sumter. Lawrence had lost a part of a hand in a farming accident a few years before. The work was difficult, but he managed. He believed in the South, he just couldn't go fight with the injury. He had a brother who lived at first with the family in Charleston but then moved north just before the war."

"Would that be Parker Stallard?"

"Yes, how did you know?"

"It fits."

"Because of the war, there was no direct mail service between the North and the South, but Parker would contact Lawrence on a regular basis. Evidently, they had friends who would run mail down through Kentucky and get it put into the Confederacy's postal service. Parker's letters, a few of which I have, mostly dealt with family news or general comments about the war. Nothing someone could take as being important information. I've read the letters myself."

"I would like to see everything you have, if you don't mind," Sparks said.

"Of course. You can make copies to take with you, but I would like to keep possession of the originals."

"Certainly."

"Sometime in July of 1863, Lawrence received word from a family friend that he had received a letter telling Lawrence that Parker would be sending some vital information to Florida and that it might come after the war was over. It would involve a large sum of money that belonged to the family. Around this same time, Lawrence and

Parker's father died in Charleston, and he was a widower with two daughters who were both already married. Then, after that message from the family friend, there was nothing. No letters. No telegrams. After the war, Lawrence traveled north to find out what had happened to Parker. There were few leads, and they didn't come to much. He evidently didn't know a lot of the people Parker associated with, so he went back down to Florida and continued farming."

The food arrived within a few minutes, and they set about eating. The atmosphere, drinks, and Coulthard's appearance in the soft candlelight provided an intoxicating mixture. Sparks was also fascinated by the story and the mystery around it. He knew he would have to study the White House report carefully in the morning.

For now, he preferred to concentrate on Coulthard.

July 25

The phone shattered the droning of the air-conditioning unit in Sparks's room. He had left an 8 a.m. wakeup call with the front desk. He sat up in a dark room, thanks to the heavy curtains. His mouth dry, he grabbed a glass of water and parted the drapes. The night before had ended with some laughter and a soft goodnight kiss in the car before she had let him out at the hotel.

Coulthard's story was interesting, and it seemed to fit with the general perusal he had given the White House file. Now it was a matter of reading it in more detail this morning. Sparks had made plans to meet Coulthard at her office, where she was to bring the old family files. That was set for 3 p.m., so he had some time before then.

After breakfast and a quick look at the *Times-Union* and *USA Today*, Sparks made a phone call to Fort Myers and got through immediately to Johnson.

"Jason Sparks, I thought I'd be hearing from you soon." Johnson's husky voice was made more so by what sounded like a bad cold. He coughed before he could continue. "Standing in that damn rain when we met sent me over the edge. Felt it coming on all that time."

"You sound like shit," Sparks said. "Any news on your investigation?"

"It's nice to know I sound as bad as I feel. Yeah, one of the lab guys lifted a clean print near the light switch in the bedroom there where all the books and the computer station were. It matches a rather dubious character from New York City by the name of Peter Coleman. His background printout sheet reaches clear across the room. Grand theft, assault, solicitation, blackmail. Been arrested for them all, but only the assault and solicitation charges ever stuck. NYPD says he has links to a small mob family but has been known to hire out to others. He's been linked to, but never arrested in, about a dozen murders just in New York City."

"Does the report say how those murders were committed?" Sparks asked.

"I thought you might ask that. It seems Mr. Coleman prefers using sharp objects to guns. His assaults were all with knives, and the possible murders were all similar. They couldn't nail him on them, though."

"Did you try to locate him yet?"

"Way ahead of you." Johnson coughed again. "They staked out his place and got a warrant. Nothing there to lead us anywhere, but they're hanging around to see if he turns up. They can bring him in just on the fingerprint on Sanibel. They're going to let me know what they turn up. The rest of the lab work from Sanibel is still being processed. The island cops are on my back to get someone nailed on this. They don't want nervous tourists canceling over an unsolved murder. Have you come up with anything?"

"I have an idea as to why Drury was killed, but I want to get everything in line before I pass it along to you. I can tell you the motive was money, and you can bet that if Coleman is the guy, then he was hired by someone else outside your area."

"I hate that need-to-know crap." Johnson was mildly irritated.

"I'll get back to you. Let me know when Coleman is brought in, and I'll make sure all the necessary information to extradite him gets to you."

"I would appreciate that, and, hey, you got any special family remedies for a bad cold?"

"I'm afraid you're on your own."

Sparks sat on his bed, a notebook and pen in one hand, turning pages in the report spread out in front of him. It was really an amazing file—a mixture of copies of old documents with longhand script that sometimes was difficult to decipher and modern printout forms with evaluations of the feasibility of locating the gold. Still another section dealt with just the potential legalities of who would own the gold if it was recovered.

As mysteries went, this was one for the books.

A regular Pinkerton operative, on loan from General George McClelland to the president and Secretary of State Seward, was killed near Sharpsburg, Maryland, just before the Battle of Antietam in September of 1862. A short list of regular Union soldiers had been compiled, and this Lieutenant Jackson Prescott was at the top.

He had shown resourcefulness, great physical ability, and great contempt for inept superiors. His peers found his opinion flawless and his character likewise. But the most important note was that his family had ties to the possible next contact with the Rebel conspirators, a Cassias Fitzroy of Philadelphia. Lincoln convinced Prescott to go undercover to try to gain information on this group.

He had left on September 24, 1862, when a fake escape was arranged, and an actual attack from highway robbers had provided additional coverage. Then, much to Lincoln's dismay, Prescott vanished for two and a half months, until a wire reached the president. Led with the words "North Star," which was the agreed-upon code, the wire message went like this:

Progress made. Shipment being processed in Chicago. Early spring move expected. Shipment destination undecided though likely from northern port. Assistance unnecessary now. Will contact when shipment ready. J.P.

The president noted his relief that the young officer was alive and very much working on the assignment. Then there was another long period of no contact, until a second wire arrived for the president. This came on February 15, 1863:

Shipment scheduled to leave Philadelphia in late spring. Will contact with specific instructions. Route unknown. Wagon passage expected. Shipment size unknown. My place is secure. J.P.

All through March, April, and May, Lincoln waited for word from Prescott on the gold shipment, with no contact forthcoming. Both Seward and Stanton believed that the gold had already made it out of the country, though contact with agents in England and France reported no discussion about a shipment's arrival.

Then, when reports came into Washington that General Lee and his army of Northern Virginia was again moving into the north and the Army of the Potomac was moving to meet the threat, another wire arrived from Prescott. This one was dated June 24, 1863.

Urgent. Shipment to arrive in Philadelphia early July. Trenton Warehouse. Shipment sailing July 7. Troops should intervene one day prior. Not all information requested available. J.P.

The last wire came from Harrisburg, Pennsylvania, barely a day's ride by rail. One could assume the gold was there on that date. But somewhere between Harrisburg and Philadelphia, the gold disappeared.

The phone jolted Sparks, and he spilled some of his papers on the floor as he reached for it.

"Jason?" It was Tracy, her voice thick with fear. "I just had a talk with a most unnerving individual. He gave me his name as Paul Smith and . . . oh, God, it was scary."

"Try to calm down. Are you OK now? You aren't alone, are you?"

"Yes, that's just it. I swung by the house for something I had forgotten this morning, and he came to the door just as I reached it. Before I realized it, we were inside."

"Did he threaten you?" Sparks asked.

"No. Actually, he acted quite pleasant, but I remembered all you said about the poor professor and . . ."

"Get in your car and meet me at your office. Don't come here to the hotel. I want to see if you're followed. Also, did you tell him about the family papers?"

"No, I told him just what you said to tell him. The general story about the family legend, but nothing beyond that. I think he'll probably try to contact me again. It kind of sounded like he would."

"Drive to your office. Give me about fifteen minutes before you leave. I want to be in place at your office before you arrive."

"OK . . . Jason, I'm scared."

"I don't think you're in any danger, but when we meet at the office, I'll want a full description."

"I'll see you in a little while."

"Forty minutes."

As he gathered up the papers, his mind already thinking of the best vantage point to observe the outside of Coulthard's office building, a small piece of paper caught his eye. It was a copy of an original document in handwriting Sparks had seen before. It was short, but the implication was significant.

Under my personal authority as President of the United States, I have dispatched special agent Col. Andrew Brison to monitor Lt. Jackson Prescott during a personal assignment for myself. Col. Brison is to view the circumstances, then lend assistance when necessary. Col. Brison is working under authority granted by myself, solely for myself, and will respond to consequences only from this office.

I make this authorization and proclamation, Sept. 26, 1862.

A. Lincoln

Chapter Eight

September 30, 1862

It was still dark when Stallard roused Prescott from his sleep in the basement of Fitzroy's house. All Stallard asked was if Prescott wanted help in getting out of Philadelphia and heading west. When Prescott answered in the affirmative, Stallard immediately indicated they were leaving.

Minutes later, in Fitzroy's private carriage, the two men set off north to where they could cross the Delaware into New Jersey, heading for the largest city in America—New York. Stallard's reason for not taking the Pennsylvania and Ohio out of Philadelphia was made clear shortly into their journey when, in the predawn, they were stopped by a detail on the main pike heading north.

The man in charge was tired but wary. "I'm sorry to delay you, sir, but we're looking for a fugitive—a traitor—who escaped just south of the city and might be headed north." He peered into the carriage's interior, which was occupied solely by a gentleman with an ivory-handled cane and a scar on his left cheek. "I must first ask you why you're traveling so early in the morning?"

"I have business in New York City, but I'm stopping at a family farm in New Jersey. I felt it necessary to start early today. My name is Parker Stallard. I'm a Chicago-Philadelphia–based businessman. Who are you looking for, Lieutenant?"

"Captain," corrected the officer, irritated by ignorant civilians, especially young, healthy ones who had not answered the call. He unfolded a flier and handed it to Stallard. "We're looking for this man. His name is Jackson Prescott."

"I have seen these notices around the city, and I read about him in the newspaper. Despicable character. I hope you catch him, Captain."

The captain took the paper back and glanced around the carriage, including checking underneath, before asking to see the face of the driver. Apparently satisfied, the captain apologized for the inconvenience and waved the carriage on.

After they were around the bend, Stallard got up from his seat and lifted the one-piece unit forward to reveal a rather cramped Prescott, who stiffly climbed out.

"Now you see why I told you it was necessary to head west from somewhere other than Philadelphia. I doubt you'll draw much attention up there. And even if you do, without your mustache and chin hair, people won't recollect you." Stallard looked at the clean-shaven Prescott. "You do look five or six years younger."

"Why do you think I grew them in the first place?"

Stallard laughed. "When the war is over and you go home to Charleston, you can grow it back again, I'm sure."

"For now, I would just be happy knowing where we're going and why you're helping me."

"There are two reasons. One, I like you, even though we have different feelings about the cause. You're an educated man, like myself, and you stand by your convictions. Second, we're both southerners, at least in how we were raised, and I feel it's my duty to help you, and more selfishly, I hope I might convince you to join with me in a little endeavor Cassias and I have been undertaking."

"You two are involved in business?"

"More than business," Stallard said, tapping his cane on the carriage's floorboard. "We're doing some work up here in the North that will ultimately benefit the South, as well as ourselves. It could be rewarding for you."

"What is the nature of your business?"

"We shall discuss it at a later time. We have a few days of travel, and we'll get to it in all good time. For now, I would like to get some sleep."

Stallard propped his feet up on a small footstool and folded his arms across his chest. Within a few moments, much to Prescott's amazement, he was snoring. Prescott turned in his seat, leaned his head back against the corner of the carriage, and looked out at the first touch of light coming from the east.

His thoughts drifted from his own situation to his friends in the regiment back in camp, wherever that was now. Certainly, McClelland must be pursuing Lee southward to press the advantage. Prescott found hope in the idea that the war might end before he would have to complete his assignment. *Perhaps that will happen,* he thought, before drifting off to sleep.

Prescott awoke to find Stallard reading what appeared to be a ledger, scribbling in some notations, fighting the carriage's movement. Prescott looked out at the countryside, soft with the pale sun of early fall, the trees and grass tinged with brown. He sensed the approach of a deepening chill and ultimately the slumber of winter.

"I haven't been through this part of New Jersey before," Prescott said.

"It's Pennsylvania." Stallard closed the book. "We're going to take the railroad west out of Harrisburg to Cleveland, then on to Chicago. That's my final destination. Yours as well, if you decide to stay with me."

"A man can get lost in the Western Territories much easier than in a city where there will be much Union Army activity. Still, your offer is intriguing, if you believe you can truly help end the war."

"My group believes we can," Stallard said. "I believe you can be a value to us. You're resourceful, intelligent. Those are qualities I can use."

"Give me some information I can use to make a decision."

Stallard looked at Prescott for a moment, then took his cane and rolled it vertically between his hands.

"Five years ago, my brother Charles, always a bit of an adventurer, headed out to the territories in search of . . . adventure, I believe. Three years ago, he found it. He saved the life of an Indian, part of a tribe that lived just east of a large mountain range in the Montana Territory. Even though Charles was a white man, the Indian took him in."

They reached a small town, and the driver pulled the two-horse team off the road into a cleared area next to a tavern. Climbing down from above, he said that they needed to water the horses and rest them a bit, and that he needed a break as well. Stallard and Prescott crossed over to the tavern for a meal and drink. As they sat at a table near the window, Stallard continued his story.

"As Charles was preparing to head into the mountains, he heard the story of what the Indians called 'Sun Cave.' It was in an area the tribe said had never been visited by the white man. Intrigued, he took a guide and went into the mountains. They were gone for a month, but when he returned to the Indians, he negotiated a safe passage through the territories north along the Canadian border until he came back down through Minnesota and Wisconsin to Chicago. He wired me from there."

"Gold," Prescott said matter-of-factly.

"How did you get that?"

"Come now. Sun cave, mountains. A sudden desire to contact you."

"We knew that war was coming soon and all it took was a careful examination of the industries of the North and South to see who would win if the war lasted a long time. And that was without taking into consideration an effective blockade. So, we decided to set up a system to move large amounts of gold out of the country in exchange for armaments, but more importantly, political influence."

"To France or Britain, asking them to exert political pressure on the Union," Prescott said, pausing to shake his head. "I don't see it being effective. A single gold strike can make a man, or a few men, rich. But it couldn't produce enough gold to sway the politics of a world power."

"Are you sure?"

"How? All of the gold taken out of California in the last thirteen years might do it, say two or three hundred million dollars. But that was from thousands of claims spread over a large portion of California. You're talking about a single mine."

"Exactly." Stallard smiled and took a drink from his beer.

Prescott leaned forward and whispered, "What are you saying?"

"That gold cave is well hidden and has a small entrance. But it opens up into a cavern. Charles did some research, and he believes it's the largest gold deposit ever found. Just working by himself, he extracted three hundred thousand dollars in fairly pure ore. He says he's barely scratched the surface."

"How have you been able to keep it a secret? The people and materials necessary must be enormous."

Stallard snatched his cane in his left hand and pointed it at Prescott. "That's where my brother Charles's true genius lies. He forged an agreement with the Indians, a pact that we have every intention of keeping. Because they trust Charles, they have helped set up a camp far enough into the mountains that no white man has been there to stake a claim."

"So you haven't made a claim yourselves."

"Of course not. If we registered a claim in that part of the territories, it would be Sutter's Mill all over again. When the war is over, we can stake a legitimate claim." Stallard's enthusiasm swelled. It had taken five years of planning and cultivating a select group of Indians who would work the site and other men to move the gold back by wagon east to Chicago. "So far the project has worked with few problems, in terms of secrecy."

Prescott shook his head.

"We offer them more money than they would ever need in return for unquestionable loyalty and absolute secrecy," Stallard said.

"Still, I find it astounding you have kept it quiet."

"Charles is an amazing individual. I'll be glad to introduce you to him eventually."

"I'm not familiar with how to process gold at a camp and melt it down. That's the sort of work they do at a mint, don't they?"

"Yes, but we have an agreement with a foundry owner in Chicago. He has helped us make the final separation of the gold from the ore. Then he melts it down and stores it for us. When the time comes, we'll ship the gold out of the country and to the individuals we're contracting with to buy influence in the English Parliament. If we show enough consistency in payments, then the cry for Confederate recognition from England will be undeniable."

"And if the war ends before your plan brings results?" Prescott asked.

"Then we'll stake a claim and become the richest men on the continent."

The proprietor brought them their food, and they ate heartily to quiet their hunger.

Switching from coach to railroad in Harrisburg went smoothly. There was a detachment of Union soldiers moving through town on another line heading west as well, but Prescott stayed clear of any place where it would be possible for someone to recognize him. To their relief, there were no notices posted at the station, and after a night of sleeping in the carriage, Stallard and Prescott purchased tickets west. The train left at 8 a.m. the next day.

Stallard paid for separate sleeping rooms, the first they had ever seen, and tipped the conductor enough so that they knew they would not be disturbed. He then inquired about any card games being organized, and when informed there would be, made sure he reserved himself a place in the game.

The day passenger car carried an assortment of people—a few soldiers on leave, two or three businessmen, two complete families from Philadelphia headed for somewhere in Indiana, an elderly man going to live with his son and daughter-in-law in Cleveland, and a stranger sitting in the very back of the car. He was dressed in a dark suit with a western-style hat. He wore a black mustache and sideburns that moved gracefully down his face. He carried a satchel of dark leather that matched his pristine boots. A careful observer could see he carried a cold face with dark eyes, alert and clear. He gave the appearance of being unapproachable—which was honored.

Except for a girl of seven who approached his seat. "Are you a cowboy?"

The stranger's face softened a bit with a small smile. "I guess you could say I'm a cowboy. I've done a little work like that."

"Where are you going?" she asked, shifting from one foot to the other in a nervous cadence. "Are you going all the way west to fight Indians?"

"No. I haven't decided how far I'm going."

"We're going to a big city. My father already lives out there, and now my mother and I are going to live out there, too."

"Well, I hope you find it to your liking."

"Betsy!" The girl's mother took her by the arm roughly and pulled her toward the front of the car, mumbling an apology to the man.

"Ma'am. It's OK. She wasn't doin' no harm." The stranger sat back in his seat and shook his head as the mother spanked the daughter and moved her back to a seat up front. Colonel Andrew Brison, special agent for the president, had two daughters of his own, and he didn't care much for seeing other children punished in public—even when being taught a lesson about talking to strangers.

The poker game Stallard had bought himself into was set up in a baggage car set near the train's rear. The swaying of the car made sitting on the overturned barrels an inconvenience, but the five men found it tolerable. The conductor ran the game, along with one of the firemen from the engine who was off duty.

With them and Stallard were two men: a businessman from Philadelphia whom Stallard didn't know, and a rough, drifter-looking type who wasn't dressed well, but who brought plenty of table money. And while he gave his name as Webster Tyler, no one at the table believed that was his real name. The game began in the early evening under the light of three lanterns, and by 10:30, the drifter had lost a great deal of his money. To compensate, he had started drinking at a quicker pace than anyone else.

To keep a low profile, Prescott had stayed back in his sleep compartment at the insistence of Stallard, who was jovial about finding a card game to pass the hours until they reached Cleveland. After a brief time of utter boredom in his compartment, Prescott had moved as discreetly as possible to one of the day cars and had taken a seat with his hat tipped forward over his face. He proceeded to listen in on the conversations going on around him.

Lee's venture into Maryland had spooked these people, at least until the battle at Antietam Creek had forced him to withdraw southward. The talk was a mixture of praise for the army and bravado about how quickly the war would now end. There was also a tinge of worry about the action taking place in the North. Two older gentlemen were arguing the merits of the announcement about the coming proclamation on the slaves—the climax of which included finger pointing and an occasional profanity. It wasn't a night of light conversation with a group of beautiful women at a Boston social, but it was entertaining nonetheless.

Still, after dozing a bit and listening some more, Prescott got up and worked his way back through the cars to the baggage compartment where Stallard said the card game would be held. He opened the door and slipped in without a word just as Stallard won another hand with three jacks.

"Thank you, gentlemen," Stallard said, pulling the chips in. "I do apologize for this recent lucky streak I've been having. It's about time, though. The last game I was in, I lost enough it hurt me for a spell."

"I don't want to hear no apologies, just set up for the next hand," said the conductor, who, judging by the pile of chips in front of him, was the only other player who had won more than he had lost.

"Yeah, get on with it. It's your deal," the businessman said.

"All right. I was just trying to keep this a friendly game," Stallard said.

The drifter named Tyler poured himself another glass of an amber-colored liquid and tipped it back with one gulp. He was drunk and his card playing was suffering. His mood matched his drunkenness.

"You, you with the cane, you've been too . . . lucky for too long." He slurred his words.

"Mr. Tyler, as the organizer of this game, I'm afraid I'm going to have to ask you to retire," the conductor said.

"I'll quit when I'm damn well ready to quit," Tyler said.

He was a big man, and the conductor looked about nervously. Seeing he didn't have any immediate help, he let the words pass.

Stallard, seated opposite from the door Prescott had entered, looked up at his traveling companion as he shuffled the cards and dealt the next hand. Prescott raised his eyebrows in reaction to the small confrontation and saw a small smile come to the corner of Stallard's mouth.

The next game progressed, with the conductor dropping out first. Then the businessman folded, leaving the fireman, Stallard, and Tyler. Each man turned in their discards and took their replacements. Prescott couldn't see anyone's hand from where he was, but Tyler, sitting to the left from his position, afforded a clear view of his hands and lap area.

For the moment, Prescott wondered if he should say anything if he caught Tyler cheating, but quickly decided that the player was too drunk and wasn't dealing this hand, so it probably wouldn't be a problem. The hand progressed and the pot grew until it was substantial—near eighty dollars, Prescott guessed. At that point, the fireman folded, leaving Tyler and Stallard.

It was Tyler's turn to raise or call, and he looked at his remaining money, then studied his cards, then flashed a glance at Stallard, who calmly turned a spare chip in his hand. The noise of the train, while loud enough to restrict all but the most determined conversations, seemed strangely in the background.

"Mr. Tyler, are you going to raise or call?" Stallard asked.

Tyler looked up at Stallard again. "You're bluffing, just like that hand you won with a pair of tens." He forced the words out without a stammer.

"It will cost you to find out, sir."

Another pause from Tyler, but this time he took his remaining money and dropped it into the table's center. "I'll raise you twenty."

Stallard paused as well. He had told Prescott earlier that he loved this part. He didn't care about the money, just that the others cared deeply about the money.

"Well, I'll be a gentleman, sir, and will not see and raise you again. I call your twenty," he said, dropping his money in the pile. "What do you have?"

Tyler, to Prescott's surprise, didn't smile but simply revealed his cards. "Straight, jack high."

Stallard looked at the hand on the table and felt the room's eyes on him. He had told Prescott before that this was the best part, the crushing blow of lost expectations.

"Full house, queens over nines."

There was a quick exhale from the players in the room, and the conductor produced a small whistle. A couple of voices murmured congratulations as Stallard pulled the chips from the table's center while thanking them. Prescott smiled as he folded his arms, marveling at the South Carolinian.

A look at Tyler, and Prescott lost his smile as the drifter took his right hand and slipped it low and underneath his coat. Everything seemed to slow down for Prescott as he saw the small gun appear in Tyler's hand, still below the table. Without a sound, Prescott propelled himself from the wall, took one step, and launched himself at Tyler, just as the drifter was standing, raising his pistol arm at Stallard's chest.

"You bastard!" is all Tyler said as he pulled the trigger just as Prescott, almost parallel to the floor, slammed into him. The pistol fired, and Tyler let out a muffled cough as the air was forced from his lungs by Prescott's shoulder. The two men fell to the floor, and Tyler's head thumped the side of a crate. Tyler was knocked unconscious, bleeding from a forehead gash.

Still stunned from his fall, Prescott was quickly aware that the car was alive with motion as hands helped him up. He immediately sought out Stallard and was surprised to see him standing, clutching his left arm.

"God damn it, I thought you said this was a friendly game." Stallard's words were directed at the conductor. "And I thought it was understood that there would be no guns allowed at the table?"

"I . . . I'm sorry, Mr. Stallard. He said he understood the rules."

"Damn it. It just nicked my arm, but the idiot could have killed me!"

"I apologize again," the conductor said. "We'll have him arrested at the next stop."

"No, don't do that. I don't have time to deal with this idiot. Just put him in a locked room and let him sleep it off. Then, have one of your rougher-looking workers kick him off the train with a warning—you obviously aren't up to the task. And make sure they tell him that the next time I see him, I'll kill him."

"Yes, sir."

"Thanks for saving my life." This was directed at Prescott, who was moving his arm around in discomfort.

"My pleasure. I saw him pull the pistol and figured I didn't have time to yell out." Prescott motioned to Stallard's arm. "You better get that attended to."

The game broke up, and the unconscious Tyler was carried to another car while Prescott and the conductor attended to Stallard's arm. It was a simple graze, and they applied a bandage.

Stallard laughed as they finished up. "How about that. Did you see those last two hands I had? Damn, I was lucky tonight. Haven't had a run like that in a long time."

Prescott was incredulous. "You almost *died* tonight."

"I know, I know. Thank you again." Stallard put his hand on Prescott's shoulder. "I'm being truthful here. Your quick thinking saved me from the stupid son of a bitch, and I owe you. First chance, I'll buy you a drink." The smile returned.

Prescott could only shake his head.

The roar of cannon shook the ground under Prescott's feet as he ran in a crouch to the edge of the cornfield. The air was alive with death—

mini-balls, shrapnel, and canister grape, all hot enough to heat the very air they were propelled through. One of Prescott's best friends, Jeremiah Smith, threw his body down next to his lieutenant and swore under his breath. A battery of Union artillery, just off to the left, exploded in retaliation. Thick, grayish smoke hung suspended just in front of the muzzles after the flash disappeared.

Jeremiah yelled something to Prescott, but Prescott could not hear him over the voluminous rush of sound. Prescott nodded in understanding, even though he didn't, and Jeremiah collected himself and tensed for a rush to the left. Prescott took one step before an explosion knocked him off his feet and slammed him to the ground. Suddenly, the sound was gone. Silence filled his head, and he tried to blink his eyes to clear his vision. It returned as the sounds did, more frightening and loud than before. A hot, sticky wetness covered his face and Prescott felt for his head to locate a wound, but was unsuccessful.

He sat up and gingerly worked his way into a crouched position again, all the while feeling for an injury, waiting for the pain to strike. But it would not come. He called out for Jeremiah. He said his name a half dozen times, like calling for a brother at dusk on a warm summer evening. A call filled with affection, a bit of annoyance, and concern. Twice more he called Jeremiah's name before he saw the shape just to the left. Prescott had to stare for a few seconds before the horror of recognition. A misshapen tangle of human flesh turned inside out and torn into pieces. Prescott's eyes followed from the body along the bloody ground to his own feet, then his legs, then his torso and arms—all wet with blood. A scream swept over him.

Prescott's eyes snapped open and his body shook as he awoke in the sleeping compartment. Covered in sweat, he swung his legs around and off the bed as he tried to regain his breath, his heart crashing against his chest. The dream came to him after a moment, and he felt nauseated. He needed air, and so he got dressed and slipped out of his compartment, heading for the day cars.

His watch said 2:30 a.m. and he was tired, but the adrenaline hadn't subsided. He was still shaking as he walked down the aisle of the quiet day car, filled with people trying to sleep. The lamps were turned low. He moved through the back door and went down a second car much like the first. When he reached the back of this car, he stopped, for this one had an extra-large entrance area where he could stand and watch the dark countryside slip past. The moon was only past its first quarter, but Prescott could still see some of the land's features. He took out a cigar. He hoped a short smoke might calm him down.

The door opened behind him and a figure stepped onto the platform. Prescott glanced back over his shoulder and saw it was a man of medium build with a hat pulled low over his face. The newcomer mumbled a hello and added something about air. He turned to the opposite side of the platform and pulled out a cigar of his own, put it in his mouth, bit off the end, and then made the movements of searching for a match.

"Excuse me, sir," the man said. "Could I have a match? Seems I've misplaced mine somewhere."

"Certainly." Prescott struck a match and lit the man's cigar.

As the man inhaled in rapid fashion, he kept his face down, and the brim of his hat blocked the match's illumination. "Obliged."

Prescott turned back to the railing where he had been standing when he heard the telltale sound of a pistol's hammer being cocked. His body froze, and he felt a pistol barrel against the back of his head.

"I have little money on me. I'm traveling as the guest of someone else." Prescott raised his hands.

"I'm not concerned with that right now, *Lieutenant Prescott*." The man accentuated the last two words.

"You have the wrong man. My name is Stevenson, not Prescott."

"Don't insult me, Prescott. My brother was in your regiment, and he introduced me to you about four months back. Name is Pierce. My brother is Private Seth Pierce. I read about you in the papers. Did you know there's a thousand-dollar reward for you?"

"No, I didn't."

"Well, you're quite the traitor, aren't you? Where you headed? Canada? Western Territories?"

"It seemed the prudent action to take."

"Why not just head south, you scum? Move this way to the baggage car." Pierce stepped back and pointed with his free hand to the door of the baggage car across the coupling from where they stood. "Let's go."

Prescott tossed his cigar away, as did Pierce, and the two of them made their way into the baggage car, the same one used for the card game a few hours before. There was a dimmed lantern on the left wall, casting a yellowish tint to the interior. Pierce closed the door behind him.

"The reward says nothing about having to bring you in alive, Prescott. Get on your knees." Pierce was standing with his back to the door and had the gun held a little above waist-high. He was a good eight feet away. Too far for Prescott to reach before the hammer came down.

"Look, I won't give you any trouble, but you're really going to muck things up if you take me in. The newspaper stories were put in on purpose," Prescott said, feeling that the truth might be his only hope. "I'm actually working for the government."

The words evoked a smile from Pierce. "The Confederate government, I'm sure."

"No, the United States. I—"

"Shut up. Talkin' won't git me my money." Pierce raised the pistol, and Prescott tensed for a dive to the back of the car. The door behind Pierce slammed into his back and sent him staggering toward Prescott, who grabbed the pistol arm and thrust it downward. Both men were now locked in a death struggle, using all they possessed to gain the advantage. With an extra thrust he surprised even himself with, Prescott forced Pierce's pistol arm against a crate, knocking the weapon away. It dropped away to the floor.

Prescott took a swing with his right hand and missed, and Pierce threw his weight against Prescott and went for his throat.

Pierce had big hands, and they were now clasped around Prescott's neck, crushing the life out of him. Pierce's elbows were out at an angle, cutting down Prescott's ability to raise his own arms in defense.

The blood pounded in Prescott's face, and his lungs began to burn as he felt his back bend over something behind him. He couldn't get any leverage. He would be a dead man in a moment if he didn't act *now*!

With his legs pinned down and his body bent over backward, the only freedom he had was with his left arm, and he used it, pulling back and launching his fist into Pierce's groin. There was an exclamation and a lightening of the grip on Prescott's throat, and that was all he needed. He grabbed Pierce's arms. As Prescott regained his balance, he threw himself back at Pierce, and the two of them lurched against the crates where the pistol had fallen.

They separated and staggered farther apart as they both fought to regain their balance. Pierce lunged for an iron bar hanging from a nail and drew himself into a throwing position.

They were only ten feet apart and Prescott had no time. He threw up his arms to block the bar but was only partially successful. The blow against his forearm and head was massive, and he fell as quickly as if he had been shot. Conscious, but severely stunned, Prescott could make out Pierce bending over to pick something up. What was it? *The pistol.* Trying to gather himself, Prescott attempted to sit up, but he fell back as the car's interior started spinning.

He felt Pierce's presence above him, but there was nothing he could do.

Then, as darkness closed in on him, he heard a muffled sound and a cry of agony. He thought it was his own.

Chapter Nine

Present Day
July 25

Coming through the parking lot's back side, Sparks pulled his rental into a lot space slightly above and away from the main lot and entrance to Coulthard's office building. He only had to wait three minutes before he saw her BMW pull into the main lot and park. Her gait was hurried. Just as she entered the building, a light tan sedan slipped into the lot from the street and casually made for a spot in the main lot with a clear view of the entrance. There were two men inside, and they didn't leave the car.

Sparks left his car and worked his way back from the lip of the lot so he couldn't be seen from below. He slipped in the back entrance.

"Jason." Coulthard, oblivious to the stares of staffers, took quick steps to meet Sparks as he entered the office, and she put her arms around him.

"You OK?"

"Just a little unnerved. The man at my house had a very foreboding presence about him. It's got me on edge. I wasn't followed, was I?"

"Two men in a tan sedan. They weren't very subtle."

"This is disconcerting."

"We'll be fine. Now, which bank do you have those old family papers in?"

"It's a main branch of First North Florida. You don't want to get them now, do you?"

"As soon as you don't have possession of them, their interest in you will wane. I'd like to move them to the main bureau office here in Jacksonville."

Coulthard took hold of Sparks's shoulder. "I don't want to give up those papers, Jason. They belong to my family, to me. I'm not giving up my rights to them."

"I understand your concern, but the big, bad government bureaucracy isn't going to steal away your personal property. I have a right to hold on to it as part of an investigation, but I would prefer not to have to go through the warrant process. I would rather get your permission. I want to get a look at what, if anything, there is to this story. Obviously, someone thinks there's something to it, because they've already killed for it once and tried to kill a second time." Sparks studied her face. Her eyes were alert with concern but still mesmerizing. "Let's see what you have and then decide what we're going to do next."

Coulthard agreed to drive with Sparks to the bank. They made their way downstairs to the back entrance. Sparks headed for the car, retracing his steps so that he approached it from behind and was out of sight of the lower parking lot until he got to his driver's side door. The two men were still in the sedan and never glanced up at Sparks as he pulled out. He picked up Coulthard at the back entrance, and they left unseen.

At the bank, it took all of twenty minutes for Coulthard to retrieve the papers from three safe deposit boxes. The papers were in numerous manila folders. She also brought out an antique box with intricate carvings on the corners and top. It was about two and a half feet long by eighteen inches wide and eight inches deep, filling up an entire deposit box on its own.

As they were putting the materials in his car, Sparks saw another car approach. There were four men inside, and the driver was accelerating toward Coulthard and Sparks.

"Get in the car, now!" Sparks yelled as he threw himself into the front seat, thrust the key into the ignition, and started the engine. Coulthard was on the back floor by the time the other car slid into position behind them. The doors were already opening, and Sparks saw in the rearview mirror at least two assault-style weapons. The parking lot had staggered spaces, and though Sparks's car now had cars on each side, there was about a five-foot gap in front and to the right. There was only one choice.

"Tracy, it's going to get rough," was all he said as he put the car in reverse and slammed his foot on the accelerator. The car leapt backward the eight feet and smashed into the partially open doors where the two closest men were trying to get out. The crash of metal was followed by an agonized scream as the door crushed the legs of the man in the backseat and forced the car to the side a few feet. Before the movement had even stopped, Sparks had dropped the shift into Drive and shot forward, aiming for the opening to the right-front of his parking space. He clipped the two cars, but made it through as he accelerated to the screech of metal.

Coulthard yelled as they sped out of the parking lot and onto the main road. A look back found the other car pulling into traffic as well, three hundred yards behind them, with eight to ten cars between them. She got up on her knees and slipped between the two front seats. "I don't want to sound ungrateful, but what the hell did you just do back there?"

"Four rather unpleasant gentlemen were about to take away property that's rightfully yours, and from the metallic ensemble they were sporting, they weren't going to ask nicely, *and* I wouldn't give a whole lot for our seeing the end of the day."

Sparks darted in front of a car in the right-hand lane, invoking a horn and an obscene gesture. He skidded and fishtailed through a right-hand turn and accelerated down a side street through a residential area. The car in pursuit made the corner and now had a clear line-of-sight with Sparks's car. The back window of the rental exploded into fragments.

"Down!"

"Already there. I had a feeling this was going to happen!"

Sparks could hear individual shots strike the car near the back on the sides. They were trying to flatten the tires without hitting the gas tank, he figured, because someone would have a hard time explaining why the material they wanted went up in a car fire. Still, they were taking a dangerous tack. And they were closing in. Their car had more horsepower, and Sparks didn't want to risk cutting off into another street and finding a dead end, or worse, kids playing in the street. This open, four-lane road would have to do for the moment.

"Do you know where we are?" Sparks cut around another car and looked back to see the pursuers less than fifty yards behind them. "We seem to be heading out into a more rural area." A high-pitched whine signaled another try for the rear tires.

"I've never been out this way, but the farther west we go, the more we head into rural areas." Coulthard had to yell over the sound of the engine and the wind through Sparks's open window. "What are we going to do?"

"It would be nice if there were some sharp turns or hills to shield us from them, but I think that's a little much to ask for in Florida." Sparks would have to take back his words, for up ahead was a turn sharp enough that there were arrows located on the turn's outside and a sign that said *25 mph*.

He waited for the car to almost reach the point of no return— he hoped—then slammed on the brakes and swung into the turn with a screech as the tires protested. The car's right side left the road for an instant, but they made the corner and accelerated down an-other straightaway. The gunmen's car also made the corner, but the driver took a more conservative approach, and it cost him distance coming out of the turn.

Sparks swore under his breath . . . an intersection was ap-proaching. The light was with them, but it had been green since he saw it, so he knew it would be changing any second. He took his foot off the gas pedal and quickly looked back and forth at the traf-fic waiting on either side of the cross road.

The light turned yellow.

He smashed his foot to the floor and the car sluggishly increased in speed. Pressing his hand on the horn, Sparks shot through the in-tersection as the light changed to red. He looked back with dread, fearing that he would see the gunmen slamming into the crossing traffic and killing innocent people. He didn't. The other drivers, experienced in city driving, had seen the pursuing car coming and had let it pass through against the light. Sparks felt relief that no one had been killed, but now the gunmen were gaining on him, and he was already topping 100 mph.

Another turn approached, again to the right. It was not as sharp as the one before, but it still required them to slow down quickly. There were heavy trees to the right, blocking his view of the upcoming road. Sparks used the same procedure as before, only he took the corner faster. The rear end slid out from behind them, and Sparks turned into the skid as they slid into the oncoming lane.

It wasn't what he had wanted to do, but it saved their lives, for just past the turn, pulling out of a dirt road onto the main road, was a cement truck going in the same direction. There was no time to react, and fortunately, there was no oncoming traffic as Sparks's car flew past the truck and the startled driver, who was just starting to get the entire truck onto the pavement.

Sparks regained control, accelerated away from the corner, and looked back in the rearview mirror. The driver of the gunmen's car, wanting to close more quickly out of this turn, had taken the corner fast and had no time to react at seeing the truck instantaneously appear. All he could do was swerve to the left, and the car became a projectile across the road and into a group of trees. The car exploded into a twirling montage of flying debris, spinning sideways in a tight rotation, hurling guns, glass, pieces of metal, and bodies into the air. As the scene slipped away in his mirror, Sparks took a breath for what seemed like the first time in ten minutes and let up on the gas pedal.

"What's happening?" Coulthard implored from the backseat.

Sparks suddenly became aware that his hands were shaking and his face and back were drenched in sweat. "They're gone." It was all he could say.

The roadside motel Sparks picked out was simple but clean. He paid cash and, with Coulthard standing beside him, drew nary a glance from the desk clerk. Registered as Mr. and Mrs. Connors, they went to Room 125, and after a few minutes of coming down from the car chase adrenaline rush, they went to work on the papers.

"Why the motel? Your adrenaline rush leading you to think of a more personal activity?" Coulthard's question came with a smile. "We haven't even had our second date yet."

Sparks smiled unconvincingly and continued to glance over the papers without looking at her. "I wanted some time to think. They found us awfully fast at your bank, and I could swear I didn't see anyone behind us on the way there from your office. Either I blew it on the drive over, or they had that branch of the bank staked out."

"Jason." Coulthard reached out and touched Sparks's arm. "I was just trying to lighten the mood a bit."

He stopped shuffling the papers and looked up at her. "Sorry. I take it personally when someone tries to kill me. It was stupid of me not to realize that as soon as they located you, they would want the papers immediately, and after what happened to Drury, the possibility of violence was obvious. As soon as we go through these papers, we're headed for the bureau office here in Jacksonville."

They began to go over the papers more closely, initially separating anything from around the Civil War era from later dates. That cut the volume by two-thirds. From there, they each took half of the remaining group and started reading. From a historical viewpoint, the papers were interesting to Sparks, even though they were letters from members of a family he knew little about. Birthdays, marriages, deaths, some nineteenth-century-style gossip, all mixed in with details of family business ups and downs.

It's a unique collection, Sparks thought. But there was nothing from either Parker or Lawrence Stallard. There were a half dozen or so letters from a Charles Stallard, but they were all dated before the war. There were none after that, and the other family letters didn't mention him.

"No correspondence from Parker or Lawrence." Sparks pulled his half of the letters together.

"I remember seeing those letters when I was younger. My father would look them over from time to time, but I don't know where he kept them. I assumed he had them with the others." Coulthard was almost done with her pile as well. They both looked over at the small chest with the intricate carvings.

"I don't know what's in the chest. My father kind of kept it to himself. I suppose they could be in there." Coulthard got up and brought the chest over to the bed.

The chest was not locked, and Coulthard carefully opened the two clasps on the front. Despite its age, the chest was pristine.

"Here they are!" Coulthard said, taking out a bundle and pulling the letters out of another envelope. "My father must have separated out the letters between Parker and Lawrence because of the family story." She counted out twelve letters. They were already arranged by date, with the first one dated May 2, 1860. Sparks and Coulthard read together, beginning with the first letter. Parker Stallard had been an educated man, and he wrote elegantly. The news was general or family related until just before the closing:

> *I do wish to address my offer to you one final time, Lawrence. I fear if you do not join us in our endeavor, we will drift apart as a family. The war will come soon and we must help the South prepare. This is a rare opportunity. I understand your reservations, but I do implore you to reconsider. However, lest you let it affect your decision, remember you will always have my love and respect, no matter your decision.*

> *Your brother,*

> *Parker*

"He's asking Lawrence to join the smuggling operation," Sparks said.

"They must have had a face-to-face discussion about it before this letter was written." Coulthard turned the letter back over to the first page. "Parker wrote 'Chicago' underneath the date. Could that be where Parker was living or where the operation was run from?"

"We'll see if there's a pattern," Sparks said.

They spent the next hour going from letter to letter, reading side by side on one of the room's two double beds. Despite his interest in the letters and the circumstances, Sparks became more aware of her presence and of his growing desire. He kept the relationship professional during that hour, but he knew it wouldn't take much encouragement from Tracy.

The next few letters were straightforward, with no mention of gold or smuggling—not even a hint. These letters, all from Parker, were dated from May 2, 1860, until March of 1862. They dealt with Parker's response to family news from Lawrence, the beginning of the war, and the news from places like Manassas, Virginia—Pea Ridge, Arkansas—Fort Donaldson, Kentucky. With the interruption of mail service between the North and South, there was mention of a trader friend who traveled between the South and Kentucky regularly—apparently he was transporting the letters across the line. He was responsible for Parker and Lawrence remaining in correspondence.

Then came a letter dated April 22, 1862:

My brother Lawrence,

Though my last letter was but three weeks ago, I felt compelled to write you on this matter. By now you have heard of the great battle held in Tennessee on the Tennessee River early this month. This battle, at a place called Shiloh, was the largest battle to date, and I fear the South will have to endure more such battles before its freedom is secured.

In excess of twenty thousand men died or were wounded there, brother. It is a number I cannot comprehend. General Beauregard's defeat has left me melancholy for the Confederacy's chances, but at the same time I am steadfast in my belief that not only will God's providence carry us, but our own work, Fitzroy's and myself, will help our just cause. That work is progressing.

I have heard from Charles, and he is well. I often think of him working alone, among the Indians, and pray for his continued safety. As I do for you and Elizabeth and the children . . .

"Did your family ever talk about Charles?" Sparks asked.

"All I remember is that he died out west in the territories that later became either Montana or the Dakotas. I don't remember."

"It sounds like he was involved with Parker in the smuggling. Does your family know anything more about him other than that?"

"Not that my father ever told me about."

The next letter was dated December 8, 1862, and contained nothing that gave any more information to help, except for a passage near the end again:

I have working with me a gentleman who belies all of our conceptions about Yankees. He does not agree with many ideas I have, but we both share a common hatred of this war. He has taught me to be humble, and I have, I believe, taught him to take life and embrace it. It is like I have a fourth brother. His name is Jackson, and I hope I will have the honor of introducing you to him when the war is over . . .

Jackson!

Sparks leapt from the bed, went out to his car, and retrieved his briefcase. Back in the room, with Coulthard looking bewildered, he pulled out the file and read the passage. The operative who had disappeared at the same time as the gold, the one handpicked by Lincoln, was a Lieutenant Jackson Prescott.

"This can't be a coincidence, Tracy. The man Parker mentions here has the same first name as the officer who was sent on assignment to infiltrate the smuggling ring. It has to be him."

"So there really was a shipment of gold." Coulthard could not contain her excitement as she swung herself up onto the bed on her knees.

"We know at least this might confirm the conspiracy existed."

"What more does your file have? Tell me all about it. Does it hint at where the gold might be?"

Sparks laughed and held up his hand. "Hold on. First, I can't tell you what's in the file—it's classified—but I can tell you that it doesn't have any information directly telling us where the gold is. I can tell you that the people who killed Drury and went after us today have in their possession a letter that details part of the information about where the gold is hidden. They just don't have the other pieces. Part of the answer could still be right here."

They ordered pizza and went back to reading the letters. The next one from Parker was dated January 19, 1863, again with Chicago as the place of origin, and contained more general information about the war and other family news. There was nothing else that could be construed as being important.

They sat on the bed, eating pizza and drinking beer, in a somber silence.

"There are no other letters?" Sparks asked.

Coulthard was apologetic. "These are all I remember. It has been a number of years. Jason, if my father had other letters, I wouldn't know where they could be."

Sparks got up and went over to get another slice when he again noticed the chest that the letters had been in. There was something unusual about the interior. He brought the chest back over to the bed, sat down, and began running his hands along the exterior. The wood was heavy. Sparks then felt along the base of the interior.

"You're not looking for a secret compartment, are you? Isn't that a little cliché?"

Sparks ignored the comment and continued to feel along the base, inside and out. "It might be cliché, but a lot of chests in the eighteenth century and before had secret compartments. Whoever designed this might have taken an old idea and used it. See here, the inside base is at least an inch and a half higher than the outside bottom." Just then, Sparks's finger found a depression in the carvings on the left rear leg and there was an audible *click*. "I'll resist the temptation to say 'I told you so.'"

The bottom, working on a hidden hinge, was slightly ajar. Sparks pulled it back, but there was nothing in the compartment underneath. Exasperated, he knocked the chest's top down in disappointment as he fell back on the bed. Coulthard got up to get another beer from the ice bucket. Almost as soon as he was on his back, Sparks was back at the chest, lifting the top and moving it from side to side in a vertical position.

"This whole chest is made of solid, heavy wood—I'm not sure of the kind."

"Cherry," Coulthard said.

"Cherry. This is too light." He continued to move the lid back and forth. "See. It has the same type of carvings on it as the rest of the chest, and it appears to be made of the same type of wood, but it's too light for the size of it when you compare it to the rest of the chest."

"I think you're reaching."

"No, look." He showed her the top, and she moved it back and forth.

"It's hollow."

Sparks ran his hand along the corners of the cover in the same manner as before. "It might be cliché to have a false bottom in the chest, but what would you say to a false top?" As if on cue, there was another *click,* and the cover's interior popped open to reveal another compartment.

And this one wasn't empty.

The only letter in the secret compartment was dated June 28, 1863, and had been written in Harrisburg, Pennsylvania. The significance of the location was not lost to Sparks. The report in his briefcase said that the final contact Lincoln had with Prescott had been a wire sent from Harrisburg on the same day this letter was written. The tone of this letter was urgent, unlike the others, which had been conversational.

The handwriting was different from the others as well—abrupt, sharper. Though he was not an expert, Sparks had consulted with enough of the bureau's top people that he had picked up a basic professional level of understanding. While Parker Stallard had written the other letters in a casual environment, this last letter was written under great stress.

My brother Lawrence,

By now you have received the news of Charles's death. The accident from my understanding was abrupt and his death was quick. We will have time to grieve in the future, but I must detail information to you now that is vital for you and your family.

We have moved a shipment into hiding near here, and for reasons I cannot go into now, I have found it prudent to put the information on its whereabouts into three separate documents that alone cannot divulge the shipment's location, but together will allow you to complete the task.

Lee's Army of Northern Virginia and the Union's Army of the Potomac are maneuvering close to each other. A major battle may be days away, but no one knows where it could be. The balance of the war could be decided within a week.

If I do not survive the conflict, here is what will happen. I have retained a law firm in Boston. Upon the completion of the war, no matter the outcome, you will receive a representative from this firm. He will have in his possession one-third of the necessary information. This letter also contains one-third of the information. The final one-third is in the possession of Cassias Fitzroy in Philadelphia. He will have instructions to give it to you upon your request.

I cannot go into the reasons why the shipment is not leaving the continent, but rest assured, my reasons are sound.

I have taken precautions in the event these letters are discovered. I only ask you to remember the word and number games we used to play as children. The truth can be found five steps on the side of our savior, who is with God. Our family is in my prayers, Lawrence, take the information and use it to better their lives.

Your loving brother,

Parker

25 1 12 12 7 13 4 11 14 25

And he showed unto him all the kingdoms of the world in a moment of time.

For a long time, Sparks and Coulthard sat on the bed against each other in silence. They both reread the letter three times over before Coulthard spoke.

"Something happened to change their plans about shipping the gold out of the country. And it is, or was at the time, hidden somewhere around Harrisburg."

"These numbers mean something as well, as does this phrase underneath," Sparks said. "Do you recognize it?"

"It sounds like it's from the Bible."

"Yes. And the numbers?"

"I don't know."

"Parker writes Lawrence and tells him to remember the times when they played word and numbers games as children," Sparks said, pointing to the line of figures. "And all those numbers are under twenty-six, the number of letters in the alphabet. So, it would be logical to assume the numbers represent letters."

"It would be too simple, wouldn't it?" Coulthard retrieved a pen and paper from her purse and wrote the numbers out in sequence and put the letters in order. Without cryptic work, she came up with Y A L L G M D K N Y. "Well, so much for being a simple puzzle."

"There's more to it than that, Tracy, but I'm tired. I need a good night's sleep. In the morning we can go over this again, and then I'll need to bring the bureau in on this. There are just too many bad guys roaming around you. They already have one-third of the puzzle, and if they get you, they'll have just one-third to go. At the bureau, they have computers that will solve this within minutes."

"Does this mean you're going to dump me off with people I don't know and force me to sit and wait while you see this through to the end?" Tracy leaned over to Sparks and kissed him gently on the lips, lingering to draw out the moment. "I would much rather remain in your custody."

"I would enjoy it, also." He brought her back to his face and kissed her in return. "But this will have to wait until we're done with this whole mess. It's too risky."

"You won't blame me if I keep trying to change your mind, will you? My family will have a legitimate claim on that gold, and my life won't be normal again until the gold is found, one way or another. You can't blame me for wanting to be part of the process."

Sparks smiled and kissed her again. Short and tender. "It would be strangely out of character for you to act otherwise."

Coulthard reached forward again to kiss him, but he leaned back and shook his head slowly. He let out an audible sigh. "We need to stay professional, Ms. Coulthard."

She tilted her head to look at him from the side, then climbed off the bed and headed for the bathroom, calling out behind her as she went, "I'll take the bed nearest the television. I want to watch the news before we go to sleep."

Chapter Ten

October 1, 1862

When Prescott was first aware of the train's motion, he wondered for a moment why someone was pounding metal with a hammer, but then he realized that it was his head. In front, where the bar . . .

He sat up in his compartment and was immediately aware that he shouldn't have—the room was spinning, forcing him to lie back down. Bringing his hands to his face, he waited for calm. Feeling around, he came upon dried blood and a gash on his forehead, along with a good-sized bump. A range of questions, from how he got back to his compartment to why he was still alive at all, surged through his thoughts. His last memory was of Pierce and the fight. Maybe the bounty hunter had decided not to kill, but take him alive to the authorities. Prescott again tried to sit up, this time slowly.

He was sitting there, his feet hanging over the side, when there came a knock. The door opened and in stepped a well-dressed Parker Stallard.

"Good morning, Jackson. We'll be pulling into Cleveland soon. I know this magnificent establishment that . . . Good God, man, what happened to you?"

"I fell down."

"A score of times, from the look of it . . . and every time on your face." Stallard went over to a basin and pitcher, the latter of which was mysteriously filled with water. He wet a towel and brought it over to Prescott, who took it and began gently dabbing his face.

"I got into a fight last night back in the same baggage car where the poker game was held."

"I told them to put that idiot in a locked room."

"No, it wasn't your gun-toting friend. This was a bounty hunter who had actually met me once. His brother was in my regiment. He wanted to collect on the reward. He was going to kill me, and we struggled. He hit me with"—Prescott felt the dark bruise on his forehead and also on his left wrist where he had held up his hand—"an iron bar or something." The words came slowly. "He was going to shoot me, I think."

"Well, he obviously didn't, thank the Almighty."

Prescott's mind was clearing. "But you must know all this, Parker. You stopped him, didn't you?"

"Not me, friend. I was sleeping quite soundly next door here. Didn't hear a thing."

"Then who saved my life, and where the hell is the guy who tried to kill me?"

"I'll ask around discreetly and see if anything comes up. For now, you rest until you feel like you can move around."

"No argument coming from me."

Stallard left and Prescott spent the next hour washing up and keeping the wet towel on his forehead. A trip to the mirror on the closet door revealed an ugly discoloration. It looked like the scar might be permanent.

Stallard returned with no news. No one had seen or heard anything, and there was no sign of anyone back in the baggage car. Tyler, the unlucky card player, had been already shoved off the train at a coal stop. There was no evidence of the bounty hunter, Pierce.

"Are you sure of what happened?" Stallard asked. "You've got a nasty bump."

"I know I got knocked out pretty good, but I'm sure about what happened."

"It will serve us well to be cautious."

Within the hour, the train arrived in Cleveland. They had two hours before taking a new train farther west, heading for Indiana, where they would board yet another train for Chicago. Stallard's first stop, with Prescott in tow, was the main telegraph office in the station, where he sent a message to Smythe-Tilling foundry in Chicago.

He arranged for a response from Smythe to be sent to an Indiana stop, then it was off to a restaurant for a big noon meal. Prescott was astounded at the number of people at the establishment who knew his companion. Stallard explained that the familiarity was because he regularly stopped there on business trips through Cleveland. Prescott realized that it was also a good indication of Stallard's ability to cultivate sources of support.

Sitting at a window table facing the busy street, and after the first beer had arrived, Stallard was conversing with a local while Prescott was left to look out over the tumultuous market scene in front of him. But his thoughts were on the night before. His memory was disjointed, but he had the sense that all the events were there. The brief conversation on the car platform, the pistol in his back, the few words and the death threat from Pierce in the baggage car, then . . .

There had been someone there! The door to the baggage car had hit Pierce from behind with enough force to drive him forward. But why didn't the person intervene, or did he?

He looked around at the faces in the tavern and then out on the street, paying particular attention to people who seemed to be loitering, with no business to attend to. He recognized no one, and there was a singular lack of interest in him from anyone else.

"Jackson."

Prescott realized that Stallard was addressing him. "Forgive me. Just lost in my thoughts."

"Still trying to put together what happened last night? You still look like hell."

"It still hurts like hell."

"I've got a remedy for that, my friend, but that will come later. We have some business to attend to first. The time has come for you to make your decision, because this is where we part company if you're inclined to go off on your own. I know people here who could get you into Canada by boat, and I also know people who have interests in California, unrelated to my own, who could use an extra man. No questions will be asked."

"I thought I could go as far as Chicago before making my decision."

"No, I need to have it now. It's best if we make a break now if it is to be."

Prescott looked into the face of the southerner across the table—the glare devoid of its usual jovial manner, the blue eyes staring him down. Prescott glanced downward and stared at a grain ridge on the table. After looking up and around to make sure their conversation was private, Prescott focused back on Stallard. "Do you honestly believe Fitzroy's contacts in England can sway Parliament to support the Confederacy and put an end to the war?"

"I believe the chances are even. Fitzroy is a remarkable negotiator. If it can be done, he'll be successful."

"I still don't understand how you can support slavery, Parker." Prescott leaned forward, almost pleading. "You're an educated man. You know that it is indecent and reprehensible . . . men putting their fellow man into bondage. You also strike me as a man who believes in God. Would God want men to own other men? Did he not deliver the Hebrews out of slavery?"

"I believe in God, and no, I don't believe man was meant to hold his fellow man in slavery. I told you I don't like the institution. But I also believe in determining one's own future, and Washington is denying this right to the citizens of the South. Ultimately, I believe the slaves will be freed one way or the other. But the South is doing nothing more than the colonies did ninety years ago. Why have a people's right to form their own government suddenly changed?"

"You also believe that if the Confederacy wins its freedom, the slaves will be freed?" Prescott asked.

"I'll be one of those working for it."

"Do I have your word?"

"Absolutely."

"And if the war ends before the gold can affect influence . . ."

"Then we'll use the gold to better our lives, but also to help those lives destroyed by the war, North and South. I sincerely mean that."

Prescott looked straight into the face across the table and remembered the words President Lincoln had said to him: *All that matters, young man, is that the union be preserved. It should be held by you with your last measure of devotion.*

Prescott held out his hand. "Then we work for a quick peace."

Stallard flashed a smile as he took Prescott's hand and shook it. "I'm damn glad you'll be with us. There's one caveat. We'll insist you see the task through to the end. There will be no quitting in the middle."

"Of course. I wouldn't have it any other way."

"You won't be allowed to change your mind. Do you understand me?" Stallard held on to Prescott's hand as the warmth vacated his face yet again.

Prescott nodded. "I understand perfectly."

The train pulled out of Cleveland, and the passengers' festive mood seemed far removed from the war, as there were a disproportionate number of young people on this leg of the trip. The banter was excited and rampant. Even with Stallard's considerable influence, there were no private sleeping quarters available, so the two men chose a wide seating area in the last passenger car.

Stallard was amazing. Fifteen minutes after settling in, he was involved in a flirtatious conversation with two women, dressed in travel dresses, seated across the aisle. Prescott shook his head and smiled as his companion regaled the women with talk of how his company was furnishing many of the needed materials to fight the war, and from the looks he received in return, the women were impressed. Stallard's ability to balance his work with other pursuits was phenomenal, and Prescott found himself envious.

After a pair of cursory introductions, Stallard invited the women, who were traveling alone, to have dinner, and the women accepted readily. The four made their way back to the dining car, which was only partially filled. This service, like the sleeping quarters, was a new addition to this line out of Cleveland and was elegantly detailed with rich draperies, carpeting, and lamps that bathed the interior in warm light against the dusk outside.

The dark-haired woman, who introduced herself as Sarah Blackstone, was more outgoing than her companion and started right in with the conversation. "It's so nice to find a pair of gentlemen such as yourselves on our long trip out west. Abigail and I were a bit hesitant about traveling on our own out to Chicago. We have heard such tales about unscrupulous people along the way."

"One does need to be careful, Miss Sarah. There are many people who would separate you from your money at the first opportunity, all the way from common thieves to your professional gambler." Stallard glanced at Prescott, who smiled briefly in return. "We're none of those. Though I've been known to partake in an occasional card game, I would never profess to be a professional. And William here's my right-hand man, you might say. He does all the work, and I get the credit."

"I'm sure you're overstating your unimportance, Mr. Stallard," Blackstone said. "Please tell me about your business. Do you plan on staying in Chicago long? Have you been there before?"

As Stallard started off, Prescott turned his attention to the young woman sitting across from him. Blackstone had introduced her as Abigail Stinson from Boston. She had a dark complexion with brown hair and eyes. Her features were perfectly proportioned and unblemished. Every detail was wholly perfect in its relationship to everything else. Her gaze was measured, and Prescott found that he was quite intimidated. He could instantly tell that this was a woman of uncommon intelligence and manner.

She leaned over the table and spoke softly. "Your friend finds talking about himself an easy task."

"Parker is fully versed in the topic, so I don't expect he feels at all intimidated about discussing it at length."

Stinson laughed with delight and sat back. Prescott moved forward.

"So, tell me about Miss Abigail Stinson of Boston. Is she going out to Chicago to see relatives?"

"No, though we do have family in the area, we're going to start our own business when we get there. A dress shop and other items."

"Oh, so you're both seamstresses."

"I am. Sarah is learning, but she has the business sense."

"Well, I find that interesting. It's nice to meet women who are confident in themselves and believe they can be successful in business. It's refreshing to see. I think that in a limited manner, women can be superior to men in certain kinds of businesses, such as women's apparel."

"There are some vocations where being a woman is a distinct advantage. You don't find women in business to be inappropriate?"

"Not at all. Times change and intelligent women are a commodity that has never been used properly. You seem a woman of education. May I inquire . . ."

"Bates College."

"What did you study?"

"English. I was planning on being a schoolteacher, but my life has taken a different road."

"Most extraordinary."

"What about you, Mr. Jackson? How long have you worked for Parker, and if you don't mind my asking, where did you get that nasty bruise on your handsome picture?"

Prescott touched his forehead. "I took a rather bad fall, you might say. As for myself and Parker, I'm joining him in a business venture in Chicago. His family and my family have done business together, mostly before the war."

"Did you attend college?"

"Harvard, Class of Fifty-Four. Quite a change for a young man raised in the South, but my father, a transplanted northerner, believed in obtaining the best whenever possible."

"So where do your sympathies lie? Raised in the South but educated in the North—it must create turmoil within you."

Prescott shook his head. "I only hope the war ends soon and slavery is abolished. But I don't want to lessen the festive mood with this talk." He tilted his head over to where Stallard and Blackstone were laughing quietly, completely absorbed with their own conversation. "It seems they have decided to leave us on our own."

Stinson smiled. "I don't find that distressing in the least. May I call you William?"

"Will, please."

"Call me Abby."

For the rest of the evening Prescott never gave the war, his mission, or the attempt on his life another thought, so taken by Stinson was he. It took him no longer than a few minutes to realize she was the most remarkable woman he had ever met.

She was well spoken, intelligent, and well versed in the correct protocols of polite society, which Prescott found distasteful in most circumstances. But with Stinson, it was different, because he noticed a mischievous way about her. She exuded a sensual presence that he found most exciting, and instead of finding himself uncomfortable, he was enthralled.

An hour later, Stallard and Blackstone excused themselves, saying they were going for a walk. Prescott and Stinson stayed on to talk. The topics ranged from school to old sweethearts to favorite childhood memories. She took his hand as she talked, eyes dancing with visions from a recent, happy past, and Prescott felt his attraction overtake him.

"I believe it's time for me to go back to my compartment," Abigail said. "I don't believe Sarah and Parker will be coming back this way."

"I'll walk you back."

They made their way through two of the seat-only cars and reached the compartment car. It was half past ten and the car passageway, which went along the car's right side, was empty. As they walked past the compartment next to Stinson's, she stopped and paused, bending her ear to the door. She held her finger up to her lips and smiled, motioning for Prescott to press against the door.

With a perplexed look, he brought his ear to the wood. From inside, just above the sound of the wheels on the tracks, could be heard the sounds of a couple having taken to bed. He felt the blood fill his face with embarrassment—not only for what he was hearing, but also from the look of delight on Stinson's face as she took his hand and led him away from the door to her compartment.

She unlocked it and slipped inside, not allowing Prescott to let go of her hand.

"Abigail!" he said in a loud whisper. "You embarrassed me, listening in on them like that. Is that Sarah's compartment?"

"Of course it is. Your friend Parker is positively devilish. He has met his equal when it comes to relations between the sexes, though. Sarah is not afraid to enjoy herself, as I think Parker is finding out presently." She laughed as she looked into Prescott's bewildered face. "I'm not going to apologize for her behavior."

"I don't follow the mandates of polite society in all cases, but I think there are proper ways to address your feelings."

Stinson brought herself up close to him and touched the side of his face. "Then how do you tell someone that your heart leaps when he smiles at you? And that you want to lie with him more than anything, even at the risk of being thought of as a street woman?" She reached up to his face and brought her lips to his. Prescott's mind fluctuated, confused by his emotions. He kissed her in response, putting his arms around her and drawing their bodies against one another.

As their kiss slipped away, Prescott protested. "I'm not a Puritan, but we have only just met. I'm intoxicated with you, but to throw ourselves together like a customer and a woman of comfort . . ."

Stinson flashed a fiery look. "I had hoped the reason I felt this attraction was because you felt it as well, that you liked me for who and what I was. If I was mistaken, then perhaps you should leave."

"I'm sorry. I meant no offense. You just have to understand . . . I've never met a woman like you before, Abigail. You're more alive than any woman I have ever met. You're totally unafraid of what will be said about you. I wish I could be more like you."

She pulled him close again and turned her head against his chest. "Don't think about anything else except our feelings now. Nothing else matters."

They kissed again, this time with urgency. He unbuttoned her top jacket as she undid his. Her aggressiveness excited him. They continued on, each movement accelerating as each article of clothing fell to the floor.

Individual staterooms on a train—the idea had merit. Prescott smiled to himself as he lay on his back with Abigail next to him, her head on his shoulder. She was stroking the hair on his chest. Their coupling had been the most intense experience of his life—they had both hurled themselves into each other with a luminous excitement.

They had finished with him on top of her, kissing her neck and gently biting the lobe of her ear as he grabbed her and pulled himself deeper. Then, tender kisses as they came down from the passion. Now there was just the rocking of the train as the time reached half past midnight.

"Why have you not joined to fight the South?" Abigail's words were soft, not accusatory.

This was a question Prescott had never thought about having to answer, as in his mind he was still a member of the Federal Army. He was surprised it had never occurred to him.

"I was a member of the Army, but I'm not anymore."

"What happened?"

"My duty was up, and I decided not to reenlist."

Abigail turned so that she could look into his face. "Did you see any battles?"

"Yes . . . I saw a lot of men die."

"What was it like? I mean, do you have time to be scared?"

"If you manage to stop and think about what you're doing, it doesn't seem real. You just concentrate on your duty and what has to be done. I saw men, and some boys as well, do some remarkable acts. Bravery you wouldn't think possible. All in the face of a hell I could never describe to you."

"Don't try. I didn't mean to bring bad thoughts."

"Being here with you reminded me of just how important life is. It's the simple things you forget about when you're in a fight. The smell of bread baking on a winter's evening near the Christmas season—the laughter of children playing baseball in the field—the beauty of clouds sweeping by on a summer's afternoon"—Prescott looked into her face—"how it feels to be with a beautiful woman, with no other thoughts than her. You never think about those things."

"Shhhhhh. My mistake to ask you about such things. We should only concentrate on us."

Just then, from the next compartment, they both heard a muffled passionate cry from Sarah.

"You're so beautiful," he said.

"Well, thank you. Such a compliment should be repaid."

Stinson slid her hand down from his chest and began to caress him. She moved over, and they kissed, tongues gently probing, touching. When he made an effort to push her over on her back, she stopped him.

"Just lie there," she said.

She straddled him, continuing to kiss him as she softly used her body to caress him.

Chapter Eleven

Present Day
July 25

"This is just the kind of bullshit that infuriates me, Sparks, and it makes you a danger to yourself and anyone who works with you." The exasperated voice of Marshall Goldberg was just short of yelling, but it still forced Sparks to keep the receiver from his ear. "Where the hell are you? You never checked in with the Jacksonville office, and this is your first contact with me in thirty-two hours!"

"You're right. I should have checked in . . . my mistake. Clark gives me a lot of latitude and sometimes I forget that when I'm not dealing with him. Sorry."

"Don't patronize me. I know how you feel about me. Well, I don't particularly like you, either, but for now, you're reporting to me. You got that?"

"Yes."

"I want contact a minimum of every twenty-four hours, and not with the office there. I mean with me directly. No turning off your cell phone. You'll follow procedures."

Standing at a fast-food restaurant across the street from the motel, Sparks shook his head. He should have realized that Goldberg would take the opportunity to be difficult. "Understood. Look, I'm in contact now, so can we dispense with the woodshed justice and let me report?"

"Just as long as your responsibility is clear."

"First of all, how is Clark doing?"

"What? Oh, he went into the hospital today. He said something about a series of tests."

"Let me know how he's doing."

"Sure." Goldberg lowered his voice. "All right, what is going on down there?"

Sparks gave him the details of meeting with Coulthard, going over the papers, and finding one-third of the clues to the shipment's location. For the moment, he left out the car chase.

"No sign of anything from the Boston family?" Goldberg asked.

"Not them directly, no."

"What do you mean, not directly?"

Sparks thought for a second. Goldberg would probably pull him in and mobilize a strike team. "Some rather nasty individuals tried to procure Coulthard's papers as we were leaving the bank here in the lovely River City. We eluded them."

"That wouldn't have been the four men in a blue sedan who crashed into a group of trees at a hundred miles an hour?"

"You heard."

"I'm monitoring reports out of Jacksonville. There was mention of a high-speed chase with a crash involving a car with four armed men after a car with a man and a woman. There was also a witness in the bank parking lot. I've also got a preliminary report on Tracy Coulthard and a quick trace got me the bank she uses. It matched the scene of the altercation reported late today."

"You're monitoring my calls, Goldberg?" The anger rose in Sparks. "That's the only way you could have known about her. Our briefing up there didn't cover her by name. What the hell kind of crap is this? You've got some control agenda you can't resist exploiting while Griffin is in the hospital?"

"You're paranoid."

"Am I? When I have something substantial to report, I'll do so. And I'll deal with the office here in Jacksonville—you keep them informed as well. Other than that, stay off my back or you'll have to explain to Griffin why you cost him a valuable agent."

"You'll follow procedure."

"Never mind using the GPS in my cell, either. We're on the move, heading to the office for Coulthard's safety and to work on some other leads."

"What leads?"

Sparks closed his cell and swore out loud. The conversation hadn't gone well, and Sparks knew he should have held his temper. He also had not raised his concern about how the assailants had known where he and Coulthard would be going. It was one of the reasons why, in the morning, he would take Coulthard in and have her put in a safe house until this was over.

He walked across the road and back to the motel just as a thunderstorm arrived, and with a quick jog to his room's door, he made it inside before getting drenched. Coulthard was wrapped in one towel, using a second to dry her hair. The motel was not high quality, so the towels provided were small, leaving Sparks with a teasing view.

"Rain, huh. I'm done if you want to use the shower," she said. "It's actually a nice shower for this dumpy place."

Sparks double-checked the window after closing the door. He didn't see any suspicious activity. "I think I will. I feel pretty grimy."

"Did your boss have anything interesting for you?"

"No, just the usual bureaucratic crap. He's actually not my usual contact. I'll be in the shower. Don't answer the door for anyone, no matter what they say. Get me first, OK?"

"Right."

The hot water felt good on Sparks's neck and back. He thought about how a case that had started off strange was getting more so. Standing under the water with his head against the wall, eyes closed, he felt cold air rush in as the shower curtain opened. Turning and wiping the water from his eyes, he felt Coulthard step into the shower.

"I decided to advance our relationship along," she said, putting her arms around his shoulders and bringing herself against him. Her supple breasts brushed against his lower chest.

"This isn't a good idea, Tracy," he said even as he brought his hands around her and grasped her back before lowering them.

"Shhhhhhh. You can't deny that the tension has been there from the beginning. It's time you stopped being the FBI guy and thought of me as a woman and not just part of the case."

They kissed . . . a hungry, deep one as they pressed their bodies together, hot water cascading down.

"There hasn't been a moment when I didn't see you as a woman I wanted," he said, bringing his left hand up to caress her breast while his right hand slipped down.

She moved a leg to the side, allowing him better access, and exhaled as his touch pleasured her.

"This doesn't mean I'm going to change my mind about your going to a safe house under guard."

"I don't care right now. Just make love to me."

"Well . . . I am a government employee. I guess I have to do what the taxpayer wants."

July 26

Sparks sat on the bed quietly talking to himself. The night with Tracy had been superb, but as soon as they were finished, the doubt in his wisdom filtered back. The best thing to do now was to get her safely to the Jacksonville office and take a shot at figuring out the Stallard letter. In the middle of this bizarre story came Tracy, and his mind kept coming back to her. She had stirred feelings he hadn't felt since his wife's death.

"I'm ready!" Coulthard, out of the bathroom, glided over to the bed and jumped onto her knees next to him. "It was very intense, wasn't it?"

"Yes, it was." He kissed her, gently holding the side of her face. "We're definitely going to have to discuss things down the road. But for now, we need to get to the bureau office, get you some protection, and see if the lab guys in Washington can help me with this letter."

"Jason, I really want to help with this. Besides, I don't like your making decisions about my life, despite the fact that you're incredible in bed." Coulthard smiled.

"This moves into official business. I'm not normally one for following rules, but we're talking about your safety. I'll decide what's best until the situation is defused. Then maybe we can see where *we're* headed."

"I still think you're going to need my help."

"I'll make sure to keep you informed all along the way."

"You're beginning to sound like a bureaucrat."

"Flag! Unsportsmanlike conduct."

"Did I tell you I'm a big Jaguars' fan?"

"A football fan as well. This is too good to be true."

Sparks met with Special Agent Robert Catwood at the Jacksonville office and arranged for Coulthard to be placed into protective custody, with the stipulation that Sparks could rescind it at any time. This last qualifier came on the insistence of Coulthard, who threatened to raise hell with the press if it wasn't included. Catwood seemed capable and cooperative. He planned to put Coulthard up in a suite maintained right at the building.

Sparks scanned in the Stallard letter and e-mailed a copy up to Washington and Tom Becker, a friend of his who worked in the Encryption Section and who was assigned to any work Sparks brought in. There was a standing order for Becker to consider anything from Sparks top priority.

Still, Sparks called Becker and finessed his way into Becker working on it right away. It was a game they played often. When Sparks needed work done, Becker pretended he was doing the agent a favor, and he would finagle a round of golf.

Sparks spent the remainder of the afternoon with the letter.

As he was sitting in the conference room, Coulthard came in and sat down beside him.

"So, there were three letters," he said without acknowledging her arrival. "One went to the firm in Boston, which is in the possession of the mysterious Boston family. One was sent to Lawrence Stallard in Florida, which I'm holding here. And a third was sent to a man named Cassias Fitzroy in Philadelphia. That's the piece of the puzzle still missing, and we—and they—don't have a clue as to where it is."

"Who do you suppose this Fitzroy guy was?"

"I know who he was. He was part of the Stallard conspiracy to smuggle the gold out of the country. What happened to the conspirators, I don't know. I suppose I'll need to head for Philadelphia and try to track down his decedents. Maybe we'll luck out twice."

Sparks held up the letter and read the final section again:

I only ask you to remember the word and number games we used to play as children. The truth can be found five steps on the side of our savior, who is with God. Our family is in my prayers, Lawrence, take the information and use it to better their lives.

Then came the numbers.

25 1 12 12 7 13 4 11 14 25

And he showed unto him all the kingdoms of the world in a moment of time.

"Parker Stallard didn't want to make it too difficult for his brother to solve this little riddle," Sparks said. "The reference to their childhood games means they used to play around with letters and numbers. We're doomed if they had some sort of master code they had developed as kids. But, for the sake of argument, let's assume the clues are right here."

"Break it down, and let's decipher it one part at a time." Coulthard leaned forward over Sparks's shoulder, then looked up with embarrassment. "Sorry, not trying to tell you how to do your job."

"So let's take this: The truth can be found five steps on the side of Jesus. If you're talking about the side of something, can we assume we're talking left or right? Or are we talking good and evil?"

"Parker was trying to help Lawrence on some part of the gold's location, so you would think any reference would have to do with the relationship between the numbers here and the alphabet."

Sparks wrote out the letters of the alphabet and assigned them each a number.

"I already tried it directly and came up with garble," Coulthard said.

"This is just a visual reference point. OK, Parker mentions Jesus, so this reference has to have some religious connection. Where in the Bible is there a mention of Jesus being on the side of good or righteousness?"

"There are plenty of passages . . . wait. I remember a prayer we would always say in church about the resurrection . . . he was crucified, dead, and buried. On the third day, he rose from the dead, ascended into heaven, and he sitteth on the right hand of God, the Father Almighty . . ."

"Five steps to the side of Jesus. Five steps to the right side." Sparks looked down at his letters and numbers.

1	2	3	4	5	6	7	8	9	10	11	12	13
A	B	C	D	E	F	G	H	I	J	K	L	M

14	15	16	17	18	19	20	21	22	23	24	25	26
N	O	P	Q	R	S	T	U	V	W	X	Y	Z

"Let's take the fifth letter to the right of the letter you would normally assign the number," he said.

With that, Sparks wrote out the letters. D for five places to the right of 25, F for five places to the right of 1, Q for five places to the right of 12, and so on, until he had the letters: D F Q Q L R I P S D.

Sparks let out a short exhale. "Well, if we're supposed to drop in the fifth letter to the right of the assigned number, the number one doesn't start with the letter *A*. There are no other references here to give you a starting point."

"Let's try going with each letter assigned the number one. We have to order in dinner anyway."

Starting with the letter *B* this time, Sparks slid all the numbers to the right one spot and reworked the letters. He came up with E G R R M S J Q T E. He moved on from there, each time getting a garbled response. Thirty minutes went by and still nothing intelligible had come from their method. Sparks put down his pen and got up to stretch.

Suddenly, Coulthard sat up in her chair.

"Do you have a map of the eastern United States?" she asked. "Damn, we're stupid. There's another way of going about this. The last wire came from Harrisburg, right?"

". . . so if the numbers represent letters, then it could be the name of a town or city near there."

"And the first letter is a twenty-five, and the last number is twenty-five, and there are two twelves."

"So, you look for a city or town where the same letters appear at the beginning and end and also with a letter repeating in the middle. Of course, we're assuming the linking of the letters and numbers remains constant through each of the ten numbers here."

"Worth a try," she said. "Keep on going through the cycle you're on, and I'll look at the maps."

Coulthard went to a hard copy atlas while Sparks continued with sliding the number one designation down the alphabet. He was close to the end, just two letters to go. With *Y* as the number one, the result was: B D O O J P G N Q B. With *Z* as the first number, the result was: C E P P K Q H O R C. He had gone through all the letters with each assigned the number one. Then he did something he later lamented would have saved them a lot of time if he had done it first. He reversed the numbers and listed them backward against the alphabet:

A	B	C	D	E	F	G	H	I	J	K	L	M
26	25	24	23	22	21	20	19	18	17	16	15	14

N	O	P	Q	R	S	T	U	V	W	X	Y	Z
13	12	11	10	9	8	7	6	5	4	3	2	1

On his first try, taking the fifth letter to the right of each number assigned, his heart quickened and within moments, he knew the answer.

"Jason." Coulthard approached Sparks from where she had been sitting. "Jason, this fits."

Twenty-five became 20: G. 1 became 22: E. 12 twice became 7 7: T T. 7 became 2: Y. 13 became 8: S . . .

"Jason, it fits!" Coulthard dropped the atlas down beside him and put her finger down. It rested just above the border between Pennsylvania and Maryland.

Sparks had just finished writing the tenth letter in the progression. "It fits here, too."

They looked at each other, then at the table where the other was pointing. In both places, there was one highlighted word.

Gettysburg.

Chapter Twelve

October 5, 1862

C hicago in the fall of 1862 was a city in the process of growth on a massive scale. In 1850, the city proper had a population of less than thirty thousand. As Prescott stepped onto the station platform on the shores of Lake Michigan, he was in the midst of a metropolis whose population was nearing one hundred fifty thousand, and he pondered the city history Stallard had imparted to him on the way out. Chicago was already the most important industrial center in the west and provided the jumping-off point for thousands beginning the move farther west.

With quick growth came quick fixes to difficult problems, and the people suffered through deplorable conditions. The Chicago River, which meandered through the city, became a cesspool of human waste and animal carcasses, never fully flushed out into the lake. The result was a history of disease and death in the decade prior to the war as cholera claimed thousands of lives. Financial panics had also led to bankrupt businesses, destitute families, and general intense poverty.

In 1855–56, most of the city was raised four to seven feet to accommodate a new sewer system. An effort to pave streets began with planking, macadam, wooden blocks, and stones. Then, with the outbreak of the war, Chicago immediately began to gain economic benefits. The raw materials of food, lumber, and metal that flowed through the city suddenly took on unprecedented significance. Wealth for the intelligent businessman was there to obtain—it only took ingenuity, some resources, and hard work. If a person wanted to be on the leading edge of where the Union was going, he only had to step onto the depot's platform.

Prescott was exhausted. The luxurious private rooms available across the eastern portion of their trip weren't available for the final two days, and Prescott, Stallard, and their new traveling companions spent that time exclusively in the ladies' cars, with the occasional foray into the smoking car for the two men. Food was only a passing thought, as it often had to be with the refreshment saloons along the way. The train would slide to a stop and the passengers would briskly move to the saloon for a fifteen-minute meal before being herded back onto the train. It wasn't conducive for either one's intestinal well-being or romancing.

Abigail Stinson continued to intoxicate Prescott. Without embarrassment for how their relationship began, Stinson delighted Prescott with tales of her youth in Massachusetts, taking summer holidays in the country at the upper peninsula of Cape Cod, walking along the beach on an island outside of Newburyport, being at the exquisite parties her family gave during the social times. All the while, Prescott sensed that she was a woman who, while fond of those memories, knew that she wanted a life away from those days.

"Will! Will, look at this. My best bag is ruined!" Stinson lamented as she held up the damaged valise. "Those intolerable baggage smashers. I'll be issuing a strong protest to the management of this railroad!"

"There's a lot of baggage to move, Abby. I imagine damage to one bag isn't going to register high on their list of priorities," Prescott said.

"No, I suppose not. Besides, what are bags for but to carry your items while you travel?" She chuckled. "It was really silly of me to get angry."

They collected their things and moved away from the platform's heavy traffic, looking for Stallard and Blackstone. They found them within a few minutes, and the four of them were able to move to one end of the loading area for carriages. The day was clear and crisp, but the unpaved areas were muddy from what must have been a strong rain.

Stallard found quickly that a lightweight Concord had been sent from the Smythe-Tilling foundry for their use, and they quickly loaded the baggage. The ride to the women's boardinghouse was entirely filled with observations of the constant activity around them as they made their way through Chicago's streets. Upon arriving at the boardinghouse, the two couples separated to say their goodbyes.

"I heard that Chicago was a growing city, but I didn't realize how much. I wonder if I'll be able to find you again. I don't want to lose the opportunity to see you." Prescott touched the side of Abigail's face. "And I do want to see you again . . ." He looked down at the two of them in mud-stained, two-day worn clothes. "But not until we've both had a chance to better our situation."

Stinson beamed at him. "I was thinking the same thing. It's a marvelous phenomenon, how you know exactly what I'm thinking. It's most unsettling."

"There's something else you're thinking about."

"What?"

"You're wondering who I am."

"Excuse me?"

"You're wondering who I am. You've asked me a couple of times about my present situation with Parker, and I haven't really given you a proper answer, I know."

"No, you haven't, but I thought you would tell me when you felt it was right. I know you aren't married, so I wasn't worried about that. But you're keeping a secret, aren't you?"

"I can't talk about it now, and I honestly don't know when I'll be able to. But I do know that I want to see you again."

"And so you shall. Sarah and I will be staying here for a while. But there's something I need to tell you, Will. I do want to see you, but I'm hesitant for the very reason you gave. You have to be honest with me if we're to have a future."

"I can only ask you to be patient," Prescott said. "Circumstances are tenuous, and I don't know when they will become stable. Please, wait on me. I'll call on you soon."

Stallard came around the carriage and with a blast of enthusiastic banter, pushed the women along into the boardinghouse. Five minutes later, he and Prescott were in the carriage alone and headed for the foundry.

"Well, they were a welcome diversion for the final part of the trip, I'd say." Stallard tapped his cane twice on the floor and used his fingers to straighten the hair of his goatee. "A right nice pair of cherries."

"I don't appreciate your comments."

"You've taken a cotton to Miss Stinson? Well, I can't say I find fault with you. Still, you need to keep details in order. Women are a nice diversion, but anything else . . ." Stallard let his thought drift off.

"We're going to the foundry now?" Prescott asked.

"Yes. You need to meet William Smythe. He's the genius behind the refining of the ore brought in from the West. He's the singular most important asset to our efforts. He's a hard businessman and has a close group of workers—many of them rather unsavory."

"I would say he's the second most important asset to your plan. Your ability to cultivate contacts up here in the North is astounding. I lost count of how many people knew you on the way here."

"Time and money, Jack. That's all it takes. I've spent three years working my way back and forth along the northern railroad lines. Spread a little money, do a small favor. You would be impressed with what you can do."

"Lord, you should have been a politician."

"When the war is over, I just might take your advice." Stallard laughed and tapped his cane again as an exclamation point.

Prescott fumbled with the buttons on his grimy overcoat. "Where will we be staying? I could use a bath and a couple of nights' sleep."

"I have stayed with Smythe and his family before, but I think it would be best if you bunked with the employees. Their quarters aren't really that bad. I believe Smythe might be uncomfortable with having you in his house—being a traitor and all." Prescott glanced up at Stallard, who held up his hand. "Apologies . . . a stupid use of a word."

"You're forgetting one thing. My face. I think we should limit my contact with the foundry personnel. The fliers on me probably rode the same trains we did on the way out here."

Stallard nodded. "You're correct, of course. I'm tired and not thinking."

Prescott and Stallard settled into a pair of chairs in the smoking room of Smythe's home, located on the Smythe-Tilling foundry property. Both men were tired and embarrassed by how they had presented themselves to Mrs. Smythe.

They looked every bit as long-distance travelers should before having the chance to clean up, thanks to an insistent Smythe, who gave them no choice but to join him immediately upon arrival at the foundry. They went from the carriage to Mrs. Smythe's table before they realized it. Now, with a full meal and a drink in hand, they had the look of persons much more suited for sleep than a discussion of business.

"Parker, and I mean this with utmost respect, but you two look like my dog after he's been out in the rain all night," Smythe said without humor as he poured himself a drink. He was a dark, forboding presence, stocky, with black-as-coal hair, thick eyebrows, and a matching mustache. "I know you're tired, but I expect that, now that we've gotten the pleasantries aside, you'll want to know about the last shipment."

Stallard lit his cigar and offered the matches to Prescott. "It would make me rest a little easier. The wire I received from you on our trip out wasn't clear as to the shipment's yield."

"It's down, I'm afraid. The trail boss said your brother was expressing concern about the vein, that it might not be as long-lasting as his original estimates. And if the yield is dropping this quickly, the costs are going to make the venture less of an opportunity. I have to be truthful with you on this. While I pride myself on the loyalty of my workers, the longer we keep this operation going, the more difficult it will be to retain secrecy."

"I understand your concern, but if my brother thought the vein was truly reaching its limit, he would have sent a more strongly worded message, don't you think?"

"I agree. Knowing your brother's character, he's very cautious. I do hold out a measure of confidence the yield will increase with the next shipment. I was just planting a seed of concern, that's all."

"Excuse me, but I believe I could contribute more effectively if you gave me a briefing on just how this whole operation works," Prescott said.

Smythe's dark eyebrows narrowed slightly. "I was under the impression that Jackson here was already part of your operation, Parker. What is this all about?"

"I guess it's time to bring all the participants onto equal footing." Stallard stood up and stepped next to the fire, feeling the heat press against his face. "First, we weren't truthful with you when we introduced Mr. Jackson here before dinner. His real name is Jackson Prescott, formerly Lieutenant Jackson Prescott of the . . ." He looked over at Prescott.

"Twelfth Massachusetts regiment."

"What do you mean, 'formerly'?" Smythe said.

Stallard stepped in. "Well, Jackson here decided to treat some Confederate prisoners with dignity and give them a chance to spend the war in a place other than a Federal prison. He was rewarded for his efforts with arrest and future trial, until he managed to escape, while, I might add, he helped his captors against a group of highwaymen."

"Pardon me, Prescott, but it sounds like if you had stayed, they would have drummed you out of camp."

Prescott was up on his feet. "I'm not a coward. I've seen a might more action than you have sitting in this fine house while you conspire to betray your country." Prescott could feel Stallard's eyes on him. "My objections are not with the Union. I'll defend my country against any outside aggressor. I only want this bloodshed to end, and Parker has promised me this plan can work to bring an expedient resolution."

Stallard held up his hand and put it on Prescott's shoulder.

Smythe tilted his head as if to light his cigar, but then changed his mind. "I suppose it's hypocritical of me to criticize any man's method. You follow your course. Mine is solely for the ledger's bottom line. And with that in mind, do you think it's wise to have a wanted man possibly bringing attention to us?" The question was directed at Stallard.

"I felt it was a justifiable risk. Let's leave it at that."

"So be it. Go on."

"Jackson, I met Smythe here about four years ago during a business deal. My brother, Charles, arrived here about the same time, bound for the West. He was always a restless soul, looking for adventure. We didn't hear from him for a year, but when he returned, he told an unbelievable story—"

"I still consider it a rather tall tale," Smythe interjected.

"But we both know Charles is not one for exaggeration. It seems he broke off from the party he was with, and on one of his side trips, he came upon an Indian trapped alone on a ledge after a landslide. With gestures to speak to him, and a rope, Charles managed to save the Indian."

"Foolhardy at best. Most members of tribes out that way would just as soon kill a white man."

"Charles has that way about him. To continue, the Indian turned out to be much more than just a *brave*, I think they're called. He was evidently a high-ranking leader, though not the chief, of the Lakota Sioux. The Indian, who goes by the name of Gray Bear, brought Charles into their community, and my brother was honored with ceremonies and such. He was allowed to stay with the tribe, and he began to learn their language. Though they're distrustful of white men, Charles's character impressed them."

Stallard finished off his drink and motioned to the table. Smythe offered his hand in permission, and Stallard went on. "Then comes the story about the sun cave I already mentioned and his discovery of the high-yield vein of gold. It was a series of mountains not known to anyone other than the Sioux, and it was considered sacred. It's a testament to Charles that he was allowed to see it and ultimately allowed to take from it."

"Come now . . . the Sioux are getting something in return," Smythe said.

"You worked a deal with them?" Prescott was incredulous.

"Charles, when he realized the gold's potential, struck an arrangement with Gray Bear and the elders. They would allow him to extract the gold, provide some of the manpower, and ensure safe passage through the plains back to civilization."

"In exchange for what?" Prescott asked.

"Guns." Smythe had now lit his cigar and was relishing the first taste. "Forged from my foundry and assembled here as well. I have a quite resourceful staff of engineers and designers."

"Guns." Prescott looked at Stallard. "So you're really fighting a two-front battle of secrecy, aren't you? I would think the government would almost be more concerned with that than with trying to buy influence in England."

"Possibly. There are so many folks heading west that a few extra wagons from us are never suspected. So, when Charles traveled back to Chicago, I was on a second trip back here and devised a plan to bring the gold here to be processed. For a large commission, Smythe here assumes significant risk, separates the gold, and melts it down into ingots for transport. With war coming, the gold was originally to be used to buy goods from overseas, but that strategy changed with the blockade. While the Confederacy has been able to hold its own and put to rest any thoughts of a quick victory by the Federals, we have come to realize in the last few months, and especially after Sharpsburg, that for the South to survive, we must have help from England."

"It doesn't bother you that these guns you're furnishing the Indians will kill innocent settlers?" Prescott asked.

"There are no innocents in this world." Smythe took another moment to savor the pale blue smoke he exhaled slowly. "Those settlers are traveling west to take a way of life away from the people who were there first. It's only the strongest who survive. That's the way it has been forever."

"You have a cynical view," Prescott said.

"Only the money I earn can give my family the things they need to survive and enjoy life."

Prescott turned away from Smythe and to Stallard. "So the gold is staged here, and when you have a large enough shipment?"

"I've decided we'll ship it east, probably through to Philadelphia. Fitzroy has contacts in the shipyards, and the gold will be smuggled to England. With a promise of a steady amount, we hope Fitzroy can garner enough support in Parliament to force pressure to bear on the Federal government."

"It wouldn't hurt if your General Lee and his army would take care of business and give you gentlemen time, would it?" Smythe said.

Prescott, still standing, walked over to the fireplace and set his drink on the mantel. "Why not ship back what you have ready now? Winter is approaching, and you won't be able to bring any more gold east from the mountains until spring. So, offer what you have now."

"Timing is as important as the amount of gold. The gold can buy influence, but it cannot be administered from a disadvantageous position." Stallard felt along his scar again. It always acted up in cooler weather. "Politicians are weak animals. They must see it as almost a certainty before they will intervene. We'll need a significant victory, preferably in the East, where the newspapers will scream the news, timed with the final push for an agreement."

"Antietam was just the opposite of what you desired," Prescott said.

"Absolutely. For this to work, we'll need Southern victories."

"And you'll need Fitzroy to be his diplomatic best."

"Yes, or we'll be on the little end of the horn," Stallard lamented.

Chapter Thirteen

Present Day
July 27

Sparks's nightmare began while he was shaving in his hotel bathroom just before nine in the morning. He had finished, but hadn't had time to wash the excess foam off, when the phone rang. He expected it to be either Goldberg screaming or Coulthard cajoling. Instead, it was Jennifer crying. Even as he raised the receiver to his ear, before he could speak, he could hear whimpering and then came her voice: "Dad."

"Jennifer? What's wrong?"

There was the sound of movement on the other end, and a male voice, thick with a Boston accent, came on.

"Special Agent Sparks. I'm going to be simple and direct. We have your daughter. I want to set up a meeting with you to discuss the terms for her safe return."

The breath left Sparks, blood pounding in his head, his brain trying to comprehend the words. "This has to do with the Civil War gold?"

"It does, indeed. First, I guarantee your daughter's safety as long as you follow the plan we'll set up. Second, once the gold has been recovered, you'll be instructed on where to find her. Third, at the meeting we're about to set up, you'll bring me a copy of all the information you have. Conversely, I'll give you the letter that we have in our possession that you undoubtedly learned about from Professor Drury. Is that clear?"

"Yes. I want to speak to Jennifer."

"Not now. Tomorrow at 11 a.m., you'll take the Green Line from Copley Square to Government Center in Boston. When you walk up the stairs to the surface, there will be a newsstand to your right. Ask the attendant for a copy of *Vermont Life*. Do you understand?"

"Yes. Copley to Government Center, newsstand, *Vermont Life*."

"This isn't a speed test to pull your chain, or a way to make sure you're not being observed. We'll know if you're being monitored. If you involve any other member of the Bureau or any other member of the police, anywhere, your daughter dies. You're alone in this. Is that clear?"

"Yes."

The line went dead.

Sparks went over the conversation again, but all he could concentrate on was Jennifer. He had always kept her out of his working life. These people were ruthless . . . calculating. They had taken this step at just the right moment, when he had found the letter they could not and would never possess on their own. So they went for the one point of leverage they somehow knew existed—Jennifer. Now they meant to isolate him.

And Jennifer would die. There would be no safe exchange if he found the gold. She would die and then he would die. They would have no other course of action. Her only chance of survival was if he could create the right circumstances. Anger rose inside him, and he seized the nearest chair, prepared to hurl it against the wall to satisfy his fury. But in mid-motion, he stopped and set the chair down.

Control . . . no room for anger without direction.

Grabbing a pen and paper from his briefcase, he made out a short list of the actions he needed to do immediately—writing calmed his shaking hands. He began attacking the list as soon as he finished. A phone call to Catwood put an immediate hold on Coulthard. Sparks instructed the agent to keep her in custody for the next couple of days and not to let her go unless he heard from Sparks personally. Next came a call to Tom Becker in Washington.

"Hey, I had a call in to you at the Jacksonville office. It sounds like we both broke the code at the same time," Becker said.

"Yeah, listen, Tom . . . I want you to mothball all the work you've done so far."

"Well, there's nothing else for me to analyze, unless you want a date on the original letter. What gives? You trying to get out of a round of golf?"

"No, I need to shift to something else."

"You're the man. Are you sure I can't help you with anything?" Becker asked.

"You'll get yourself another round of golf after I get back to you. Until then, everything's cool—nothing to worry about."

"One thing: I'd advise you to call Goldberg, like, now. He already called me this morning, asking if I had talked to you."

Sparks had expected this and nodded to himself on the phone. "He's my next call."

Actually, Goldberg came one call later, and he was already practically shrieking when he got on the line. "God *damn* it, I'm pulling you in right now, mister, unless you can give me a very good explanation about your disobeying my direct order."

Sparks took a deep breath before carefully measuring his words. "Marshall"—it was the first time Sparks had ever used the assistant director's first name—"I'm not trying to undermine your authority. This investigation is going to go all right, you just need to be patient. We have a strong lead on the gold's general location."

"Yes, yes." Goldberg was exceedingly impatient. "Gettysburg. I find it hard to believe that the shipment could be hidden there."

"I've got a lot of research ahead of me, and I would appreciate you giving me some slack. I work better alone, Marshall. Clark knows this, and I've had a good arrangement with him. Besides, he's not going to be out for all that long. He'll be back soon, and you can move on to other matters and be done with me."

"Until then, you give me what I want. Consistent, timely updates—or I'll pull in a reprimand so fast, you'll think you were hit by a truck. And no special relationship with the director will keep that from happening."

Sparks was getting tired of the conversation already. "Don't make me embarrass you by bringing Griffin in on this. You and I both know who he'll back."

Goldberg fumed on the line's other end, swearing to no one in particular. "Just give me the reports regularly."

"Done." Sparks hung up and went right to another call. He had Becker on the line within a minute.

"You again already?"

"I've just got one question," Sparks said. "Did you tell Goldberg about breaking the code and what the location is?"

"Yes, I told him we both had broken the code, but no, I didn't tell him the town—figured you would want to tell him about it. Did I screw up or something?"

"Has anyone had access to your work there in the lab?"

"You know the setup here. Extremely limited-access area. No one, not even Goldberg or Griffin, get in here without my permission. Security is as tight as it can be."

"Thanks. We never had this conversation, Tom. Understand?"

"Whatever you say. Just don't sound so ominous."

"I wish there was nothing to it, but I'm afraid that's not realistic."

Sparks hung up and walked into the bathroom. Goldberg, in his fiery verbal rebuke, had made a mistake. And it was one that would cost him his career. But Sparks didn't feel sorry for the assistant director—Jennifer's life was at stake.

Sparks stood in front of the sink and looked into the mirror. His face was streaked with dried shaving cream.

The blue-gray Ford moved with precision, a cloud of dust behind it, up the dirt road off Vermont Route 117. The stones thrown up from the front wheels pinged against the undercarriage and side panels. Streeter, the man in charge of this undertaking for his Boston employer, mulled over the schedule in his head.

First would come instructions for Dorman, who was taking care of their special guest, then a check of how the other men were progressing with the kids' vehicle. Following would be a quick pack and the four-hour drive back down Interstates 89 and 93 to Boston for a meeting with his employer before a good night's sleep and tomorrow's meeting with Sparks.

Streeter swung the Ford into the parking area of the mountainside cottage, which was rarely used except as a base camp for fall deer hunting. He exited the car. A man of average height, he was solidly built from years of martial arts work. His sandy blonde hair was worn long enough to hang over the sides of the sunglasses he almost always wore. He strode from the car, detoured away from the cottage, and went over to the garage-sized barn off to the right. The doors were open, and a two-man crew was dismantling the car belonging to the two college students.

"How long until you have it totally taken apart and the parts loaded up for shipping out?" he asked.

The brown-haired one, Jake, looked up from the side panels he was removing from the already detached driver's side door. "Well, if we work until late tonight, we can get it done by early tomorrow afternoon."

"Not good enough. Work all night if you have to, but I want this automobile in pieces and shipped out in your truck by 10 a.m. tomorrow. I'll double what we're paying you."

Streeter went on up to the cottage, a simple but well-kept structure built a few decades ago. While not lavishly appointed, it was more than a simple hunter's lodge. The front porch led to the door with windows on either side, but the shades were drawn and the lights were on. Streeter went through the front door, but Dorman wasn't in the front living room area. Streeter paused and listened for a moment. From the back of the cottage, he heard muffled movement and Jennifer Sparks crying. In an instant, Streeter was at the door to the bedroom.

Dorman had the blindfolded and tied-up girl pinned down on the bed and was pawing at her breasts, grunting as he kissed her neck, thrusting his lower torso against her. He was a smallish man, with sparse, greasy hair and wire-rimmed glasses that were always dirty.

Streeter seized him by the back of his grimy collar and hurled him against the wall. "God damn you. If you touch her again, you stupid ass, I'll put a bullet in your head."

"Just tryin' to have a little fun." Dorman collected himself. "It's not like there are any strip clubs or whores around here to help a guy—" He lunged at Streeter and threw the two of them against the wall opposite Jennifer's room. A knife appeared in his left hand, and he brought it up to Streeter's face. "You may be the boss man, but don't you ever give me shit over something like that again. You understand, blondie?"

The sides of Dorman's mouth curled up, leaving that toothy smile Streeter hated and breath that was a foul combination of beer and food. But the smile dissolved as Dorman felt the cold steel against his temple and the sound of a safety catch.

"I've killed smarter men for a lot less than what you just did."

Streeter's tone, devoid of emotion, left Dorman chilled, and he slowly brought his knife away. "I'm just havin' a little fun, is all. No need to get riled up and nasty."

Streeter kept his gun to Dorman's head and pushed him out to the living room, his blue eyes never leaving Dorman's face. "You have done an adequate job for the man and myself in the past, but I want to make this clear to you, and I won't ever repeat it. Touch her again in an unprofessional manner, and you'll be in a barrel off Nantucket like Coleman. Do you understand?"

"Yeah, I think you fancy her yourself."

"You should concentrate only on what instructions I give you. I'm heading back to Boston. Is everything clear on what you need to do?" Streeter dropped the gun from Dorman's head.

"After the guys clear out with the car parts, I take the two love-birds to the house in Lawrence. Tony and Sam will meet me there to get them in the house undetected. I'm to drug them before moving them to the van."

"Make sure you do that. The college kid may try something if he thinks you're alone with him."

"Right, no worries."

Streeter sent Dorman out to the barn with a six-pack and strict instructions not to have any additional alcohol until the job was finished. Then Streeter went back to Jennifer's room and softly sat on the edge of the bed. "I'm sorry. His conduct was unfortunate, and he has assured me it won't happen again. I know this experience is upsetting, but we've contacted your father—"

"My father will hunt you down until you're either in prison or dead." Jennifer was still shaking, but her voice was angry.

"We're just using you as leverage, Miss Sparks, nothing more. When your father has helped us recover what we want, then you'll be let go."

"I don't believe you."

"Given the situation, I don't blame you. But you have my word: no matter what happens, I'll return you to your father. And if the other man tries anything again, let me know, and I'll take care of him." He got up from the bed. "Do you need anything right now? The bathroom?"

"Yes. And I would like something to eat."

"Of course."

"And what about Bret? Is he all right? Can I see him?"

"He's all right, but you two will remain separated. One thing: don't mistake my kindness for softness. If you or Bret try anything in the way of escaping or calling attention, my men have orders to use deadly force. I know you understand what I mean."

The trip from Jacksonville to Washington went quickly for Sparks. Work was a relief from visualizing what his daughter was going through. In less than twenty-four hours, he would be in possession of two-thirds of the necessary information. In a few more hours after that, he would be in Gettysburg.

He continued to read the file on the disappearance of the shipment in late June of 1863. He reread the wires sent by Lieutenant Prescott, including the last one, dated June 28, which gave specific instructions on when the shipment would be in Philadelphia.

Something happened in those days following the final wire, but what could it have been? Did Prescott change his mind and keep the gold for himself, to try to disappear into history a wealthy man? Was he discovered and eliminated, and the gold shipped someplace else? Or is it still there, somewhere around Gettysburg, waiting for recovery?

Sparks then came upon the short document with the simple signature of *A. Lincoln* at the bottom. Lincoln had sent a second man to shadow Prescott on the mission, but the file contained no other reference to the man: a Colonel Andrew Brison.

Why were there no reports on his progress following Prescott, and why, if the gold was lost, was there no mention of Brison's testimony or report?

The questions came at Sparks faster than he could reason.

At Dulles, he tracked down his luggage and made his way to the taxi area for the ride into the city. Stepping to the curb, he scanned the waiting cabs and instead walked across the lane to a cab off to the side with a driver alone behind the wheel. Sparks peered in through the passenger side window and nodded at the driver, who responded in kind. Five minutes later, they were out of the airport and on their way into the city.

Sparks spoke first. "I appreciate your doing this. I don't think they have a tail on me yet, but they will begin sometime tomorrow morning. This will be my last chance at a face-to-face."

"I'm sorry, Jason. God, you know I would wish anything else rather than have Jennifer involved in this." Clark Griffin, disguised with a wig and dark glasses, handed a file back to Sparks. "This is all we have on the Drury murder. By the way, Maggie is extremely pissed off at you. The doctor wanted to keep me in the hospital another day. She says not to expect a dinner invitation for a while. Of course, she doesn't know about Jennifer."

"This is what I need for you to do. You can go back to work when you want, but I want you to keep Goldberg on my case," Sparks said. Griffin's eyes shot up to the rearview mirror. Sparks continued, "I have a very good reason."

"And you aren't going to tell me, are you?"

"Because I have suspicions about him, and I'm afraid you're going to call me certifiable."

"Try me."

"He's working for the same people who are after the gold shipment, the same people who had Drury killed, the same people who tried to have me taken out, and the same people who have Jennifer."

"You're certifiable."

"When I talked with him earlier today, he mentioned Gettysburg by name when I hadn't brought it up and neither had Tom Becker. Up until I called you, there were only three people on the earth who knew the letter said Gettysburg. He got the information from only one source, and that source has to be tied in with the people who have Jennifer."

Griffin was quiet for a moment. "What do you want to do now?"

"I want Goldberg to stay in place. If Jennifer is to have a chance, we've got to keep their pipeline flowing. His harm will be minimal as long as I can control what he's passing along. And I can use him."

"I was planning to be back at work later this week."

"Stay on whatever schedule you were planning. We can't risk using the bureau to try to backend these people, at least not with the usual channels. That's where I need your help. I may be able to maneuver the principals into position, but I'll need backup to finish it off. We need a strike team that can mobilize instantly."

"You'll have it. When are you supposed to meet with them?"

"Tomorrow at 11 a.m., somewhere in downtown Boston."

"I'll start some very discreet inquiries as to who in Boston would be the sort to take on this kind of action."

"I would feel better if we played this strictly straight-on. One mistake spoken to the wrong person, and Jennifer could die."

"Jason. Jennifer is like a daughter to me, too. I'll handle it delicately."

Sparks paused. Any information on whom they were dealing with would be valuable. Griffin was right. "OK . . . discreet."

"There's one other thing you haven't mentioned."

"What's that?"

"The source of Goldberg's unique knowledge of Southern Pennsylvania geography?"

"Tracy Coulthard."

"Are you going to keep her in Jacksonville?"

"No, I was hoping the other party would allow her to work with me on finding the gold's location."

"Another angle to work?"

"Another angle."

The kids' car was dismantled and stored in the unmarked truck sitting in the parking lot of the cottage. The two mechanics received their envelopes containing a generous amount of money, and Dorman stood on the porch, hands on hips, as they pulled away for the trip down the back road to Route 117.

He looked at his watch. It was almost 10 a.m.—time to put the kids in the back of the panel truck and head down to the house in Lawrence. First came the girl, and Dorman had no trouble with her. Hooded, he put her blindfold on and bound her hands behind her back, then led her out to the back of the truck. He lingered over her, putting his nose in close to her neck. They had kidnapped the pair in a parking lot after the couple had returned from a mountain biking excursion. She had no scent of perfume, only an odor of dried perspiration. He still found it exciting.

"I don't care what the boss man said, little lady," he whispered in her ear. "I'm going to have a good time with you before all of this is over." With a laugh, he closed the door to the van and locked it. He checked his handgun and stuck it in the back waistband of his jeans as he walked back to the building.

Coming to Thomas's door, hooded again, Dorman opened the door and found the young man sitting on the end of the bed. The student was everything Dorman despised out of jealousy—young, good-looking, with an athlete's physique and a thatch of unkempt, blonde hair. He looked strong, but Dorman was confident because he had the gun. He ignored Streeter's orders about first drugging the kid.

"Down on the bed, facedown," he said, pulling the gun from behind him and waving it in the student's general direction. "I don't want any trouble from you."

"Where are you taking me?"

"We're taking you to a new place. This is just a stop along the way."

Thomas climbed on the bed and lay down, but left his right knee bent slightly, keeping his right side slightly off the bed.

"Hands behind your back." Dorman approached the bed, preparing to bind Thomas's hands. As Dorman knelt on the bed's edge, Thomas used the leverage gained from keeping his knee bent under him to throw his weight up and back into Dorman. The athletic move threw the back of Thomas's head into Dorman's face.

The killer's nose was crushed, and he cried out as he fell back off the bed. Thomas spun his body so that as he landed on top of Dorman, who was facing downward. He planted his forearm firmly on the throat of his captor. He pulled back the hood and found that the man was unconscious, blood seeping from his nose.

Thomas scrambled to his feet, his adrenaline-powered heart thumping. He rolled Dorman over and retrieved the handgun. Leaping to his feet and running out the door, Thomas checked the other rooms, calling out Jennifer's name but finding no one. He paused in the living room and looked out the windows down to the parking lot.

The van!

"Jennifer!" he yelled as he charged down the steps and swiftly made it to the back of the van. He could hear the muffled sounds of Jennifer yelling through her mouth gag, and she started to kick at the van's interior. Thomas pulled on the back door latch, but it wouldn't budge against the lock. A check of the doors found them locked as well.

The keys!

Thomas didn't relish going back into the house, but he had the gun. He glanced down the dirt road and surveyed the open area around the parking lot, trying to assess the situation.

Better to risk going back in for the keys and drive off in the van instead of smashing the glass, getting her out, and trying to make it to a main road ahead of him if he wakes up. Better still, there's a way to make sure he doesn't follow.

The van was between Thomas and the cottage, and as he rounded the back end, the gravel at his feet sprayed up and hit him as he heard the crack of a high-powered rifle. Dorman stood on the porch, leaning against one of the two pillars at the top of the stairs, blood covering the lower part of his face and his shirt. His expression was devoid of anger.

Thomas reacted with quickness that Dorman again underestimated, and he brought up the handgun and fired off three shots toward the cottage, forcing Dorman to slide behind the pillar.

I've got to draw him away from the house!

Thomas dove for the wood pile off to the right and behind the van, using it to shield him. Without hesitating, and as another shot thudded into the logs, Thomas sprinted across a short clearing and made it into the trees before Dorman could get off another shot.

The killer stepped down from the porch and walked toward the woods. As he passed the van, he turned to it. "I'll be back in a moment, honey. I just have to take care of something."

He smeared the blood from his face with his shirt sleeve.

This is going to be fun.

The morning was heavy with moisture, and Thomas slipped as he made his way along a ridge that ran just below the cottage. He was confused about which way would take him near the road and down to whatever main road was around. But he had to move fast, and that was where he had an advantage. The man with the rifle was older, and Thomas knew he could outrun him. But outrunning a rifle bullet was another thing.

Thomas glanced over his shoulder up the ridge he had just come down and saw a figure standing at the top. He thought for a second to turn and fire, but there was no clean shot, so he kept going. The brush was thick, and the branches were cutting into his arms and face as he circled toward where he thought he would intersect the road.

Where is he? Can't hear a thing over the sound of my own movement. Stop! Listen!

Thomas stopped and crouched low to the ground. His breathing was not yet labored.

Thank God for the wind sprints in football practice.

He scanned the area, looking for any kind of movement, and listened.

Keep going!

The woods were opening up slightly, and he made better progress, but then he stepped into a hole and fell forward into a small brook, landing with his shoulder against the far bank. Dazed and panicked, he scrambled up the embankment and continued on.

Road. I've got to find the road and follow it down to find help!

He was suddenly aware of pain in his shoulder where he had just fallen, but he forced it out of his mind again.

You've played with pain before. Get rid of it!

He ran on, throwing his arms up to protect his face against the brittle branches. His heart felt thick, pushing out against his chest while his breathing now came with deep, quickened bursts. By his own estimate, he had made about four or five hundred yards and was coming upon a more open area when he saw the road sweeping from his left down to his right before it disappeared in a bend.

Just as he approached the area, which was canopied by a group of maple trees, Thomas stopped and got low behind a boulder. He tried to still his breath as quickly as he could, listening for the crack of wood, a rustling of branches, anything to give him a reference point. He held his breath and listened.

There was no movement in the trees. No wind. Only faint sounds from birds disturbed by Thomas's charge through the woods. He listened for movement, for the van starting up by the house, for the shouting as his escape was reported. Anything!

There was nothing.

He peered from behind the boulder up the road. It was empty. On his feet, Thomas darted out onto the road and sprinted downhill, looking back over his shoulder every few seconds. He would stay on the road briefly, but when he caught its general direction, he would get back into the woods. They would use the main road as a starting point when they would come.

He had run another hundred yards when his left leg collapsed under him, and he crumpled to the dirt. The pain jolted his brain so that he never heard the report of the rifle as he threw up his hands, inadvertently throwing the gun a few feet. Blood poured from the front and back of his thigh.

Dorman emerged from behind a group of rocks on the left side and walked in measured steps over to Thomas, who was by now clutching his leg, trying to stop the blood. Dorman kicked Thomas in the wounded leg, eliciting a gasp.

Dorman's voice crescendoed to a yell in one sentence. "You fuckin' son of a bitch, you broke my nose! Damn it!" He looked down at the college student. "I don't have time for this shit."

He pointed the gun at Thomas's head and pulled the trigger.

Chapter Fourteen

November 9, 1862

Prescott lay on his back, looking up at the ceiling in his rented house. It was set away from the main street, and Stallard handled all the negotiations so Prescott could stay safely anonymous. The house was simple, two stories with the kitchen and living room on the main floor and two bedrooms upstairs. The second bedroom went unused, since Stallard remained at the Smythe house, with a regular exception when the southerner would entertain a lady at the house for a few hours of "recreation," as he called it.

Stinson moved against Prescott, shifting her head from the nearby pillow to his shoulder, wrapping her arm around him, her left breast slipping in nicely against his side. He smiled as she kissed his shoulder in her sleep.

It had been over a month since their arrival in Chicago—a month of change for him. Working at the foundry, he had eased his way quietly into a group of the men who manned the Number Two furnace. It was hot, exhausting work, and it kept Prescott away from Stallard for large amounts of time, something he had protested but which was dismissed. Stallard said only that the critical time for preparation wouldn't come for months, and until then, he expected Prescott to work with the crew.

Prescott let it lie. There was no real gain to be made until two things happened: one, Fitzroy provided information on his negotiations with the English representative; and two, the final plans for moving the gold came out. Neither would happen until the new year. Prescott could not move to unveil the conspiracy until after all the principals were revealed—including their link to the administration in Washington.

Besides, it was beginning to feel like the mission would be rendered moot. He gazed down at Stinson's face in the pale light of the dawn. She had changed everything. A brilliant beacon had wiped away the darkness that the war had left at the edges of his soul. He found himself moved to tears on occasion as he watched her. He knew he was in love, and he was sure she felt the same.

The unspoken truth was there, revealed during long carriage rides as fall turned into winter, especially on those days as the last taste of summer fought for its final moments against fall's inevitability. Bundled together, full of laughter, they had told each other their secrets and dreams, their weaknesses and fears—all those things lovers tell each other that they tell no one else.

But through it all, Prescott held true to his charge from President Lincoln. Jackson Prescott was still William Jackson to Abigail. And he regretted it every moment. So now his thoughts had turned to leaving Chicago and taking her west in search of a new, anonymous life.

Climbing out of bed, Prescott put on his long johns and walked over to the table where a newspaper lay. The headline drew his eye to the page:

Burnside Replaces McClelland—President Appoints New Commander Of The Army Of The Potomac

The war will continue on until the president finds a general willing to use the materials at his disposal. McClelland waited too long. There might have been a chance to catch Lee right after Antietam, crush him before he slipped back into the South. Now the long winter is here . . .

Prescott dropped the newspaper on the table. Stinson turned over in the bed, still asleep.

Whether the gold makes it out of the country or not—is it important? This war is going to continue on and, with it, the death that walks the same path. Will everything really change if Stallard's gold reaches England? Will the Confederacy really benefit?

"Will, come back to bed." Abigail held out her hand from underneath the covers. "It's warm here."

"I was just watching the day arrive." Prescott climbed back into the bed and kissed her gently. She responded by pulling him closer to her and raised the intensity of the kiss. He felt his desire for her stir as he warmed to the bed and her body.

Their two bodies moved as one, each trying to surpass the other. Building with anticipation, delight as the moment of ecstasy arrived. First for Abigail, her arms holding with all her strength, pulling Jackson tighter against her. He followed moments later, releasing himself. They waited until their breathing subsided before he moved to her side, savoring her. He kissed her gently just beneath her ear.

"You're especially passionate this morning," Abby said.

"I felt inspired by you, and I was able to clear my head of much that has been troubling me," Jackson said. He touched her cheek. "Sometimes, when you make a decision, it gives you clarity not accessible before."

Abby looked at him quizzically, not sure what she was reading in his face.

"What decision are you speaking of?"

"The decision to be completely honest with you."

"Am I going to cry?"

"You, cry?" Jackson smiled and propped himself up on his arm. "You, Abigail Stinson, are one of the strongest women I've ever known. I don't believe I could ever make you cry, nor would I want to. You're too much the New Englander, first of all. You hide your emotions well . . . except your temper, I might add. You keep your true self just underneath the surface. I've been privileged to see it."

"And you have kept your true self hidden as well, have you not?" she said, mirroring his position on the bed. "Your job with Parker— there's much more to it than you have intimated. And I don't believe you've been entirely truthful to me about your personal self."

Prescott paused. Suddenly, the decision to tell her about the whole deception became tentative.

Abby broke the silence. "In your heart, you're a good man. Whatever you have done, I believe I'll be able to forgive you. You don't share what we have in the past month without believing that." She took his hand and squeezed it before interlocking her fingers in his.

"Most everything I have told you is true, about my background, my family, how I grew up. These are all the truth. But my name and why I'm here isn't. And it's such a significant lie that I don't know if you'll be comfortable forgiving me. My name isn't William Jackson, and I'm not an employee in Parker's company. I'm Lieutenant Jackson Prescott, and I have been and still am a member of the Federal Army."

Jackson thought it was a credit to Abby's character that she reacted with more interest than anger and hurt. Her jaw dropped an inch or two, but to his relief, she tilted her head and simply said, "I knew that wasn't your real name. It didn't fit."

"There's more."

"You're a deserter?" She pulled up the covers, withdrawing her hand from him. "Oh, God, you ran away from your men?"

"No, no. That's not what happened. Believe me, I couldn't have respect for myself if I didn't face my responsibility. I left for a reason. Let me tell you."

"Tell me, then."

And so he told her everything—from the horror at Antietam to the nighttime order to report to a train in western Maryland, the meeting with Lincoln and the decision to work in the service of the president, then came his meeting with Fitzroy and Stallard and his luck at working his way into the organization.

Through Prescott's revelation, Stinson listened without interruption, though he thought she must be overwhelmed with questions. She remained silent until he was done.

"What is going to happen now? Are you going to arrest Parker and his men?"

"That's not possible. I can't, until I have a list of the conspirators. And that won't happen until the gold reaches the East Coast.

I'll then have the entire operation in line. I'll be able to give Mr. Lincoln and Mr. Seward all the information necessary to bring all those people to justice, but . . ."

"What? There's still something troubling you," she said. "Don't keep anything more to yourself—not now."

Jackson sighed. "I have another person to consider. You've changed everything. Before, I had only brief glimpses of the happiness a man and woman could share, but they were only moments. There was never anything permanent. But I want there to be now, and if I continue on with this mission, I might lose what I've found."

"Then you feel the same for me that I feel for you?"

"Yes." He leaned over and kissed her softly. "Of course I love you."

"Oh, how I hoped . . . I love you." She wrapped her arms around him, but then pulled away. "From a practical view, I would not expect you to tell me the truth until we had fallen in love, so I forgive you for not revealing me everything until now. But if you had waited much longer"—she smiled—"I would have given you such a difficult time, you would have regretted the day you boarded that train."

"I thank God for your practicality, Miss Stinson. But we must discuss my other worry—for your safety," Jackson said.

"I can care for myself quite well, thank you."

"Of that I have little doubt, but these men are dangerous, and they will not let anyone, even a beautiful woman, keep them from completing their efforts. There will be a time when I'll have to insist you leave. You'll need to go home to Massachusetts until this business is finished."

He expected her to protest, and for a moment it appeared she would, but she only kissed him on the check, as one would kiss a brother.

"I can't have you until this is done," she said.

The morning was overcast and damp as Prescott stepped out the front door, pulling up his coat collar and drawing his hat low. He walked around to the back of the house where there was a small stable shared by the two houses on this section of the block. He blanketed and saddled his horse, swung up onto the back of the chestnut and headed down the street.

A solitary figure stood at the entrance to an alley, the reins of his horse in one hand and a rifle in the other. He wore a dark coat and pants with a broad, brown hat that obscured most of his face. When he looked up, his eyes followed the rider. He then climbed onto his own horse and steered the animal past a pair of carriages parked to the side and made his way at a fast trot.

Chapter Fifteen

Present Day
July 28

Sparks stood in the half-full trolley car with his right arm wrapped around a pole, alternately pulling against it as the car swayed. As instructed, he had gotten on the T at Copley Square, and the car was now making its way along the Green Line to the Government Center stop in the heart of the business district—a short walk from the market and shops of Faneuil Hall. Sparks could get a good look at the faces of the people around him, as he had at Copley Square.

Which one of these faces belongs to them?

He knew he would be followed, beginning with his arrival at Logan Airport last night. It was of no consequence, since it didn't matter if they watched him or not, at least not now. He had only one intention this morning, and that was to meet the voice who had called him yesterday—for Sparks could only think of Jennifer. He didn't care about the gold, or Drury, or even the attempts on his own life.

No, that wasn't true. He did care about the gold. It had to exist somewhere, and he had to find it. Jennifer's life depended on it.

The car reached Government Center, and he exited, climbing the stairs that led to the concrete mall that fronted City Hall. Right at the top of the stairs and to the right was a newsstand, operated by a surprisingly clean-cut, middle-aged man with a Red Sox cap and a golf shirt and shorts. He was in constant motion, making change and pulling magazines for his customers, who arrived in well-timed intervals, allowing just enough time to wait on them but not enough time to carry on a conversation. Sparks cut in front of a businessman and asked if the vendor had a copy of *Vermont Life*. The man glanced up at Sparks and without a word stepped to the side and pulled a copy of the magazine from behind a series of bundled newspapers.

As he took the money from Sparks, he said, "Page thirty-seven."

Sparks paid the man and stepped away from the stand, not bothering to ask about the unusual instructions or who gave them. It would be pointless. A twenty and some brief words was all it would have taken. Turning to page thirty-seven, Sparks found words printed in marker.

Go to the Common. Sit on the bench facing the pond on the opposite side from the swan boat launch.

Rather than go back the opposite direction on the Green Line, Sparks walked back to the Common. As he moved past the mixture of tourists and businesspeople, he scanned their faces, looking for a sudden averting of eyes. Whenever the crowd forced him to step to the side, he was able to glance back without appearing to do so. No one was visible, but he knew they were there somewhere.

He was beginning to perspire on his back from the muggy air and blazing sun cooking the Common when he saw the bench in the shade, near the pond. There was already a woman and child sitting there, but Sparks didn't hesitate as he approached. Whoever he was waiting for wouldn't show unless he was alone. Ten minutes later, the mother and child left. Within seconds, a man with brown hair, a mustache, and a goatee and wearing dark glasses walked up to the bench and sat down next to Sparks. He carried a black attaché case.

"You weren't followed," the man said with a distinctive Massachusetts accent. "I appreciate your being professional."

Sparks fought to control his anger. "I want substantial proof my daughter is unharmed."

"Your daughter and her companion are safe. They will remain so for now."

"Her companion? Why would you take someone other than her? That only adds to the situation—complicates it."

"It was unavoidable. I want to make this transaction as quick as possible. I took this picture of your daughter yesterday. As you can see, she was fine. She and her boyfriend are being moved to a new location today. I'll let her speak to you briefly in a few days. After that, there will be no communication between yourself and her until the gold is recovered or proven lost."

"That's the first time you've hinted she'll be returned even if I don't find the gold."

"I work in a dirty world"—the man turned and looked directly at the FBI agent—"but I don't harm needlessly. The threat against your daughter is real if you try to deceive us, but if you make a genuine effort, I'll do my best to see she's returned safely to you."

"Are you authorized to promise that?" Sparks asked.

"Do you mean to ascertain if I'm in charge?"

"Yes."

"I only work for individuals who allow me broad discretionary powers."

"Why do I feel your leash will be shortened at some point?"

The man sounded annoyed. "Don't try to dig anymore." He opened his briefcase and pulled out a folder, holding it while he waited for Sparks to do the same. "Here's the letter held by the Boston law firm one hundred and fifty years ago. It was a letter from Parker Stallard to his brother Lawrence in northeastern Florida. I believe Lawrence was a farmer. The letter states there were three parts to the puzzle and that all three letters together would lead his brother to the gold."

The two men exchanged letters. It was clear to Sparks the two letters were in the same handwriting—Parker Stallard's. The letter given to Sparks was dated June 28, 1863—the same date as the hastily written one that was stored in the Stallard family's old papers. It was simple and direct and plainly disclosed Parker's intentions:

June 28, 1863

My brother Lawrence,

I have been involved with Cassias Fitzroy of Philadelphia in a plan to help the Confederacy gain political favor overseas. To that end, Charles and I have found and utilized a gold mine he discovered. We have had the ore processed and have in our possession almost five tons of high grade metal. We have moved the gold almost to port, where it was to be shipped to Europe among other goods. Events have forced me into holding the gold in a location of safety until we can complete the journey. As a precaution, I am sending information to you and Cassias in three parts.

The first letter you no doubt received a while ago. This letter has been held by this Boston law firm with the instructions to hand-deliver it to you once the war is over. That first letter contained a numerical puzzle, much like the ones you and I would play with when we were children. After the numerical puzzle is a short passage I hope you will remember. These messages give you the town and a slightly more specific clue to the gold's location. At the same time as I am writing these two letters, one to you and one to the law firm, I am writing and sending a third to Cassias, for him to hold on to until the time arrives when you both can recover the shipment yourselves.

His letter has specific instructions on the gold's location. You must follow the directions precisely and you will need to use significant man- and horsepower. Since you are reading this letter, it means I did not survive the war. I have come to realize that for all my vocal bravado, I am not a true hero of the South. The true heroes are the men who carry the musket into battle and march headlong into the roar of cannon. If I have a chance, I would like to join them. I can think of no higher calling than to fight for South Carolina. Perhaps, because you are reading this, I was allowed my chance.

Your loving brother,

Parker

Sparks finished the letter and looked up to see the bearded man reading the Stallard letter he and Tracy had found in the hand-carved box. Streeter was just finishing up when he read softly, out loud, the words written at the bottom. "'And he showed unto him all the kingdoms of the world in a moment of time.'"

"Do you know where that's from?" Sparks asked. "It sounds like a Bible passage."

"It is . . . from the beginning of the fourth chapter of Luke. The devil tempts Jesus by showing him all the kingdoms in the world and telling him they will be his to command."

"The devil tempts Jesus? What could that mean?"

"I don't know off hand, but I'm sure once you learn the connection, it will prove invaluable. Here, I've written down the numbers and the line of scripture. You can keep the original. And don't bother trying to lift my prints or DNA. I have worn latex gloves all the time I have handled the document."

"You don't miss much."

"No. Would you like to write a brief message to your daughter? I'll see that it gets sent to her immediately."

Sparks raised his eyebrows. "Yes, I would like to." He produced a pen and a notepad and wrote a short note to Jennifer. There was no need for subterfuge—all he did was tell her that he loved her and that he was doing all he could to get her and her new boyfriend to safety. He handed the note over. "If harm comes to Jennifer, I'll hunt you and your employers down."

"I was hoping we'd be able to carry on this transaction without the melodrama. But I guess it is to be expected. There's enormous pressure on you." The man stood up and paused in front of Sparks. "Just stay on track, focused on your objective. And don't have any contact with the bureau. We'll know if the bureau is trying to investigate for links to us."

As the man walked away, Sparks called out to him. "One more thing. I would like to have Tracy Coulthard help me on this. She already knows the score, and she's pretty perceptive. She actually has already been a big help. I also put her under bureau protection after your attempt in Jacksonville. If she gets antsy, she could start to raise a big stink within the bureau, and I would be powerless to stop it."

"A valid point. The attempt in Jacksonville was unauthorized, by the way."

"I trust you'll have better control over your people in the future."

The man nodded and strode away. He was gone into the crowd within a minute.

Streeter, now without the facial growth but still with his light brown hair, stood in the Lawrence house kitchen, leaning against the sink area while filling his pipe. Dorman sat at the table, having just explained how the two hostages had now become one.

Dorman waited for Streeter to respond, but when a reply wasn't forthcoming quickly, he got impatient. "I expect you're pissed off at me, but once he was free, there was nothing else I could do," Dorman implored. "I didn't mean to kill him. I tried to just wound him, but I missed high. You can't blame me for missing a target in the woods from a couple hundred feet away."

Streeter looked at Dorman as he lit the pipe, drawing hard on it to get the tobacco burning well. "You wouldn't have been in that position in the first place if you had done as I instructed and drugged them first."

"Yes. He was stronger than I expected, and he broke my fuckin' nose, for Christ's sake."

"It's an improvement."

"Screw you. I did the right thing. We didn't need him. Only the girl is important."

"Perhaps. I don't like complications because of incompetence."

"I took care of it. No one will find the body."

"All right." Streeter walked over to where he was standing over Dorman. "Don't screw up again."

"I won't. I still don't think you're giving me any credit for having taken care of the problem."

"I'll make sure the old man puts a little something extra in your pay."

Dorman smiled. "I'll go get the food for our little missy upstairs. How much should I get?"

"No more than a week's worth."

Dorman held out his hand, and Streeter handed over some cash.

Streeter watched from the kitchen window as Dorman left in one of the cars. The fact that Dorman had been smart enough to move the body from the property was small consolation. Streeter knew Dorman too well to accept the accidental shooting story, though the broken nose was real enough.

No, Dorman had gunned the kid down in anger. The only question Streeter needed to answer was whether he should take Dorman out now or wait until the job was over. Streeter took a deep breath away from his pipe smoke and rubbed his temples. He relit his pipe and walked into the living room, settling into the lounge chair to think.

"No, I don't want to talk to her right now," Sparks said from Boston, speaking with Catwood in Jacksonville. "Just put her with a courier and send the two of them up on the next plane to Washington."

"All right, but she's been asking about you. Demanding to know what's been going on."

"Just tell her I've made some progress, and I'll let her know about everything when I see her up in D.C."

"OK. She'll wonder why you didn't want to talk to her yourself after speaking with me. What do you want me to say?"

"Just tell her I didn't have time."

Chapter Sixteen

December 16, 1862

The sleet tapped at Prescott's bedroom window, the sound unworthy of the brutal conditions outside. It wasn't winter yet by the calendar, but the scene outside the glass said otherwise. The dormant season had arrived in Chicago.

Wrapped in a blanket, Prescott didn't feel the room's chill except on his face, so close to the window his breath could bring moisture to the surface if he moved slightly forward. But he chose to remain as he was, sitting hunched with his elbow on the inside sill, surveying the assault on man and animal outside.

Early morning remained the best time for him. Away from the foundry, the charade, this was the time he could think most clearly. It was a comforting time. Since their commitment to each other weeks ago, Prescott had taken Stinson's words and pondered them as he balanced her against his duty. And despite his love, when he was finished thinking the matter through, duty stood above all. As it had in the beginning, as it did now, as it would in the future.

His gaze traveled from the outside to the small desk by the window. Resting on the surface was a theater bill dated from the day before. It was from McVicker's Theater, where Stinson and Prescott, along with Stallard and a lady friend, had spent the evening watching an uncommon talent headline a Shakespearean performance before a filled house. John Wilkes Booth was the actor's name, and Stallard had insisted the group go backstage to meet the actor. The women were quite taken by his dashing presence, and he didn't disappoint, presenting himself as just as charming off stage as on.

With production people and actors moving around them in constant motion, Prescott had shaken Booth's hand and looked into the man's eyes, as he did with anyone he met, to gauge the character. He felt Booth was doing the same, and for a moment, Prescott felt awkward, uneasy. The eyes revealed brilliant passion tinged with a wild, almost mad quality to them. Prescott found it an unsettling acquaintance, but then remembered that just minutes before, the young actor had been center stage in the role of Hamlet. Perhaps dropping from character was a gradual process.

Abby was not feeling well, and so Prescott had spent the night alone. His sleep had been restful, but he had awakened earlier than normal, even for him. He had spent the last two hours in his chair, thinking on the last eleven weeks. His life had been transformed. But had not the lives of thousands of men been changed every day of this war?

It was time to send a wire.

As the weeks passed and there was no further mention of the search for the traitor Lieutenant Jackson Prescott, Stallard had allowed him to venture out on his own almost exclusively, with the previous night's theater visit being the exception.

Of course, clean-shaven and with wire-rimmed glasses for public appearances, Prescott looked so different only a close friend would know him. It was this man, with a plain suit and heavy overcoat, who came through the telegraph office's front door, the wind darting in as he stepped in and closed the door behind him.

There were three workers: one was off in the corner, his back to the room as he pored over stacks of papers; the second tapped away at the telegraph key, intently reading the message he was sending; the third, a very young man meticulously dressed and standing by the front counter, directed his attention to Prescott. "Can I help you, sir?"

"I need to send a wire."

"Of course, sir. Please write out your message here, and we'll send it out as soon as we can."

"It needs to be sent today," Prescott said. "Actually, it needs to go out as I stand here."

"Well, we try to get everything sent out by the end of the day, but it will be a long wait if you wish to be present."

The metallic sound of a coin slapping down on the counter was followed by the continuous scrape as Prescott slid it across the counter. "It won't be a long wait. Is a twenty-dollar gold piece enough to get me moved to the top of the list?"

"Well, yes, sir," the clerk said, looking off to either side. His two coworkers seemed oblivious to the conversation.

"Good. I also have a couple of other special requests that, if you agree to, will bring you more gold pieces like what you have in your hand. The first is, you're not to speak about this to anyone else. What's your name?"

"Patrick, sir."

"All right, Patrick. This is to be kept secret. I don't want it logged, and I'll keep the only copy of the message sent. Is that clear?"

"Yes."

"It's against the rules, Patrick." This came from the clerk, who had been hunched over the papers and now approached the counter. He had not been so focused, after all. He also was young, barely out of his teens.

"I'll handle this, Jacob. And you keep your mouth shut, or I'll have a mind to knock you down," said Patrick. "We'll split it if you don't tell old man Fitzgerald."

"You two argue as you like," Prescott said. "I just want to know if you'll do my bidding."

"Yes, sir," Patrick said.

Prescott carefully filled in the spaces for each of the letters he wanted for his message. As was prearranged with Lincoln and Seward, he would lead the wire with two words and the wire would be sent to Washington, where each operator on duty was instructed to contact Mr. Lincoln's assistant, a Mr. Nicolay. The message would then be delivered to the president.

Prescott looked over the message:

December 16, 1862

Chicago, Illinois

North Star. Progress made. Shipment being processed in Chicago. Early spring move expected. Shipment destination undecided though likely from northern port. Assistance unnecessary now. Will contact when shipment ready. J.P.

Prescott paid the fee, and as Patrick turned away from the counter to hand the message to the third clerk at the key, Prescott grabbed his jacket and pulled him back. "There's one additional request that I have. It's unusual, but it's vital that you follow my instructions. If you do so, you'll get another gold piece."

Charles Stallard loved the smell of burning wood. Squatting before his small stone fireplace, the heat enveloped his face and chest as he poked at the ashes underneath the logs. The popping and a gentle hiss were the only sounds. The flue on this one-room shelter's fireplace always drew well, so little smoke came into the room, but he could still breathe in the biting aroma with satisfaction.

With a sigh, he replaced the iron bar he used as a poker and stepped back from the fireplace to the only door. Opening the solid door brought a different scene to the cabin's lone occupant. Where once was subdued light with warmth, now came the white brilliance of an early snowstorm . . . a continuous whirling of white with the moaning wind as its companion, changing the landscape by the minute.

It had been snowing for two days now, and there was three feet of fresh snow—more in places where the wind had swept its hand. The cabin was placed, and smartly so, on the crest of a small hill, so access was possible through any of the snows Charles had encountered the last four years.

The small hill was about a hundred yards from the base of a broad, steep rise that became one half of a deep valley between two jagged peaks in the mountains of this territory. It was a valley few men had ever seen, but Charles had lived here almost continuously for four years, since the day he had arrived at what the tribe had called the Sun Cave.

Five years ago, searching for excitement away from a boring life, he had come west, and through a fortunate turn of events, he had saved the life of a tribal elder. Accepted for his heroic deed, he had been cautiously brought into the tribe family and had gradually gained their trust. He had learned their language and culture quickly and adopted them without hesitation. After a year, he felt a kindred bond with the people, despite their great difference in cultures.

Then had come the talk of the Sun Cave and his visit to the site. The opening was on the east side of the valley, about a third of the way up the mountain. Protected from detection from the valley floor by trees, the cave had easy access. Charles had simply walked straight in with his Sioux guide. What met him that day he would never forget: a huge vein of gold stretching the entire side wall and part of the ceiling. After acquiring some tools from the tribe, he returned for a month of work to determine the potential yield from the vein. To his astonishment, it seemed endless.

Charles presented the tribal elders a proposal where, in exchange for access and help in extracting the ore, he would bring them supplies and weapons from the white man. With it, he gave his blood oath to never reveal the valley to others from the East. And so had begun the plan to bring gold from the West to Chicago.

With money and supplies from Parker and physical help from the Sioux, the crude operation here between the mountains had taken just the summer of 1859 to establish. With five men, they had extracted close to nine tons of gold-laden ore and shipped it out two times a summer across the plains south of Canada and into Minnesota and Wisconsin and down to Chicago.

The process had gone on unabated in the warm weather months for three years. Now was the time for rest. The four Sioux workers were gone, having returned to their families to winter with the tribe. Charles preferred it this way, for he had no use for civilization. He had finally found true freedom.

For today, though, his solitude would be broken.

As he stood in the doorway of his cabin, his eyes followed the tree line until he caught the movement he had sensed before. From the shadows came a lone rider on a palomino, wrapped in buffalo skins, with a small headdress of feathers. As he approached, the rider's long hair, which appeared black from a distance, was revealed to have streaks of gray aside from the accumulated snow.

His face was weathered with a leathery texture, and the lines around the eyes revealed knowledge. Charles was not afraid, for he had looked into those eyes before, including when he had reached down with a rope from a ledge to save a warrior from an embarrassing death.

Gray Bear brought his horse to within a few feet of Charles. "Would you offer shelter for a traveler?" Gray Bear spoke in English.

"You forget, my friend, that I have grown accustomed to speaking with the words of the Lakota. I prefer it," Charles said in the elder's language.

"You honor my people."

"And you honor me. Come and rest from your journey."

The elder Sioux climbed down, tied his horse, and stepped inside next to Charles. He turned down an offer of coffee from the southerner, wrinkling his nose with distaste. They left the door open. Charles knew Gray Bear preferred it that way, disliking enclosed places.

"Why has Gray Bear traveled up from the winter home of his people?" Charles asked, knowing also the elder always spoke to the point, and sensing sternness.

"I have come to talk with you about the words you spoke long ago. You said we would trade the important sun rocks for supplies from the East. You spoke of blankets, new medicines, new things that would help my people. And you spoke of the weapons, the rifles that make it possible to extend a warrior's ability to strike. You have spoken of a great many things. My people are grateful for the things your people brought us back in the warmth of the summer. But there has been only the one time, and there are many in the tribe, some more powerful than me, who feel the trade has not been balanced. I have come here to talk with you about this." Hands on his knees, back straight, Gray Bear stopped and awaited the answer.

"I came from a land where one's word of honor is sacred, as your people say. I came to this land, not as a warrior, not as a settler to take your land, not as a soldier to kill and take away. I came as an explorer to find what the land and the sky can offer any man if he chooses to seek it out." Charles looked directly into the elder's eyes—he didn't want his gaze to stray for an instant.

"The sun rocks in that cave are valuable to the leaders from the East, and as we have discussed before, there's a great war going on now that will determine how all our peoples live together. And the gold I have sent east is more valuable than the things I have had brought back in return, I will agree. But I have sent instructions that more be brought with both of the wagon trains coming this summer. I promise the new wagons will bring important supplies for your people."

"You have never lied to my people. I believe you are not now. But I must warn you of times to come. There are those within the tribes of the Lakota who believe you are like the other men who have pushed and fought our people. And I fear it will continue. I do not know how long my words will be heard before they turn away. But when that time arrives, it will be dangerous for you. I fear it will arrive soon."

Charles took a deep breath. "Tell those who do not trust my words . . . no more of the sun rocks will be taken from your mountains until more supplies have come from the East. I will not take more until I have gained their trust again."

"But what of your brother?"

"Whatever my brother demands will have to be met with what we have already sent to him. My word stands alone."

"There is wisdom with you, Charles Stallard. I am hopeful my people will listen to me when I return."

A gust of wind swept snowflakes into the open doorway. Charles shivered and stepped up to the hearth to put another two logs on the fire. With his back still to Gray Bear, Charles spoke. "I have not heard news from the East for some time, but the last words I heard spoke of a great battle between two great armies. The battle was near a town in a place called Maryland, at a stream called Antietam. A great many men died. I am afraid there will be many more such battles before there is a victor."

"When I was young, an elder once told me a man's life is a river. There will be times when the water is swift, when life is wild and uncontrollable. Then there will be times when it is quiet, when the water is still. The river will take the path it chooses. The man must stand and face where the river takes him. How well he faces the river determines his worth." The Sioux elder stood, shifting his bear skins in preparation for leaving. "Those battles will run their course. You must have faith in the gods."

"You do not understand, Gray Bear," Charles said, turning around. "Once the fighting is over there, the victors will turn their eyes to the West—to this land."

"It is you who do not understand, my friend. I know they will come. My people will stand and face where the river takes them."

Gray Bear climbed on his horse. He adjusted the blankets and skins to maximize the warmth. He took his horse down to the tree line, retracing his steps in the snow. Charles stood in the doorway until the Sioux elder was gone. The oldest Stallard son moved his gaze from the tree line up the mountain's side.

The snow was going to be heavy this winter.

The dinner at the Smythe home was again superb. Stallard, Prescott, and Smythe had retired to the library where the fireplace roared with ferocity. Brandy and cigars were passed around. As the other two lit their cigars and settled into chairs, Smythe went to the double doors and closed them behind him as he faced the interior. There was but one weak lamp lit in the corner, so the only light came from the fireplace, the glow failing to soften Smythe's cold face.

"Gentlemen," he began, "I hate to change the tenor of our evening so quickly, but there's a matter we must discuss, and it must be done now. Parker, why did you choose Prescott here for this business? Why didn't you just help him along his way down south or north to Canada? Why include him in with us?"

"We've already discussed the events surrounding how Jack came to join us."

"And I don't like the tone of this, either," Prescott said.

Smythe ignored Prescott and addressed Stallard as he walked to where his cigar and brandy lay on the table. He didn't pick them up. "There's much at stake, and while I understand the need to replace the man you lost back in September, I wasn't comfortable with you bringing in an outsider who brought with him a Federal Army officer's uniform. I have progressed from being uncomfortable to suspicious."

"What reason do you have to be suspicious of me?" Prescott asked.

"Tell Parker of your visit to the telegraph office." Smythe's voice was barely a whisper.

The realization hit Prescott hard, but he tried his best to hide his panic. He kept his eyes on Smythe's face. The black eyes bore right back at him without blinking. "You had me followed." It was a statement. Prescott turned to Stallard. "I'm sorry, Parker. Smythe here has a legitimate reason to be suspicious, since he had someone follow me to the telegraph office. Especially with my background." He turned his attention back to Smythe. "But I can explain the reason for my sending a wire."

"And that would be?" Smythe pulled a small pistol from beneath his suit jacket.

Stallard stood up and stepped between the two men.

"Enough with the drama, Smythe! Put that damn gun away. This isn't some doggery where a drunk has challenged you. We're here as businessmen having a sociable drink after a fine meal."

"Out of my way." Smythe moved so he had a clear view of Prescott. "Go on with the explanation. And be aware I have posted three men at the exits."

"You're joking with us!" Stallard gasped.

"The explanation is simple," Prescott said. "Being on the run as I am, sending a wire, particularly when the government is so involved with the telegraph these days, is a dangerous decision. And one, I can see now, should have been cleared through you first, Parker. I did send a wire this afternoon. It was to Boston, to a very impressionable young lady who is used to receiving letters from me regularly. Unfortunately, I forgot an important day, and I felt the need to get something to her quickly."

"You risked someone recognizing your name in Boston for a woman?" Smythe was skeptical.

"Not just a woman. My cousin, Elizabeth. She's mentally deficient . . . has been since birth. But she adores me, and I have always written to her on her birthday, without fail—until this year. I missed her birthday, it was last week. So I sent her a message using my own name, but just my first two initials. And I bribed the clerk to destroy the sheet and not enter the message in the log. You can go and ask them yourself, but I paid them to keep quiet. They might deny it."

"For your sake, I hope they will be forthtelling," Smythe said.

"Enough!" Stallard was smiling as he stepped to Smythe and firmly lowered the foundry owner's arm with its burden. "After you received your messenger this afternoon while I was there, Smythe, I went myself to the telegraph office and spoke with a pair of enterprising young men. Jackson's story is corroborated. He did send a wire to Boston—to an asylum. They had already destroyed the message, but they remembered the destination. I believe this takes care of your concerns."

Smythe placed the pistol back underneath his jacket. "I suppose it's a believable reason. But it was careless, something I would punish severely if it had been one of my men. They aren't so stupid, of course."

Prescott glared but simply said, "I felt the personal importance was worth the risk."

"You have done smarter things in your life, I'm sure, Jack, but I'm willing to overlook it," Stallard said. "Come now, let's enjoy this fine brandy and your cigars, William. Nothing finer in the world than this."

An hour later, Prescott sat on the edge of his bed in the rented house, tossing the last of his clothes on the nearby chair. Still in his underwear, he crawled between the sheets and pulled the blanket up to ward off the night chill.

Smythe was a dangerous man. He could almost see in Smythe's face the decision-making process of weighing risk against reward with him. Smythe wasn't satisfied, even with Stallard's story that backed Prescott up. Every future move would have to be done with care—Smythe would be watching.

The young man slipped in the side door to the well-kept house into the kitchen where two older prostitutes were eating a snack, still sitting in their pantalets, talking as he made his appearance. They both called to the young man by name and gave him a smile.

"Hey, there, Timothy, my boy," said the older of the two women, who went by the name of Betsy. "What brings you here so late at night? You're too young to be a customer coming in the front door, so what's this?"

"I am too old enough. I'm near enough seventeen. But I'm here to see Mr. Smythe. He's here tonight, isn't he?"

"Ah, I knew you were a runner for him. I saw him earlier," said the younger prostitute. "He's with Edith and Marie. They're upstairs by now. I wouldn't go tramping up there without telling Miss Sophie. You know how upset she gets when people who aren't supposed to be upstairs interfere with the business."

"I know, ma'am, but he sent word to my family that he wanted to see me tonight, no matter how late."

"Maybe so, but I don't think he'll want to be bothered right now," said Betsy, laughing.

The boy flushed with embarrassment and stammered to get out a reply, but his effort was interrupted by the entrance of an imposing figure in a broad, blue silk dress. Miss Sophie was not an older woman like many of the city's madams. She was still young, in her early thirties, and auburn-haired, with strong, attractive features. Her neckline sloped down to reveal an ample bosom, but her manner conveyed a distant attitude. She saw the boy and her eyes flashed with recognition. "Timothy! Mr. Smythe wants to see you right away, young man," she said. "Go on up. It's all right."

"But the ladies said he wouldn't want to be disturbed."

"He told me personally to send you up when you got here, no matter the time. He's in Room 5. Go on!"

The boy made his way through the hall, past the velvet décor in the rooms on the first floor, and climbed the stairs quickly. Within a few moments, he was in front of the room. He brought his hand up to the door, pausing with his knuckles inches from the door. He waited and listened. With no noise coming from within, he lightly knocked.

"What is it?" came the muffled, masculine voice from inside.

"It's Tim, sir. I came as fast as I could."

"A moment," was the reply.

In a few seconds, the door opened and a bare-chested Smythe motioned for the boy to enter the room. As the boy did, he at once noticed the two women sitting up in the bed, clearly naked and looking at him with amusement.

"I . . . I came as fast as I could, sir." Timothy again had difficulty. "Your message said as soon as I could."

"That it did, boy," Smythe said. "We'll make this a quick visit, and then you can be on your way home. Listen to me, you work in the back of the telegraph office. I want you to answer a couple of questions about some of the goings-on there today."

"I'll try, sir."

"A man came in there during the day and offered the three clerks in the front some extra money to send a message back east and to keep it out of the logs. Did you see the man yourself, or hear about it from the other three?"

"Both, sir. I saw him when he came in. He had glasses, no mustache or beard, dark hair. He was wearing a very fine overcoat. The clerks later said he gave them both twenty-dollar gold pieces for them to send a wire and to keep it out of the log, just as you said."

"This is important, Timothy. Did they tell you where his message was sent?"

"Yeah, but not until after the other man came by and asked about the first man."

"The second man?"

"Yeah, he was a sure dandy, sir. He was dressed up in right fine clothes, and he carried a fancy cane with the head of some animal or bird on it, I really couldn't tell. Oh, he also had a scar on his face."

"That would be Mr. Stallard."

The boy nodded. "I believe that was the name, sir. The clerks told him the first man sent a message to Boston."

"Did Mr. Stallard seem pleased by the news?"

"I guess so. I didn't see—just heard what was being said from the doorway I was near."

"Well, I guess that's it. You can go," Smythe said, handing the boy a gold piece.

"Thank you, sir, but I don't think you heard me correctly."

"I don't understand."

"I don't like those clerks, sir. They treat me poorly. They always talk like they're so much smarter than me. They wouldn't split the money with me . . . I heard them tell that Mr. Stallard that the wire was sent to Boston, to a hospital."

"So what?"

"I said they didn't tell me about where the wire was sent until *after* the second man came by."

"Get to the point."

"I heard them boasting about how they lied to the second man, because the first man had promised them extra money would be coming. He told them, if anyone came by, to tell them about this hospital in Boston."

Anger stirred in Smythe's face. He grabbed the boy by the shoulders. "The first man told them to say Boston?! He told them to lie to anyone who might ask?"

"Yes, yes, sir," the boy exclaimed with abrupt fear. "That's what I said. They said he told them to lie, and that's what they did!"

"Where? Where was the wire really sent?" Smythe's voice was suddenly loud, demanding.

"I don't know for sure, because I haven't learned how to operate the key yet, but what—"

"Where, I said!" Smythe shook the boy's shoulders again. "Where did they say the message was sent?"

"Washington." The boy's voice quivered. "They said it was sent to Washington."

Chapter Seventeen

Present Day
July 29

With an agent stationed discreetly a few steps away, Coulthard stood against the building with her bag, trying to avoid the afternoon sun. She wore a simple blue dress, her eyes behind sunglasses and her hair around her face.

She heard a short horn, and a car pulled against the curb. Sparks emerged from the driver's side and motioned for Coulthard, then signaled the agent, all while hitting the automatic trunk latch. Coulthard met him at the back of the car, placed her bag inside and held out her arms for him.

"I missed you," she said. "You need to let me know when you go off into the night. I was worried about you. Why didn't you call?"

"I'm sorry." He gave her a firm hug, but kept it short. "I should have talked to you, but the situation has changed. Let's get in the car and out of the sun. We'll talk on our way to Gettysburg."

Within a few minutes, they were away from Pennsylvania Avenue and the Hoover Building and were headed out to take the circular beltway around the city. Coulthard's few questions went unanswered by Sparks as he negotiated the traffic, periodically checking the vehicles around him.

Once on I-495, Sparks felt more relaxed. "I'm sorry for the cool reception, but I wanted to get on the road as quickly as possible, and I wanted to make sure we weren't followed away from the bureau."

"Why? What is going on?" she asked. "You disappear for a couple of days and I'm left cooped up in that office, then I get moved here in the middle of the night. You don't call. I feel like a prisoner, Jason."

"That's my fault, I'm afraid. I told Catwood to put pretty tight controls on you. They've got my daughter."

"What?" Coulthard's surprise was genuine. "Oh, my God! They kidnapped her? Why?"

"To keep the official investigation out of their way while I find it for them. They learned I often work alone, and so they found the best way to cut me off from the bureau without raising suspicion. It was dangerous, but smart. They now have no competing interests."

"Oh, Jason, I'm so sorry. Have they let you talk to her? Is she all right?"

"I haven't spoken to her yet. I'm hoping to talk to her today or tomorrow."

"I can't believe this," Coulthard said softly.

"We now have two of the three letters. I was given the letter found in Boston, and with the one from your family, we should have a good start. Take a look at them here. Read them both and tell me what you think."

They rode in silence as Sparks reached the exit for I-270 and they headed northwest, away from Washington and into the Maryland countryside.

"So, my family's letter reveals the town and a general location of where the gold is hidden," she said. "Well, we know the town, but the Boston letter also says we should have the general location."

"The phrase underneath the numbers," Sparks said. "Remember? We didn't get to it after we figured out the number progression."

"'And he showed unto him all the kingdoms of the world in a moment of time,'" Coulthard read the copy of her family's letter. "You said it was from the Bible, right?"

"Whoever we're dealing with, he knew immediately, and he was right. I checked. There's a Bible back there on the backseat. Look up Luke and read from the beginning."

It was quiet for a few moments while she read. "This is when the devil is tempting Jesus during his forty days in the wilderness, isn't it?" she asked.

"The devil, indeed. I don't suppose you know anything about the Battle of Gettysburg?"

"Just kind of general knowledge. The Union won the battle . . . turning point of the Civil War."

"Well, if you're going to help me on this little gold-hunting expedition, you're going to need to learn more. Look at that book on the backseat where you got the Bible from." As Coulthard pulled the book from the back and settled into her seat again, Sparks continued. "I've marked a few pages. I'll give you a synopsis as you look at the battlefield diagram."

"You've done a lot of research in the last few days?" she asked.

"No, I've read a few books in the past. I have an ancestor who fought in the war. Anyway, in the summer of 1863, the war had been going on for more than two years and there had been significant Union victories in the West, but the war here in the East had not gone well. Robert E. Lee had not suffered a true defeat since taking over, and there had been two major victories—at Fredericksburg, Virginia, the previous December and at Chancellorsville in May.

"In June, Lee took the Army of Northern Virginia across the line into the North, through Maryland and into, ultimately, Pennsylvania. Meanwhile, the Union's Army of the Potomac, having just been put under the command of General George Meade just two days before, had been moving in a parallel movement northwest, keeping itself between the Rebels and Washington. The two armies stumbled into each other, and the battle was fought in and around Gettysburg, just north of the Maryland border. The battle lasted the first three days of July. Lee's army was defeated and withdrew, but Meade failed to follow up and probably squandered a chance to destroy Lee's army."

"Why is it so necessary to know about the battle?"

"Because your ancestor, Parker Stallard, wrote those letters in Harrisburg, just north of Gettysburg, days before the two sides fought there. And as we have already learned, it appears he hid the gold somewhere around Gettysburg. The first day of the battle, the action was centered west and north of the town and progressed to where, after that first day, the Union line was shaped like an up-side-down fish hook that ran along Cemetery Ridge south to just north of a pair of small hills called Big Round Top and Little Round Top. The Confederates were to the west and formed a line along Seminary Ridge that ran southwest in a parallel line.

"The second day, most of the heavy action took place in the south as the Confederates tried to take both the round tops and failed. The third day, Lee decided to attack the center and sent twelve thousand men marching across the open expanse between the two armies and toward the Union center. The attack, which became known as 'Pickett's Charge,' after the general who led the assault—George Pickett—reached the stone wall on Cemetery Ridge but was bloodily repulsed. The battle ended, and the next day Lee took his army south and out of harm's way."

"I'm still catching up here," Coulthard said. "History doesn't tell of any gold being involved in the battle, right?"

"No."

"Then why do you think the battle might matter?"

"The Civil War is filled with famous names of specific pieces of land where men fought. At the Battle of Antietam, there were the West Woods, the Cornfield, or the Sunken Road. At Shiloh in Tennessee, there was the Hornet's Nest and Bloody Pond. Gettysburg has its own. There's an area just north of a copse of trees that was at the Union center that became known as The Angle. And there was a farmer's field west of the round tops that's simply known as The Wheatfield. Well, just south of that wheat field was a rough, boulder-filled area where some of the heaviest fighting of the battle took place on the second day. Civil War historians know it simply as . . . Devil's Den."

Coulthard looked over at Sparks, the car's air-conditioning the only sound. "It's right here on the map. Could it be as simple as that?"

"The biggest question in my mind is, if the reference in the letter is to that part of the battlefield, then how did Parker Stallard know about it six days before the battle even took place?"

"That makes sense, but this can't be a coincidence."

"I agree. If the gold was hidden in a place that later became part of a battlefield—the most walked on, studied, and photographed battlefield in North America—it's logical the gold would have been found."

"But it hasn't been."

"And it could very well still be there."

For the remainder of the drive to Gettysburg, Coulthard read through the material. Sparks was thankful. His emotions swirled, still with the toughest time of his life ahead. They reached a hotel near the town. Contact with the kidnappers was at 11 a.m. the next day. He would get to talk to Jennifer and receive further instructions. The number given him carried a Massachusetts area code, but likely was just a relay or a throwaway, untraceable cell phone.

After checking in, Sparks collapsed on the bed with a cold towel on his face.

"When was the last time you slept?" Coulthard asked, emerging from the bathroom.

"I can't remember—oh, I slept four hours last night. Before that, about twenty-four, since I got the first phone call. I'll get some sleep tonight after dinner."

"Let me order in while you take a shower. Then you need a good, solid eight hours or more. A tired man makes mistakes. Isn't that high up on the agents' list of rules?"

"Very much so, but you'd be surprised how often it's broken."

"Not tonight, Special Agent Sparks."

The food was takeout chicken along with a bottle of soda. Blindfolded, with her hands tied in front of her, Jennifer Sparks sat cross-legged on her bed as her kidnapper sat in a reversed chair, his plate on a table. Food had been infrequent, so Jennifer ate with abandon, while her captor regarded his single chicken leg with a disappointed gaze.

"I would have figured you to be a vegetarian, Miss Sparks," he said.

"I don't believe animals should be tortured or treated cruelly, but we're omnivores. I eat mostly fish, chicken, and turkey. Given my circumstances, though, I'd eat anything."

"Sensible."

"I could rip off my blindfold and see who you are."

"The blindfold is for your own protection. Take it off, and it will become exponentially more difficult to keep you alive. Not so much for me, because I'm well versed in disappearing and changing my appearance. But the others working here are not so, and they, along with the gentleman I'm working for, would want to eliminate you."

"Like Bret," she said softly.

"A tragedy. I am sorry. He made an unwise attempt to escape, and my man made a rather stupid error in judgment."

"An error in judgment? Bret is dead because all he was trying to do was get help. What would have you done in the same position?"

"As he did, except I would have taken the gun and killed my jailer before running out of the house to the van. If he had taken a moment to look at it logically, studied the situation, you both would be alive and free today. You're studying law, Jennifer. Logical thought process is the core of your future profession."

"Bret wasn't the type of person to take a life. And the logic of a killer cannot be compared to that of an attorney's."

"Of course it can. Attorneys are paid to skirt the letter of the law. No, not just paid—it is an attorney's *duty* to present the best defense, the strongest case possible. If the law is bent and bruised a little in the process, well . . ."

"I plan to practice law for people who are otherwise unrepresented by the system," she said defiantly.

"You were born fifty years too late," he said. "The sixties are nothing but documentaries, geriatric rock stars, and Time Life music offers. We've been through a generation of change since then, fought another feel-good war, and had to deal with 9/11, Iraq again, and Afghanistan. Your kind of social consciousness has been replaced by a politically correct consciousness—similar in appearance but singularly lacking in substance."

"You're pretty philosophical and intelligent. You're obviously an educated man. How did you end up in this line of work?"

"I have two bachelor's degrees and a master's. Education is a wonderful tool, but it isn't the end-all. Pure knowledge without being tempered by the outside world is weak." The man picked up the leftover containers and put them in a trash bag. "I apologize if I belittled your career choice. I think you'll make a difference in many people's lives. The world just needs many more people like you than it has, or ever will have."

"But to go from a man with three degrees to someone outside the law—why?"

"I'm a nonconformist."

"You're going to kill me in the end, aren't you?"

"I'll do everything I can to prevent it . . . my word on that," he said, "but life doesn't have guarantees."

"Why are you spending time with me?"

"I have a sister who is very much like you . . . idealistic, stubborn, tough when she has to be . . . very much her own woman."

"And I look just like her," Jennifer said. "That's cliché. She didn't die tragically, did she?"

"She's alive and doing well by herself, I believe."

"You don't see her?"

"I'm *persona non gratis* in her home. It's for the best. With the circles of people I travel in, it's wise to keep any family members distant. Someday, I hope to stop by and mend fences as best I can."

Jennifer took a long drink from her soda. "What do you want from my father? Why am I here?"

The man got up from his chair and drank the last of his beer, adding it to the trash bag. "A fair question, and I'll answer it—to a point. Your father is helping find some valuable property that has been missing for over a hundred years. Your presence here guarantees he'll work alone on this and not bring the entire FBI into it. If he makes a legitimate effort to find this property, we'll let you go.

As long as he doesn't try to come after us, we'll stay out of your lives from then on. Simple?"

"What is this property?"

"A gold shipment that was lost in the summer of 1863."

"My dad is very good at what he does," she said. "If anyone can find it, he can."

"We're relying on just that."

Sparks left Coulthard sleeping and slipped out of the motel room door, closing it softly behind him. Sleep would have to be postponed for a short time, but not long—she had been right. Sleep right now was as important as anything, and he was desperately in need. But one important phone call still awaited.

Walking out to the main road, he crossed over to a twenty-four-hour convenience store and went immediately to where there was a sitting area. He used his cell to call a long distance number he retained from memory.

Three rings later, the deep voice of someone half-awake answered.

"Sam," Sparks said. "We need to talk business."

"Jason . . . haven't heard from you in a while. I'd ask you how things are going, but when I get a phone call at 2 a.m. from you, it usually means my bank account is due for an increase."

"I've got a serious problem, and I honestly believe you're going to be my ace out of the bullpen. That's if we get to the ninth inning."

"I love your baseball metaphors. Go ahead."

And so Sparks did, starting at the very beginning, with his visit to the bungalow on Sanibel Island, until that moment. Sparks felt better as he unloaded the details because he was talking to the one man in the world he trusted as a brother—Jon Samuel Anderson. An ex-Navy Seal, Anderson was a little older, nearing forty-five, but as he had been his entire life, he was in excellent physical condition, equaling that of a man twenty years his junior. He operated his own security firm and was used frequently for unofficial business.

Though Sparks had never pressed Anderson on it, he believed that his friend had been used on occasion by the CIA and Interpol. Possessing a genius IQ, Anderson was ruthless in the field and an expert in martial arts and various weapons. His training level surpassed that of any of the armed services.

Aside from his professional skills, the most important advantage was that he was the most honest man Sparks had ever known. They had met twenty years before when Sparks stepped into a fist while trying to stop a barroom fight between Anderson and a couple of drunks who didn't take kindly to a black man having a drink in their favorite bar. Out of that scrape, the two had become friends.

It had also been Anderson who had introduced Sparks to his wife. And Jennifer was his goddaughter. "Damn it, Jason, why the hell didn't you call me right away on this, two days ago?" Anderson lectured.

"This has been my first chance. The situation is such that I'll need your services without a lot of notice. But it should happen within a few days, I hope."

"But Jennifer? Are you trying anything from the back side on this? It would be a hell of a lot easier if we could come up from behind while spending their time watching you dance the dance."

"I've got Clark doing some discreet inquiries, but I've got to keep the bureau out of this one entirely. These people have already killed once and have tried twice with me before arranging my cooperation. They'll kill her if they feel it's necessary, and I believe, ultimately, that's what they'll do. I need your help to get her out."

"Give me your cell phone and twenty-four hours. Do you expect all this to go down there in Pennsylvania?"

"We may have only a general location for the gold. They're holding Jennifer somewhere in Massachusetts. My contact was in Boston, and I've been given a first contact number with a Massachusetts area code. But you can be certain I'll make sure she's brought here before they learn anything."

"Leave all the outside details to me," Anderson said. "I'll give you a 24/7 contact number. And I'll set up an ops center near the battlefield. When the time comes, we'll break down the situation." He paused. "Don't worry, Sammy's coming to the party."

July 30

To Sparks's genuine surprise, Goldberg was almost contrite when they spoke, six hours after Sparks's call to Anderson. Sparks made the call to the bureau despite what the Boston family representative had said. He had to make brief contact with the bureau whether Griffin was planning an early return or not. As they discussed Griffin's return, the voice from Washington sounded sincere and compassionate—and Sparks didn't believe it. When they were finished, he gave Goldberg his cell number and told him he would keep to a twenty-four-hour contact schedule.

After hanging up with Sparks, Goldberg went right to his office door and told his secretary to hold his calls and cancel his next appointment. He then left the bureau by a side entrance on Ninth Street and walked until he crossed E Street. Now, just down the street from Ford's Theater, he found a spot to sit down and use the disposable cell phone he had purchased just for these calls. He punched in the number he had retrieved from his wallet.

"Yes," said the voice upon answering.

"It's Goldberg. Subject is distancing himself from home. He's not asking for assistance."

"Good. Notify me if that changes."

"Absolutely. Ah, Richardson. We haven't discussed payment."

"You'll be compensated in accordance with our original agreement."

"But the nature of my information is taking on a more, shall I say, valuable tenor. It's worth more than before."

"I don't usually renegotiate terms, but I'll consider it. Keep me informed."

"We'll talk about this?" Goldberg asked, but the line was disconnected. The second-in-command at the FBI sat on the bench in awkward silence before looking at the cell phone and then, still stunned, turned off the screen.

Chapter Eighteen

December 15, 1862

The tavern was not one of Chicago's finest. It was placed between a livery stable and a dry goods store, and now that night had settled in, it was filled with workers attempting to find warmth from the hearth and whiskey. The room was poorly lit and that was why Stallard said he chose it. The day before, a man had come around Stinson's boardinghouse asking if anyone had seen a man matching Prescott's former description.

The questioner hadn't identified himself, but Stinson had thought that he was a bounty hunter and had steered him away. She had informed Stallard and Prescott, and the former had been concerned enough that when Sarah Blackstone had suggested that the four of them go out to dinner, Stallard had insisted on this place. After much cajoling on Stinson's part, Blackstone had agreed.

Stallard chose the establishment for another reason as well. The tavern was also the unofficial meeting place for many of the Southern sympathizers living in Chicago. From the simple worker to the more influential power broker, with divergent opinions rampant through the city, there was always a need for the copperheads, as they were called in the Northern press, to meet and discuss ways of furthering the cause.

Camp Douglas, the prisoner-of-war camp, was right on the southwest part of the city and took a prominent place in many discussions. Conditions were said to be poor, and while all the former

Confederate prisoners had been paroled or transferred for now, the time would come when Confederate prisoners would return. And there had been talk of helping those prisoners out in most illegal ways.

But on this night, the discussion remained lighthearted.

"Parker, darling, you must take us all to the theater next week," Blackstone said. "I've heard there's a delightful new play coming to town. And Abby and I haven't been to the theater together since we arrived here. And you promised, need I remind you."

"You need not, and I believe it will not be difficult to ask if William here and Abby will agree to spend the evening together," Stallard mused. "It seems they're together all the time as it is."

Prescott and Stinson smiled with embarrassment, but didn't offer a protest.

"You both have caught each other's fancy, we all know that. There's nothing to find fault with. You two are quite a well-formed match, if I'm allowed to say," Blackstone commented.

"You're never without words for any social situation," Prescott said. "I'll thank you for bringing Abby into my life, but we need not concentrate our conversation here. I want to hear more about the shop and how well you're both doing. Details are always difficult to pry from Abby."

"We can't expect to turn a significant profit yet, but business has been brisk, and I believe we'll be moving onto the profit side of the ledger soon," Blackstone said.

"I'm impressed, ladies, I—"

"Excuse me, I apologize for my interruption, but I wanted to give my regards," said a strong voice that carried despite the room's noise. Everyone at the table turned and found that the voice belonged to a dashing figure with dark hair and the same lightning eyes three of the four people at the table had seen on stage a few nights before. John Wilkes Booth bowed slightly from the waist and extended his hand to Parker, who was sitting in the chair closest to the actor. "Parker, it's good to see you again. I was hoping we would get a chance to meet again before I left Chicago. It seems providence was in my favor."

Rising, Stallard took Booth's hand. "John, it's good to see you. I believe you've met everyone at the table with the exception of this beautiful young lady here." Stallard motioned to Blackstone, whose hand was taken by the actor. "Sarah Blackstone, this is John Wilkes Booth of the famous acting family."

"It's a pleasure to meet you, Miss Blackstone." Booth bowed to kiss her hand. "Parker, you are the worst kind of Southern scoundrel, are you not? You've been in Chicago for some time and you knew I was in town performing at McVicker's, and yet you've kept this beautiful woman a secret from me."

Blackstone tittered. "Mr. Booth, I have certainly heard of you, sir. I have seen the notices up around town for weeks. And you've played to sold-out performances, I understand."

"We have been pleased with the response."

"Join us, would you?" Stallard asked.

"I would like to ask you if we could meet later, after you've escorted the ladies home for the evening. There's something I would like to discuss with you."

"I can't speak for Sarah, but I'm feeling a bit tired," Abby said. "I wouldn't mind if you sent us home now with the carriage."

Blackstone displayed a pout. "I suppose we could leave you gentlemen alone, but only on the condition that we arrange a dinner with Mr. Booth soon, before he leaves Chicago."

The group murmured an agreement and while Booth called for drinks for himself and Stallard and Prescott, the ladies were escorted to the foursome's waiting carriage. As they said their good nights, Stinson and Jackson agreed she would stay at his house that evening, waiting up for him upon his return. Back in the tavern, they found Booth regaling another table with a small scene from a play. Stallard and Prescott sat down and Booth joined them a few minutes later as he enjoyed the applause following his impromptu performance.

"A life on the stage has rewards, gentlemen," he said. "Not just with the ladies, but you find many a free drink and meal as well. Such is the case with these whiskies."

Stallard laughed and put his hand on Booth's shoulder. "William, here's one man whose commanding performance with women surpasses my own. And I say that with all modesty." They both roared with laughter again. Jackson smiled at the two and shook his head.

After a few more minutes of light talk, Booth shifted his mood almost in mid-sentence. "I have only met Mr. Jackson here just last week. May we speak freely here? Does he believe as you and I do?"

"Truthfully, Jackson has a bit of a story behind him that you would find surprising."

"Parker?" Prescott said.

Stallard looked at Prescott with the eyes of a schoolteacher on a protesting student. "The only item you need to know is that he's with me, and while he's a northerner by birth, he was raised in the South, and he hates this damn war as much as any man. I trust him, and . . . owe him my life."

"No doubt because of some married woman or too much luck at the card table," Booth said with a smile.

"It was the latter," Prescott said.

"He doesn't cheat. Emerson says 'shallow men believe in luck,' and certainly in Parker's case, I would agree with him." Booth looked at Stallard. "But I still want to hear you say I can trust him."

"You're not on the platform, my good man," Stallard said. "I keep little from William. To ease your fears, I offer you only this. With the exception of myself and a certain young lady, he's a man alone, and he will be for the rest of his life—in the Union's eyes."

"I believe you," Booth said. "The reason I wanted to talk is that I have information that may be important to you."

"Important to us?" Prescott asked.

"Yes, it can help you in your efforts."

Stallard's eyes narrowed and his hand was back on Booth's shoulder, this time with a forceful grip. "What are you talking about? What do you know of our efforts? You and I have never had the occasion to discuss my business affairs."

"You and I know this is not strictly a business affair. Rest easy, I don't know the specific workings of your group. I only know that an organization I've been involved with has been contacted by a friend of yours, a Cassias Fitzroy, and . . ."

"Thank God, John, you had me fearful. You talked with Cassias directly?" The relief in Stallard's voice was obvious.

"I belong to an organization that's working to help the Confederacy in her righteous fight, and Cassias contacted me through my brotherhood and asked that I talk to you when I was out here on this part of my circuit. He said our group's resources may be able to help you. Can you tell me what you're planning?"

"I would rather not for the moment." Stallard was thinking as he spoke. "But I can say that it is ambitious, dangerous, but ultimately can have a decidedly positive result for the South."

"What resources does your group have that can help us?" Prescott asked.

"We have courageous men in many important positions in the North, and we have smugglers who are helping us past the blockade. Whatever your needs, I'm sure we could be helpful. Our resources are limited out here, but in the East, they're considerable. We're going to make a difference in the war, and in the end, the South will cry our names out as heroes."

"If you're as strong as you say, then you could help us in the coming months, perhaps the spring," Stallard said.

"It all might be for naught anyway," Prescott interjected. "We haven't even discussed Fredericksburg. It was not a good result for the Federals."

Booth nodded. "This new general they have, Burnside—I haven't read much about him, but I know McClelland could be beaten by General Lee. The papers said the Federals failed and suffered many casualties. We can only hope this Burnside is as poor a general as McClelland. Lee should go straight to Washington, attack, and take that scoundrel Lincoln prisoner. He's a tyrant of the worst sort."

"The Federals should be worried if the spring holds more Fredericksburgs," Prescott said.

"And yet, we need Confederate victories if we're to be successful," Stallard said, glancing at Prescott.

"For what purpose?" Booth asked.

Stallard smiled and then finished his whiskey. "Your offer is genuine and welcome, John, but the details are best left to us—for now."

"I'll give you my itinerary for the next few months, and if you need help, just send me a message. Cassias also knows how to reach us in Philadelphia."

"What is this group that you belong to?" Prescott asked.

"We're known as the Knights of the Golden Circle," Booth replied.

"An apropos name," Stallard said with a raised eyebrow, his finger running along the scar on his face. "Very apropos, indeed."

A brisk December night had become fierce under the influence of a northwesterly wind sweeping down from Canada. Stallard's carriage had returned from dropping the ladies off and had been waiting for a good hour when Stallard and Prescott gave their regards to Booth and left the tavern. Prescott, uncomfortable as he was, still spent the time riding back to his house mulling over the implications of Booth's presence.

If Booth was connected to a secret society, one with many members and significant influence, then the opportunity was clear—the information he could ultimately give the president would be far more valuable than Stallard's conspirators or perhaps even the lone spy in the administration. When the gold moved east in the spring, Prescott could bring Lincoln an entire network of traitors and opportunists. The enormity of the possibilities kept him from noticing Stallard's gaze from across the carriage.

"Damn cold. These are the times of the year up north that I do miss South Carolina the most," Stallard said. "The winters are softer, kinder . . . more gentlemanly, I dare say. Jackson, are you listening?"

"My apologies, I was in my own thoughts, I guess."

"Concerned about Booth?"

"He's quite a presence, even off the stage. But there's something about him that worries me."

"Oh, he does look to himself more than I care to see in friends, but I believe the same complaint could be made about me." Stallard chuckled. "We'll be cautious. I have heard of his organization through others, but I didn't know he was involved with politics enough to work as he portrays. I'll do some investigating. Besides, we may not need his assistance."

"The important words you just said were 'as he portrays.' He's an actor, and more than a bit pompous. He could be exaggerating his importance."

Stallard nodded. "We'll see. As for you, I believe this is your house."

Prescott climbed down from the carriage, holding his collar against his neck. "I'm working the afternoon shift at the foundry. Will I see you?"

"Perhaps . . . I'll be doing a check of Smythe's security around the shipment. I think his foreman is becoming too at ease."

"You know I don't trust him, Parker. He sees me as a liability, I think."

"I understand your concern about Smythe . . . and Booth." Stallard nodded. "Trust me."

Prescott nodded his goodbye and trotted up the walkway and steps to the front door. The wind was speckled with ice and stung his face as he watched the carriage move down the street. Once inside, he exhaled in relief from the cold.

He discarded his overcoat and climbed the stairs. He hoped that Stinson would be awake for him tonight. The cold made a perfect counterbalance to the warmth of his bed with her beside him. A slight movement of the door revealed two candles and Stinson, elbow bent to support her head, reading a book.

"I heard the wind picking up outside and the sleet against the window," she said, closing the book. "Not a fit night for anyone. How was your business discussion with the actor?"

"Let's just say the actor is not afraid to carry the stage with him wherever he goes. He's a strange person."

"Well, he's an actor. What did he want?"

"Do we really need to talk about him?" Prescott was now in his long johns, having been disrobing since he walked in the door. "I would much rather worry about getting myself warm after that frightful ride in the wind." He climbed into the bed and found that she was naked under the covers. "That's my girl. Always thinking. I really have been most fortunate." They smiled together and kissed, their hunger mutual and building.

Prescott's eyes flew open, and he found himself awake in the room, a single lamp burning in the corner. The wind had not lessened, and it brought a soulful moan, though there were no sounds against the window. The sleet had stopped. Prescott sat up in bed as Stinson rolled over. He supported himself with his hands, listening.

Something had awakened him. Sleeping in the field with hundreds of other men, you learn to tune out almost any sound, but what the skill really involved was training yourself to ignore all the normal sounds and still recognize something that shouldn't be there. That was what happened here. His ear had caught something out of place.

There it is again!

A muffled movement of something downstairs and a creak came from a floorboard on the first floor. Was it just the house settling, adjusting to the cold? No, this was different.

Someone was in the house.

Prescott leaned over and covered Stinson's mouth and gently woke her.

She only looked at him questioningly, for which he was grateful.

"Be quiet and get dressed without making a sound. There's someone in the house. It could be a thief or a tramp trying to get in from the cold," Prescott said. He reached over and quietly slipped on his clothes, all the while listening. He reached the chest and pulled out the top drawer. On the left side in the back was his revolver, already loaded. Abby was struggling to put on her simple work dress, having already put on her pantaloons for warmth. Her eyes were filled with fear, but she was calm in her movements, not panicking.

A finger to his lips, Prescott moved along the wall to the single door that opened inward. He could hear a sound through the door that he could not recognize. Pressed against the wall, gun in his right hand, he reached across and slowly turned the doorknob to peer into the hallway. His face was immediately met by smoke surging into the room.

"Abby, we've got a fire. Hurry!" Prescott stepped into the hallway and closed the door. The smoke was already thick, and he now recognized the sound he had heard through the door. It was the fire on the first floor. He moved to the top of the stairs, holding his handkerchief over his nose and mouth, squinting to try to fight back the tears. The smoke thickened, and Prescott coughed as he looked down the stairs. The flames were already prevalent everywhere he could see down on the first floor, which was the main hallway and part of the front drawing room.

The way was not only blocked to the front door, but to the entire first floor. The flames were at the base of the stairs and in minutes, if not seconds, they would be up the stairs. The heat was already flush against Prescott's face. He took another few seconds to survey the situation, but then he was back at the door just as Stinson stuck her head out, also something over her mouth and nose.

"How bad is it?" Her voice was muffled by the material.

"Bad. We can't go downstairs and the fire's going to be up here soon," he said. "We'll go out the front window of the other bedroom. The porch roof only has a short drop and there are bushes that can break our fall. We'll get scratched up a bit, but it shouldn't be bad."

They moved along the wall and reached the door to the bedroom that faced the front of the house. Prescott tested the doorknob—it was cool—and turned it to move into the room, but the door was unyielding. Bewildered, Prescott moved his weight against the door, but again he met resistance.

"What's wrong? Is it stuck?" Abby asked.

Prescott's shoulder and the weight of his body pounded into the door. Again, there was no give. "It's more than stuck," he said. Now he moved to the hall's far side, measured the distance and took two steps forward and threw his foot against the door just to the left of the doorknob and keyhole. "Damn! We'll find no way out through the door."

Prescott kneeled down and felt the floor with his hand, but quickly pulled it back.

"The floor is hot," Stinson said. "The fire is spreading, isn't it? The only way out is the window in our bedroom."

Without an acknowledgment, Prescott took her hand, and they swiftly moved back into their bedroom. Stinson had wisely closed the door behind her before, so the smoke level was tolerable. The house moaned in death as burning wood shifted in answer to a sudden voluminous wind outside.

Prescott scanned the room to assess what they had available to use. He lived a sparse life in the house, spending most of his time away, so there was little besides the bed, the bureau, and a couple of chairs. There was a closet in the corner he had merely glanced into once or twice during the last two months.

"Open the window and check and see if there's any fire on this side of the house, quickly!" he said. "I'm going to check the closet for anything useful to help us down the side."

Prescott grabbed the candle and opened the door to the closet. It was sparse: a couple of hat boxes, a trunk that yielded nothing, a box of candles next to the door, and a couple of dresses—nothing that could be used to drop down to the alley behind the house. They would have to hang outside and drop to the ground, maybe use a bedsheet. They would be risking a twisted ankle or knee, or a broken leg, perhaps, but they would survive.

"Jack!" The apprehension in Stinson's voice came through the rush of air. She was bent over the windowsill, looking down.

Prescott reached the window, and she stepped back. The sight below made his stomach churn. The alleyway between the house and the opposite building was filled with discarded junk—most of it appeared to be farming equipment. It was packed in from fifteen feet to the left all the way across his view to the right and down the alleyway a good fifty feet. The metal edges pointed skyward and beckoned them with a yellowish flicker of light. The fire had reached the outside of the wall and to jump down to the alley meant certain injury and possible death.

He turned from the window to Stinson and looked into her face, expecting to see fear. She instead carried a quizzical expression—and she wasn't looking at him at all. She was looking past him and upward.

"There's a man on that building," she said. "He's moving around like he's trying to do something. I think he saw us in the window."

Prescott saw the form now as well. The person was moving on the roof of the three-story building above them. After a few seconds, he stopped and approached the edge of the flat roof and to Prescott's amazement, waved.

"Can you help us?" Prescott shouted but his words were drowned out by the wind outside and the roar of the flames that now were breaking through the wall on the first floor. The form didn't respond, so Prescott pointed down to the alleyway and the steel deathtrap. The man waved in response and then, again to Prescott's shock, motioned for the two of them to move away from the window. Within seconds, there was a solid *thump* against the outside wall next to where they stood. A quick glance revealed the source of the noise.

"He's trying to throw a rope through the window," Prescott said. "We might as well just jump and take our chances on the junk in the alley."

The smoke was thicker now, and Stinson was having difficulty breathing. Prescott put his arm around her. The room's temperature had risen swiftly. The speed of the fire was incredible.

Thump!

Prescott moved into position so he could see the man pull the rope back in from his position *standing on top of the railing!* He had something heavy attached to the rope, and as Prescott watched, he started swinging it around his head like he was trying to throw a grappling hook. Three . . . four . . . five . . . six times he swung it around, gaining momentum with each turn until he released the rope and the object hurtled down and squarely through the window, showering Prescott and Stinson with glass. It was a fireplace andiron. Prescott jumped to the andiron and pulled Stinson to it and forced it into her hands.

"Hold on to this," he said. Moving across the room with his head bowed to see better against the increasing smoke, Prescott pulled the bed across the room and next to the window. He stuck his head out and waved to the figure, then took the rope and, not bothering to remove the andiron, wrapped the whole assembly through the vertical pillars on the brass headboard and then around the frame itself. In a moment he was at the window again and waving at the man and the message was instantly communicated—the line pulled taut.

"Jack, I can't make it across there," Stinson said. "I'm not strong enough to carry myself across. Maybe I can wait here, and they can stop the fire. You go without me."

"Do you think I'm a nit? We're both going and we're both going together. You're going to put your arms around my neck and shoulder, and I'm going to haul us up the rope."

"You can't do that."

Prescott grabbed Stinson with both hands on either side of her face and brought it up to his.

"We're going to make it across. You only have to concentrate on holding on."

Stinson nodded.

Flames burst into the room along the floorboards and in the corners. They had only seconds. Prescott moved onto the windowsill and sat facing outward. Giving Stinson a smile of confidence, he tied a large bandanna around Stinson's right wrist and then had her move her left arm over his left shoulder and then her right arm up underneath his right arm and in front of his chest. He then tied her hands together, but allowed for her to grab her left wrist with her right hand.

"Ready?" was all Prescott said.

"Yes."

On the count of three, he swung out the window and brought the full weight of the two of them onto his hands and arms. The immediate difficulty was apparent. He was trying to cross a fifty-foot alleyway going up to the roof of the next building, an angle steep enough to try alone, but with Stinson's weight on his shoulders,

Prescott was overwhelmed with hopelessness . . . because of the wind.

It quickly twisted the two of them around so they faced up the alley and not at the building. Prescott was forced to use added strength to keep himself facing up the rope. He made five overhand moves up the rope when his hands encountered a sticky substance on the rope. *Tar!* The man had put tar on the rope. He had to be careful, but the tar was just the right consistency to help him maintain his hold. Still, his arms were burning already, and he was only halfway across the alley.

He considered himself a strong man for his size—he had won many an arm-wrestling match back in the 12th Massachusetts—but nothing he had faced before equaled this. The angle was increasing as they moved closer to the building, and after just minutes of work, they were still fifteen feet from the ledge. Prescott was at the point of exhaustion already. The burning in his shoulders, forearms, and hands was beyond anything he had ever experienced. He looked up to see the man on top of the building, whose face was still in shadows.

"I can't make it," he yelled up.

The man pointed down and for a moment Prescott couldn't imagine what he was trying to signal, but then he heard a voice.

"Get ready to jump to the balcony," it said.

There was a balcony, a small one in front of a single door on the second floor now below where Prescott and Abby were hanging. Prescott gauged the distance—it was too far away for the little strength he had remaining. He looked down to see the sharp edges that filled the alley and knew the ledge was their only hope and time was almost gone.

"Get ready to swing against the wall and drop to the balcony," came the voice from above.

Prescott gasped in agony. He looked up to see the figure, rifle in hand, aiming across the alley at the window they had just come from. "What are you doing?"

The rifle fired and the area near where the rope went around the window frame splintered. The man worked the lever and took aim again. More splintered wood. A third time he fired, but the line remained. Prescott's upper body burned, his grip beginning to slip. The lever was worked again and the fourth shot severed the line neatly.

The sudden slack caught Prescott by surprise even as he realized what the shooter was trying to do. Stinson had been strangely quiet during the whole crossover, but now she screamed as they swung, twisting and accelerating. The force of their impact above the balcony forced the breath out of Prescott, and he let go of the rope. They dropped the ten feet, landing half on a railing, but then dropping to the floor.

Stinson's face drifted from a blur into a clearer image with a yellowish glow. The next sensation he felt was one of heat. The fire was fifty feet away, but the house was fully involved and the heat, coupled with the exertion, had Prescott sweating and gasping for clean air.

"Jack, darling," Stinson said, wiping his forehead with the bottom of her dress. She had freed herself from the bonds, but he didn't remember her doing that. "You were unconscious for a few moments. Do you have any injuries?"

Prescott worked his way shakily to his feet.

"You had a rough time of it," she added, "but from what he says, you can take it. Seems you and he have been through a difficult time before. You never told me about the wagon ride and the bandits on the road outside of Washington."

"What are you talking about?" Prescott queried. "That was part of my plan for establishing my identity as a—"

"And it worked mighty fine, if you take almost getting killed by a bounty hunter on a train as proof of your success," said the figure leaning up against the door frame, his head bent down as he lit a cigarette, chuckling to himself. "God damn, Prescott, this is the second time I've had to save your hide."

Prescott looked up into a familiar face. "Brison!"

"Don't you just love surprises?" Brison said, turning his head down the alley as whistles and voices grew from the south end of the way. "I suggest we move along out the back. I've got two horses waiting and a room over on the south side of town where you can stay."

"What the hell are you doing here?" Prescott asked.

"The president wanted an insurance policy on you, and I was in a position to provide the protection. Let's move on. I don't want anyone to see us."

The three of them moved out of the building, opposite from where the water crews were trying to fight the fire. The house would be gone in minutes, and the houses around it were in danger, too, but there was hope, for the volunteers were now bringing up a small pumping carriage, and the sleet from earlier had changed over to a biting rain. Brison led the way with a still-incredulous Prescott and Stinson.

Forty minutes later, they were inside a room at a boardinghouse south of downtown and east of Camp Douglas. With the lateness of the hour, there had been no one around as they climbed the stairs, the front desk empty for the few moments they were in the lobby. Brison offered Stinson a bathtub room at the end of the hall. There was no attendant to draw hot water for a bath, but he managed to scrounge up some men's clothes she could use and a towel to dry off from the cold ride.

"All I can offer you are these." Brison tossed a pair of trousers and a shirt to Prescott. "You and I are about the same size. It will hold you until you can buy something of your own."

"I've got clothes at the foundry I can use," Prescott said.

"You should reconsider going back there, at least until you've heard me out."

"First, I would like an answer to my question. What are you doing here?"

"As I said, I'm an insurance policy. The president asked me to shadow you, observe what I could, and contact you only if the situation called on my intervention."

Prescott shook his head. "He didn't trust me?"

"Quite the contrary. He thinks highly of you. Not many men would allow their reputation to be destroyed with no sure guarantee it would be restored. Your resourcefulness was well documented from reports, especially coming out of Antietam. Lincoln thought you were the man who could complete the mission. He just wanted to double the chances of success."

"So, you were on the train?" Prescott straightened up in his chair.

Brison laughed. "I saved your hide. The bounty hunter was about to cash in without having to bring you in alive. I hog-tied him and took you back to your room, or whatever they call those things—first time I've ever seen one on a train. Anyway, I stored him away until the train stopped for coal and water, then I dropped him off with the local law with instructions to hold him for a week, then send him along with the word that if he pursued you again, he would be shot on sight."

"I owe you thanks."

"More than you know, Jack."

"What do you mean?"

"Tell me about what has happened since you all have arrived in Chicago."

Prescott spent the next twenty minutes giving his overview of Stallard's and Smythe's operation, the general size of the processed gold ready for shipment, and that they were waiting to hear from Fitzroy on whether the gold would be needed in England. Brison listened without interruption, only getting up when Stinson returned to the room. Prescott was thorough, even retracing his thoughts to bring up any information he thought relevant. The last episode he relayed was the incident with the wire office.

"I don't trust Smythe," Stinson said. "He doesn't seem like an honorable man."

"He's still suspicious of me, though I believe he's so in general terms, not because of anything he learned from the confrontation over the wire I sent."

"You weren't cautious enough. Tonight's a clue as to that," Brison said.

"The fire? You could be correct," Prescott said.

"What about the fire?" Stinson asked.

"Something awakened me. There was someone in the house. I didn't hear anything specific after I was awake, but something out of the ordinary woke me. Someone was there."

"There were two of them, actually," Brison said. "I saw two men running away from the building to the south, and I thought I heard hooves on the boarding, but the wind was strong enough that I couldn't be sure."

"You were watching the house?" Abby said.

"Well, I saw you leave with the other young woman, but I stayed here with the lieutenant and followed him back from the tavern. It's my way to stay around for a spell and see if anything comes about."

"You ever sleep?" Prescott asked.

"Certainly." Brison smiled. "I've even had a few nights off. But tonight, I stayed around. Providence was in your favor. I cut around to the front, but the fire had already spread enough on the first floor that I couldn't reach you. So I thought your only chance out was going to be the bedroom window or the front second-floor window. When you didn't come out there within a few minutes, I hightailed it around to the back."

"The reason we didn't go through the front bedroom was because the door was jammed shut," Stinson said.

"It wasn't jammed. It was nailed shut," Prescott said.

Brison nodded. "They obviously did some preparation work before you both arrived back there. Not enough to raise suspicion if you both went straight to bed, but enough so they could block your only easy escape route from the second floor."

"The whole downstairs was blocked when I got to the top of the stairs," Prescott lamented. "I never saw this coming. I'm an idiot, Abby, and I could have gotten you killed tonight."

"Do you think it was Smythe?" Stinson asked.

"Only one who comes to mind," Prescott said.

"That's why I said you ought to reconsider going back to the foundry," Brison reminded him.

Prescott sat for a moment, his head tilted back and his eyes closed. "No. If Smythe tried to have me killed tonight, it was because he's suspicious of me—or he might be using this as just a first parry in trying to take all the gold for himself. Parker will be next."

"One quick telegram and we'll have a detachment here to use," Brison said. "Let's take them now. You already have enough evidence to hang them all. This is what the president sought."

"I also know the president wouldn't want the job half done." Prescott got up from his chair. "If I see this through until we get the shipment to the east, we can bring down the entire organization. And there's someone else . . ."

"The spy within the administration?" Brison asked.

"I don't have a name yet, and, with this actor Booth, we might have a link to another group the president would want as much information on as possible: this Knights of the Golden Circle."

"Who is this Booth?"

"An actor and an acquaintance of Parker's. He could be of some use to us."

"I don't know, Jack, the president asked me to step in when I thought it was necessary. It seems to me your mission can be completed to satisfaction without going back in. Besides, what will stop Smythe from killing you outright when he realizes his failure to do so tonight?"

"I don't aim for him to have another chance." Prescott shook his head for the second time. "My work isn't done. There's too much at stake. We go on . . . unless you have the authority to stop me?"

"If the president put the emphasis on finding the spy, then . . ."

"Good . . . what to do next? I'll make an appearance to Stallard and Smythe tonight, make up a story about getting out, put forth the idea that I think the fire started with the stove downstairs."

"And hope he believes the lie," Stinson said.

"We'll need to set up a method for me to communicate with you in case something unexpected happens," Prescott said to Brison.

"We will, and I believe there will be many unexpected events to come," Brison said. "I cannot say I'm overly fond of the prospect."

"Good god, Jack, the two of you are well?" Stallard's face showed genuine shock at the news, his face flushed with emotion. He grabbed

Prescott by the shoulders. "The entire house is gone? What happened? How did you get out?"

Prescott did his best to give the story as he and Brison had worked it out. After finishing at Brison's boardinghouse, Prescott and Stinson had gone by where the fire brigade was putting out the final embers of the house amidst a chilling rain. The other building next door had been singed but otherwise was intact.

After making the suitable statement to the authorities, with a promise of a more complete statement later the same day, the pair had accepted a carriage ride from a nearby businessman. Prescott had dropped Stinson off at her boardinghouse and then proceeded up to the foundry, where, precisely at 4:15 a.m., he was knocking on the front door to Smythe's house.

The Negro servant had allowed Prescott in, and Stallard had been the first one downstairs, no doubt because he had only recently retired.

"Let's have a drink, Jack. You must have had a rough time of it," Stallard said, guiding the pair to the liquor in the library. "Abby must have been scared to death."

"Yes, she was quite disturbed by the experience. We had to drop down from the second-floor window and there was farm equipment in the back alley . . . made it difficult to get by without injury, but we were fortunate."

"Most extraordinary." Smythe stood in the library's doorway with his smoking jacket over a shirt and a pair of trousers. "I heard the word *fire* as I was coming down. What happened, Prescott?"

"We had a fire at the house where I was staying. A total loss, I'm afraid. Thankfully, there were no injuries either inside or outside the house. The rain helped enormously with that, though Abby and I got pretty well drenched."

"Sounds like you were fortunate."

"Yes, but I'm very tired now."

Stallard passed a brandy to Prescott, who took it gratefully. He was nervous being in front of Smythe, but at the same time, he was calmed by the fact that any odd behavior on his part would be explained away by the hour and the evening's events.

Smythe leaned against the door frame, still not coming into the room. "How did the fire start, do you know?" he asked.

"It started downstairs, but it was fully involved when I was awakened. It had to have been the stove in the front sitting room. I didn't check it when I returned home tonight after our visit to the tavern, Parker, because it felt quite warm in the house when I entered. I was tired and went straight to bed."

"Miss Stinson was waiting for you?" Smythe asked.

"She was already asleep. It must have been two hours later when I woke up smelling smoke. It had to have been the stove. Abby said the caretaker had stoked the stove with wood just as she was coming home before me. He probably left the door open, and some sparks started the fire. He's left the door open before."

Smythe raised his eyebrows, but remained unperturbed. "You two are fortunate to be alive, and those tending to the fire were lucky the rain came. That whole part of town could disappear quickly with a fire and fierce wind. Since you and Miss Stinson are safe, I'll be retiring again. Prescott, you're welcome to bunk down on the bed just off my office in the main building. Tell the night watch I said it was all right."

"Thank you," Prescott said.

"See you in the morning, William," Stallard called out to Smythe, who was already moving up the stairs. Stallard glanced at Prescott and shrugged his shoulders. "How about another drink before sleep?"

Prescott stepped forward, his eyes on the staircase, watching as Smythe disappeared from view on the balcony above. He moved close to Stallard. "I'm leaving presently, but you and I must talk later today—alone. Something is very wrong here, Parker, and we need to discuss it."

"What do you mean?"

"If we want the gold to make it safely to England, then we have a problem," Prescott whispered.

"Explain yourself," Stallard implored, matching Prescott's whisper.

Prescott shook his head. "Later today, or tonight." He didn't give Stallard a chance to respond, instead slipping out the front door.

December 18, 1862

Across the valley and up the western mountain's slope, the snow had fallen steadily for seven weeks. Every day blended into another as gray and white became indistinguishable between sky and mountain. Charles Stallard was in his third winter here, and he was looking at more snow than he had seen through the entire first two seasons.

He made the most of every daylight hour, clearing away the area around his cabin. The storage shed thirty paces away from his door was lost in a mass of white, and he cleared it away as best as one man could. The daily exertion was difficult, but it was keeping him in the physical shape he would need once the snow receded and the mining continued.

Even with snowshoes, the climb to the entrance that took fifteen minutes in the summer became a one-hour struggle in the winter. But each day he made it, just to clear away what snow he could. Even with no one there to help him, Charles was still at work, poring over the walls and fissures, searching for the one precious spot where the vein lived. He was confident it was there, but with the limited resources he had in men and materials, the operation had gone as far as it could for now.

Today brought heavy winds and light snow, the skies dark, full of anger. Charles decided to shift his schedule around. He would climb to the mine this morning rather than in the afternoon as he was accustomed. He put on his wool shirt and pants over his long underwear and then his buffalo hide boots stitched with fur all around. He strapped on his snowshoes and pulled on the fur skins and hood.

The trail up the slope was easy to follow, even with the daily snowfall. With the snowshoes, he sank down to his knees with each step, and so he rested frequently. Shovel in hand, he was fifty feet inside the tree line when he felt the surge of an immense wind. It blasted through the trees above him, and he felt the immediate effects on the slope as snow swirled around him. He had difficulty keeping his balance.

The wind roared through the evergreens and the wood moaned as it yielded to the force above. He was familiar with heavy winds through the pass—it happened frequently—but this wind was extreme, and it lasted much longer. He swore out loud as the icy pellets stunned what part of his face was exposed.

Then, as he braced himself against a tree, breathing hard, he could hear the wind leaving as it moved away. But that sound was replaced by another. For a moment, he stood still, turning his head to make out the strange, muffled noise he heard. Was it from farther out in the valley? It was a rumble, not unlike the buffalo when they were on the run. No, it wasn't from the valley, it was from above him. The rumble grew, and he gradually became aware of the earth's vibration.

The realization shocked him, his brain trying to comprehend the conclusion.

Avalanche!

He glanced around him. *Too far to make it to the cottage. It might be buried anyway. Too far to the other side of the pass. Can't outrun it. What to do? Think! Now!*

"Climb!" he shouted. Loosening his snowshoes, he fumbled with the straps because of the cold. The rumble reached a crescendo above him. He had only seconds. Being on top of the snow meant he had many branches with which to begin his climb in the nearest pine, the very one he was leaning against. He looked up only to find his view obstructed by the snow-laden branches. Five steps, eight steps up he climbed, the roar of sound filling his ears, the shaking dropping the snow on him from above.

Higher, I must get higher!

Without turning toward the mountain, he knew he was out of time. Debris flew past him, first a few intermittent pieces, then an increasing flow of small trees, branches, ice chunks, and snow. His mind marveled at the roar. He wrapped his arms around the tree and the leading edge of the snow pounded into it, tearing him from its shelter as the snow shattered the tree. The force threw him end over end, twisting, twirling his body like a child's doll thrown through the air.

Debris battered at him in a continuous assault. For forty-five seconds the snow swept down into the pass, swallowing the cabin before crossing over to the other side. Like a fading storm the thunder dissolved, movement slowing with less anger . . . the strength of its fury released forever.

Chapter Nineteen

When Sparks called Griffin at his Arlington home, the director didn't bother with any question other than the one the agent expected. "Have you heard from Jennifer?" he asked.

"In just a few minutes, I'll be calling a number, and then they will call back from another. I'm sure they have anti-trace software."

"I'm sure she's fine for now. I wanted you to know I have two men working on the back door to this Boston family and hopefully they can nail down a location."

"Have them be extremely careful. Whatever your men find, let me know first before proceeding. I know I'm asking a lot, but this is Jennifer."

"I agree," Griffin said.

"Has the disappearance raised any concerns with the local police or with her friend's family? If they file a missing persons report, we could start to feel heat from the media and from the locals."

"The boy, his name is Bret Thomas, right? His family is in Europe and won't be back for two more weeks. I don't think they'll raise an alarm, but if they do, we'll contact them directly."

"What about Goldberg?"

"I have him under surveillance. He's already given us a lead directly to the family. I'm getting a preliminary report this afternoon."

At 9 a.m. exactly, Sparks dialed the number he had been given in the packet on the Boston Common. The call went through but was unanswered. Five minutes later, with Coulthard sitting on the bed beside Sparks, the phone rang.

"Dad?"

"Jen, honey, are you OK?"

"I'm doing all right. They haven't harmed me."

"How is Bret? Have you gotten to see him?"

"I was told not to talk about anything else."

Sparks's heart felt like it would burst against the inside of his rib cage. Jennifer's voice sounded strong, but there was a distance to it, a sadness tinged with acceptance. When he spoke again, his own voice wavered, but then he caught himself. "Jen, I'm going to take care of this and get you back home again. I promise. Haven't I always kept my promises to you?"

"Yes, you have. I love you, Dad . . ."

"You now have confirmation," came the kidnapper's voice. "I'll call you on the cell phone number you gave me each night at 9 p.m."

"I'm meeting with historians and guides with the national park here," Sparks said.

"Until tomorrow night."

The line went dead. Sparks slowly closed his cell phone.

"Is she all right?" Coulthard touched Sparks lightly on his shoulder.

"Her boyfriend is dead."

"Oh, my God, Jason. Did she say that?"

"No, it was the way she answered about him."

"Thank God she's OK. I can't imagine how difficult this is for you. We'll get her back."

Sparks let a small smile appear, and he took Coulthard's hand. "I appreciate you being here." Inside, he fought the desire to slap her face.

The appointment with the director of the Gettysburg National Battlefield Park was at 1 p.m., so Sparks sent Coulthard off to bring back lunch as he sat at the hotel room's desk and went over the White House file on the Stallard group. The last piece of information he had seen concerned another operative Lincoln had sent to help Prescott.

After a few minutes of rereading the material he had already seen, he went through a small bunch of synopses. The papers recounted that Lincoln had sent a man named Colonel Andrew Brison, an operative who had been hired secretly by Lincoln for special investigative assignments.

Brison had followed Prescott out to Chicago, where the conspirators were evidently preparing to ship the gold east in the spring of 1863. Brison's report, a copy of which was in Sparks's hand, was filed in August of 1863, after the gold had disappeared. It told an amazing story of treachery, murder, and survival, resulting in Brison and Prescott both being wounded in late June. However, the report had no details of what had ultimately happened to either Prescott or Stallard. It lacked details, and, in fact, its final pages were removed.

A separate report turned up interesting but puzzling facts. Cassias Fitzroy remained in Philadelphia and, during interviews, denied having been in contact with Stallard for more than a year. He also denied having seen the spy Prescott, though he knew him through family.

The foundry owner in Chicago who was a key link in the conspirators' chain, a William Smythe, was also mentioned without any reference to his being arrested. All the remaining names connected with the shipment were lost with Prescott. All, that is, except one that was casually mentioned in the portion of Brison's report on the Chicago activities:

In Chicago, Stallard and Prescott came into contact with an actor—John Wilkes Booth. Prescott said Booth had definite ties with the Confederacy, knew Fitzroy from Philadelphia, and was the member of an organization called the Knights of the Golden Circle. Though my investigation has not linked Fitzroy to any known group, it is my recommendation that both men be investigated further . . .

Sparks whistled to himself. It was incredible! The eventual assassin of President Lincoln mentioned in the very report Lincoln himself would have read. The irony was shocking.

It was near noon when Coulthard returned with the burgers and milkshakes. It was time for a quick lunch, then a meeting that would start them on their fact-finding.

"What does the FBI want with information about the Battle of Gettysburg?" Ted Simpson, the head of the park, was a large man in his forties with a full mustache and goatee that tried to hide such a weak chin the line went directly from his upper lip down to his Adam's apple. He wore a park ranger's khaki uniform shirt and was seated with his stomach up against the edge of his desk. He carried about him the air of someone of great importance—in his own world.

"My associate and I are on a basic fact-finding effort, but the nature of that effort, outside the material we're gathering from your staff, is classified." Sparks was trying his best to sound apologetic, but the look from Coulthard told him he wasn't off to a great start. "I don't mean to sound heavy-handed, it's just that I don't have permission to discuss the specifics at this time. I just would like access to your best park guide, and I'd like to pick his brain."

"Well, you don't need my permission for that," Simpson said. "For the regular fee, you can reserve one of our guides for the day and get a thorough tour of the battlefield. Don't you all have guys in white coats who sit in front of computers all day to analyze data? With the Internet and online services from a vast number of Civil War Web sites, you could learn a lot without coming directly here. Or is this a lot more than just general knowledge? You looking for specific information? A specific regiment or something?"

"Something like that. I guess you could say we need a general briefing on the battle, and then I need someone who can give me details about the town and the surrounding area at the time of the battle."

"All our guides are what you could call experts, but we have one who fits your needs best. Complete knowledge of the town and all the legends and lore created by the battle."

"Great, can I get access to him for a couple of days?"

"Of course, but the him is a her."

"Your sexism is showing, Agent Sparks." Coulthard gave him a small smile.

Sparks gave her an annoyed look and turned back to Simpson, who was already punching in a phone number. Someone on the other end answered, and judging by Simpson's side of the conversation, it was the guide in question. After a minute, he finished and said she would be joining them shortly.

"Her name is Brenda Munson. She's the best I've got," Simpson said. "You're damn lucky, she's off today and tomorrow, but she must have been hanging around her apartment, not planning on going anywhere. I have a hard time keeping her out of the park on her days off. She's relentless about her work."

"Really into history?" Coulthard offered.

"Undergraduate and graduate degrees from Gettysburg College and Pennsylvania. She's studied the battle for sixteen years, since before she was in college. She could write a book—what am I saying? She could write a dozen books. She'll get a kick out of helping you out. She's that way with anyone."

"Sounds like she's perfect," Sparks said.

Simpson said Munson would meet them in the main lobby of the visitors' center in forty-five minutes. Sparks and Coulthard crossed the street and took a walk on the manicured pathways and evergreens of the national cemetery where many of the battle's casualties lay. Set in a semicircle around a main monument, the Federal graves were marked by state and a listing of the number of bodies.

Sparks and Coulthard were silent during this time. After a half hour, they made their way back toward the street and the visitors' center, where Sparks stopped and sat down on the steps of a nearby reviewing stand in a shady area. He rested with his eyes closed, leaning against a railing.

After a few minutes, Coulthard broke the silence. "How much did you sleep last night?"

"Some, but not much."

"I know this is difficult and you're worried about your daughter, but you've got to try to rest at night. And I wish you would let me help more. I helped with the note from my family—I can help with finding the last clues we need. I have a stake in this, too."

"But it's purely a financial one, isn't it, Tracy? I'm here because my daughter's life depends on us being successful. That's all I'm concerned about."

"I'm . . . sorry, Jason." Coulthard pulled herself away. "I didn't mean to minimize the situation. I know your daughter's life is all that matters."

"You surely know that if the gold is here, it's most likely not on private land, but on land owned by the park service. Just who has rightful ownership over it will most likely be decided in the courts. You're in for a long fight."

"You sound pleased."

Sparks looked at Coulthard's face—it was masked with disappointment and sadness. She was a good actress.

"I'm sorry. I didn't mean to snap at you," he said. "It's hot, and I'm tired. I know you care about Jennifer. It's also not normal for me to have anyone with me while I'm roaming around bumping into obstacles."

"I think you're incredibly exciting and intriguing. Besides, you're fantastic in the shower." She smiled.

"You know how to make a guy feel better. Come, our history major should be arriving pretty soon."

Brenda Munson was exactly the information source Sparks needed. That opinion came within a few minutes of meeting her. She began by taking them on the automobile tour of the battlefield, which began at the visitors' center, went through town, and then headed out to the northwest where the first day's fighting took place.

Heavy fighting it had been, with the Federals being pushed back late in the day to a position just south of town on Cemetery Ridge. Sparks had decided he wanted to have a general overview of how the battle had gone, even though he was really only interested in the fighting that took place on the second day—the battle for the southern end of the field, down in the rocky valley at the Devil's Den.

The tour, which was open to anyone with a car and a map, took them back down south and onto Seminary Ridge, which ran parallel to Cemetery Ridge, a mile or so to the east. The one-way road ran tourists south along the ridge, which was the Confederates' position for the last two days of the three-day battle.

The three of them soon arrived at the large Virginia monument located next to the road about halfway down the ridge going from north to south. They left the car and walked down a path to an area where there were benches and an information plaque.

The heat was oppressive, the rows of corn seemed to bake in their husks, and the symphony of sound from the insects weighted down the ear. They arrived at the benches. While they had been surrounded by other tourists back at the monument, they were alone now.

"If you look across here, you can see the vast expanse of open field the Confederates had to cross during the attack on Meade's center on the afternoon of July third," Munson said, pointing to Cemetery Ridge, distinguished now by the slight rise in the ground, but also by the plethora of monuments dotting the ridgeline. "The decision to try to strike against the center is the most talked- and written-about decision of the entire Civil War. History shows it was a tragic decision, but as it was, they almost made it through. It's known as—"

"The high tide of the Confederacy," Sparks interrupted, wiping his brow and putting his dark glasses back on. "He asked too much of any group of men—a mile of open ground to cross with enfilade fire awaiting them on the other side as they climbed up to the Union line. It was stupid."

"Hindsight is twenty-twenty." Munson sounded defensive. "There's no doubt it was the wrong decision, because it failed, but if the Confederates had been able to break through, the war might have been over. It was the closest they would come. France or England might have come in and put real political pressure to bear on Lincoln to find a resolution. As it was, the war would go on for almost two more years."

"Only because Meade failed to act aggressively in his pursuit of Lee. It's interesting you should mention the European powers. It's because of that very political situation that we're here."

"Why are you here, then?" Munson pulled her sunglasses off and put her hands on her hips. It was only then that Sparks realized that in an evening dress she must have presented a stunning appearance. She was a strong figure of a woman, with black hair and fiery hazel eyes that bore right at him from three feet away. Her tone refocused him. "You obviously have a decent working knowledge of the battle and the movements around it. Just what do you need me for?"

"I think she would be of more help, Jason, if you gave her specifics," Coulthard said.

"Why would the FBI have any interest in this battlefield? What criminal connection could there be to us? Fake artifacts on the Internet . . . something dorky like that?"

"Trust me, there's a lot more involved than counterfeit guns and bullets."

"I think you should clue me in. Ask me more specific questions. What are you looking for?"

"Something that may or may not be here. Something that may or may not have been here almost a hundred and fifty years ago."

"Jason, I don't think you would be putting her in danger by telling her what we're after," Coulthard said.

"Danger? What is this all about?" Munson asked.

"If you work with us here, then you could be prosecuted if you reveal anything we talk about." Sparks tried to sound foreboding, but Munson wasn't impressed.

"Whatever."

A small laugh came from Coulthard, drawing a look from Sparks. "Despite the cavalier attitude of Ms. Coulthard here, we're here for a very real and high-stakes reason."

"Again, what possible reason could there be for the FBI to be interested in Gettysburg?"

"Actually, there are a hundred and fifty million reasons why we're here," Sparks said.

"There are a hundred fifty million and one, and it's only the one that counts." Coulthard squeezed Sparks's arm. He nodded at her.

The water cascaded over Jennifer's shoulders as she stood in the shower, arms outstretched against the wall. She rotated her head as she savored the feeling. This was her first chance at getting clean since she had been kidnapped. She didn't know what time it was, though she was pretty sure it had been five days since she and Bret had come down from the mountain trail. Under the water flow, her face contorted in pain as she thought of Bret again.

She felt the sorrow, but she resolved she would not grieve. Not yet. Not until she was safe and the people responsible were in jail, then she would grieve. What had her dad said to her many times before sending her off to college? *Identify the most important challenge and focus on it until it's accomplished.* That advice had helped her immeasurably when she was thrown into college life. She thrived on it.

When left alone, she was allowed to remove the blindfold and was given free movement within the room, but that didn't help her much in terms of finding a way out. The room had two windows, but both had heavy storm shutters. They were the kind of shutters that protect houses in Florida against hurricanes, and they were attached on the outside.

The room was simply furnished, with a bed, a table, and a dresser. The connected bathroom had an opaque window that would have opened, except that it, too, was nailed in place. It wasn't large enough to crawl through anyway, but she thought about breaking the glass and yelling for help. It was something to consider, but she had no idea if there were any nearby houses. She could not hear any activity, such as kids playing, automobiles, or sirens.

The house did seem old, judging by the room's molding and the aged hardwood floor, but she couldn't begin to guess the house's age. It really didn't matter, she supposed, because she had no idea what town or even what state they were in, though the trip in the van had been long enough to put her in New York, New Hampshire, Massachusetts, or maybe Connecticut or even Rhode Island—but probably not. They had been on the interstate system the whole way since leaving Stowe, which meant they had been on I-89 or maybe I-93. Or they could have headed north, which meant she was in Canada—but, no, that would have meant going through customs. It had to have been south.

Jennifer used the shampoo and soap that had been provided and went about the task of getting clean. Because it was stuffy in the room to begin with, she left the door to the bathroom ajar. She was uncomfortable about it, but there was no lock for the door. If she had looked through the semi-opaque curtain, she might have glimpsed Dorman. He had crept in from the outer hall and was moving into the bathroom doorway, his face alight with anticipation.

The girl's form was clearly visible through the curtain, and Dorman licked his lips with delight as he gazed as her youthful, athletic body. Her breasts were firm, as he had imagined, as were her hips and buttocks.

Oh, man, he thought to himself, *when Streeter gives me the OK to off her, I'm going to have a lot of fun first.*

Chapter Twenty

December 16, 1862

The day after the fire, Prescott worked at the foundry, then went into the city to arrange for another place to stay. While talking to the other workers, he advanced, at every opportunity, the story of his lucky escape from the fire. The other workers had heard the news and were keenly interested in how Prescott and his lady friend had survived. He was interviewed again by the authorities, and he stayed with the story he had detailed the night before.

The caretaker was adamant in his denial of having left the stove open, but he did admit to keeping some kerosene-soaked rags just inside the stairs going down to the basement, near the living room. The general consensus was the fire, which might have been contained at first, had spread quickly because of those rags.

Prescott had checked on Abby and found her rested but still shaken. He did his best to comfort her, then he rode back to the foundry near dusk and ran into Stallard coming out of Smythe's office.

"There you are, Jack. Where have you been? I was beginning to think that the fire had spooked you out of the city entirely!" Stallard laughed and slapped Prescott's back. "Let's go get some dinner. I know a place where the ladies definitely take your mind off the food. Ha!" His voice was loud, but his eyes flashed a look that said "beware."

"I am hungry."

The pair went over to Stallard's carriage, and after hailing a driver from the bunkhouse, they piled in and started out the front gate and onto the street.

"I've been busy today, but I've had our discussion foremost on my mind all day," Prescott said, but he was immediately stopped by Stallard, who held his forefinger to his lips before carrying on talk about the beauty of the barmaids at their next stop. Whatever Stallard's beliefs were, Prescott knew the South Carolinian had taken his warning to heart. At the tavern, they ordered food and drink, and then Stallard went right to the subject. "What the devil were you talking about last night?"

"The fire was set on purpose, and I believe it was Smythe," Prescott said. "He still doesn't believe me about the damn wire. He wants me dead."

"He's a ruthless son of a bitch, I'll give him that."

"And there's a hell of a lot of gold sitting in his warehouse that doesn't belong to him. He could be preparing to take it all."

"I have always considered that a risk with him, but I had hoped the lure of more to come would weigh more heavily. How do you know the fire was intentional?"

"I heard noises that awoke me, and I know someone was downstairs. I moved pretty quickly to the top of the stairs and the fire was already coming up. And I smelled lamp oil."

"Kerosene lamps?"

"There were two or three downstairs. And an easy escape route through the front bedroom and simple drop to the ground outside . . . someone nailed the bedroom door shut from the inside and left through the window."

"Are you sure?"

"Abby and I wouldn't have made it, except for one thing. There's more to the overall story than I've told you."

"Oh?"

"I ran into someone I know from my days in Boston. He's a good friend and, you'll like this, he's not political. He doesn't give a damn who wins the war for what cause . . . as long as he gets paid. He's good with a gun . . . very good."

"I don't like you having more contact with people than is necessary. Who is this friend, and if he's so interested in being paid, then why do you not think he'll turn you in?"

"Trust me on this man. He could be invaluable to us. I would trust him with my life without hesitation."

"I don't believe adding another person is in our best interest." Stallard spoke guardedly.

"You took a chance on me, and I'm a larger risk than Andrew Brison will ever be."

"Brison?"

"Yes, and if my suspicions about Smythe are correct, we'll need someone like Brison. He's damn useful."

"I'll meet him, my friend," Stallard said as the barmaid brought them chicken stew and some drink that Prescott couldn't immediately identify. Stallard liked to try new cocktails on occasion, and Prescott found protesting far more laborious than just trying the new concoction. They set about eating.

Stallard continued, "Before I meet this Brison, we need to devise a way to deal with Smythe, if, indeed, he's a problem."

"The fire wasn't an accident, and having it look like a fire would keep him in good standing with you. And have you considered that you may be in line for an accident, as well?"

"Smythe knows that I have friends from here to Philadelphia and that my death would bring retribution." Stallard looked for a moment at Prescott. "But if it looked like an accident, or if I disappeared altogether . . ."

"We need to be cautious."

"I'm going to have you stay out of Smythe's way. We need to come up with a task for you that will take you away from the foundry . . . . . . at least for now."

"Could we get the gold out of the foundry by force if we had to?" Prescott asked.

"Frankly, I hadn't even considered that possibility. My first answer is no. His men are well equipped and extremely loyal."

"Then the time will come when we'll need a Philadelphia lawyer for sure."

"Yes." Stallard offered a sigh. "It will take a foremost effort."

January 2, 1863

A solitary figure on a chestnut colt made his way along the ridge, just along the tree line as it swept from north to south. From a distance, he appeared to be moving at his leisure, taking in the majestic view—a solitary man on his way while the good weather allowed. His horse broke stride and snorted, pausing for a moment before the man gently prodded the animal's sides with the sides of his boots, not the heels.

"Come on, boy. I know they're there. It will be all right," he said.

Within moments, melting from the trees on two sides were a score of men on horses moving to the clearing's edge, holding their positions. The solitary man reined in his horse and absentmindedly felt for his rifle, wrapped in pelts but with the stock facing rearward, next to his right hand. It was useless, and he knew it. He might pick off two, but that would be all. But he also knew he wouldn't need to be defended. Not today, not here—for he had been invited.

The man was a British subject, and while he spent most of his recent life in Canada, trapping and generally staying the hell away from authority, he was presently in the Dakota Territory, just west of the United States. He had heard that there were opportunities to be taken there in the coming years as the country would seek to expand its dominance to the Pacific. It was inevitable.

From the middle of the group came an elder with an elaborate headdress. As he moved away from his men, the Canadian felt others close in from the sides and behind him. He felt that uncomfortable feeling between his shoulder blades and tried his best to ignore it.

The Sioux elder stopped just feet away, saying nothing.

"Gray Bear"—the Canadian held his hand up in greeting—"I have come to you as you asked. Little Stream came to the fort and sought me out." The man's command of the Sioux's language was rough, but he had been told before that it was passable.

"You show much courage to ride alone away from the trails that spread the white man from the East—perhaps too much courage." Gray Bear kept his eyes transfixed on the trapper. "There is a white man who has been a friend to my people. He has died, and his spirit calls on me to tell his brother. This brother lives east in a large settlement called Chicago."

"I know of it."

"Good. The man you will seek is named Parker Stallard. His brother's name was Charles Stallard. You will travel with me to near this settlement, Chicago, and you will bring this Parker Stallard to me."

"We have crossed paths before, and your warriors have left me alone because I traded with you and brought you knowledge about the men with blue coats. I have honored you at all times, and I'll continue to do so, but I don't see why I should go to the east with you. Why is this important?"

"The dead man's brother must be told. I owe his spirit, and you owe me your life. This Parker Stallard is also a powerful man there, and I know he will honor you with whatever you seek most."

The Canadian weighed the possibilities. A trip east during the winter would be hard, but he would be traveling with Indians who knew the land and the hardships and accepted them with no complaint. It would be a change from the whimpering settlers and weak-kneed prospectors in Virginia City and elsewhere.

These people were one with the land, while the people and governments in the East just overwhelmed it. The Canadian knew which he respected the most. Still, having an influential friend in Chicago could mean money with which to set himself up nicely in the territories, or even California. Still, Gray Bear could be wrong about the "gratefulness" of this brother in Illinois.

"Can you trust the brother of this Charles Stallard?" he said. "With the battles fought in Minnesota during the warm season, the troops will make our journey difficult and dangerous."

"I can only tell you that Charles Stallard brought much honor on himself and his family. I trust his brother will have honor, as well. You will join us." A statement, not a question from the elder.

"I will join you." *Do I really have a choice?*

"We leave at once, as the skies are clear for travel."

"How many warriors are to be included in our party?"

"There will be three besides myself and you."

A small group, better to hide and slip close to civilization, the Canadian thought. *At least we'll have that.*

January 8, 1863

Prescott shook hands with the foreman of the small carriage business and walked to the side of the barn that served as the assembly area for the wagons and carriages now under construction. The business was located in Indianapolis, and Stallard had sent Prescott here after the fire so as to keep him at arms' length from Smythe, and as it came about, this was a necessary trip.

Stallard had decided that his contacts on the railroads had already been well-used, so it was advantageous to delay using them again. They would move the gold east by way of wagon along the northern sections of Indiana and Ohio and into Pennsylvania, then on into Philadelphia.

Stallard sent Prescott to this business because he had done work with the owner before and the workers here were known to be sharp craftsman who were also discreet about their work. They were also sympathetic to the South. Prescott had expressed concern for Stinson, but Stallard had promised to watch after her while he was away. And so, for the past week, he had been working with the foreman on what they would need.

Stallard had been very specific on the design. The foreman, named Travis O'Reilly, was a likable sort. He listened well and asked only precise questions. He reminded Prescott of an instructor at Harvard who had given the latter a particularly difficult semester. He had asked Prescott to join the crew in some drinks, but Prescott decided it would be best to keep to himself. It made for a number of quiet, boring nights.

"Mr. Jackson?" It was O'Reilly, summoning him over to a partially completed wagon in the far corner.

"You can take a look and see what we're doing here," O'Reilly said. "As you ordered, we've taken the heavier suspension that we normally use with a freight wagon and put it on this smaller frame. You really want this on a drummer's wagon?"

"Is that a problem?"

"No, just a bit odd. Will you be transporting heavy goods? I mean, most drummer's wagons have enough iron in the frame to support most things shopkeepers need. And to put it on your standard wheels just means you're going to have more strength than you really need."

"We have special needs."

"A Conestoga, something like the army has, will give you what you need. It will cost you less than what we're going to charge."

Prescott smiled and clapped his hand on O'Reilly's shoulder. "Trust me, just make the two wagons the way we want, and you'll be paid the price we agreed to."

"I just think it would be a sin to Moses if we stole money from you. But if that's what you want, then that's what you'll get. You still want us to do the painting for you?"

"Absolutely. Just have your men design it with the words I gave them."

"They'll do a right fine job, no seven-by-nine painting done here. You know, you're lucky Mr. Stallard remembered us. Most of the wagon makers in three states here are all tied up with government work. Plus, material is hard to come by, but we've got our own stretch of timberland. Not as good as timber up north or out west, from what I hear, but good enough for us."

"When do you think you can have it done and delivered to Chicago?"

"Early next month, if that suits you."

"We won't need them before then, I don't expect. I'll be staying around a couple more days and then I'll head off to Chicago."

"Just what kind of goods are you going to be moving?"

Prescott offered the other man a small smile. "Heavy ones."

Chapter Twenty-One

Present Day
July 31

"It was a day much like this one . . . oppressively hot. The kind of day that sucks the breath from you," Munson said.

The three of them climbed out of the car, now parked under the shade of a tree opposite some of the largest boulders Sparks had ever seen. They were massive—towering forty, fifty feet above the floor of the valley. Immediately upon closing his door, Spark noticed the small sign sheltered from the sun by the mature trees on either side of the paved road. It carried two words: Devil's Den.

"It is truly hard for someone to imagine the hell on earth that took place in this area that day," Munson continued. "The land was much more open than it is now, especially the land south of here. The Rebels—members of the Forty-Fourth and Forty-Eighth Alabama, along with the Second and Seventeenth Georgia—came sweeping from the south and west. The fighting over the rocks to the south and through this area around the diabase boulders of the Den was some of the fiercest of the entire battle."

Sparks, facing north directly into the face of the largest out-cropping of rocks, started his gaze to the left and followed along the boulders until he looked out over the open stretch of field that led up to the rocky hill almost due east from the Den. It was the hill made famous in history books and in movies: Little Round Top. The driving tour had just taken them right along the back side of the summit and had swung around, down the north side, and through the field to the small parking lot where they stood. He turned around to look at the heavy woods and smaller boulders. "The Slaughter Pen," he said quietly.

"Yes," Munson said.

"The what?" Coulthard asked.

"This area here near the Devil's Den and leading up to the area between Little Round Top"—he pointed at the rocky hill—"and Big Round Top"—he moved his arm toward the wooded area. "After the battle, the bodies covered the ground in and around the large boulders. Some were caught in crevices. The area out there in the field leading up to Little Round Top is known as the Valley of Death."

"Gruesome names," Coulthard said.

"It's hard to imagine with the way it looks today, but it was a gruesome place," Sparks said. "There are photographs taken right after the battle."

"It took days for the dead to be buried, and some were in places where they could not be extricated. You can try to image the condition of the bodies after four or five days in July," Munson said.

They walked over to the boulders and climbed the built-in stairs to the top of the boulders. Sparks surveyed the battlefield as Munson found a rock to sit on. Coulthard did the same. Munson waited for a small group of tourists to walk past and get out of earshot before she spoke.

"The Alabama and Georgia regiments were engaged against members of the Fourth Maine and Ninety-Ninth Pennsylvania, stationed right up here on Houck's Ridge, which runs northeast here from the Den. Positioned to the right of those two regiments were the One Hundred Twenty-Fourth and Eighty-Sixth New York, plus the Twentieth Indiana. Coming up the ridge from the west was a Georgia brigade with the Seventeenth and Second on the right—our left as we look to the west—then the Twentieth and Fifteenth regiments.

"On the Confederates's far left were the First Texas and the Third Arkansas. The Georgians and Alabamians who came through this area, from where the parking lot is now southeast up the slope of Big Round Top, encountered heavy fire from two regiments that swept in from the north: the Sixth New Jersey and the Fortieth New York. The Confederates also tried to take Little Round Top, but were stopped thanks to some fast thinking by . . ."

"Gouverneur Warren," Sparks interrupted, looking back over to the hill. "He was the army's chief engineer. He saw the strategic importance and moved Federal troops up on the hill fifteen minutes before the Rebels, led by Colonel William Oates, tried to take it."

"You do know your share."

"They tried all the late afternoon to take that hill and failed each time. Tracy, we just drove through the area where Joshua Chamberlain and the Twentieth Maine fought off another Alabama regiment, the Fifteenth. If the Rebels had taken the hill . . ."

"A layman can see this terrain must have been terrible to fight over."

"Some of the worst of the war." Munson paused to wipe her glasses and put them back on. "You said one hundred and fifty million reasons, Agent Sparks. I can assume we're talking dollars."

"It's an approximation. In the spring and early summer of 1863, a band of Southern sympathizers were transporting five tons of gold ingots through the Pennsylvania countryside on their way to Philadelphia, where it would be smuggled out of the country on a ship to England. The gold was to be used to buy influence in Europe to exert pressure on Lincoln to sue for peace and give the Confederacy legitimate standing. Only, the gold never got there. It disappeared despite the best efforts of a government agent within the organization and what I can assume was a thorough search during and after the war."

"What has this got to do with here, Devil's Den . . . Gettysburg?"

"We have evidence the shipment was hidden somewhere in the Gettysburg area—before the battle, apparently—and the phrase 'Devil's Den' figures prominently in our information."

"Give me the specifics," Munson said.

Sparks described the details of the three letters, how they had two in their possession, but still needed the third, and how the first two letters carried a crude code that left them with Gettysburg as the town and a link to the word "Devil," which had led them to where they now stood.

Munson listened intently, but began to shake her head as Sparks was finishing. "You say the three letters were sent around the twenty-eighth of June, three days before the battle?"

"Yes."

"Then the reference to Devil's Den can't be correct."

"Why?"

"It isn't clear just when the name was placed on these rocks," Munson said. "There are conflicting accounts about when the name became popular. It's possible the area was known by the name 'Devil's Den' in the years before the battle, but at the very least, it wasn't a common reference. There are no known published references to the area by this name. Only after the battle did the name begin to appear with regularity. If this man Stallard was using the Den as a hiding place, I don't think the term was widespread enough that he could be certain his family would know where to look in Gettysburg."

"I see your point, yet we know we have Gettysburg for sure as a starting point," Sparks said.

"And the Bible verse, it has to be a reference to the devil," Coulthard stressed. "It was put in that letter for a reason."

"OK, for the sake of argument, let's say the letter was a direct reference to this area." Munson stretched her legs out across to another small boulder. "And this Stallard guy used this area to hide the gold. Just how big a hole would you have to dig to hide it?"

"Depends on the size of the ingots, but five tons wouldn't really take up that much space, maybe ten feet square and five feet deep. I really don't know. Why?" Sparks asked.

"Because it would take a fair amount of dynamite or a lot of men with pickaxes and shovels to dig a hole that size in this area. There was a reason a lot of the dead rotted aboveground after the battle. The land is one big rock pile."

"But it still looks like there could have been plenty of crevices and natural holes where they could have stashed the gold." Sparks got Munson's point, but he desperately wanted to find an easy solution.

"That might have worked for a few days or weeks, but this area was a popular picnic area before the war, and since the battle, this land has been gone over meticulously for decades. And before they were outlawed, there were people here with metal detectors. The gold, unless it's hidden extremely well—and I mean *inaccessible*—would have been found."

"And history shows us it was probably never found," Sparks said. "That much gold would have made news."

"This area was a heavily traveled tourist stop for years and a lot of boulders have been removed and buildings constructed and eventually torn down," Munson added.

Sparks looked over the Valley of Death up the slope to the hill's top, the area littered with boulders, small trees, and strategically placed monuments. There were a few people walking along the top and in the tower placed on the southern side of the summit. For a moment, he tried to place himself here on that day amidst the roar of cannon and musket, the whir of mini balls screaming inches away. The area's history was overwhelming.

"We've got to find the third letter," he said. "It was supposed to go to a man by the name of Cassias Fitzroy in Philadelphia. Ever hear of him?"

"No, it doesn't come to mind," Munson said. "The name Parker Stallard sounds familiar to me, but I can't place it. But we do some research here, as well, going through official county records and general documents that came out of the battle."

"Well, if you could fish around for any possibilities, we're on a tight deadline. I have your park director's permission to monopolize your time for as long as I need."

"I love mysteries, so I'll help you as much as I can."

Coulthard sat in front of the air conditioner in the hotel room, letting the cool air blow in her face. She was drinking a glass of ice water. Sparks seemed oblivious to the relief of the cool air. He looked over the Lincoln file.

"Jason, the land out there just looked too foreboding. And if what Munson says is true about the land being heavily gone over, then how could the gold still be out there?"

"It may be or it may not be. We just have to try to track it down, if possible. And we can only go by the information we have."

He looked again at the letter from Parker Stallard to his brother, the letter held by the Boston law firm.

> . . . *The first letter you no doubt received a while ago. This letter has been held by this Boston law firm with the instructions to hand-deliver it to you once the war is over. That first letter contained a numerical puzzle, much like the ones you and I would play with when we were children. After the numerical puzzle is a short passage I hope you will remember. These messages give you the town and a slightly more specific clue to the gold's location. At the same time as I am writing these two letters, one to you and one to the law firm, I am writing and sending a third to Cassias, for him to hold on to until the time arrives when you both can recover the shipment yourselves . . .*

"The third letter never reached Fitzroy. He would have contacted Lawrence Stallard," Sparks said to himself.

"What?"

"But we still have to make sure," he continued in a low voice.

"What are you saying?"

"Sorry. I was saying that I've got a phone call to make. What time is it?"

"Three thirty."

"I've got time, then." Sparks pulled his laptop from his suitcase and plugged it in. He was on the Internet in a few moments, and after searching for five minutes more, he came upon the Web site for the Philadelphia Historical Society.

"What are you looking for?"

"This whole operation was based in Philadelphia. The gold was going to be shipped out of Philadelphia. Maybe we can find records on this man, Fitzroy."

Ten minutes later, he was on the phone with an assistant director with the historical society.

"You're looking for anything we might have on a person named Cassias Fitzroy," the assistant director said. Sparks could almost see her reading the handwriting from the secretary who had first taken his call. "And you're an agent with the Federal government?"

"FBI. We're in the middle of an investigation, and it has taken us on a rather unusual lead."

"Our records are open to the public, provided we get a written request, and you visit us here in Philadelphia. The records never leave the building."

"I understand, and I can have Marshall Goldberg, the deputy director, have his office make the formal request, but we don't have much time, Miss . . ."

"Walker."

"Miss Walker. All I need to know for a start is whether there are any personal papers in the archives there."

"Hold on, and I'll check the database. We just got everything referenced into the computer last year. We have copies of every document on file now. It's really quite amazing."

Sparks was rubbing his eyes with his free hand. "I'm sure it was a long, difficult task."

"Oh, it was . . . OK, we do have material for a Cassias Fitzroy."

Sparks jerked to attention. "Can you give me any details?"

"There's a brief synopsis on the man based on a former student's paper."

"That would be great for starters. Would it be possible for you to fax me that information here at my hotel? I'm in Gettysburg and my associate and I will be driving to Philadelphia tomorrow to see the complete file if possible."

"Goodness, you do want to move fast on this."

"It's very important."

"I . . . I suppose I can fax the thesis here to you, but I'll need a formal request to let you see the files."

"I can have it in your hands tomorrow morning," Sparks said. He needed to make a courtesy call to Goldberg anyway. "My associate and I will be in Philadelphia tomorrow afternoon."

A minute later, Sparks was off the line with the Walker woman and on the phone with the front desk, arranging for the receipt of a fax from Philadelphia. A half hour later, he had the fax in his hand.

Cassias Fitzroy was a prominent Philadelphian who was born in 1807 on a plantation in South Carolina. He was raised there with two brothers and a sister until he went to school at William and Mary in Virginia and graduated in 1827. He spent an undetermined amount of time in the thirties and forties building his wealth through business dealings in the South, but had at some point moved to Philadelphia permanently.

Sparks finished the rest of his coffee, part of a takeout order brought in by Coulthard. She was now sitting next to him, trying to read the profile he held in his hand.

His business concerns at the start of the Civil War spread from manufacturing to shipping, agriculture to finance. He was not one of the wealthiest men in the city, but he was a significant player, to use a modern-day term. He was a Copperhead, many in Philadelphia society believed, but he stayed clear of demonstrations and organizations that rallied against the war.

Many of his business enterprises supplied goods to the Federal Army, which many voices in hushed support of him used as evidence he wasn't a Southern sympathizer. He was a man of recluse, yet he was frequently seen in public with a close circle of friends that extended beyond the normal boundaries of polite society. He never married, but he was thought to support some of Philadelphia's best brothels single-handedly.

"Here," Sparks said with annoyance, handing Coulthard the first two pages and moving to one of the two plush chairs supplied to the suite. He went on . . .

One of the most damaging rumors to his business life came after the war when the Federal government under Andrew Johnson's administration investigated Fitzroy. It was not a public investigation, but it was common knowledge to Philadelphians. Fitzroy was never arrested or tried for any crimes, but his business associates gradually severed ties with him, and while his wealth was greatly diminished as a result, he did live a comfortable life until his death.

He lived in the city all that time, but did travel to South Carolina during the harshest of the winter months. He died in August of 1887, just short of his eightieth birthday, leaving no heirs. His estate was given to a pair of charities in Charleston. For someone who loved the South as much as Fitzroy did, it was surprising to Charleston society that he did not return in his later years, but perhaps he himself made the reason clear in a note to a business friend in the city:

"Philadelphia provides me with a home and it is where my body rests, but my soul remains in South Carolina. But it is subject to pain for the place of my birth is gone, only a foggy wisp remains on cool, still mornings by the river. The heat of oppression takes even that away . . ."

"He sounds like a man without a country," Coulthard said.

"For a lot of southerners, the rest of their lives after the war was spent lamenting a time passed. This Fitzroy certainly had the resources to be the mastermind behind the gold shipment," Sparks said, "and he probably had shipping contacts to get the gold to England undetected. So I think it will be well worth our visiting the historical society tomorrow. We need to leave in the morning."

Coulthard looked at her watch. "It's almost 9 p.m."

The phone call from the kidnapper was brief. He assured Sparks that Jennifer would be moved into a position where she could be exchanged with quick notice. He said he was making the call away from her location, so Sparks couldn't talk with her, but he would arrange for them to speak soon.

"We're going to Philadelphia tomorrow to follow up on a lead with this Fitzroy," Sparks said. "I feel strongly that if he had received the letter, he would have acted on it and the gold would have been recovered. A historical society in the city has some of his personal papers. I also have one of the guides here at the park going over whatever material from that time is available. Also, we'll want to check with the Adams County Historical Society and other official records from Gettysburg."

"Keep me apprised," the voice said. And with that, the phone went dead.

Chapter Twenty-Two

January 30, 1863

Being that his traveling companion was a southerner of fiery temperament and used to the mild winters of the Carolinas, Prescott thought Stallard would be the one to issue the first expletive-laden complaint about the cold. Instead, the words came from his own lips and were muttered under his breath, head bowed against the freshening wind.

He had traveled many times on the roads in Massachusetts during this month, and he had never experienced the raw suffering he and Stallard were facing now as they rode on horseback along a frozen trail in what he could only believe was still Wisconsin. It had been getting steadily colder with each mile they had made since leaving Chicago.

They were dressed as warmly as a man could expect, with furs over most of their body, layered beneath with work clothes and long underwear next to the skin, but still the bitterness of their travel was undeniable. Prescott glanced over at Stallard, whose face was hidden by the upturned collar of the fur and a wide-brimmed hat pulled low. He had seen the southerner occasionally pull off a glove and rub the exposed, scarred cheek. It must be bothering him, Prescott thought. But other than that, Stallard had not changed position or said anything for two hours.

It had been four days since he had learned of his brother's death. Parker had taken the news with measured grief, then had immediately set forth organizing their trip north. They had left just twelve hours after the news had been delivered. Nothing would change his mind, though both Prescott and Stinson had tried. The desire to speak to the man who had last spoken to his brother was too great.

And so, in the middle of a plan with exacting detail and much at stake, Stallard had put all that aside to make a dangerous winter trip on horseback through the north country. And Prescott had gone along—not because it would benefit his mission, but out of a genuine respect for Stallard's loss.

And they weren't traveling alone.

They were being led by a heavily bearded man who said he was a Canadian, but who carried with him an English accent. He reeked of wet fur and whiskey, but remained clear of eye when he had found Prescott and Stallard at a local tavern. He had addressed Parker directly with an educated voice, and Parker had listened from the first moment, quite literally like he knew that the words from the visitor would change his life. The Canadian had given his name as Henry Wilshire, though Prescott didn't believe it to be his real name, but the rest of his words sounded as truthful as they were disturbing.

He was a trapper and a scout who had worked in the Dakota and Montana territories both before and since the recent gold discoveries. He had come to know a Lakota elder named Gray Bear, who weeks ago had insisted he travel with the Indian and some of his men east to search for Stallard. They had stayed clear of any U.S. Army or militia units and had made their way to a camp four days northwest of Chicago.

When Parker asked what all of this had to do with him, he did so with the dejected tone of someone who already knew the answer. The Canadian told Parker he didn't know the details, but he did know Gray Bear wanted to meet with Parker, and he said, as easily as he could, that it concerned the death of Charles Stallard.

"Wilshire, how much farther to the trading post?" Stallard coughed at the end of the question as he had to breathe in the frigid air without the benefit of the scarf that had been pulled above his mouth.

"There has been a change in plans." Wilshire reined in his horse and waited for the two southerners to do the same. "We should have already met up with Gray Bear by now. We haven't met him, and that tells me something has changed. You need to understand the Lakota. They aren't big on letting you in on what they're thinking. This Gray Bear is even more so. Tough old bastard. Don't get me wrong, I wouldn't give you a Federal greenback for any one of those Indians, but Gray Bear is different. He demands and gets respect from Indian and trapper alike, all through the territories."

"Charles had mentioned him. Can we trust him? Did you sense whether there was a problem with my brother or our arrangement?"

"His words about your brother were spoken only with respect," Wilshire said. "No, we're not heading into an ambush. Something just spooked him. A patrol, perhaps. Remember, the feelings are running high on both sides here since last summer's uprising in these parts. This whole area is brittle as dry tinder."

"So we just wander around until Gray Bear decides he wants to meet?" Prescott asked.

"There's a sheltered ridge about an hour from here. It's near where we came due west from. Gray Bear will find us quick enough." Wilshire kicked his horse and the three of them were off again.

True to his estimate, an hour later and near dusk, they came to a ridge that, indeed, provided a place out of the prevailing west wind. They settled into a grove of evergreens and cleared away an area to build a fire. In a short time, they were eating thawed-out beef and bread, the darkness enveloping the surrounding sky.

Prescott had pitched a tent and piled snow up against the sides to further insulate them from what he knew would be a bitter night. The wind died and the stars were showing up as the pink sky became dark blue and then black above them.

It was then that Gray Bear arrived.

There was not a sound to hint of their approach—not even the horses stirred from the shelter of the evergreens. It was to the credit of all three men that they didn't shout in exclamation and dive for their weapons. Instead, the instant of recognition came seconds after all three were aware of the Indians' presence. Wilshire stood first and signaled a greeting to the two younger men who preceded the elder into the light of the fire.

"Gray Bear. It's good to see you. Join us by the fire," Wilshire said.

The two guards looked over Prescott and Stallard and the weapons leaning against a boulder just far enough to be too far away, seemed to take in the campsite as a whole, and then immediately stepped back from the fire and into the shadows. Gray Bear spoke a few words to Wilshire, who relayed them.

"He says I'll speak for him and for the both of you. Neither of you speaks his language, I assume?" Wilshire said. Getting a shake of the head from both, he continued with introductions. "Gray Bear"—he motioned to the Indian and then to the two others— "Stallard . . . Jackson."

Gray Bear directed his gaze and his words to Stallard. He spoke for almost two minutes, by Prescott's estimate, before pausing to let Wilshire translate.

"He gets right to the matter, Mr. Stallard. He says he's saddened to bring you the news of your brother's death. There was an avalanche in the valley where the caves lie, and he was killed. A scout party found the destruction of his cabin and eventually the body. He says your brother was an honorable man, one who saved his life, and one who became a brother to him. He found your brother to be, what's the word? . . . uh, resourceful. He found him to be unlike any white man he has ever known." Wilshire gave a slight look of distaste.

"Tell him I'm honored that Gray Bear would come this great distance to council with me. My brother, Charles, sent me word of his work with the great elder of the Lakota Sioux." Stallard's words were clear until he spoke his brother's name, but he recovered to continue. "My brother loved the country your people live on. And he held great respect for you. That's why he worked to have our agreement."

Wilshire translated Stallard's words. Gray Bear listened intently, never letting his eyes wander to Wilshire, but keeping them directly on Stallard . . . studying his face. Prescott shifted his weight on the log where he was sitting and looked around. There was still no sign of the two braves. He was most uneasy.

After the exchange, Wilshire responded, "Gray Bear says his people have waited patiently for a time beyond what was agreed to. He's inquiring about when his people will receive the goods the agreement called for."

"When the final snows are gone in the spring, we'll send the wagons as we have before."

Gray Bear didn't wait for the translation but instead interrupted. When he had finished, Wilshire gave the elder a most peculiar look, Prescott would later recall.

"He says the last time he spoke with Charles, your brother promised that the supplies would be arriving. His word was as strong as a mountain, and he said Parker Stallard's was as strong. He says he's adding a condition to the agreement, and I don't like this at all, Stallard," Wilshire said. "Gray Bear wants me to lead the supplies out to them in the spring. God knows why he would want me. The Lakotas and the other tribes tolerate me, but I'm not exactly friendly with them. Besides, I have other work. I can't be spending months leading a team out into the territories again."

Gray Bear spoke, his gaze trailing slowly from Wilshire over to Stallard.

"He says this is how it must be. There will be no more talk about it," Wilshire said. "Look, we can agree to it now and then leave them hanging later. I wouldn't put it by them to take what is here and be done with us." He glanced over at the guns, still lying naked to the cold, just far enough away to be too far.

Prescott's voice was barely over a whisper. "I have a bad feeling about this, Parker. They're out there and we're here in the light. Settle the matter and let them go."

Stallard looked at both men without expression. He focused on Wilshire. "We have in our possession more gold than in all the banks in Chicago. We'll honor our agreement with the Sioux, and you'll lead the team out in the spring. Is twenty thousand enough to satisfy you?"

"You don't have that money," Wilshire said.

"He does, indeed," Prescott said.

"That kind of money will set a man up nicely in any business he would want." Stallard's tone hinted of persuasion. "I'll pay you a quarter before and the rest when you return with this." Stallard stood up, reaching for his haversack, and withdrew his cane. He unscrewed the eagle's head from the staff and handed it to Gray Bear. "Wilshire, tell him you'll lead the supply train and will meet with him. He'll return the eagle's head to you, and when you present it to me, I'll give you the other three-quarters."

Wilshire thought for a moment, then smiled with a nod. He told Gray Bear he would, indeed, lead the wagons out to the Sioux in the spring. For the next half hour, by Prescott's estimation, the old Indian and the Canadian trapper discussed what he could only guess were the details of the exchange. Then, they were done.

"We have a meeting place worked out. I'll give you the details later," Wilshire said. "He's leaving now. I'm to travel back with you to Chicago."

Gray Bear made a motion with his arm and spoke loudly. One of the braves appeared with a wooden chest and placed it next to the fire. Gray Bear spoke and Wilshire translated a final time. "He says he recovered this chest from your brother's cabin. He didn't know all the things your brother believed were important, but he did his best. He said he understands your family finds value in written words and pictures, of which your brother had much. He returns them to you."

Stallard knelt down and opened the chest, running his finger along the crafted designs on the outside as he looked inside. There were family letters, four guerrotypes of family, including one of the three brothers—himself, Charles, and Lawrence. He nodded with satisfaction and gratefulness and looked up at Gray Bear, but the elder was gone and so were his men.

"What is the chest all about?" Wilshire asked.

"Memories from years ago," Stallard said. "Seems far more distant."

"Your brother's personal papers," Prescott said.

Stallard nodded, closing up the chest.

Wilshire went to the rifles and carried them to the fire. The three men moved around in an attempt to get warm. Despite the healthy fire, the cold hung like a shroud over the camp.

Chapter Twenty-Three

Present Day
August 1

"If anything, Jason, you're punctual," Jon Samuel Anderson's voice boomed on Sparks's cell phone as the FBI agent stood around the back of his hotel. It was 7 a.m. and the appointed time for their call. "Any progress on your end? I want to move my men into position as soon as possible."

"I've looked over the terrain and talked with a local expert. Let's just say I'm not optimistic about finding a spot on the battlefield with a big *X* beckoning for us to come and dig," Sparks said. "This area has been picked clean for generations by the curious and opportunistic. All we can do is continue as we're going, string this thing out, and give Griffin a chance to locate Jennifer before this group decides I've had enough time."

"I've got a small team ready to go. You know my specs—independents I've used before. These guys are the best."

"Former payroll guys?"

"One, yes, the other, no. But they've been employed by our friends at Langley more than once. Just a few nasty jobs they didn't want to chance anything coming back on them."

"If they're good enough for you . . ." Sparks let the sentence die off.

"Do you want the team in Gettysburg?"

"Go ahead. If Griffin can't locate Jennifer ahead of time, this is where they'll bring her when I find the gold."

"We'll be in place by tomorrow."

Ninety seconds later, the phone at Clark Griffin's Fairfax, Virginia, home rang, and Sparks heard Griffin's voice on the private, secure line. He sounded relieved to hear Sparks's voice. "When you didn't call last night, I became worried," Griffin said.

"My fault entirely. I was working on a lead, and then I went through the Lincoln file again. We're going to Philadelphia today to look at some documents pertaining to Cassias Fitzroy. The third letter was supposed to go to him. We've got to determine whether he ever received it."

"Why is there no reference to a full investigation of this Fitzroy and the operation in Lincoln's papers?"

"Someone removed them from the file at some point . . . perhaps even Lincoln himself," Sparks said. He listened as Griffin paused.

"Have you spoken to Jennifer?"

"She sounded pretty strong on the phone—as well as can be expected."

"She's a strong woman, just like her mother." Griffin hesitated, then continued, "How are you doing?"

Sparks found the question annoying. "You just have the team ready when I need it."

"Of course . . . we now know who we're up against. The man's name is Jonathan Richardson. The family is a wealthy one, based in Boston. The old man is into some oil, mostly import/export and some real estate. He's somewhat of a recluse, while his wife is on all the usual society committees. Two children. Both boys are away at college. Locals think he has some illegitimate dealings, as well, but his name has never come up in any other organized investigation."

"Any line on who would be his point man?"

"No," Griffin replied. "I have Boston personnel asking some discreet questions about who Richardson might employ. We're trying to expedite, but we're being cautious. The combination is difficult to control. The one thing we've learned so far is that Richardson is an egomaniac and carries a ruthless reputation in business. He'll cut your legs out from under you if it's to his advantage."

"This all came through Goldberg?"

"He's a moron, Jason. He called Richardson directly on an unsecured phone just a short walk from the bureau. I'm keeping a couple of men on him."

"You'll need to step in if he rants about bringing me in."

"I'll time it right. If he becomes a real problem," Griffin added, "I'll return to work full-time and take over your case. It will all be official."

"I need to see what you've come up with on Richardson."

"I'll send to an expanded, secure e-mail. Pick it up on your laptop."

"Keep working on finding Jen. If we can pull her out before this is completed, the better the chance she has. I don't want to go through a face-to-face exchange. Too much can go wrong."

"Agreed. Let me know what you learn in Philadelphia."

"All right . . . Clark?"

"What?"

"Are you OK? The doctor's work was top shelf, right?"

"Yeah, they did so many tests I'm out of blood and piss. I should know for sure soon."

"You keep me informed. No bullshit, right?" Sparks asked.

"No bullshit."

The drive took Sparks and Coulthard along a secondary road before getting on the Turnpike, which took them on their way east to Philadelphia. Sparks was thankful for the excuse of his daughter's kidnapping to keep his emotional distance from Coulthard.

Their first few days together had been like the time after a spring shower when everything was fresh, reborn with the anticipation of summer. She had lightened his heart with her personality—challenging, yet with a hint of vulnerability; businesslike, yet playful in her exuberance. She had interested him more than any woman since he had lost Casey. He had thought that perhaps, when this job was over, he would take some time off and find out where they might be going.

But that was before Goldberg's slip. She might not have talked to him directly, but the information came back to him from the other side—and Tracy had been the only other person to know. And then came Jennifer's kidnapping. And his desire for Tracy had vanished. She had made a deal with them. The only question that now remained for Sparks was how he could use her to his advantage.

"I'm sorry I haven't been a very good companion the last few days," Sparks said.

Coulthard had her head back on the seat with her eyes closed, though he knew she wasn't asleep. She smiled without opening her eyes. "You've been an absolute bear, and I wouldn't stay two minutes with you except that you're wonderful," she said. Then she opened her eyes. "And you need someone while you work to free your daughter. When this is over, we can revisit what we started when we met."

"Very practical." There was a ruthless side to her. You couldn't be successful in business without having it. If she was to get what she wanted out of this endeavor, he would be dead and so would Jennifer. The thought chilled Sparks, and he kept his eyes on the road as a semi-truck eased past the car. "I never asked you how you've been able to just leave your firm and go off with me."

Coulthard's eyes were closed again. "I've been keeping in touch. I have good people working for me."

Two FBI agents, Stewart Grimes and Taylor Wallace, looking like twins with their dark blue suits, white shirts, and dark ties, nodded simultaneously as they walked past Griffin's secretary. She frowned at them but let them pass, as the director had told her to. They were expected.

The pair knocked on the door but entered without an answer. They found Griffin sitting in his desk chair—only it was near the window, where he sat with his feet propped up on the sill, as was his custom—reading through some paperwork. Wallace closed the door behind them, and Grimes handed a folder to Griffin. "The report," Grimes said simply.

"Give me a synopsis."

"As I told you on the phone, the guy's name is Richardson. Family is some old Boston money for sure, but the old guy himself has worked some major deals over the years, especially in real estate. Family is clean, wife and kids have stayed out of trouble. Not so much as a speeding ticket. But the word has been circulating about this guy. He's one badass motherfucker, business-wise. He's stepped on his share of people, and he's ruined a few, too. But people he's partnered with swear by him. His business decisions are sound."

"He's an egomaniac, if you ask me," Wallace interjected.

"What's his personal worth?" Griffin asked.

"Somewhere in the four-hundred-million-dollar range," Grimes replied. "And he's right, the guy has an ego. The family corporate offices are in downtown, and he already has a statue of himself in the lobby."

"I need a motive as to why this guy would risk what appears to be a successful company for a venture that has now escalated to kidnapping and murder. I know a hundred and fifty million is awfully enticing, but greed seems too easy a motive."

"It would increase his wealth significantly, and if he sheltered it right and gradually added the gold to his reserves, it would be untraceable," Grimes said. "Perhaps he thought it would be a simple treasure hunt at first, but things got out of hand."

Griffin took some more of his medication and swallowed a full glass of water. He took a deep breath and collected his thoughts for a moment. "What about any illegal activities? What's the word on the street? Anything about a kidnapping of two college students, or the attempted murder of an FBI agent in Florida?"

"Nothing," Wallace said.

"I want to know as much as possible about the people he uses." Griffin spit out the words. "He's got to have a guy running the show and he's got to be good or Richardson wouldn't undertake something like this. Check with our own database, Interpol . . . NSA . . . CIA. See if any name players are known to be in the Boston area. For God's sake, continue to be discreet. Work the rest of the day on it, and then I want the two of you on surveillance on Richardson's home in the morning. I'll let the bureau chief know you're going to be in the area, but I want to keep them out of it. I want the Sparks girl located and out of the equation as quickly as possible."

Sparks and Coulthard arrived at the downtown Philadelphia hotel in the mid-afternoon. While Coulthard went upstairs to the room with the bags, Sparks called the historical society from a lobby phone and reached Walker and arranged to see her in an hour.

She apologized for forgetting to tell Sparks that the building was going to close early because of maintenance work that would interfere with the reading room. They could still come by, but they would have to view the material in a smaller, less inviting room at the other end of the building. She also said she couldn't guarantee sufficient quiet. Sparks thanked her for the warning but insisted that he and his assistant would be over immediately.

Chapter Twenty-Four

February 3, 1863

Prescott made a decision that when the war was over, he would give serious consideration to living in the South again. The cold night after Gray Bear had left had moved by quickly enough, and the next three days of travel had been relatively comfortable: there was little wind and the temperature had moderated. But this day dawned overcast, and now the darkening clouds from the west foretold of snow before nightfall. There was no wind, but a shroud of gray pressed down from the sky.

Prescott didn't know the name of the road they were on, only that they had run into it two days ago, when it had led them to a small town where they discovered they were back in the Union—Minnesota, to be precise, close to the Wisconsin border. The town had had a small boardinghouse, and the three men had shared the only room available. Even though Prescott had lost the coin flip and had slept in a chair with his feet propped up while Stallard and Wilshire had shared the bed, the warm accommodations had been a welcome change.

Last night had been another matter: a bedroll in a tent. Now the threat of snow loomed, and by Wilshire's estimation, they were now just near the Wisconsin and Illinois border. They wouldn't be back into Chicago until tomorrow evening—if the weather held. And as Prescott looked to his right and above him, the prospects were ominous.

"I know I'm but a humble Southern gentleman," Stallard said, his horse next to Prescott's, "but it seems to me the sky tells us of snows to come. Does it say the same to you, Jackson? You are, after all, from the land of steady habits."

"You're in much better spirits today," Prescott observed, looking ahead to where Wilshire was thirty yards ahead of them. "And yes, it's going to be snowing hard very soon. Traveling is going to be difficult. I recognize that ridgeline over there—we came by this way. If I remember, there's a sharp drop-off to that river of ice we crossed a few days back."

"If we push on and only give the horses the rest they need, we could beat most of the worst weather to Chicago."

"Perhaps you're correct." Prescott paused to change the subject. "There have been a couple of questions rummaging around in my head, and I haven't had a chance to ask you with Wilshire about. You up for answers?"

"Why do I get the feeling I've got some . . . what do you soldiers call artillery shells in flight?"

"Lampposts."

"Yes, lampposts. I feel like I've got lampposts headed my way. Should I be lying flat to the ground?"

"Why did you agree to deal with Gray Bear? Was it only to guarantee us getting out of there alive? You working a deal with Wilshire to wagon-train supplies out to those Indians? It raises a point for me."

"Why would I honor a deal with the Sioux?" Stallard asked. "Because I honor my brother by completing the agreement he forged. My family's honor, as well. Wilshire will take one of the first trains out in the spring, and he'll give Gray Bear what was agreed upon. Then he'll return to Chicago for his payment."

"So honor is upheld and the possibility of future gold shipments is secured?"

"No, at least not the second point. In his discussion with Wilshire while making plans, Gray Bear told him the avalanche apparently sealed off the mine."

"No more shipments."

"It would seem so."

"So why honor the agreement when you have what you desire without payment? Family honor aside, could it be you respect Gray Bear and his people?"

Stallard cast a reflective glance at Prescott and a small smile appeared. "You're some pumpkin, aren't you?" He sighed, more for effect than need. "You're acquiring as to why I would show respect for the Indians and, at the same time, be working to keep the Negroes as slaves. The Indians, though primitive to us, have at least forged a life in a harsh land. They have been on their own for generations. The slaves that populate my homeland—and yours, too, I remind you—have lived here under a guided hand, not on their own. They know nothing else. I fear that if they were set free, there would be great hardship."

"For them or the South?"

"Both." Stallard was quiet for a moment as he scanned the ridgeline away from Prescott. "I suppose it's inevitable that they will be freed. But that isn't what this war is about—it's about having the ability to determine your own destiny. The people of the Confederacy have every right to that."

"The war isn't about states' rights anymore, Parker. The president's proclamation changes everything."

Stallard chuckled. "That document means nothing. No one will pay attention to it. Why should the Confederacy recognize a document from a government it doesn't consider to have jurisdiction?"

"The world will recognize it. And it means your gold will have no effect when it reaches England."

"Whether our gold will have the desired effect will be based on how General Lee does in the spring and summer, not because of some words from a Sam Hill of a despot in Washington. Bobby Lee will whip Burnside again just like he did at Fredericksburg."

"You move away from the point," Prescott said. "You show respect for one race that many people believe are savages and you deny it to another. You say you fear the time when the Negro will be free, but you have to know the race has much to offer. Don't you see the inconsistency of your position?"

"You and I will always be on the opposite side on this. You abolitionists led this continent to war, now I just want to help bring a political solution before many more men die. And ensure the survival of the Confederacy. It's a goal I thought you shared with Cassias and me."

Anger stirred within Prescott. Self-righteousness was always a trigger for his temper. Each time Stallard spoke like this, justifying deceit became easier. "Don't talk to me about the noble effort you and Cassias are executing on behalf of the land of our birth. And don't say it's because you can't stand to see more blood shed. You haven't been there to see the black hand of death sweep over a field. At Sharpsburg, we fought over the same cornfield, back and forth, for hours, until the corn that had been over head high was cut down just above the earth."

Prescott leaned over so that he was in Stallard's face, while the latter looked away. It was the first time he had ever seen Stallard avoid looking him in the eyes. "You couldn't walk through the field without stumbling over the bodies from both sides. I saw two thousand men fall in twenty minutes. Do the mathematics: that's one hundred men a minute. Do you know how many casualties there were at Antietam? Do you? They were still counting the bodies when I was arrested.

"I never saw what I thought to be an accurate number in the papers, but I heard from the colonel at the Old Capital Prison. Twenty-three thousand men, Parker. That's how many fell that day. There has never been a battle like it in human history. I saw men with arms, legs shot off as they marched, men on their knees with their guts in their hands as they watched the life bleed from them. Some worked to put them back inside their belly. I saw men explode in dozens of pieces—"

"Enough!" Stallard said sharply. "I know what you saw."

"My point is you don't."

"So that makes you a better man, aye? Well, you weren't at Fredericksburg, and you won't be in the battles to come. Lately, I haven't seen you suffering much. Not with Abigail in your bed every night."

Prescott reined in his horse and Stallard did the same. Before Prescott could decide what to say, there was the crack of a rifle shot from up the road. Wilshire's upper body twitched backward and he fell without a sound as his horse sidestepped in panic. Now came a spitting of bullets biting the air around them. A pair of bullets slammed into Stallard's horse, which stumbled, exhaling, a sound Prescott had heard many times in battle. Stallard reacted well and was able to sling his leg over as the horse fell, and he landed on one foot and one knee.

"Highwaymen!" he shouted.

"Your gun! Now!" Prescott yelled and held out his hand for Stallard to climb up behind him in the saddle. As Stallard settled in, another series of shots came, one flicking at his arm. Prescott kicked the horse into a gallop, or as much of one as the gelding could handle with the extra load, and guided him toward a stand of trees on the east side of the road—the left side, as they were traveling.

They dismounted, took their rifles and ammunition pouches, and fell against two trees, one standing and one of good size that had recently fallen. They both peered up the road to where Wilshire's body lay and a hundred feet closer where Stallard's horse lay laboring, unable to get back on its feet. They listened but their attackers made no sounds. The wind stirred through the bare limbs of the trees above them. Prescott didn't feel the chill—his heart pounded the blood into his extremities.

"Robbers or Indians?" Stallard asked.

"Could be either . . . or someone else?" Prescott surveyed the scene. The road before them led up a rise as it traversed the east side of a ridge that ran parallel to the road. Heavy woods lay along that stretch of the road, with some boulders visible nearby—a good spot to take shots at any travelers coming along this north-south stretch of road.

Right at the heaviest grouping of boulders, the road turned to the east and slipped away into an open area—at least, it was open on the side he could see. From the boulders, he could see the road in either direction for near enough a mile. "If I was going to ambush someone, I'd sit myself right amongst those boulders at the turn in the road. See them?" Prescott said.

"How many different shots did you hear?"

"Four or five in rapid succession. Even with breech loaders like we have here, those shots came quick enough. I would say, if they all fired, of course, that we're looking at about five men."

"As I said, highwaymen?" Stallard asked.

"No. I don't think so. This road isn't well traveled. There can't be that many valuable possessions carried through here, at least not this time of year. I've got to believe the pickings would be too slim, especially for that many men in the group."

"Indians?"

"Too far south and east, I would think. We're close to the Illinois border."

Stallard sighed. "What do you think of Wilshire's condition?"

"If he's not dead, he's not moving," Prescott said. "All right, what have we got to fight with?" He made a quick assessment. "Both of our pistols with about thirty rounds apiece. And the two Sharps Carbines. How many cartridges?"

Stallard looked in the two pouches slung over his shoulder. "Maybe as many as we've got for the pistols."

The trees next to them emitted a thumping sound from the other side and they could hear the reports from up the road. This time, Prescott peered around his tree, and now he could see them, for they weren't hiding now and the smoke from their rifles hung in the air by the boulders. There were three of them reloading as they moved, well sheltered from any return shot.

For someone who had never seen battle, Stallard appeared calm as he loaded his Sharps. First opening the trigger guard that also served as the lever, he placed the paper cartridge and bullet in the chamber and closed the breech. He did so with a steadiness that belied the chill and the circumstances.

"You do that pretty smartly," Prescott said.

"Comes in handy when you travel and are prone to winning in card games, of which I do both."

"I saw three, but I would wager we've got some of them moving to one side or the other or both. In small skirmishes, the gray backs are fond of doing that, only in larger numbers. You can get enfilade fire on the enemy that way." Prescott put the cartridge pouch over his shoulder and took his carbine. "Stay here and look to the right. They'll keep firing from the boulders, but they won't come directly because the road is open ground. Look to the right because that's where they'll try to swing around from. Our only chance is to pick them off until our numbers are more even. You are a good shot with that, aren't you?"

Stallard gave Prescott a bored look. "What about yourself?"

"My colonel said my being an officer was a waste of a good sharpshooter," Prescott said as he moved off. "I'm going to swing around to the left and see if they're coming from both directions. For God's sake, keep your head down."

Prescott moved cautiously through the east woods. There was still no sound other than the reports of the rifles as they continued to fire on Stallard's position. As he moved, he evaluated. These weren't road agents—they wouldn't shoot down men in cold blood when they had the advantage. Then he remembered the night in September when he and Brison had been ambushed by the robbers on the pike between Washington and Baltimore. Maybe they would shoot first and find out what they had earned later.

He situated himself behind a boulder that offered him the best position. Just as he heard the report from Stallard's carbine from his right, Prescott saw the man. He was dressed in an ordinary overcoat and a black hat and had a heavy beard. He was making his way through the most open area in the trees, looking ahead without so much as a glance to the sides. Prescott figured the man must have made up his mind that the trouble was ahead of him and never thought someone would do to him what he was planning to do himself.

Prescott didn't hesitate to debate the morality of the easy shot he had. The .52-caliber bullet caught the man in the right side of the chest and spun him around, and he slipped to the ground. Prescott watched for any reaction from the woods around him, but none came. But they might come running after hearing the shot. The Union lieutenant, back in an element he had grown familiar with, moved over to the body to confirm the man was dead.

He turned him over and, upon seeing his face, let out a breath quickly and took in the implications as he scanned the woods around him again. He took the man's carbine and moved off farther to the east to make sure no one was following along. He then swung around to the north and made his way back to Stallard, getting there just as shots started coming in from the west. Prescott dove to the ground next to where Stallard was held up with his back to the boulder.

"Glad to see you're still with me," Stallard said. "I've aggravated my damn leg with all this crawling around these trees and rocks. I heard a shot from over there."

"One of our adversaries. This was his." Prescott leaned the carbine against the fallen tree. "He won't be in need of it. You recognize it?"

"No, why should I?"

"Never mind, we'll talk about it later," Prescott said. He loaded his carbine and moved around a boulder to get a clear look at the new menace. It was a single man. He was nestled between a pair of boulders not a hundred yards away. He fired just as Prescott looked around, and the bullet split the air near Prescott's head and struck a tree behind him. They were effectively cut off from moving to the north.

"They're keeping hot fire on us." Prescott moved back next to Stallard. "They'll replace the man I just took out and then slowly work their way to us from the sides while the fellow over there keeps us down. Then they can just keep coming until we run out of ammunition."

"This is a public road."

"It's February, it's close to dark, and a heavy snow is coming. Would you be out traveling?"

"I see your point. Can't expect those wonderful Federal horse troops to appear to save us."

"No."

"You have a solution, Jackson?"

"We take the horse and swing around through the woods and out into the countryside to the east. It will be dark soon enough, and they'll think twice about following us in the dark, especially after seeing one of their own in the snow back there."

"I yield to your military tactical experience, sir."

Now it was Prescott's turn to look bored. They gathered up their weapons, reloading as more fire bore down on them from two sides. Prescott saw the three men from up the road working themselves along the tree line on both sides. They were thinking as Prescott had deduced. The two South Carolinians moved back to where Prescott's gelding had trotted off at the start of the firing. They mounted with Prescott in front, and he kicked the horse into a gallop along the tree line behind their position.

Just as he reined the horse over, Prescott saw the man west of them stand up to deliver a shot, but then there was some sudden, unusual movement. Prescott didn't bother to look, for he heard the shouts of the other men up the road. They charged around the trees and into an open field north of the woods where Prescott and Stallard had just been. The ground was, thankfully, level and crusted over with snow that cushioned the horse's steps.

"I've got a peculiar feeling between my shoulder blades," Stallard shouted, "but I still believe they're not pursuing us."

Prescott glanced over his right shoulder, and, indeed, there was no sign the men were on horseback behind them. Then, as the horse struggled with a deeper section of snow, Prescott caught sight of them from the right. The three men from the road were now on horses and had worked their way south of the woods and were coming into the open area with pistols drawn.

Prescott beat them and fired off a shot without much hope of hitting anything. Stallard fired as well, with the same result, but the men did hesitate for a moment before again coming on after them. They were a hundred yards to the rear of Prescott and Stallard and were taking aim. Prescott heard the report of the revolvers, but felt no result.

The horse came to an area where the snow had drifted away and so began to pick up speed. They were approaching a small stand of trees that Prescott could see was along the edge of a ridge, and he thought for a moment that he would cut down the ridge to the valley below where he remembered there was a river. But then, with a yell of surprise and a string of cuss words, he turned the horse away from the ridge.

"What the hell is wrong?" Stallard asked.

"It's a straight drop-off. The river is down there, but we have to get back closer to the road. There was a bridge around here somewhere. There's a sharp ridge on the other side, if I remember correctly. If we reach the other side, we could defend ourselves quite well. Reminds me of the hill above the lower bridge at Sharpsburg."

"What?"

"Never mind." Prescott continued to lead the horse along the ridge's edge, sometimes coming within a half dozen feet of the edge. The horse's breathing was coming hard now and he was building up a lather despite the cold. "How far back?" Prescott asked.

"They've slowed down a bit. They aren't as crazy as you are. You're going to get us killed and save them the trouble."

"How far?"

Before Stallard could answer, the horse stepped into a hole. The left front leg snapped like a dried tree limb, causing the two men to be pitched forward and to the left as the horse dropped its shoulder in collapse. Both men were hurled through the air, over the edge and down the side of the ridge.

Prescott remembered later that he didn't even have time to scream, but he knew in his mind that death would come within a moment. After falling away fifty feet down from the edge, they both pounded into the branches off a large evergreen filled with snow. Prescott felt his entire body being attacked with a relentless vengeance. In a macabre manner, everything slowed down. And then came darkness.

Prescott awoke to the sound of Stallard's voice. Consciousness came with the crawl of cold sap tapped from a tree, but come it did with pain from, as near as Prescott could tell, every part of his body. He tried to move at first, but when the pain intensified, he held off. Still afraid to open his eyes, Prescott listened as Stallard continued with his verbal tirade against an unseen adversary, coupled with the frequent gasp of pain. The fog lifted, and he realized that Stallard was talking to someone. The voice was subdued, but familiar.

"Your arm is broken," the voice said. "Can you move everything else?"

"Of course I can, you damn well think I'd be concentrating on my stupid arm if I had other injuries?" Stallard spat. "Besides, what do you care? You're the reason we went over the damn cliff in the first place."

"Hardly. You would be dead if it wasn't for me, so I would take careful choice in your words, mister, that is, unless you want me to leave you here."

"We'd be dead if it weren't for you? What kind of bullshit is that?"

"Parker?" Prescott called out. "I'd like you to meet Andrew Brison. He's a friend of mine, and I truly doubt he's the reason I'm lying flat on my back in this snowbank with fifty broken bones."

"I already checked you, Jackson," Brison said. "You've got nothing sticking out where it shouldn't, but take it easy trying to sit up."

Stallard was incredulous. "This is Brison?"

"How come we aren't dead?" Prescott ventured a glance with his head spinning in response.

"The tree you're lying under." Brison chuckled. "Damnedest thing I've ever seen. You two hit about twenty feet down from the top of the tree and just tumbled through the branches into this snowbank. You two are the luckiest sons of bitches."

"How the hell do you know each other? Damn, you're breaking my arm all over again," Stallard barked as Brison felt around as best he could through the overcoat.

"I told you we ran into each other in Chicago awhile back." Prescott struggled to sit up, gingerly testing his extremities. He looked up the tree to where they had just come from and stared in amazement.

"The welcoming party back there on the road is gone, Jackson," Brison said. "I took care of two of them. The other two headed off down the pike toward Chicago. I let them go. I figure they're assuming you're dead and their work is done."

"There was another, but I took him down," Prescott muttered.

"All right, damn it, set my arm," Stallard said. "Then tell me how the hell you two know each other."

The snow began minutes later as Brison set the break in Stallard's lower arm. They were small flakes, but great in number, which Prescott knew meant a heavy accumulation would take place in the following hours. To his astonishment, he was bruised and scraped up around the face and hands, but he had escaped with no apparent breaks.

Brison, as prepared as Prescott had come to expect, had with him a flask of whiskey, and after three hard swallows each, Prescott and Stallard were feeling marked improvement. Stallard bit down on a leather glove as the break was set, and after Brison had finished with the makeshift splint and the whiskey had taken hold, he was moving back toward being his usual self.

"Well, Jackson, my friend, we have looked death in the face again and we're still walking, so to speak, although I haven't yet tried to get up again," he said. "Thank you for your assistance, sir. Now, what the hell are you doing out here in Wisconsin in the middle of a damnable snowstorm?"

Brison looked over at Prescott for help.

"Andrew and I ran into each other in Chicago." Prescott climbed onto his feet, still testing whether everything worked. "We actually met in Boston before the war. I was there on business. Andy is . . . well, what would you call yourself?"

"An adventurer for hire." Brison smiled. "Though I draw the line at battle. Too many chances for incompetent men to get you killed. I've always said, if you're going to get killed in an unnatural manner, make it at least by your own decision."

"Now don't get your anger stirred up here, Parker, but I hired Andy in Chicago to keep an eye on Smythe's operation while we were gone. He did a superb job." Prescott waited for Stallard's eruption, but was instead greeted by a laugh.

"It's awfully difficult to get angry at a man whose decision saved you from blazes a mite earlier than you desired," Stallard said. "I already know what you two are going to tell me next. You're going to tell me those men back on the road were Smythe's men."

"The one I got in the woods was, I think, called Wilkenson," Prescott said.

"And I followed this bunch all the way from Chicago," Brison said. "I had done some drinking with one of them the night before, and he and his mates were heading up north to take care of some troublemakers for his boss, Smythe. They made their way along until they set up camp just over the ridge from that turn in the road where they ambushed you. They then sent one of them farther along. My guess is, they knew this was the best route back from Minnesota and their scout ran into you all somewhere north and west of here."

"We stayed in a town the night before last. He could have seen us there," Stallard said.

"Then he hightailed it back here, and they waited for you three to ride down the road," Brison said.

"Wilshire!" Prescott exclaimed.

"He's dead," Brison said. "I checked him out before swinging down the ridge to check on the two of you. He took a bullet in the heart."

Stallard struggled to his feet, muttering something about the cold, and took a few steps away from the other two. He stood with his back to them for a time as Brison packed away the blanket and extra carbines on the only good horse they had.

Stallard turned back. "We need to get Wilshire's body to a town so he can get a proper burial, and then we need to get back to Chicago. I imagine we'll need to make plans to recover our property." He then directed his last sentence to Prescott. "Smythe has obviously decided to keep it for himself."

"And Cassias was to arrive a few days ago, so his life may be in danger, as well," Prescott said.

"Undoubtedly, but he may be safe for a time once those two report that we had an accomplice. But they will also report that you and I are dead, which means in his mind that if he disposes of Cassias, he retains the property."

"What is this property you mention with such reverence?" Brison asked.

"Gold, Mr. Brison," Stallard said. "And we should very much like to retain your services. You'll be paid handsomely." He turned to Prescott. "And you and I will need to prepare a way to eliminate Smythe. I'm assuming Cassias will bring us good news from his negotiations with the Englishman. But for now our immediate need is shelter, horses, food, and some more whiskey . . . my arm is killing me."

"About a mile south of the bridge, there's a fork in the main road. About another mile to the east is a small town. I don't know what type of lodgings they have, but we should be able to buy a pair of horses," Brison said. "At inflated prices, of course. Horses are an expensive commodity."

"So is time," Prescott said. "Especially for Cassias, if we delay."

Brison handed the reins to Stallard. "You two take turns riding. You've had the worst of it today."

Above them, the darkness was about to settle in, the snow relentlessly filtering down from the sky. Stallard climbed on the horse with assistance, and the three of them trudged their way along the river toward the bridge.

Chapter Twenty-Five

Present Day
August 1

Dorman wiped his glasses on a kitchen towel attached to the stove and eyed the man called Stubbs, who stood before him in the Lawrence house.

"Just what does Richardson want you to do? Why did he hire you?" Dorman's voice was quiet, but honed to a sharp edge. "I've got everything under control here. Did Streeter complain about our little spat up at the cabin?"

"Hey, man, I don't know anything about any trouble you might have had." Stubbs was a short, dark-complexioned man with thick legs and wide shoulders, leaving a distinctly square appearance. "All I know is he hired me to help out. You know, sort of an extra pair of hands. I'm not trying to muscle in on your deal, man—I'm just trying to make some extra bucks. I've been doing some extra work as a collector, you know, and Mr. Richardson heard about me."

Dorman put his glasses back on and glared. "Whatever he hired you for, I'm the fuck in charge here, you understand? Did he tell you about the girl upstairs?"

"He just said she was, like, 'a vehicle through which I could come into some serious money.'"

"She's my responsibility, you see, *mine.* I don't want you fuckin' with her at all. I'm the only one to see her, you get it?"

"Sure, man," Stubbs said, turning his hands upright. "Like I said, I'm just supposed to help out."

Dorman swore again, this time softly to himself, and went over to where he had prepared a tray of food. He retrieved a beer from the refrigerator and placed it on the tray. "I'm going up to give the girl her food. You can have any food you want, but keep your hands off my Sammy Adams. There's some other beer in the back you can have."

"Whatever, man. I'm hungry."

"You'll have to make a run out to get some extra food. Streeter hasn't let me know when we're going to move the girl, or where. I don't know what the fuck he wants."

"I don't know the guy. Is he an asshole?"

"He's Richardson's number two on this job, but if you ask me, he's just a screwup." Dorman gave a sarcastic laugh. "Always smoking his faggy pipe and quoting some dead writer. He thinks he's a lot tougher than he is."

Stubbs shrugged and opened the refrigerator door, and Dorman moved up the stairs to the second floor. When he reached the girl's door, he pounded twice on it. "Put the hood on."

"What do you want?" Jennifer's muffled voice responded.

"I've got your food, so don't give me any shit."

After a moment, she told him it was all right to enter. He unlocked and pushed the door in and found her sitting on the bed at the room's far corner. She sat with her back straight and her hands on her knees pressed tightly together. The corners of Dorman's mouth came up and he showed a shark's grin. He set the tray down on a table by the bed and stood before her.

With the hood on her head, he had free rein to look over her body without a rebuke. She was still wearing the tight, elastic biking clothes she'd had on when they'd kidnapped her. They accentuated her breasts and the tightness of her legs. He remembered watching her in the shower before, and the corners of his mouth moved higher.

"I got you some Chinese food—some fried rice and a couple of egg rolls," he said. "I also got you beer. Don't know if you like beer. I can get you something else if you want, but we don't have much."

"Some water."

"All right."

"I want to talk to my father again."

"That's up to the boss man, and he ain't here, so I'm in charge."

"Can you call him?"

Dorman reached over and brushed his hand against her left breast and laughed when she stiffened in shock to the contact. He expected her to cower into a ball on the bed, so he was stunned when she lashed out, swinging both hands together blindly, missing his groin but making solid contact just to the left of his stomach. He staggered back two steps, but when he realized that he wasn't injured, he threw himself back at her, pushing her down onto the bed.

"You little bitch! I'll bet you're used to being in charge of the boys you fuck," he hissed. "But you aren't in charge here—I am." He had his left arm pressed down across her throat, pinning down her arms with his body and his left hand. With his right hand, he roamed over her, squeezing her, rubbing the material. "I'm going to let you in on a little secret." And he leaned down and whispered into her ear. She was crying now, breathing hard. The corners of Dorman's mouth were back up again. "Now you go and eat your dinner. Enjoy it. Maybe tomorrow we'll have another talk. You know, I really am good. You'll come to realize it."

He pushed off her and walked back to the door. As he stepped out and brought the door to the frame, he saw her lying with her knees drawn up to her chest. She had pulled the hood off, but made no effort to look his way.

The room at the Philadelphia Historical Society where Sparks and Coulthard were situated was unlike the rest of the building. It was not air-conditioned, the musty air oozing around. There was plenty of light from three fluorescents—two on the ceiling and one freestanding that Walker turned on before she left them with the journals of one Cassias Fitzroy. They were impressive upon first glance—leather covers, bound with woven material and filled with what must have been top-quality paper at the time.

They were dated and began with an entry in August of 1858, making him fifty-one years old. The urge to start with the war years was strong, but Sparks felt they should at least skim through the years leading up to the war in case there was a helpful reference. They settled into chairs opposite each other and began.

The diaries of a successful man can reveal much about his character, or nothing at all if the words he chooses are superficial. Cassias Fitzroy's thoughts, left behind for a century and a half, were somewhere in between. He was a true believer in the South and her right to self-determination. He felt the "darkies" were inferior and needed care, but his tone was one of measured disdain, not hatred. He thought the abolitionists were vile and muddied up the issues and were bringing the country toward a desperate confrontation.

Like much of the continent at the time, he knew war was coming. He did make one direct reference in the winter of 1860 that he would remain in Philadelphia if war came, and he made a veiled reference to his being more help to the "cause" if he stayed in the North. But while Fitzroy made it clear where his loyalty lay as Sparks and Coulthard approached the second summer of the war in his journals, there was no mention of the Stallard family, the gold-for-political-influence plan, or whether he was contacted at all by a group planning such an effort.

"It's ten minutes to nine," Coulthard said. "Is your cell phone reachable in here?"

"The call?" Sparks stared at the entry he had just finished. "I need a break anyway. Let's go outside and get some air."

The pair stepped out onto the porch attached just off the room. A minute later, Walker appeared, asking how long they intended to work and telling them that she needed to leave. Sparks negotiated the ability to stay until 11 p.m. They would lock up and leave through the rarely used porch entrance. Sparks thanked her and told her they would return in the morning to continue what they wouldn't finish tonight.

At one minute past nine, his cell phone rang. It was the same voice he had come to recognize as the kidnapper in charge. "Any progress?" the voice asked.

"We're here at the historical society, going over Cassias Fitzroy's journals. It's tedious at best and we have no leads yet. I want to talk to Jennifer."

"Impossible at the moment."

"I want to talk to her at least every other day," Sparks demanded. "You know damn well I won't give you anything unless I know she's unhurt. And I've only spoken to her the one time."

"'Love is the chain whereby to bind a child to his parents.'"

"What?"

"Words from the time we're seeking the truth from, I believe."

"I want an answer from you."

"You cannot speak to your daughter because I'm not with her at the moment. I'm attending to some other matters. But I can arrange to have you speak to her tomorrow."

"Make sure you do."

"I admire your steadfastness, but keep foremost in your mind what your objective is. I'll not falter when it comes time to take the necessary measures if you fail. Remember, Agent Sparks: 'Beware of rashness, but with energy, and sleepless vigilance, go forward.'"

"You're beginning to worry me more than I already am."

"Lincoln. Those two quotes are from the sixteenth president," the voice said. "I thought a little verbal inspiration from that time would inspire you. Same time tomorrow night, and you'll talk to your daughter."

The connection was gone and Sparks closed the cell phone. "I think we're running out of time."

"Why?" Coulthard touched his shoulder.

"The man is quoting Abraham Lincoln to me. Let's get back to reading."

The Fitzroy journal entries continued as the prewar ones had, mentioning major political and military events. There were also entries concerning days filled with business dealings and personal household issues. There were no gaps of any significance until they reached January of 1863, when he wrote of a trip to Chicago. The entries began again upon his return in February.

"I don't think I can read much more." Coulthard yawned and moved her head from side to side.

"There doesn't seem to be anything here," Sparks said. "If he was heavily involved in the conspiracy, it isn't mentioned here. He seemed to be an arrogant man, so it would be logical for him to write about his exploits in his journal. If he thought of himself as a hero of the Confederacy, he was writing his journal so he could write his memoirs for after the war."

"Unless he feared arrest."

"He could have a second set, but it isn't here. I asked Miss Walker for everything they had."

"Can we finish up in the morning? I can hardly keep awake." Coulthard said.

"I want to push on through."

They continued for another forty-five minutes until an entry struck Sparks like hot iron to skin. The entry was dated August 9, 1863.

> *I received an interesting visitor today, unannounced, but he was cordial. He was a good-sized man with the appearance of someone who has seen much of the war. He presented himself as a special attaché from the War Department in Washington. He wanted information on Parker Stallard and Jackson Prescott. Of course, I told him I had seen Jackson before the war, but not since, and I had read of his escape and the charges against him.*
>
> *I told him also of my closeness to the Stallard family, as well, a business relationship going back twenty years. I made certain of my willingness to speak with the attaché, but I had no other information. He seemed unsatisfied, but left nonetheless. I am concerned that I, my friends, and business associates are being investigated by the War Department. I will have to inquire as to what proceedings, if any, are going against me.*

"This is the only mention I've seen of anyone connected to the operation," Sparks said.

Coulthard finished reading the passage herself. "There's no mention of a letter or of Lawrence Stallard in Florida. Fitzroy was intentionally being coy in his journal. Either he planned to write his memoirs separately, or he was never going to reveal the truth of his activities."

The phone on the desk by the interior door rang, and after a second of hesitation, Sparks answered it.

"Agent Sparks, I took a chance you might still be there. I was also going to leave a message at your hotel. This is Mary Walker."

"Yes, we were about to finish up for the night and come back tomorrow."

"I wanted to let you know about something in case you wanted to make a call first thing in the morning, seeing as you said this matter was urgent."

"Yes?"

"Those journals are not the property of the Society. They're on loan from a descendent of Cassias Fitzroy."

"Does he live in this area?"

"Yes, he lives just outside of the city. I don't have the address with me, but I can call you in the morning with it when I get to the office. It's in a locked cabinet, or I would lead you to it now."

"I appreciate it very much," Sparks said. "I'll expect your call in the morning, then. I'll leave our number here with the journals."

"When the gentleman gave me those journals, he said he had other papers from Cassias Fitzroy, but that he wanted to exclude them from the gift to us."

"Did he say what type of papers he was talking about?" Sparks pointed at Coulthard to get her attention.

"He just said they were papers that dealt more with business dealings, expenditures. But I remember this distinctly: he seemed evasive about it. I thought it odd at the time, that's why I remember. It was just within the last year."

"Thank you, we'll talk to you in the morning."

Sparks replaced the receiver and raised his eyebrows.

"What is it?" Coulthard asked.

"We just got ourselves another lead."

Chapter Twenty-Six

February 5, 1863

The storm faded off to the east as day drifted into night and was replaced by a deeper cold. It settled over the city, the new snow bringing it down from the black sky. Horses on the streets walked with muffled steps, heads down with clouds of breath. Occasionally, a saloon door would open and voices would spill out onto the street, but just as quickly, it would close, and the quiet night would continue.

Stallard, with his arm now in a sling underneath a cape, and Prescott, now in a less insulated overcoat than what he wore on the trail, stood in the shadows in a narrow alley, stepping from foot to foot in an effort to keep warm. They gazed up and down the street, nearly empty except for one carriage approaching slowly, still two blocks away. On the opposite side of the street, also in shadows but motionless, was Brison, his Spencer carbine resting in the crook of his right arm.

They had arrived in the afternoon and had visited yet another one of Stallard's lady friends who had a house. She was a widow, her husband having been killed at Shiloh last spring. Prescott got the impression Stallard had been offering his condolences on a regular schedule.

What was important was that, when they had gone to inquire about Stinson at the dress shop, Blackstone told them she had been taken away, after leaving the shop, by two men in a carriage that was from the Smythe-Tilling foundry. Blackstone had not been alarmed because she had assumed Prescott had sent the carriage.

With Stinson taken, it would force them into having two objectives instead of one—but only one really mattered to Prescott now, and he castigated himself as he stood in the cold. He should have taken Abby out of harm's way long before now. If she died, he would be to blame.

The lone carriage now approached the saloon and turned just before it reached the alley, which led all the way through to the next street over. When it passed by Brison, he stepped from the shadows and tipped his hat. The carriage stopped just down the alley. Stallard touched Prescott on the arm as a smallish, rotund man bundled in a heavy chesterfield with its distinctive collar came out of the saloon. He placed his silk hat on his head and turned to walk down the street. Stallard smiled and shook his head. Fitzroy always overdressed for the occasion and underdressed for the weather.

"Good," Prescott said.

The two crossed the street unhurriedly, glancing back and forth up the street to see if anyone was taking notice. They needn't have worried, as the few people in sight were in far too much of a hurry against the cold. Fitzroy looked up just as the pair arrived close to him. He recognized them immediately, but before he could speak, Stallard put his hand over the Philadelphian's mouth.

"Not a word, Cassias. Into the carriage," Stallard said. The three moved into the carriage as Brison held open the door, and they climbed inside. Fitzroy protested for a moment, then seemed to think better of it when he looked into the faces of the three men around him. At least, until they were settled inside and the carriage had moved off.

"It's good to see the two of you," he began, "but damn you, why the sudden rough handling right off the street? Where the hell have you two been the last week? Smythe didn't have an explanation, and you didn't leave word for me. You two knew I would be arriving at the end of the month—"

"Cassias, you have the occasional fault of having a mouth that goes off ahead of your thoughts," Stallard said. "Especially when you should be skeery instead."

"Don't be insolent to me, Parker. I want an answer to what is happening here."

"No one has noticed us." Brison finished peering through the curtains at the alleyway. "The driver's been instructed to take a long way back to the house."

"And just who the hell is this man?" Fitzroy was becoming red in the face, the spirits in his system roaring.

"Fitzy, we had to leave. It was very important," Prescott said. "Perhaps we should wait until morning to give you all the information."

"Perhaps you're correct," Stallard said.

Fitzroy held up his hands as if to quiet a classroom. "I had a good amount of whiskey back there, and I was on my way to visit a lady friend of mine. I'll not begrudge you for forcing me to break my appointment." He smiled. "I haven't had so much as to be drunk without my faculties. I'll listen. Besides, I'm just glad to see the two of you. Smythe had me all worried about you going off on some winter march into the wilderness."

"And that's exactly where we've been," Stallard said. He paused, leaving the horses' muffled steps and the carriage suspension squeaking in the frost. "We received word from a trapper who had dealings with the Lakota that an elder—the one that was helping us at the gold's source—was four days' ride away from here with a message for me. Cassias, Charles is dead."

"Good God! How?"

"An avalanche in the mountains somewhere in the Dakota Territory," Stallard said. "You know Charles never really gave us a location. It's supposed to be on sacred land."

"Do you have proof? Are you taking the word of a savage?"

"That's why we rode out to meet with Gray Bear," Prescott said.

"Gray Bear?" Fitzroy said.

"He's the tribal representative who was working with Charles," Stallard said. "A very foreboding figure, especially at night in the middle of Minnesota. We talked briefly, Cassias, and he gave me a small chest Charles received as a present from our father in Charleston long before Charles headed west. The story seemed true."

"A tragedy." Fitzroy shook his head.

"More than you know," Stallard stressed. "The avalanche also closed off the main cave supplying the gold. What we have in Chicago is all that we're going to be obtaining. It's all we can negotiate with."

"It's a considerable amount, to be sure." Fitzroy was already attempting to decipher the news. He tipped his head back on the leather seat. "We'll just not tell my intermediary that the source has been cut off. I believe I can make do with the amount we already have. Smythe said we have close to five tons processed. It that correct?"

"Yes, but it's not in our possession anymore, Cassias."

"What!"

"Smythe has tried to have us killed."

"Twice for me," Prescott said.

"He had a group of his men ambush us up near the Wisconsin-Illinois border," Stallard said. "Brison here, a friend of Prescott's and now our employee, was thoughtful enough to follow the group and intercede when they attacked us. Smythe will no doubt have a similar fate for you planned, perhaps as early as tonight."

"This is astonishing." Fitzroy was incredulous. "He has decided to keep the gold for himself, aye? He's a ruthless man. I underestimated his greed."

"So did I. The moment has come for us to decide how we'll retrieve the gold," Stallard said.

"That foundry is like a fortress in many ways," Fitzroy said. "The gold is being kept in a building set away from the others, and it's hard enough just to get on the grounds. We need some time to plan this. We don't want to bungle around like some Federal general."

"Abigail," Prescott said to Stallard.

"There's another problem aside from the gold." Stallard took his gaze from Prescott to Fitzroy. "Smythe has taken my friend's lady and is holding her."

"You have acquired a lady friend?" Fitzroy was back to being incredulous. "You know damn well that serious women complicate matters. Jackson, why couldn't you have taken Parker's attitude on women? Stay away from entanglements until this whole business is over with. Who is she?"

"Don't chastise me," Prescott retorted. "I didn't go courting her to make our job a harder task, and we weren't going to see a squire . . . at least, not for now. Her name is Abigail Stinson, and we met on the train out here last fall. And she's as fine a woman as any man could hope for. Our plan must include a way to get her free from him."

"Even if it runs contrary to our recovering the gold?" Fitzroy asked. "We have worked on this too long to risk it for a woman. Don't let some fleeting romance take you from us."

"I'm not the schoolboy you knew in South Carolina." Prescott glared. "I don't need a talking-to about the world or what's important. If we don't try to rescue Abigail as a group, I'll do so alone without your help."

"I encouraged Parker to bring you in with us because I thought you would be of service to us." Fitzroy leaned forward. "Don't make me regret that I did so. You're being insolent and stupid. You can always find another woman."

Prescott leaned forward and moved as if to prepare himself to strike, but Stallard placed his cane between the two men.

"Will you all bicker like old women, or will you try to get something done?" Brison said.

"Both of you need to remember something," Stallard interjected. "You, Cassias, are to remember that I'm in charge of this operation, not you, and I'll decide the best course of action. Our efforts to retrieve the gold will also include assuring Miss Stinson's safety. It is the right course—it's what gentlemen do. The subject is closed. Parker, you need to remember that I warned you of romantic interests while we were out here. Now the situation is more complicated and dangerous. But we still have an opportunity to do a great service for the Confederacy . . . and the North."

Both Fitzroy and Stallard moved back in their seats, casting their eyes to the side.

"I apologize for my harsh words," Fitzroy said. "I would surmise Miss Stinson is a rare jewel."

"I apologize, as well, to both of you," Prescott said. "My actions have made our efforts more difficult . . . and, yes, Cassias, she is."

"Now, then, we must get ourselves some hot coffee when we get back to my friend's house." Stallard tapped his headless cane on the floor. "Then we can work for a few hours on what we need to do. Correct? Excellent!"

Brison pulled the curtain to the side and muttered, "Unbelievable."

With the fire's warmth in his face, Prescott suddenly was exhausted. They had been hard in the saddle, been shot at, and fallen through the branches of a one-hundred-and-twenty-foot tree, followed by an additional hard ride in snow into Chicago.

Then had come the news of Abby's kidnapping. Prescott, even as he lay on the sitting room's sparse sofa, marveled at Stallard, who continued working by candlelight at the table, drawing a map of the foundry to use for their discussion. Stallard's ability to push himself left Prescott in awe.

"Cassias, in all the excitement of our travels back to the city and spiriting you away by carriage, we have failed to ask about the news you bring from the East." Stallard continued sketching without looking up. "Can you give us the details of your negotiation with the English contact?"

"Albert Crowley represents a number of men in the British Parliament who are sympathetic to the Confederacy—"

"And her cotton, no doubt." Brison sat in the corner, cleaning his carbine.

"Ah, yes, and that's where we hope the ultimate favor lies with us," Fitzroy continued. "Since the war began, President Davis has had three gentlemen in Europe attempting to garner support. A James Mason is in England, and a John Slidell is in Paris. There's also a third, named Mann. Their efforts, while noble and extensive, have been met with many words but few deeds. Our efforts, coming as they do from an entirely independent means, strike not at bolstering those already sympathetic to us, but at those who care little for the outcome. Their support can be purchased. Couple this with victories by General Lee this spring, and Mr. Crowley believes we can bring about a brokered peace on the part of the European powers, if not direct military support. Still, I don't trust the man, and I suggest I travel to England along with the gold."

"What's the attitude of Parliament at this time?" Stallard asked.

"They're waiting to watch the military developments over here," Fitzroy said. "Forcing Lee from Maryland in September hurt us in the eyes of many in Europe. However, the victory at Fredericksburg should be reverberating around Parliament as we sit here."

"Has the amount been agreed upon?" Stallard asked.

"There are many hands that need to be paid, Parker."

"How much?"

"Four million. We have that much, correct?"

"Smythe has that much," Prescott said from the couch, eyes closed.

"We have that much, but the avalanche that killed Charles also, according to Gray Bear, sealed off the source," Stallard said. "Charles was the linchpin in this endeavor. His relationship with the Indians is gone now, and we'll have to make do with what's in Building Five. How sure are you of our getting results with the gold we ship across the ocean?"

"As with anything, there's never a certainty"—Fitzroy up-turned his hands—"but our agents in London will be there to put whatever pressure is needed at the proper time."

"Physical as well as political?" Brison asked.

"Yes."

"We'll leave the continuing details of the England question to you, Cassias," Stallard said. "Now to the problem of getting our gold back. I have sketched out a layout of the foundry as I can best remember—"

There was a knock on the kitchen door, just a few steps from where the group was, and it caused a commotion. Brison was the first to the kitchen entrance with carbine in hand, a cartridge already bolted into the chamber. Prescott and Fitzroy sat up and became on edge. Only Stallard moved with deliberate cause past Brison. "I'm expecting someone."

Stallard slipped outside. His voice and the stranger's were muffled through the closed door. In a minute, he was back. "That was a man of mine who still has access to the foundry," Stallard said. "He confirmed what we assumed. Miss Stinson is staying at the house, and there are guards posted discreetly around it. Smythe is spending the night in his office and the family is away. It doesn't appear she's being held against her will, but he cannot tell."

"How decent of him," Prescott muttered about Smythe.

"He could have told her anything," Fitzroy said.

"My man also said that two of Smythe's men rode into the foundry early this morning, then after meeting with him, they resupplied themselves and headed back out." Stallard returned to the table.

"Miss Stinson won't be leaving the foundry anytime soon," Brison said.

"And how do you draw that conclusion?" Fitzroy asked.

"I would wager those two were the two men who got away up near the border." Brison didn't bother to look at Fitzroy. "They probably reported your demise at the river, but if Smythe is as smart as you all say he is, he'll want proof. He sent them back to find your bodies. The fact you two had help, namely myself, will cause Smythe to take precautions until your deaths are confirmed. He doesn't know what he's facing, but with Miss Stinson, he has insurance. For that reason, we can hope he won't kill her outright."

"We'll have about a week before that pair returns without bodies," Prescott said. "Less if they somehow get a telegraph message through."

"We need to keep a close watch on Smythe," Fitzroy said.

"It will be difficult," Stallard said. "He has more than a hundred men working for him, and he has a group of guards who watch over his men."

"His own little army," Brison added.

"And they're extremely loyal. Most of them know our appearance, so we can't slip in and blend in with the workers," Stallard continued. "We'll have to think carefully about this. And when we strike, it's going to have to be fast, with superb timing. We'll need some help."

"Quite a formidable task," Fitzroy's voice hinted at despair.

Stallard tapped his cane. "Before we get to the plans of how we actually do this," he said, "there are additional plans that need to be carried out . . . beginning tomorrow."

Chapter Twenty-Seven

Present Day
August 2

Sparks had called Walker just after 9 a.m. and, true to how she had been the last couple of days, she kept her word. She had the name of Fitzroy's distant relative who had loaned the papers to the historical society. His name was John Peters, and he lived just a short drive northwest of downtown Philadelphia. Walker had said Peters was set in his ways but might be amenable to helping them.

The next ninety minutes were frustrating because there was no answer at the house and there was no answering machine. Sparks was ready to drive out to the house unannounced when he tried for a fifth time with success. Peters was at first distant, but warmed up some when Sparks told him it was official FBI business, then became almost friendly when Sparks mentioned he got the number from Walker. They arranged for a visit after noon.

Coulthard kept to herself on the drive out to Peters's house. She spent the ride looking over what part of the Lincoln White House file that Sparks felt she could see. She read without comment.

Peters's house was at the end of a tree-lined street with large houses on expansive acre lots. They reminded Sparks of his home growing up as a youth in Massachusetts—yards large enough to hold mini-baseball games where the Green Monster in left field was the back of a garage and a home run to right field had to go over Mr. Brock's hedge. Old Man Brock never complained when a ball ended up in his roses. Instead, he would sit in his porch rocker and clap when a ten-year-old connected for a home run.

Sparks's first thoughts of the old man always began with those hot summer days of baseball, but they always finished with why Sparks became interested in the FBI as a career. The old man had come home on a dark winter afternoon only to surprise a burglar in the house. He had put up a fierce struggle, from what Sparks's father heard from the police, but had been beaten and left for dead. The murderer had never been found. Sparks was fourteen, and closure had never come, and for a teenager, closure is everything.

Now he was driving down this beautiful street, and his thoughts remained with Jennifer—and how he feared that, again, there would be no closure. He found Peters's address—a blue house with black shutters and an eagle over the garage door. Five minutes later, they were sitting in the living room.

"I went ahead and brought out the papers since you were coming," Peters said. He was a balding man, in his seventies, with a white mustache that drooped like his shoulders. He walked like he was arthritic in the hips, but without the benefit of a cane, though Sparks noticed one sitting in the corner.

"We appreciate your allowing us to see the papers," Sparks said. "The matter is most urgent. I was wondering why, when you donated his journals to the society, you didn't turn over these papers here?"

"My great-great-great-grand-uncle was what they used to call a copperhead," Peters said. "He lived here in Philadelphia, but he was just a transplanted southerner. I've read his journals—he kept most of his politics out of them. But these papers are business-related, and he often would make notes. Those notes are embarrassing to my family, frankly. Don't draw a conclusion yet, I'm really not trying to protect him all that much—just my family. I personally find it hurtful to know I come from a family that once owned other human beings."

"You're not alone, sir, many families have those ties from back then. You can't be held accountable for the sins of your forefathers," Coulthard interjected.

"I suppose not, but the feelings are there just the same." Peters moved to show them to a family room where there was plenty of light and a table to work on. With the acceptance of coffee to come, Sparks and Coulthard began reading through the business papers. For someone who didn't want the papers left for posterity, Peters had meticulously endeavored to do just that, with each correspondence encased in a plastic covering—not quite like laminating, because you could peel back the sheet to touch the actual document. The files were dated with colored tags and were in chronological order. By his first guess, there were probably two hundred of them.

"This is quite impressive," Coulthard said.

"Very impressive. It's going to take us some time to go through these and see if there's anything to glean," Sparks said.

Peters brought in a tray with coffee and three mugs. "I have no plans for the day, so you're welcome to stay the afternoon. That is, if you let me sit next to Miss Coulthard here. I never have beautiful women over to my house anymore, not at my age—at least, until now." He laughed.

"It's pleasant to see there are some real gentlemen left in the world." Coulthard grinned, taking the tray. They both chuckled with their joke, but Sparks didn't hear them. He was already focused on what was in front of him. And his heart raced with its importance.

Munson had finished with her only guided tour of the day and was sitting in the shade at the base of a tree next to the Cycloroma, just a few minutes' walk from the visitors' center. She was looking over her own notes.

> *Because the name seems familiar, logically I would have had to have seen it recently, or been exposed to it multiple times a longer period of time ago. That's how my mind works. I can't remember my damn PIN for my debit card, but I can remember a name from one hundred and fifty years ago when I've seen it two or three times in the course of my work. This is why I'm making this list.*
>
> *There was the cross-referencing we did for the ACHS . . . then I worked on the 1st Minnesota project, then I reorga-*

nized and with Bob set up the new guide procedures, then I oversaw the additional building of a fence in the Devil's Den area, then we began the monument restoration project on Seminary Ridge. Then there was the cleaning of the display cases in the museum portion of the visitors' center . . .

"Ughhhhhhhhh . . ." Munson threw down her hands and banged her head against the tree. It was useless. There were hundreds of places where she could have come across the name in the last two years. She had promised Sparks she would try to find a reference to Stallard or Fitzroy, but she didn't know where to begin.

They weren't soldiers in either the Army of the Potomac or the Army of Northern Virginia—it would be easy to search the archives for a name. We have the records of all the families living in the borough and the surrounding countryside at the time. But strangers to the town? They had to have had a connection with someone here, the odds of them leaving the gold, not knowing anyone in town, the land . . . there had to have been a reason they came here. And that was where I have seen the name of Parker Stallard. I'm sure of it. Somewhere . . .

It had been two hours since Sparks had picked up the first document and seen a bill for supplies out of a Chicago company dated in 1860. Mining equipment and wagons, teams of horses—these were the items that Sparks noticed first, then the handwritten notes in the margins. Sentence fragments like:

. . . remind Parker of advantages of Conestogas . . . advantages of hiring experienced miners . . . set date for trip to Chicago for inspection of foundry facilities . . .

Then came letters between the Smythe-Tilling foundry in Chicago and Fitzroy, most of it boring dialogue about specifications of their contract or the need for large quantities of cyanide and coal to be shipped to the foundry. All the references would not really draw attention, unless one knew the bigger picture.

This group of documents confirmed that Fitzroy and Stallard had been setting up their gold operation a full year before the first shot at Fort Sumter and three years before the gold disappeared. As the documents approached 1863, there were three correspondences with an Englishman. While, again, the language was vague to the uninformed, it was clear this was the man whom Fitzroy was using as a go-between with England.

Then came the letter that was in Sparks's hand.

It was dated November 28, 1863, and was written by an investigator obviously hired by Fitzroy and mailed from Chicago.

Dear Sir,

It is with great regret that I am unable to inform you of the location of either Mr. Stallard, Mr. Prescott, or the shipment that was entrusted unto them. I have spoken with people in Harrisburg and two or three cities along the route from Chicago with whom they spoke, but none of the people are forthcoming with further information. Mr. Smythe, the owner of the foundry you asked me to investigate, died in a fire at the foundry in February of this year. No body was recovered, but witnesses put him in the area where there was horrible damage.

I did speak with several former employees of Mr. Smythe who were forthcoming. They spoke of rumors of a shipment of gold, but could not tell me of events beyond the foundry. They led me to another individual who gave me details of gold processing that did occur. He had no knowledge of the shipment's whereabouts except that it was gone in the days following the fire.

Upon retracing my steps, I found people in Harrisburg who knew Mr. Stallard and Mr. Prescott, but they also knew a third man. They did not know his name, but they believed he was working with the two gentlemen. I have not been able to track them from Harrisburg, and this now brings me to the resolution. I have been approached by an agent of the

Federal government who told me in plain terms to refrain from further inquiries.

There were words, sir, and I must say I was threatened with arrest if I persisted. Therefore, I am canceling our agreement and returning a portion of the expense monies not used. I will also be forwarding to you a detailed listing of the persons with whom I have been in discussion. If you choose to continue this inquiry, this information will be invaluable to my successor.

Your obedient servant,

Payton Howell

"What do you think?" Sparks handed the letter over to Coulthard. She had just finished reading it when her cell phone rang.

"It's my office. I'll take it outside," she said. "I have a feeling it will be important."

Sparks watched Coulthard as she left the room and stepped onto the backyard porch. He gave her a couple of minutes and then slipped to the porch door.

"Trouble at work?" Sparks's question made Coulthard jump, and she shut her phone without ending the conversation.

"No . . . no, just more problems I'll have to solve when this is all over," she said.

"Read this again." He handed her the letter from the investigator. "Then read the notations in the margin. I don't think you saw it the first time."

Coulthard reread the letter, then tried to make out the writing on the sides.

. . . government may know I am looking for Parker and the gold . . .

Must stop for now . . . no word from Parker since Harrisburg . . . shipment unnecessary . . . opportunity lost . . .

"What does this mean?" Coulthard asked.

"I checked the rest of the letters—there weren't that many—no mention of the conspiracy. No report from the investigator. It's clear Fitzroy never received the gold shipment, and he never received word from Stallard. We know he was never arrested, so Prescott didn't recover the gold. The third man mentioned in the investigator's letter may have been Brison, the operative who was working with Prescott, but I can't be sure. What we can be sure of is that the third letter never got to Fitzroy."

"And that takes us back to Gettysburg?" she asked.

"And that takes us back to Gettysburg."

Chapter Twenty-Eight

February 15, 1863

Prescott paid the stableman with a double eagle and made his way through the structure, past the two newly painted drummer's wagons with their side lettering and heavy suspension—the finest turnouts available.

The trip back from Indianapolis had been uneventful, the weather had held, and now the wagons contracted for early last month were in Chicago, in storage until they were needed to transport the gold east. This had been Prescott's calling for the past ten days, since the morning after their taking Fitzroy off the street and moving him into hiding. The plan had been Stallard's, and he had listened little to objections pointed his way.

The next morning, Prescott had taken the train to Indianapolis to oversee the completion of the wagons and buy horses and hire drivers to bring them back to Chicago. He had sent a messenger boy to the house that now served as their headquarters to bring Brison and a carriage back to the stables. Prescott had been waiting an hour when a buttoned-up Concord slid up to the side of the street and Brison poked his head out from behind the curtain. Prescott climbed in and a word from Brison sent the carriage out into the light traffic.

"I really do hate running around in these things," Brison grumbled. "It's pilin' on the agony if you ask me, making a man of my skills run around the city like I was a squire. I suppose it's necessary, but I'd much rather be on a horse."

"Well, good day to you, Andrew." Prescott afforded himself a smile, but then became serious, for Brison had news he needed to hear. "What of Abby?"

"Our informant at the foundry hasn't seen her since the day you left, but we believe she's being held in that Building Five, the same one with the gold. Food is being brought regularly, but none of the regular workers are allowed near the building, just Smythe's select guards. The two men I scared off after you and Stallard took your dive over the cliff got back into town two days ago. We got third-hand knowledge about a lot of yelling coming from Smythe's office that day. I figure those two got ridden out on a rail, but they could have gotten worse."

"So he knows we survived the attack."

Brison nodded.

"What plan has Parker come up with?" Prescott asked.

"He has not been completely forthcoming to this old soul," Brison said, "but I think he was waiting for you to return. Also, Fitzroy has returned to Philadelphia."

"Why?"

"He needed to work on the details of getting the gold out of the port. Stallard had him send a message to Smythe, brimming with pompousness, telling him that 'when Stallard and Prescott get back from their little excursion, to kindly send a message as to why they felt it necessary not to be in Chicago when I arrived.' We're hopeful this will explain his absence. We also hired a bodyguard for him."

"Good."

"There's something else we need to discuss."

"Washington?"

"A message must be sent to the president to appraise him."

"You're correct, of course."

"And I'm going to say it another time. You should consider calling in the army on this now. Confiscate the gold and save your Miss Stinson. Our testimony alone will put away the whole lot of them."

"I have considered it, but you just said the important words yourself," Prescott said. "Fitzroy has gone back to arrange for the shipment to get out of the country. If we can take the gold east, we can get information on the people Stallard and Fitzroy haven't told me about—the people in the north smuggling contraband out for profit. More importantly, the name of the traitor in the administration."

"Your friend Stallard is a traitor, as well. He'll hang for what he's doing," Brison said. "Listen. When the president instructed me to watch over you, he told me you were in charge on matters."

"I appreciate that . . ."

"But he did instruct me that I had the authority to call in the entire Federal Army if need be, if I felt it was necessary to save your life or salvage part of the operation. I have the final say, Jackson."

"Are you ready to quit on this?" Prescott asked.

"Are you prepared to lose Miss Stinson?" Brison waited for an answer as the carriage jostled them.

"I'm not prepared to lose her, but I'm not ready to accept that we can't take her away and still get the gold safely. I desire to hear Stallard's plan first."

"I insist we send a wire to the president," Brison said. "I'm then willing to see what Stallard has come up with."

"Smythe could have spies at the telegraph office or just around in general." Prescott showed concern. "My face is well known enough I could be seen."

"I doubt Smythe has that many people in his employ. This is a big city . . . but I see your opinion has merit. I can send the message for you."

Brison took a small book and pencil from inside his vest and gave it to Prescott. It was difficult with the carriage moving, but he managed to write down the brief message:

February 15, 1863

Office of the President

Washington

North Star. Shipment scheduled to leave Philadelphia in late spring. Will contact with specific instructions. Route unknown. Wagon passage expected. Shipment size unknown. My place is secure. JP.

"Is this sufficient?" Prescott handed Brison the paper.

"For now."

"Let us wait until we see what manner of plan we can devise. If the plan fails to meet a comfortable level of success, we shall do as you suggest."

"And how do you feel about that?" Brison asked.

"I don't understand."

"Are your priorities clear?"

"I swore an oath to my country when I enlisted." Prescott leaned forward for emphasis. "I made a promise to Mr. Lincoln that I would try to find the truth behind this group. I respect Parker for his personal honor. I respect much that he has accomplished in his life, no matter that I believe he's misled. When this is over, I'll fight to have him receive as lenient of a sentence as possible. But he'll be brought to justice."

Brison nodded. "I'll not speak of it again."

Stallard had not been sitting idle while Prescott had been in Indianapolis. The ten days had been put to good use, and Prescott's hopes were infused with Stallard's positive outlook. At least, at first glance. Before him on a table was a miniature design of the foundry, complete with building and trees, smokestacks, and tiny figures.

"Why the children's play set?" Prescott asked.

Stallard gave him a look and felt for the scar on his face. "I have used pieces from a children's play set, but this is far from child's play. With the help of some certain inside information, I have obtained survey maps of the foundry and its support buildings. I have re-created them here, attempting to keep the distances to scale. I have also, while you were relaxing on your trip, come up with a plan I believe holds the best chance for success."

"I'm eager to hear it," Prescott said.

"As am I." Brison walked in from the kitchen with a turkey drumstick he was gnawing on.

"We'll need to coordinate our movements and anticipate anything Smythe might have planned," Stallard said. "He knows we're alive, and he'll have guards posted in all the correct places. I have some information on their movements, but it is far from complete."

"To have anything is quite remarkable," Prescott said.

"There's not much cover between any of the entrances and Building Five, is there?" Brison said.

"No, that's why we'll need to have a demonstration elsewhere on the grounds to draw as many people away as possible. A military tactic that's well tested, is it not, Jackson?" Stallard asked.

"Tie up the enemies' resources on a part of the line, then strike him hard elsewhere when his attention is concentrated there," Prescott said.

"There are only three of us, and you have a broken arm." Brison's skepticism was evident. "He has a security staff alone of twenty, then there are the workers who are there at all hours. I don't like those odds."

"The odds will not be close to even, but there will be more than just the three of us," Stallard said. "I have gained the employ of three men who know the foundry intimately. They are employees who, shall I say, don't fancy the way they're treated. They would like to respond in kind—for a healthy price. We'll use them for the demonstration."

"It will still be six against thirty or forty." Prescott spoke as if to himself.

"I have been figuring what resources we have, and I believe we have a chance for success . . . with luck and God's providence," Stallard said.

"I'm more inclined to rely on my own abilities," Brison said. "And those of people I trust. You're asking us to rely on men we're not familiar with."

"Have you heard me question Jackson bringing your services into our plans?" Stallard retorted.

It was Brison's turn to smirk, then nod his head gently. "Point taken."

"I managed a smile out of ol' stone face there." Stallard laughed. "Did you see that? When I'm through giving you my theory on how to do this, you'll shake my hand and graciously admit defeat, that you will."

"I look forward to that handshake, for it will mean I got a chance to walk away with all my faculties," Brison said.

"Have faith, sir." Stallard took a drink of whiskey. "I always do."

February 23, 1863

Prescott turned his back to the wind but didn't turn up his collar. He had experienced this before on the battlefield. Men reacted differently going into battle—some prayed continuously, some bragged about how many Rebels they were going to get, others vomited from nerves, others sat in silence.

And some, like Prescott, had the ability to focus only on what was needed so strongly that everything else was ignored. So he now looked carefully over the foundry grounds from the tree on a rise to the north. It was one in the morning, and there were but a few lights coming from the buildings. The massive furnaces continued to work through the night—the war effort moved forward.

Stallard's plan was direct but would take careful timing. There were four guards patrolling the four sides of the wooden fence that surrounded the foundry grounds. There were two entrance gates: the main entrance faced south toward the city, the second faced east and allowed easy access for unloading from a rail spur that ran along the east fence.

They would use neither to get in. There was a lone door and a single guardhouse on the north fence, about two hundred feet from Building Five—the northernmost building. All approaches to that building were in the open, but the best chance came from going directly from the fence to the building.

The single door on the north fence was padlocked, and the guardhouse unmanned at night. Employees used the entrance when it was available, but from what could be viewed, it was not open on any set schedule. The guards, one to each fence side, walked along the base from corner to corner of the rectangle that ran from north to south.

The result was that the guards walking the north and south fences were required to wait until the east and west guards returned from their longer routes. The guards were apparently instructed to make contact with their counterpart, then begin the walk again. But the guards weren't sharp about it. Inevitably, the north or south guard would wait only for the other to approach before beginning his rounds again. Stallard himself had spent two nights watching this behavior. He would use it.

What moon there was lay hidden behind thick clouds, but there was no feeling of a coming snow. The effect was that it was especially dark, with just enough light from the foundry to keep a man from tripping over his own feet. Prescott slipped down the tree and dropped to the base, then made his way fifty feet to the fence next to the door. At his feet was a lantern with its sides closed so it would radiate no light until a panel was opened. A hundred and fifty yards to Prescott's left, at the meeting of the north and east fence, Brison was climbing the twelve-foot-high fence as quietly as possible.

This night was also ideal for their purposes because the wind was strong enough to hide an occasional stray sound. At the top, Brison peered over the edge in time to see the east guard approaching his corner. The north side guard moved from one foot to the other as he waited twenty feet along his own side. The two waved briefly, and the north side guard, apparently thankful to be moving again, trudged off to the west and faded into the darkness. After a brief moment, the east guard did the same.

Brison slid down the rope and opened the flap on his own lantern in Prescott's direction.

Just as the signal came, Stallard arrived at Prescott's position. "There, the signal," he whispered to Prescott. "The guard is on his way."

They moved the ladder into position against the fence and Prescott moved up until he was just below the top edge. For two minutes, he looked over the edge until he could see a shape, darker than the surroundings, moving closer. Listening for footsteps was useless because of the wind. Then he saw the small moving light. Smythe's men were insufficiently disciplined—now smoking on duty.

As the guard moved just under Prescott's position, the Federal spy swung his leg over and dropped, club in one hand, without so much as a scrape on the fence, onto the guard. Prescott's weight dropped the guard, and before he could even cry out in surprise, Prescott tapped him on the side of the head. Within a minute, Brison and Stallard dropped to the ground and moved into the shadows of the empty guardhouse.

"Move it, we have only got seconds," Stallard said, helping with his one good arm to get Brison into the guard's coat and hat. "Hopefully, they will miss the difference in boots—you're both wearing dark pants, so we're lucky."

"We have to keep the perimeter normal to all appearances as long as we can," Prescott said to Brison.

"I know my job." He pulled his hat down to shield his face and moved off to the west along the fence.

Prescott bound and gagged the guard. He might freeze to death if he was in the guardhouse long, Prescott thought, but in an hour, everything would be over one way or another. They gathered their two bags with rope, extra ammunition, gags, and dynamite with fuses, tucked in their revolvers—Prescott's army-issued Colt and Stallard's Kerr—and crouching, made their way toward the unlit Building Five.

Brison tried to imitate the gait of the guard he had replaced—a kind of a shuffle with a slight limp on the right side. Hat down low, he carried the carbine taken from the guard, leaving his own Spencer back behind the guardhouse. The path was well worn beneath his feet, and as he could see the corner approaching, he realized that he had reached it before the west guard.

He moved back and forth on his feet as the north guard had done before. Within a few minutes, he saw the west guard approaching with head bowed to the wind almost directly out of the north. Brison waited for him to look up when he was thirty feet or so away, then he gave the guard a half wave and began his own walk back to the east. For a few steps, he felt uneasiness, but when he glanced back

to his right, he saw that the west guard had already turned around, probably thankful he was traveling downwind.

Stallard and Prescott reached the back side of Building Five. There were no windows and only two entrances—one the double-door freight entrance for wagons on the south side, and the other a single door on the west side. There was light coming from underneath the door. They both stood away from the wooden step and adjusted their clothing. A quick glance and nod signaled their readiness, and they approached the door.

"So I told the asinine barmaid that I had already paid for the whiskey," Stallard said as they casually strode into the building with Prescott right behind. "And then she called me a liar to my face. I told her I had not come for no quiltin' bee and that I was there—"

He stopped in midsentence as they took in the scene before them. In the middle of the warehouse were two wagons with heavy tarpaulins strapped on. There was a pulley and winch still hanging over the back of one, as if work had been just completed.

"You said she called you a liar?" Prescott asked, stomping his legs as if fighting off the cold.

"I told her I had a mighty grist of anger buildin' up if she didn't take back what she said," Stallard continued. He looked around as if looking for someone. "Hey, where are you?" A louder voice this time.

From a dark corner, they heard the *click* of a hammer, and two men stepped into the light with pistols drawn.

"Walkin' in on people like that can get yourself killed," said one of them, "especially when you walk into this here place."

"Don't be gettin' ornery on us," Stallard said, his Southern accent noticeably missing. "Mr. Smythe roused us up and told us to come up here. He said we were going to have work beginning first light, but he wanted us to come up here now 'cause he wants to see you at his house."

"Smythe never sees us at his house," the second one said. "What's this all about?"

"Shit, we don't know," Prescott said. "Put the damn pistols down. You'll make a man piss in his pants."

"No one is allowed in this building unless he's with Mr. Smythe or is one of us guards," the first one said. He lowered his gun slightly and stepped closer.

"We know the rules. We've been working for Smythe outside the foundry on this job, dealing with some people that were a problem to him." Stallard eased down his sack and adjusted his sling. "I got this in our last meeting."

Seeing his ease and noticeable infirmity, the two guards lowered their pistols. The second one stayed back while the first moved to put on his overcoat. "I don't think we both should go, since we don't know you two."

"It's all right." The first one pointed to Prescott. "I've seen this one before around here, I think."

"Yeah, I've been on the grounds many times," Prescott said.

"Still, I'll stay behind," the second one said. "Just tell Smythe I wanted to be sure."

"Suit yourself," Prescott moved closer to the second guard as he made to put his sack down and get closer to the stove. As soon as he was close enough to the second guard, just behind his field of vision, Stallard cried out in pain. "Ah, damn it. I bumped my arm again."

The second guard could not have expected to remain focused on Prescott as he turned to see what had happened. As he did, he felt cold metal pressed against his throat and his arm bent back underneath his shoulder blade. At the same moment, Stallard's Kerr appeared next to the first guard's head.

"Open your mouth to shout, and you'll be dead before the first sound reaches the wall," Prescott said.

"Both of you on the floor, hands behind your back." Stallard moved to the door. "No lock. That's rather peculiar, given what's stored in here. I'll need to stay at the door."

Prescott, with Stallard covering him, tied and gagged the two guards to an inside post away from anything they could kick to draw attention. Then he quickly made his way to the only two doors. The first was a storage room. The second was latched from the outside, and he slid the bolt back and eased the door open, his Colt drawn.

Stinson was sitting up on the cot, fully dressed, blinking in an effort to focus on the figure in the doorway. He waited for her to recognize him before he moved to meet her at the edge of the bed. There were no joyous cries. They simply clung to each other for a moment.

"We must move quickly," he said.

They moved out into the main room. Stallard was still near the door, watching the two men on the floor.

"Thank you, Parker," Stinson whispered. "I had given up hope."

He smiled at her. "Never give up as long as we're alive."

"That's just it. I thought you were dead."

"Land sakes, woman, did Smythe tell you that?"

"Yes, but I was hopeful . . . at least for a while."

"Above all else, the man's a liar." Stallard smiled and motioned to Prescott and the door. "Get her out of here. I'll stay with these two."

Prescott and Stinson slipped out the door and made their way up to the north fence, his arm around her waist. Within a few minutes of reaching the guardhouse, Brison came along and helped Prescott up and over the fence. A minute later, they had the ladder down on the inside and Stinson was dropping down to the outside with Prescott's help in easing the fall. Brison continued on his walk to the east side. Prescott led Stinson to a single horse tied to a tree in the woods.

"Take the horse and follow these directions." Prescott placed a piece of paper into her hand. "Under no circumstances are you to go back to the boardinghouse or to the store, or to anywhere to try to talk to Sarah. Do you understand?"

"Yes."

"The woman at this address is expecting you and you alone. We'll be along eventually to take you away. But we have business with Smythe we must attend to."

"I don't want to lose you again, Jackson." She grabbed him by the shoulders and put her head to his chest. "I'm free. Why can't we all just leave?"

"My mission is far from over, and to continue on, Parker needs to get his gold back," he said. "Simple as that. We don't have any more time. Go."

Stinson nodded, climbed on the horse, and headed north to circle around the woods where she would meet the road heading south into the city. Prescott made his way back to the wall and was waiting for Brison when he reached the guardhouse.

"Eventually, one of these guards is going to want to have a brief conversation, and then we'll have only a few minutes before he's missed down at the southern end of the foundry," Brison warned. "Where are Stallard's three inside men?"

Kneeling in front of the lantern, Prescott risked a look at his pocket watch. "Five minutes and they should be here. Keep going on your rounds. We'll catch you on the return."

Impressively, the three men appeared from the direction of Building Five, and when Brison reappeared, the first one went off with him to the east fence. Ten minutes later, Brison returned with an unconscious figure draped over his shoulder.

"Everything go all right?" Prescott asked.

"He didn't like trying on the guard's coat," Brison mused. "He thought it smelled."

As Prescott gagged and tied up the east guard, the remaining hired men walked off after Brison as he went west. For fifteen agonizing minutes, Prescott sat at the guardhouse with the two prisoners. Then Brison appeared from the west, clutching his left arm.

"Trouble?" Prescott helped Brison pull his arm from the coat sleeve.

"No trouble with the west guard, but when I reached the south fence, the guard there wanted to talk. As soon as he got close enough to recognize me, he made to shout. I managed to keep him quiet, but he had a knife. I had to kill him."

Neither spoke while Prescott surveyed the damage to Brison's arm. "It looks uglier than it is."

Prescott cleaned up the wound and wrapped it with a bandana, a difficult task in the near dark, but he dare not keep the lantern open. "That will have to do. Are we all set with the guards on the fences, then?"

"For how long, we don't know."

"We're halfway home—Abby's safe. Now it's time to take care of Smythe."

"I still think the odds are long." Brison eased his coat back on and picked up his carbine.

Prescott was already moving down the slope to Building Five.

Chapter Twenty-Nine

Present Day
August 2

"Brenda?" the coworker called to her for the fifth time from across the bar. Uncomfortable with her lack of response, the friend wandered over through the crowd to where Munson was sitting alone at a small table in the corner. "Hey, Brenda, what are you doin' over here all by yourself? Come on over and join the group. We're discussing whether, since men are usually pigs, we should just send them all to Australia. Right now, the group is split fifty-fifty. Come on, you can cast the deciding vote."

"I've got a problem I'm working out in my head." Munson smiled. "The beer and the noise help lubricate the wheels. I'll be over in a bit."

"You sure?"

"Put my vote in for keeping the men here. I'm for a more sophisticated plan—just weed out the assholes and keep the rest, no matter how few."

Her friend laughed and left, leaving Munson alone with the problem of why she remembered the name Parker Stallard. She had gone over the last eighteen months of projects, but nothing had jumped out at her. The whole effort was fatiguing, but now she was gradually getting a feeling that the name had recently appeared to her.

Munson abruptly took a final swig of beer and left. She would swing by the visitors' center office. It was after hours, but she would begin sorting through the paperwork connected with the First Minnesota project. It was as good a place as any to begin.

His breath fouled by stale beer hung heavily on her neck as he held her down on the bed. For a consecutive day, he was assaulting her through her clothes and laughing while telling her what he was going to do. Underneath the hood, Jennifer Sparks cried, struggling against his weight with no success. She realized now she would die soon.

Anonymity or not, these men were going to kill her, no matter what the leader had said. This one was too strong, she could not survive on strength, and she had already exhausted herself on other options. The violations were too much—she felt nauseated as he continued.

"You know, I might not wait until the boss man says we don't need you anymore," he whispered. "I might just take you now. I'll bet you're one fine piece of ass. Oh, I bet you are."

"Leave me alone!" she screamed. "I'll tell the other one. I'll tell him!"

"Don't matter, and don't scream at me. I don't like it when you scream."

He shifted his weight and reached down to unbuckle his pants with his free hand, still using his left to pin her down by her throat. Despite her lashing out at him the day before, he eased up on her restraint as he fumbled with his pants, his confidence in her weakness unfazed. When she felt the pressure lessen, she brought her left knee up and to the right as hard as she could.

This time her attempt hit right on his groin, and the air escaped through his lungs like squeezed bellows. He fell off her and onto the floor, swearing under what breath he could muster. Jennifer struggled to her feet and tried to peek under her hood for the way to the door. Before she had taken three steps, there was a figure standing in her path, framed by the doorway. When she saw her way blocked, she slipped down to the floor and moved on her hands and knees back to the bed's foot.

"It seems this is the second time I have arrived when you were molesting the girl as I expressly forbade you." Streeter's voice was frigid. "Dorman, I told you to leave her alone. I warned you of the consequences!"

"You said my name," Dorman whined. "You asshole, you said my name. We've got to kill her now, you asshole. You stupid fuckin' asshole!"

"Shut up!" Streeter spat. "If you had been professional and had kept your hands off of her, we wouldn't be having this conversation." A gun appeared, leveled at Dorman. "Downstairs." The killer, having regained a little mobility, got to his feet, took off his glasses, and wiped them on his grimy shirt. "I said, downstairs," Streeter repeated.

"I'll talk to the man about this, Streeter." Dorman put the wire rims back on. "You're fuckin' in deep shit. Him and me go back long before he hired you on for this job."

"Really? And what do you think he'll say when he finds out you were thinking with your dick and not your head?" Dorman didn't respond but moved to the door as Streeter stepped aside, gun moving with Dorman. When they were through the door, Streeter spoke up, making sure Dorman knew the girl could hear him. "You're disgusting. The only way you can have a woman is if you attack her or pay her. Either way, I'm sure you're sadly lacking in the skills or equipment for the job."

Dorman suddenly turned to strike out at Streeter, emitting a growl as he threw his body at his tormentor. But unlike back at the cabin, Streeter was ready this time, and he sidestepped the attack, swinging his gun hand and arm down on Dorman's neck.

The blow stunned Dorman, his anger escalating to fury as he got back up, now armed with a knife he had pulled from a sheath tied to his ankle. He moved forward as Streeter retreated from the top of the stairs. Despite the silenced gun pointed at him, Dorman took Streeter's place in the hall with his back to the stairs.

"You really are just plain stupid, aren't you?" Streeter shook his head.

It was at that moment that Jennifer stepped into the doorway, hood off, eyes glazed by the scene. Streeter looked over at her, and as he did, Dorman lunged for the girl, moving behind her in two steps. The knife moved up underneath her chin and the top of the blade rested just under her right ear.

"Put the gun down and kick it down the stairs," Dorman croaked.

Streeter stood with the gun measured at the pair. "No."

"Do as I fuckin' say!" Dorman shouted, then went on in a lower tone. "I'll cut her. You know I'll do it." Arm around Jennifer, he moved her to the top of the stairs.

"I have no doubt you would. The girl is still valuable to our employer. That's what you should consider."

"To hell with him and to hell with you, you puke!"

Jennifer was looking straight at the gun when she saw the muzzle flash in the darkened hall and simultaneously felt the jerk of Dorman's body. A small, crimson blotch appeared on Dorman's forehead as the back of his head exploded onto the wall backing the stairs. His lifeless body, still wrapped around her, fell backward, taking her with it on a chaotic roll down the stairs.

The bruise on Jennifer's forehead was ugly, the swelling obvious. Streeter placed a cold towel on it and checked her eyes. The pupils reacted well to the penlight and the action itself caused her to begin to stir. It appeared to be just a bad bruise and perhaps a slight concussion.

As she awakened, the memory of what had happened to her a short time before filtered into her consciousness, and her body became tense as she cried out in panic. He managed to calm her down after a moment, when she realized that she was on a couch in a living room.

"I'm truly sorry for what you've been through," he said. He was wearing dark glasses and a faded, blue baseball cap with a red *B* on the crown. Blond hair stuck out from underneath the sides. "Unfortunately, my employer and I made a terrible choice in personnel, and you, I'm afraid, faced the consequences. However, you won't be bothered by him again."

"You . . . you shot him," she said, taking a glass of water from Streeter. "I remember the gun, but no sound."

"You fell down the stairs with the late Mr. Dorman, took a nasty spill, and hit your forehead on the wall. You'll be OK, just might have a headache for a while. I can get you something for that."

"It doesn't matter."

"I've got painkillers in my bag." Streeter dug into a large shoulder bag next to the couch.

"You're going to kill me. I'm too tired to go on with this," she whispered, almost like it was their own secret. "Just don't hurt my father."

Streeter took her hand and squeezed it. "I know you've been through more than most young ladies, but you need to be strong. I'm going to get you back to your father."

"You're just saying that to keep me calm."

"You have no reason to trust me, I understand." He smiled. "If you're able to stand up, it's time for us to take a trip."

"Where are we going?"

"To where your father is, I believe."

"Where's that?"

"How much do you know about the Civil War?"

Sparks answered the phone back in his Gettysburg hotel room after the first ring precisely at 9 p.m. Jennifer's voice welcomed him, but she sounded tired, her nerves shredded. She told him she was all right and that she loved him, then she was gone.

"You got to talk to your daughter," the voice said. "Now, what do you have for me?"

"We just came in from Philadelphia," Sparks said. "The third letter never made it to Fitzroy."

"Where does that lead you?"

"The last telegraph message to the White House came from Harrisburg. I could go up there and look through the historical records there, but our best lead is still here in Gettysburg. The park ranger here says she's familiar with one of the principal's names. She just can't place it."

"That doesn't sound like much."

"It's not."

There was a pause, and then the voice continued, "There has been a change. I don't have time to give you instructions now, but I will soon. Continue on with your search, but if you're approached or contacted by anyone else, remember that I'm the one who holds your daughter's life."

"What do you mean?" Sparks implored. "I'm working the best I can under the circumstances!"

"The change will benefit you and your daughter, but you must continue on with the search. I'll call again tomorrow."

The line went dead.

The stress was turning Goldberg's stomach and head into constant annoyances. The late-night pizza slice had quieted the hunger but given him indigestion. His head pounded from fatigue after having spent five hours going over cost projections for the next year.

Griffin had come by Goldberg's office just as the deputy was ready to leave and demanded that a thorough analysis of the data be completed by midday. That meant a very late night, on top of his worry over Richardson's lack of concern. It all made for an unpleasant drive home to Manassas.

His mind occupied, he didn't see the dark sedan that picked him up outside the bureau and followed at a discreet distance while he stopped for the pizza and then headed out of the city. It was closing in on 2 a.m. when Goldberg turned off the main road and started through the ungated, yet exclusive, development with homes placed on three-acre lots.

Goldberg was approaching an intersection when a car pulled out of a driveway to his right and stopped at the stop sign. Goldberg approached and stopped behind it, but the other driver didn't continue on. Suddenly, lights appeared from behind him as the dark sedan pulled right up, almost touching the bumper of Goldberg's car.

"What the hell?" Goldberg said, not noticing the car behind him, still concentrating on the car ahead that would not move. "Let's go, you stupid moron!"

Fatigue, the pain in his head, and his aching stomach all stole his attention. He never saw the shadow move along the side of his car until it was upon him, and then, in his side mirror, he caught a glimpse of a long-barreled semi-automatic with a silencer. There was only a split second of realization, an instant of adrenaline, before the shock of knowing that he was about to die. He didn't even cry out as the multiple shots turned his window into a star field, the bullets slamming into his chest.

Chapter Thirty

Brison and Prescott joined Stallard in Building Five, and after brief words, Prescott and Stallard strolled casually toward the Smythe house. Their plans had changed for the better—the gold was already loaded onto wagons, a sign Smythe was preparing a move. As Prescott and Stallard made their way, Brison moved off into the shadows. There was a single lamp burning on the front porch, and the first floor inside was illuminated, but gently so.

The two men walked past the house, trying to determine whether anyone was taking an interest. It appeared that there was no one, so when they passed behind the house, they moved quickly to the rear porch door that led to the kitchen.

It was locked, but Prescott was able to pry it open, hoping any noise was masked by the wind, which even now was increasing in intensity. The stillness inside contrasted with what they had just come from, and for a moment, they stood without moving and listened.

"Servants?" Prescott whispered.

"One cook, one butler," Stallard said. "Cook is off, as we planned. Butler is upstairs, first room on the left at the top of the stairs."

They soundlessly moved up the stairs. The door to the butler's room was unlocked, and thankfully, didn't emit a noise when Prescott slowly opened it far enough to see inside. The butler was fast asleep, his back turned to the door.

Five minutes later, they were back in the hallway moving to the master suite door. The butler had been easy to subdue and had emitted no shout of warning. Having the black hole of a revolver's muzzle six inches from your face as you awoke would sensibly have that effect.

They had bound, gagged, and left him on the bed. Prescott repeated the process as before, barely slipping the door open. He could see that Smythe was asleep, as well, in the single candle-lit room, his breathing steady with a slight snore. Prescott gave Stallard a glance, and they moved into the room.

Sudden movement brought the sound of a hammer being cocked, then came the numbing sensation of steel against the back of the neck.

"Gentlemen, you really are making yourselves available at a most peculiar time of day." Smythe was sitting up, a pistol of his own waving in their general direction. "I'm so glad to see that the initial reports of your deaths were inaccurate. You've proven very resourceful at staying alive."

Their weapons were taken away from them, defeat sweeping over their faces. The two killers from the highway up in Wisconsin took the pistols and also found the clubs and knives the two had hidden.

"We only came for the woman," Stallard said. "That was our foremost task. You had no right to abduct her."

"Parker, I had every right." Smythe climbed out of bed. He had been fully clothed under the sheets. He walked over to a table and poured himself a drink. "I must say, you've always impressed me with your ability to organize the network of people who seem willing to help you with this plan to deliver gold to England. But both you and Fitzroy have become too narrow in your views. You continue to look at the goal without reevaluating its merit, or more carefully scrutinizing the dangers around you."

"What rubbish are you talking about, Smythe?" Stallard asked. "The only serious mistake we made was not taking precautions with you. I should have realized that the lure of the gold would far outweigh your stake. And knowing how ruthless you are, it was stupid on my part."

"True, but that's not the limit of your stupidity on such matters. The man standing to your right is proof of that."

"I know you were suspicious of me from the start," Prescott interjected. "I assume you had me investigated. I assumed Parker did, as well. I never hid my feelings. I don't have a great love for the South, or a great love of money."

"Oh, we've discussed this at length before." Smythe laughed quietly. "You've seen too much death and carnage. You wanted to stop it in any way possible. You're so altruistic."

"What nonsense are you speaking?" Stallard asked.

"You didn't believe me when I told you there was something about his sending wires from here back east," Smythe said. "You accepted his explanation of a mentally ill family friend. But I did not. I subsequently learned that he sent a wire not to Boston as he told us, but to Washington. Now, I didn't learn the contents of the message, but the young operator did remember the first two words of the message—'North Star'—and to whom it was addressed. It was addressed to someone in the Executive Mansion."

Prescott could feel the blood rush to his face.

"Is this true?" Stallard's words came to Prescott, but he continued to look directly at Smythe.

"Why are you trying to cause dissent between us when you're going to kill us anyway?" Prescott directed his words to Smythe.

"Answer me. Is what he said true? Are you working for the Federals?" Stallard grabbed Prescott to face him.

"No, he's not telling the truth," Prescott said. "If I was working for the government, I would have called in the troops by now, before this attempt at rescuing Abby. I would have had enough evidence to stop you all now. The gold is here, the conspirators are here. Why are the troops not?"

Stallard's face softened, and he started to nod. He gently patted Prescott on the shoulder. "Indeed, they're not."

Smythe shook his head. "I gave you my reasons. Take them for what they are. Regardless, the end result is the same. The gold stays with me, and you both disappear."

He motioned to the two killers, and Stallard and Prescott were prodded out the door and down the stairs. The five of them went out the front door, and Smythe motioned toward Building Five. Stallard and Prescott moved ahead of the other three, walking side by side.

"This was not in the plans we talked about," Prescott lamented. "You have something planned for this outcome, I hope."

"I'm afraid the river is dry," Stallard replied. "The pot is full and our hand is weak, but we do, I believe, have one more card to play."

"That we do," Prescott said, wondering just what it was. Brison had proved immensely resourceful, but Smythe had changed things, and they were now—as his father used to say—working a new stream. A new stream meant everything was fresh, unfamiliar. The odds heavily favored the fish. Prescott almost muttered out loud about why he would be thinking of his father.

They were a hundred feet from Building Five when the first storage building nearest the foundry exploded with a spectacular force that knocked all five of them off their feet. Anticipation of some event didn't stop Prescott from lying on the ground in shock as he saw shards of timber and other material sweep with a wave over the area around them and against the south wall of Building Five.

Seconds later, a section of the foundry building itself exploded, with flames thrusting out of the open expanse left by the blast. Prescott heard someone swearing in loud, staccato bites. It was Smythe, and he was looking at Prescott, his gun already pointing straight at the Federal.

"Where the hell is that third man, Prescott?" he roared. "You son of a bitch!"

The five of them staggered to their knees and then awkwardly to their feet. There were shouts and the compound was already in turmoil. Smythe grabbed one of the two guards by the arm. "Take them to the building, make sure the gold is secure, and then put a goddamn bullet in their heads! You understand me?" Smythe yelled above the noise of men and frightened horses.

The guard understood, for he again directed them toward the building. Smythe ran off in the direction of the foundry, yelling instructions to the swarm of men filing out of the bunkhouse. As

Stallard and Prescott reached the building, the four of them were shaken by another explosion, this time from a building on the south side of the compound.

"Inside," the one called Cramer said. He began to form another word, but his mouth twisted up in a grotesque sneer from the bullet that completely blew off the top of his head and splattered Prescott with blood and brain. The other man stood, openmouthed, before Stallard kicked him in the groin and he bent over in agony. A second blow to the head with the butt of Stallard's own recovered revolver, and the man fell unconscious.

"Come on!" Stallard winced in pain from the exertion with his bad arm. They slammed through the door, not bothering to check if it was safe. The two guards lay as they had left them, tied to the side timber, eyes wide behind the gags. Brison had, indeed, been busy. Both teams were hooked up to the wagons, pawing at the ground with nervousness at the chaos outside.

Brison crouched against the stables and placed his Spencer against the wood. The compound was filled with swarming men, alarm bells ringing, horses and their riders rearing with each new burst of flame from the foundry building. The front gates were opened, allowing activity in and out as men were organized to fight the growing menace of flame spurred on by the wind.

Brison had placed four charges of dynamite in four different buildings and had lit fuses of varying lengths. The first three had been successful, detonating seconds apart, but the fourth should go in moments. The fuses weren't effective a hundred percent of the time, and as the seconds passed, he worried that the final distraction wasn't coming.

Already, though, Brison's thoughts were elsewhere. Amid the turmoil, he could see four men casually walking in a coordinated movement, each on a different side of the compound. Pistols in hand, they weren't helping in the fire-fighting efforts. They were searching for him. It would be only a few minutes before the one closest to him would be in proximity.

He couldn't risk taking this guard down as he had just done the others. One of the guards falling down dead in the compound would bring a dozen or so men his way. And this was where he had to stay, for if Prescott and Stallard were to bring the wagons through the front gate, this was where they would have to go by. And they would need his help.

The closest guard was fifty feet away, looking down each alleyway. There were no barrels or such near Brison's position—even in the shadows, he would be seen in moments. Scanning the compound, he caught sight of Smythe standing in front of the main foundry building, directing men in fighting the fire. But he was turning around frequently, interested in the search. Brison took the carbine and revolver and laid them down, moving a couple of loose boards over them.

He took his knife from his leg sheath and moved against the wall, far enough back as to not be seen easily from the compound. He could only hope the guard wouldn't call everyone over when he spotted Brison. Now it would only be seconds. The guard would be at the entrance to the alley. Would he call out and bring a group of men over, or would he come down between the buildings to investigate the figure on the ground? Brison moved his hand and gripped the knife tighter.

Seconds now . . .

At the very moment the guard came into view, the main foundry building exploded.

"How much damn dynamite did he use?" Prescott staggered back from opening the doors. The horses were fighting against their harnesses, close to bolting through the opening.

"I find it quite a sufficient usage." Stallard climbed on the first wagon's seat and gathered the reins with his good hand, trying to use his bad arm as much as he could despite the pain.

"We go now?" Prescott asked.

"Yes. Brison will have to find his own way out."

The guard and everyone else in the compound were knocked off their feet by the fourth explosion. Some were killed outright by the projectiles slamming into their bodies—deadly missiles of wood, metal, and glass. The guard abandoned his search and climbed to his feet, facing the huge, fiery spectacle before them. As the guard ran to help those closest to the foundry building, Brison collected his weapons and moved back to the corner position he had occupied before.

He scanned the scene, looking for the other guards. *Will they resume their search?* He could see no one doing anything other than dealing with the burning buildings and the wounded. He looked for Smythe, who had been standing by the main entrance, and saw a body, lying where he had been standing, smoldering with heat from the blast. Even from this distance, Brison could see the twisted and separated body parts.

Stallard moved his wagon out and around Building Five with Prescott moving right behind him, the horses agitated but manageable. The scene before them reminded Prescott of a battlefield—noise, motion, and death in a horrible crucible of destruction. They moved the wagons at a quickening pace along the west side of the compound on the opposite side of the carnage.

From his position in the shadows, Brison immediately caught sight of the two wagons. He tossed his Spencer and ammunition pouch into Prescott's trailing wagon, then jumped between the massive wheels and swung himself up and over the sideboard. Prescott recognized the figure now kneeling between the tarpaulin-covered stacks of gold ingots.

"Good job with the diversions," Prescott yelled above the noise. "Don't you think you overdid it a touch?"

"Just continue with the harsh words, we're far from being out of here," Brison countered.

The two wagons approached the open main gate, but one of the guards put up his hands and motioned Stallard to stop. Prescott subconsciously felt for the pistol in his belt under his unbuttoned coat.

"We need the wagons for water and men," the guard shouted. "Where the hell are you going?"

"Smythe told us to get these supplies to safety, away from the fire," Stallard said impatiently, "and he told us to be quick about it."

"What's in the back?" the guard asked, peering back at Prescott and Brison in the second wagon. "You should stay until I get this approved."

Stallard later told Prescott he thought about shooting the guard outright. There was so much confusion—they might have made it away from the gate without drawing attention.

There was another smaller explosion from the foundry building. The furnaces were clearly visible from inside the shattered exterior. The guard's attention returned to Stallard.

"It's all right. I was there when Smythe gave them the order to take the wagons. I was there," a voice said. The man Brison had left as the replacement for the guard on the west wall trotted up to Stallard's wagon. "He said for them to get them out of the foundry straightaway and take them to the staging warehouse on the waterfront. I'm no bootlicker, but when the man says move, I do it."

"I still want to know what's inside the wagons," the guard insisted.

"Damn it, man, I'll take the responsibility!" Stallard's hire said. "Smythe didn't tell us what was in the wagons, just that they had to be moved to safety! Let them go!"

The guard shook his head, finally giving in to the fire's distraction. He motioned them to move along. Stallard's man jumped on the back of Prescott's wagon, but then cried out in agony as a pair of bullets slammed into his back, throwing him off the wagon.

"Stop the wagons!" It was Smythe's assistant Joshua, coatless and just in his long johns and boots, charging toward the gate, pistol up and aiming at the wagons pulling away. The guard, realizing his mistake, brought his rifle up but died before he could aim. Brison swung around, dropped his pistol, and picked up the Spencer. Bullets spit at him and Prescott as he drew on the large man with the dark sideburns, but as he pulled the trigger, the man dove to the frozen mixture of dirt and snow. Brison swore and reloaded the carbine.

"Let's move or we're dead!" he screamed at Prescott, who didn't need the reminder. The two wagons broke away and the horses reached a gallop that left Brison with the difficult task of staying upright on roads rutted from previous thaws. They continued down the road away from the foundry, which moved swiftly from view as the road took a natural bend.

"They'll be along quick enough," Brison said, moving closer to Prescott.

"We only need ten minutes," Prescott replied. "Here we go."

At the next intersection, the regular grid of streets began, and while Stallard went straight through, Prescott reined in the horses and directed them to the west down the cross street. Two targets could divide a pursuer's attention, making him half again as effective.

In half of Prescott's ten minutes, Joshua and five other men were on horses and headed along the south road, two carrying torches, and the other three, including the leader, already with guns drawn. When they arrived at the intersection where Prescott had turned west, they held up.

Joshua studied the wagon tracks, which was difficult because there had been much traffic, but there was a fresher set turning west down the side street, and another set continued on. He pondered his dilemma for a moment but then split his team. He sent two men headed down the main road and took the other two with him.

The group of three had gone a half mile when they came over a rise in the street. Joshua was in the lead, so he was the one to take the bullet in the right shoulder. The report from the Spencer split the cold and echoed off the storefronts. Joshua fell from the horse, landing squarely on his back. The two riders' reactions were understandable. They reined in their horses and looked around wildly, seeking the direction from where the threat came.

Another shot came, and this time one of the men grabbed his left arm, forcing him to drop the torch. He cried out, turned his horse around, and headed back up the street, trailing his mounted companion as they sought the safety of distance.

Two buildings away, Brison reloaded his carbine and moved off from the corner of a store's sign and crossed over to the ladder placed against the west wall. The climb had been difficult because of ice on the rungs, but he had managed to make it to his position with three minutes to spare. He now made his way down, returned the ladder to the ground, and made his way on foot through the back alleyways.

Stallard found maneuvering the wagon challenging . . . and painful. Each time he made a turn with the team—and that was often—his slowly mending arm reminded him of the fall through the tree in Wisconsin.

He had not seen the pursuers during his frequent glances over his shoulder, but he knew they would be there. How many was the question. He only needed a few seconds more without being seen. He turned one last corner and stared straight into the blackness of an open barn, a solitary figure holding the door.

He directed the team straight into the barn, and the woman immediately closed the door. Stallard brought the team to a stop and jumped down, racing through a side door and joining up with the woman to pull a decrepit, snow-covered wagon in front of the door. Just as they had moved it into place, they heard a whistle from up the street.

They had only seconds. Stallard and his accomplice moved back to the side door and inside. He retrieved his revolver and positioned himself where he could see the outside through a small opening between the weather-worn boards.

The two riders had slowed to a canter. One of them was trying to make out the tracks, but the torch was almost out. They had pulled even with the barn when their heads snapped to the right. They saw a wagon cross the street three blocks up, and they kicked their horses into a gallop.

"Uncle Petrov is right on time." The woman lightly kissed Stallard on the cheek.

"You and your Uncle Petrov are wonderful," he said. "I love you both."

"If only that were true, my Parker." She smiled. "You only love me for, well . . . and you only love Uncle Petrov because he loses to you in poker."

"I'm so misunderstood."

Chapter Thirty-One

Present Day
August 3

Alex Pierce was a summer intern from Gettysburg College, working between his junior and senior years, and as the lead intern, he was given the vital job of purchasing the morning doughnuts twice a week. This morning, promptly at 6 a.m., he walked into the main visitors' center between Washington Street and Steinwehr Avenue.

He placed the three boxes on the counter and continued on into the center's museum portion. This morning, he found Munson in a back room, working on the computer. Her chin was in her left hand, while the right worked the mouse, eyes glazed over, face reflecting the glow from the screen.

"All night?" he asked. "You didn't just come in, did you." The second question was a statement.

"No, I have been here all night, and no, I'm not going to tell you what I'm doing," Munson croaked in response.

Pierce shook his head, made a motion of defeat, and continued past the room. As he left, Munson called out to him, and he reversed himself.

"Does the name Parker Stallard sound familiar to you? Like you've seen it around in the archives or markers or monuments, anything?" she asked.

"Parker Stallard? No . . . I don't think so. You trying to find a reference?"

"I've gone through everything I've worked on in the past year, and I've run out of possibilities."

"Did you check the archived letters you and I did last summer?"

Munson sat up in her chair. "Those letters—my God, yes! But I haven't seen them on the database. Are they on here?"

"Don't you remember? We were going to catalog them for the historical society because they were letters from the town's residents at the time of the battle, mostly personal correspondence donated from families. But we didn't do it, because we ran out of time before the fall semester started. I thought you all would have done it by now."

"Where are those boxes?" Munson couldn't contain her excitement.

"They're probably right back here." Pierce motioned down the hall.

Munson grabbed him by the arm and led him down to the storage room. Once inside, he pointed to a corner, and Munson remembered the boxes.

"Tell Ted I'm working on something for the government folks," Munson said. "He'll understand."

Munson closed the door and moved the boxes onto a folding table she had placed underneath the light. She started taking the documents out in handfuls, then scanned each one, looking for the name that had hounded her since Sparks had mentioned it. She went through the first box and was halfway through the second when she noticed a single piece of yellow legal paper that had been on top of the contents of the first box. She had moved it off to the table's corner without examining it. It said simply:

> *Stallard letter, 6/28/1863, taken from unidentified Confederate soldier, killed in action 7/1/63. Letter in main case, campsite display.*

Munson's breath left her, and the memory appeared like details emerging from a morning fog—not quite real but becoming more so. She hurried from the storeroom, almost knocked over a coworker entering the museum, and circled over to the display case. There was a campsite scene and next to it a vertical glass display with civilian letters and military orders in plastic sleeves. She had reorganized the display the previous year, and she herself had pulled the letter from the box of uncategorized documents. It had caught her eye because of the unusual wording.

She moved to the rear entrance of the display case and took the letter down. Even as she scanned the document, her left hand was punching the keys on her cell phone.

Sparks was drying his hair and Coulthard was in the shower when Munson's call came into the hotel room on Route 15.

"I've got it!" Munson almost screamed with delight.

"The letter!?"

"It's got to be it. It was in some documents recovered from the battlefield or town around the time of the battle or just afterward when they were burying the dead. It was without an envelope, which is why it was never delivered to that Fitzroy man in Philadelphia. And the notation here attached to it says it was recovered from an unidentified Confederate soldier."

"Is the letter signed by Stallard?"

"Absolutely!"

"Is there a date on it?"

"June 28, 1863."

"Damn!" Sparks turned to the bathroom, hearing the water in the shower still running. "What does it say? Does it give the location?"

"If you read the letter without the information from the others you showed me, you would never understand what the letter meant. But with what we know from the others, it's pretty clear where they hid it."

Sparks's mind filled with the possibilities of what would come next, but he had already decided what he wanted to do. "I need your help with something, but I can't talk now. I'll call you back in one hour."

The shower had just ceased when Sparks knocked on the door. Coulthard opened it, holding a towel in front of herself, though not in a modest way.

For the first time in days, he smiled at her. "Munson, the park ranger . . . she found the third letter."

Sparks made his way back into the restaurant from the parking lot, where he had made his promised call to Munson. Coulthard was waiting for him at the table.

"I thought I was going to have to ask the waitress to have a busboy go in and see if you were all right," Coulthard mused. "You OK?"

"As I was coming out, I got a call from my boss, departmental crap. I went outside to take it. I have to call him later with an update."

"You didn't tell him about the letter?"

"I thought I would wait until we see what we have," he said. "I didn't ask Brenda to read the whole thing to me. Come on, there's one place I want to see before we go to the visitors' center."

"You're kidding, right? I thought you'd be hell-bent to see that letter," she said.

"I am, but this place is related to it."

They had to pass the bar area before leaving the restaurant, and the television screen caught Sparks's eye. There was a graphic photo of Marshall Goldberg in the upper right of the screen, and the rest of the image was the media room in the Hoover Building. At the podium stood a noticeably tired-looking Clark Griffin.

"Can you turn up the sound?" Sparks asked an employee.

An anchor spoke over the press conference. "You can see that FBI Director Clark Griffin is speaking to reporters concerning the apparent murder of Deputy Director Marshall Goldberg. Jonathan Stiles has been covering this story for us today . . . Jonathan, anything new from the scene in Manassas?"

"Thank you, Barry. I'm standing here in a neighborhood in Manassas, and as you can see behind me, the police have cordoned off this area. You can see there, in the distance, a dark sedan at the stop sign. I don't know whether our cameras can pick it up clearly, but the driver's side window has been shot out. Officials removed the deputy director's body from the sedan a few hours ago. The deputy director lived just two blocks from here, and police have cordoned off the house."

"Thank you, Jonathan, we're going to listen in on the press conference now from the Hoover Building . . ."

Director Griffin was speaking. ". . . we'll be trying to ascertain in the following hours the nature of the shooting. We have some indication that robbery was involved. His wallet, watch, and a ring were taken. But we're too early in the investigation."

There was a question from a reporter. "Is there any indication this was an attack against the bureau in general, a terrorist incident?"

Griffin responded, "Terrorists want an audience. This was done late at night on a secluded street without much lighting. It's too early into the investigation, but we also have received no recent threats against the bureau. A security check with other intelligence agencies, and within our own, hasn't turned up anything that would lead us to believe terrorism was involved."

Another question: "Will the FBI be taking over the investigation?"

Griffin replied, "We'll be working with the local departments. If this tragedy is in any way connected to his work with the bureau, we'll investigate fully from within."

One final question from a reporter: "Was the deputy director alive when he was found?"

Griffin's response: "No, the police officer dispatched to the scene after a call by a motorist determined that the deputy director died at the scene. That's all the information I have at this time. Again, I want to publicly express my condolences to Marshall's family. This is a terrible tragedy for his family and the Bureau. I worked with him for a number of years, closely. He was a dedicated professional, and he did many things daily and long-term that made the FBI better than when he first joined. Our job will be all that much harder because of the loss. Thank you."

Sparks was surprised and impressed that Coulthard didn't react outwardly, other than the usual gasp of "Oh, my God" when one hears bad news. As he led her out of the restaurant, though, he detected a noticeable tremor in her hand.

They drove into town on Business Route 15 and went down Lincoln Avenue, turning left onto Carlisle Street, and moved into the center of town. The center square was heavy with traffic, as it usually was during the summer months.

They kept to the right and turned onto York Street, heading west before turning onto Route 30 and moving northwest out of town. Coulthard was quiet at first, but then seemed to recover herself. She asked again about their destination and wanted to know if this was where the gold was hidden.

"You remember our tour with Brenda?" he replied. "What we're traveling on was Chambersburg Pike back in 1863." They approached turnoffs that were part of the auto tour with numerous monuments and markers visible from the main road. "This is where the first day's fighting took place, west and north of town. Most of the attention from the public has always focused on the second day's fighting, south at Devil's Den and Little Round Top, or on the third day, when Lee sent thirteen thousand men against the Union center with Pickett's Charge.

"Yet it was the fighting done here, a delaying action, by John Buford's cavalry that enabled two corps of Federal troops to reach and engage the Confederates. The battle would have possibly had a different result if the Rebels had taken the town, and the high ground. A much different result."

"Is the gold buried on this part of the battlefield?" she asked.

"Yes and no."

They approached a dirt road on the right, and Sparks turned onto it. The road angled until it was heading almost directly north, and they went a half mile before they approached a tree line and entered the woods.

"Quite off the beaten track, isn't it?" she said.

"I'm sure it has grown up a lot in almost a hundred and fifty years."

They came into a clearing with an old house set comfortably in the open. The brick exterior was in excellent shape for its age, and there was a more recently built barn. It was a two-story house with vertical windows on the two floors, with a third set of small ones set near the roofline. There were two chimneys, one on either end, though the one on the west side was larger than the other.

The grounds were moderately well kept, but there was evidence that work was being prepared for the house. Loose scaffolding was piled off to the left, and building materials were sitting under tarps. They could not follow the circular path around to the front of the house because of a chain drawn across the road. It had a sign hanging from the center that read, "No trespassing. Gettysburg National Military Park."

"I thought the battlefield was back there?" Coulthard asked.

"She said the house wasn't part of the fighting, but the grounds were used as a staging area for the Confederates when they arrived that first day." Sparks got out of the car and stood in the open door, the engine still running. "The house was here when the battle took place."

"I hope this is where it is. Maybe we can see an end to all this."

Sparks stared at the red brick front. "Jennifer's life depends on it."

Chapter Thirty-Two

April 7, 1863

D awn filtered in from the east over the woods, which were just beginning to bud up so that the branches spread out against the sky like veins under the skin. The morning was cold enough to cause a cloud of condensation when Prescott exhaled. He held in his hands a tin cup of strong coffee, the steam bringing warmth to his face. Winter's death grip was loosening—nights and mornings like this were almost gone.

Spring was coming, and behind it was the third summer of the war. It would be a summer of decision, Prescott thought. He and Abby had talked of it often in the last five weeks. The action would begin anew. Hooker was the man in charge of the Army of the Potomac—had been since January. Prescott only knew what he had heard about Hooker, and most of it wouldn't be complimentary in polite society.

The nightmares of the Wheatfield at Sharpsburg still came, though not as frequently. They still troubled him, and he wondered how he would respond when battle came. He thought there was a chance he would not see action again. Lee was proving to be a formidable general, and so far, the succession of Federal commanders had been disappointing.

The papers were full of editorials criticizing Lincoln and the war effort and now there was the Conscription Act. The rumblings of discontent were coming from people in the North, and if Lee continued to have success this spring, yes, the summer would bring a resolution.

Prescott took another drink of his coffee and moved around on the front porch. He was restless, having to wait here during March while Stallard traveled east to meet with Fitzroy and finalize plans for the gold's trip across the ocean. The wait had been beneficial in helping Abby recover from her ordeal, and Prescott himself now felt refreshed from the difficult time of the trip up north, the ambush on the trail, and the rescue from Smythe. The papers had been filled with details of the massive fire that had destroyed the foundry and killed four workers and the owner. The transfer of the gold that night and the next day had gone without incident.

The two wagons were in separate barns in different parts of the city, and the gold was loaded into the two drummer wagons. With Stallard and Abby driving one team and Prescott and Brison the other, they had rendezvoused and taken a road south to Danville, a town located on the Illinois-Indiana border. From there, they had traveled east until they reached Indianapolis, then it was on up to the main road heading into Cleveland, near Lake Erie. But they had never reached the city. Stallard had taken them off onto another road, which led to another road that took them to this farmhouse, not two miles from the lake. And there they remained while Stallard went east.

Brison had been concerned about any effort to track down the two wagons and the contents, but no search parties had come. The farmhouse belonged to Stallard and was worked by a family of recent immigrants from Europe. They were told to farm the land and take care of the house until they had saved up enough money to purchase it. They were a hardworking family, whose efforts were only exceeded by their desire not to know anything about Stallard's business. Prescott and Abby were posing as husband and wife, and Brison was the handyman and business partner to Stallard.

The last few weeks had been a welcome diversion from the war and from what Prescott was facing. He had attempted to suggest he travel with Stallard back to Philadelphia, but he had been rebuffed. The opportunity to gain the identity of Stallard's source in the government was strong, but he could not push the South Carolinian for fear of suspicion. And so they waited.

He felt a presence on the porch with him.

"One of the last cold mornings," Brison said, his own coffee causing steam to rise to his face.

"I must commend you, Andrew," Prescott said. "You haven't once asked me why we don't just drive off with the gold and arrest Stallard when he returns, which should be soon. We could get him to reveal his conspirators in exchange for not hanging him in the Old Capitol Prison."

"You know he would never give us the information," Brison replied.

"Southern gentlemen honor their compatriots with silence."

"He's a remarkable man. He could have served the Confederacy better in another position, I believe. It's a day I don't look forward to, when we have him arrested. But we have our duty, and that duty is clear."

"Before he left, he never asked about Smythe's accusation to me when they took us in the house," Prescott said.

"I pondered that when you told me the story. He must suspect. We must be careful when he returns, though the fact that we'll still be here should give him less cause for concern."

"Unless he knows that we're waiting for his ally in Washington. The president only told me that he suspected someone in the upper levels of the administration, perhaps even a cabinet member."

"He didn't tell me, either," Brison said, catching a glimpse from Prescott. "When he sent me after you, I'll tell you I thought I was crazier than a loon to accept the assignment. But as I have saved your backside on a few occasions here, I feel I have served my purpose."

"You've saved our efforts. All things considered, they'll probably make you a general because of this." He clamped a hand on Brison's shoulder.

"We still have a long ride ahead of us."

"That we do." Prescott nodded as he took the last of his coffee.

April 9, 1863

Two days later, a warm wind came through the country. Prescott and Abby took a ride over to the edge of the large lake and watched huge flocks of birds take to the shoreline and ride the breeze. It was warm enough that in the afternoon sun, the pair had to unbutton the tops of their tunics when they were at a standstill.

Prescott was riding a sorrel he had purchased on their wagon trip from Indianapolis north. Abby's ride was a draft horse from the farm. He had a gentle nature, and since she was new to riding, he was ideal, although his size caused her some anxiety. They stopped on a tree-lined hill so they could look out over the shoreline and the blue expanse sweeping on both sides of their view north.

"Except for the Atlantic, of course, this is the largest body of water I have ever seen," she said. They sat upon a blanket, a basket with bread and jam keeping one corner in place. "Riding on the train out from the East, you miss much of the country."

"I always prefer riding myself over taking the train, if I'm not in a hurry," he said. "You become acquainted with the land. You understand it. You smell the changes . . . you can feel it, too, on your backside as the miles move by." He laughed, more so when he saw that she was smiling. The weeks following the rescue had been a godsend. The ordeal had left her sullen, tired. She had said little for a while and just moved along with the group.

Prescott had comforted her when he could, but he mostly let her be. The farm had been a tonic, and gradually, despite the dreary days of March, he had seen the brightness in her eyes return. Now she looked more beautiful than ever. It made telling her what he had decided all the more difficult. Now was not the time, the moment too lovely.

"The war seems far away from here." She looked into his face. "I don't think it is ever far from you."

"Each time I look at you, it slips away a little more."

"I even forget why we're here, sometimes, especially like today when we're alone, no Parker, no Andy . . ."

"Andy? He lets you call him Andy?" he teased.

"Does that make you jealous?" she mused.

"If I ever used a name other than Andrew or Brison, he'd call me out for pistols at dawn. And that prospect I would much rather avoid."

They both laughed for a moment, then without another word, she leaned over and kissed him softly on the lips.

When she pulled away, her face carried concern. "What's going to happen now?"

"When Parker returns, we'll find out what he has for plans to move the gold east. It will be difficult with spring rains, but it will be best to avoid the trains or main roads."

"I meant about us?"

"You know I love you, Abby."

"Yes . . . my fear is that we'll not have time together."

"The war will not last forever. I believe this summer could see it come to a resolution."

"Mr. Lincoln doesn't seem to think so, calling for a draft of troops. When this . . . assignment . . . is over, you'll want to return to your regiment?"

"It will be my duty. They went through hell at Antietam, and they'll be in the thick of it come summer. Parker talks about the South's cause, its divine soul that is self-determination. I look at this war from our side, and I see two reasons why my life or thousands of others may be sacrificed. I see a people enslaved that are meant to be free, and I see a country still shy of ninety years old, founded on the words of great men who said all men were created equal. Well, it's time we lived by those words, and we'll not be able to if the Confederacy is allowed to continue. The British or the French or someone will find their way over here, and our country could very well die."

"I'm scared of losing you," she said softly.

"Would you feel the same way about me if we rode off tomorrow . . . knowing I turned my back on my country?"

"No."

"Would our time together ever be as sweet as the last weeks have been?"

She shook her head, tears forming at the edges of her eyes.

"The army can save the Union and make us whole again," he said. "And I can be a party who did more than his share. That's what I want to take from this time."

"I'm not normally a selfish person, but I find myself increasingly more so when it comes to a certain lieutenant from Massachusetts."

"You'll always have my heart." He returned her soft kiss from before, touching the side of her face. He felt the wind brush wisps of her hair against the back of his hand. He could tell her now, but it was not the time. This day would be another small gift to her.

April 23, 1863

The day Stallard returned from Philadelphia, it was raining and chilly, running counter to his mood. He was jovial, slapping Prescott and Brison on their shoulders and kissing the back of Abby's hand with enthusiasm.

All three of them were taken aback by his manner, but they found reassurance in it, and the entire party had a glorious meal set forth by the wife of the Dutchman—baked beans, pan-fried chicken, fresh bread, boiled potatoes, and an apple pie that had been baking when Stallard rode up to the house.

The conversation, with the family present, was forced to be a long dissertation by Stallard on the goings-on in Philadelphia and the war in general. Burnside had blundered his way on something being called the "mud march" and had been replaced by Joe Hooker, and both the Army of the Potomac and the Army of Northern Virginia were still eyeballing each other across the Rappahannock River at Fredericksburg, Virginia. The politicians in Washington were clamoring for action, and Stallard said he felt something was going to happen soon.

Following the evening meal, the three principals retired to the parlor on the house's opposite side from the kitchen and sat in front of the fire, a glass of whiskey each. Abby and the husband and wife were in the kitchen, cleaning up after the meal.

Stallard's arm had healed well, and he said there was some discomfort, but he was gradually getting his strength back. He said something about being glad that spring had arrived, for he hated the north's cold winters. The room fell silent for a few minutes as each man savored his drink. When the silence ended, it was Brison who broke it.

"I suppose this is as good a time as any. Might you let us know what went on in Philadelphia and how soon we will be heading east?"

Stallard leaned forward and a smile came. "Our negotiations with the English are complete. We'll send them three-quarters of what we have now, then, upon England's political and military pressure being brought upon Lincoln, we'll send the final payment when a treaty is signed and the Confederacy's survival is assured. The shipments will be sent out of Philadelphia on a northern merchant ship. I have assurances from people I know that our shipment will be protected out of Philadelphia, but it will be up to us to get it safely there."

"When are we supposed to move?" Prescott asked.

"The entire venture swings on a hinge with General Lee. If there comes another victory, the pressure will build. As resentment grows over the Conscription Act, the pressure will grow. As Lincoln and the politicians in Washington yell for a defeat of the South, the pressure will strangle Hooker. And as the kettle rumbles from within, selected men in the British Parliament will bring us absolution. Victory will belong to us, and the war will be over." He looked over at Prescott directly. "And the killing will be over."

Prescott nodded in response.

"There's still the matter of the Federal Army—remnants of it are all across the North—not to mention, the militia is very active in Pennsylvania," Brison said.

"We could bring it down from Canada into New York, use the canals," Prescott said.

"Secrecy would be more of a problem, changing methods of transportation," Brison countered. "It might be safer because of less contact with soldiers, but the route is longer and each change of port complicates the equation."

"Spoken like an educated man," Stallard said. "Where did you attend?"

"University of Vermont in Burlington, but I never finished. Never took to book learning completely. Too quiet—not enough action."

"Why did you not join the Yankee army?" Stallard replied. "Seems to be plenty of action there, though I dare say not in the Yankees' favor!" He laughed heartily.

"I prefer to die on my own terms. I saw Manassas from the hilltops, much like the elite of Washington. Damn fools running around like chickens, shitting in their pants as they ran back to the city. And I read about Shiloh, Antietam, and Fredericksburg, and how men charged into fire from entrenched positions and were butchered like cattle. No, I'll pick my fights, and I'll die on my terms, not on the order of some other man."

"Rarely can a man accomplish that," Stallard said. "We all have reasons for undertaking this task. Mine is simple: my home is South Carolina. It's where my family has been for generations, and it's where we'll continue. The decisions that affect my family should be made there, by people who know and love our land."

"So here we sit, a Confederate fighting to continue slavery, a Union deserter, and a fighter for hire," Prescott said. "Are we not a ragged group of souls? God, what must he be thinkin' about now?"

"He'll be thinkin' at least they're staying true to their convictions." Stallard chuckled. "The travel route, it will be through Ohio and into southern Pennsylvania and on through to Philadelphia. We may stop in Harrisburg for a time—I have friends there."

"You have friends everywhere," Brison said.

"Are these of the feminine variety?" Prescott asked.

"But of course. When we're stationed in Harrisburg, we'll finalize the plans for loading onto the ship. I don't want the gold sitting in Philadelphia. We move in, arrive, and load immediately."

The other two men nodded with approval. Stallard took another drink of his whiskey and paused to feel it nestle in with the meal. He took his glass in both hands and stared into the remaining liquid. "Contrary to my mood, I do have serious and disturbing news. I received a letter from one of the men we'd hired to impersonate the guards that night at the foundry. He slipped away well enough in the confusion, but he's been keeping watch for me in Chicago, and he has unsettling information."

"It's Smythe, isn't it?" Brison whispered.

Stallard's eyebrows went up, and he rubbed his scar. "Indeed it is."

"He's dead. Andrew, you said you saw him killed in the explosions," Prescott said.

"I said I saw him in front of the building, and after one of the explosions, I saw a body near the same spot, but I never said I saw him die." Brison leaned back into his chair.

"But we read in the papers about the fire, and it listed him among the casualties," Prescott said.

"False information could have been given to the newspapers," Stallard said. "Smythe was an influential man in that town. If he's alive . . . he'll be coming after us."

"He'll do it on his own with his own men," Brison said.

"He'll be after the gold and revenge." Stallard finished his whiskey. "The first task for us, Jackson, is for you and me to head back to Chicago and determine if this information is true. He'll have spies about, so we'll need to be careful."

Brison pointed at his chest. "Why not send me? I'm not known by Smythe or his people."

"True, but you don't know the people I do. I have many ways of gaining information. We have people we haven't yet utilized who could be of service. We must ascertain whether Smythe remains a threat. Upon our return, we'll begin the move east with the gold."

"There is still much that can stop us," Prescott said.

"But if we succeed . . . I feel confident England will change fortune in favor of the South." Stallard tapped his cane and studied the headless end by his hand. "There's another reason we must go back to Chicago. I have a debt to pay."

Prescott looked at the cane and realized Stallard's point. "There's no more gold from the source, as far as you know, and you have what you want. Why send the supplies the Indian asked for in payment? You'll never see him again, you can be sure of that."

"It's a matter of honor, even with an inferior, Jackson. He took care of my brother proper. Besides"—he pointed to the cane's top—"he has something that belongs to me."

He lay with his arm around her waist, underneath the covers. The wet day had turned into a cold, wet night, and the bed warmer had been brought out one last time—a welcome completion to the evening. Abby was already asleep. Her breaths were steady and deep. She had sighed when he had moved against her, yet remained asleep. His thoughts drifted back to what he now faced. He was not ready to tell her that not only would he and Stallard be leaving immediately, but also she would have to remain behind.

Beyond that, he dreaded even more what he needed to say—that he was going to send her away to Boston, back to her parents, until this business was done and the war was over, as well. She had been right. He would return to his unit with a commendation from the president and slaps on his back from his regiment boys. If the war continued, he would be fighting it as he had intended when he had enlisted—up front with Johnny Reb coming at him straight-on.

When the war was over, he would return to his Abby, and they would begin a life together. They would have children, and he would carry them on his shoulders on late summer afternoons. And he would teach them to ride, hunt, and fish. There would be much time for this, as he and Abby would grow old together, relishing the joy of closeness that comes with having lived a complete life together.

He climbed out of bed and took the warmer from beneath the covers, moving it to the side of the room. The floor was cold against his feet, but comfortably so, not like when winter was here. He climbed back into bed and resumed his place against her body, covered softly with a linen nightgown that still allowed him to feel her. She was facing away from him, and he kissed her gently on the back of the head, running his hand down her side and hip before placing it around her waist, pulling her close.

She murmured something in her sleep, and he thought he could see a smile come to her face.

April 27, 1863

Chicago still found itself under the effects of the mud season. The streets—the ones not of macadam—were thick with the common mixture of rainwater, mud, horse dung, and the chamber pot dumpings from above, leaving most of the secondary roads barely passable. In fact, Stallard and Prescott were now traversing a side street where five carriages were "up to the hub" and abandoned for the moment.

At the end of the street connecting with the main thoroughfare, two men were arguing over how to get a wagon and its team up onto drier ground. Their efforts were comical, with broad gestures and swear words. Prescott smiled as they struggled past on their mounts. He was pleased with the animal they had purchased for him, a fine bay he was confident would have speed on drier land. The day was sunny and cool with some clouds, and the overcoat Prescott had half-unbuttoned was warm as long as they stayed out of the wind.

They came to a small tack shop next to a livery stable, and Stallard motioned that they had reached their destination. They tied their horses up and went inside. There were two customers finishing up their business with the owner, a portly, middle-aged man already balding, with broad whiskers, who eyed the pair but showed no recognition until the first customers had left.

But as soon as the door closed and left the three alone, he started in on Stallard. "Damn you. What the hell are you doing in *my* store? The word was you were out of Chicago altogether. The old man's people with the foundry have been looking for you, and if they git word you all were here, I could lose my business or worse."

"Easy up on the reins, ol' Tom," Stallard said. "No one saw us come back into town, best as I can tell. You have nothing to fret about for now. All I desire is to talk on what has been going on while I've been away."

"Word around is you and your boys were responsible for the fire at the foundry. You know, five men died in that fire. Damn near spread to part of the city, but luckily the wind changed. Damn city is built too close together—someday you get a fire started and a good wind, and the whole city will go up. You mark my words." He stopped himself and retraced his thoughts. "You didn't start that fire, did you, Parker?"

"No. Now, I won't say we weren't there and I didn't have a fallin' out with Smythe, but I wasn't out to kill no men. We just had a business deal gone bad, is all." Stallard reached over the counter and put his hand on the owner's arm. "But I do need to know what you've been hearing about Smythe's men. Also, I've heard that Smythe's alive, even though the papers say he was one of the ones who died."

"Aye, come back here to the back of the store." The owner went to the door and placed a sign in the window saying he'd be back in an hour. "There have been some strange tales coming around about the old man."

"Smythe?" Prescott asked.

"Aye. They announced he was dead and all, but when they had the funeral, the family wasn't there. Word was the missus was too grievin' for public. Then there was a rumor she was down with consumption, but I haven't heard for sure. Then as word came the foundry would be rebuilt, that big man Smythe had with him, not the foreman, but the other—he goes by the name Joshua—he came around telling all the business folk that he would be handling the family affairs, not any lawyers. And the talk started about someone seein' Smythe, and that he was still alive and healing up from the fire and such, but I haven't seen him, and I provide plenty of leather to the foundry. I think it's just a lot of gum. Nothing to it."

"Are Joshua and his men still looking around town for me?" Stallard asked.

"Can't say one way or another."

"There must be some talking going on," Prescott said.

"They haven't been around here, I tell you," the owner implored. "I can't tell you anything more. Do me the courtesy of leavin' out the back way into the alley and head back to your horses that way. Joshua and that bunch have eyes in many places."

He pushed them out the back door and closed it.

"It takes a hell of a threat for a man to be as scared as all that," Stallard said. "And my scar is beginning to give me fits in the worse way."

"You think the rumor is true? Smythe's still alive?"

"We have to move ahead like he is."

"What now?"

"We go to the bank. I must make arrangements for the supplies to be delivered to Gray Bear. Then"—Stallard then wrapped his good arm around Prescott's shoulder—"you and I are going to find out if Smythe's alive and what his intentions are."

April 28, 1863

The night was spent at a brothel in the southeast part of the city. Stallard had taken the rest of the day to work out details for the shipment of supplies and the attachment of the wagons to the next train headed west. The scout was to separate from the trains and take the two wagons north. A single red flag was to be flown from the front of the first wagon. This is what Wilshire had agreed to with Gray Bear on that cold night back in January.

After crossing into the Montana territory, the scout would be met by Gray Bear and his men. The wagons would be turned over, and the eagle head would be returned. The scout would then return to Chicago and would be paid the second half of the agreed-upon price. The trip would be dangerous. There were a number of different tribes, and Gray Bear's influence among them might have been waning. But for the substantial money offered, the scout agreed to do the job. Stallard took the extra precaution of making the final payment contingent upon the eagle head's return.

So while Stallard disappeared into one of the establishment's back rooms, Prescott was given a canvas cot to sleep on near the kitchen. He was exhausted and slept so well he was awakened by a smiling Stallard well after sunrise. Over a large breakfast of eggs, fresh ham, and biscuits, accompanied by the harshest coffee Prescott remembered having since camp, they talked over the plans for that night.

Prescott stood in the shadows of the building, ankle-deep in mud, with a cold rain relentlessly coming down. He had spent many a miserable night in the army, both on the march and in camp, but he was hard-pressed to remember a night like this.

He bowed his head forward, and water spilled from the brim of his hat. He swore and gave a menacing glance across the alleyway to the figure opposite him. He couldn't see Stallard well, but he no doubt had a smile on his face. Five times, men had staggered along the street from the row of saloons, and five times, Stallard had held up his hand.

They were waiting for a man named Gaines, who worked for Smythe at the factory and was known to be in on most everything going on. He also had the reputation of being loose with his mouth, a trait Stallard said he found surprising. Smythe was not one to tolerate such a manner. But then he had remembered that Gaines was Smythe's brother-in-law, and it made sense. Even Smythe was subject to the demands of a wife who wanted to further a younger brother's position.

Prescott heard a soft whistle and saw a man walking on his side of the street. The figure he took to be Gaines was attempting to make his way, at first trying to avoid the deep mud, but then seeing it was impossible, starting in straight through. Prescott checked the street and found it empty as Gaines reached his position. Two quick steps, and the sound of a revolver hammer being cocked brought Gaines to a stop.

"This way or you're dead." Prescott pulled the man from the street and down between two buildings. There was no protest from

Gaines, for he felt the cold metal against his neck. Stallard followed close behind as they hurried along the alley and through a door into a storage room. Prescott pushed Gaines up against the wall while Stallard turned up the lantern they had lit in preparation before beginning their wet vigil.

"I ain't got but a half eagle on me," Gaines said.

Prescott jabbed the gun into Gaines's ear, drawing an exclamation of pain. Gaines's eyes widened in fear when he saw Prescott's face, then shifted to Stallard, who now had a hunting knife, blade upturned and just under the foundry man's nose.

"What . . . what do you want of me?" he asked. "Smythe is dead and you all got the gold, so why are you here?"

"You talk to us, Gaines. Why would we be back here, standing in the rain, middle of the night, pulling you off the street and stuck in this drafty, cold storeroom with the likes of you?" Stallard hissed. "We want information, and you're the best source around. We mean to have answers before we leave, or they'll find you with your guts spread out on the floor."

"I'll tell you whatever you want to know, but"—Gaines had long ago given up on being brave, except when it came to money—"you can't make me tell you without, uh, compensation."

"Aren't you just a huckleberry over a persimmon?" Stallard said. "I do believe he has underestimated us, asking for money." He nodded at Prescott, who then brought Gaines's arm farther up until his hand was between the shoulder blades.

Gaines yelped in pain, begging them to stop before they broke his arm. Prescott eased off but kept the gun against Gaines's neck and his arm high on his back.

Stallard continued, "We don't have time to bicker about this. You answer, and you answer without pondering. You understand?"

Gaines nodded.

"Where's Smythe?" Stallard asked.

"He's dead, I told you. He died in the fire—" Gaines was cut off by a blow to his groin, and he slid down to the floor. As he gasped for breath on his knees, Stallard brought the knife's tip underneath the man's chin.

"That was your last chance to answer us straight," he said. "Tell us the truth or we'll be done with you presently."

Gaines's breathing became steadier as he recovered. "All right, just leave me alone, please."

Stallard lowered himself down so he was directly in Gaines's face. He kept the knife under the man's chin. "Where's Smythe?"

"I really don't know."

"But you know he's alive."

"I saw him not too long after the fire. He was in poor condition and had a powerful amount of hate in his soul. The only time I saw him, he was yellin' about how he would hunt you down until the devil himself would come for him. He killed the guards that you all had tied up. Like I said, he was in poor condition, lost an eye and busted up his knee. Don't know whether he'll be a gimp or not, only saw him the one time."

"Again, where is he now?"

"Joshua was keeping him at a house away from the foundry. But that was some weeks ago, and I was told to take care of my sister for a spell. You know, make sure she and the children were given what they needed."

"And a brother would be perfect for that, and it would keep you out of the inner circle," Stallard said almost to himself. He pressed the knife against Gaines's throat but not enough to break the skin. "Is he still at that house?"

"I don't think so. I heard he and a group of his men had taken out after you. He's got men all over, you know. He knew you all had headed south to Danville, but that's all I know."

"How many of them were there?"

"Ten or so. I don't know for sure. I tell you, that's all I know."

"Anything about where they went after Danville?"

Gaines looked away into the dark of the storeroom and held his breath a moment. Stallard pushed him up against the wall, shoving Prescott to the side. He brought the blade across Gaines's throat, bringing a hint of blood.

"Parker?" Prescott said.

"You *know* more, you bastard." Stallard's eyes bore into Gaines. "Smythe would let his wife know about where he was going. He might not tell her his business, but he would for sure give her a general idea of his whereabouts. And that would be relayed through *you*. Wouldn't it?"

Gaines opened his mouth, but no words came forth.

"*Now*, you little lickfinger"—Stallard was spitting the words out, spittle hitting Gaines on the face—"or the next person we talk to is your sister."

"All right, damn it. Leave my sister be. She don't know what this is all about. She knew you all had done him wrong, but nothing as far as the particulars."

"Talk!"

"He sent a message, came by personal courier up from Danville," Gaines said. "It said he was heading up to the Cleveland area. He had gotten a wire from Cleveland. He had scouts along the main pikes between Chicago and Philadelphia, looking for a couple of wagons and you two. He was headed up that way."

"Damn!" Prescott whispered.

"How many days ago was this?" Stallard asked.

"Three . . . no, four days ago, when she got the message," Gaines said with trepidation. He paused for a second while Stallard took in the news. "That's all I know. God's truth."

Prescott started to speak, but Stallard shook his head.

"This is how things are going to be," Stallard directed Gaines. "I could kill you right here and now, and there wouldn't be a pig around to mourn you. But I don't wage vengeance against someone who hasn't directly done me wrong. So we're going to let you go, but I don't trust you. As soon as we're gone, you'll be sending a wire off to Smythe in Cleveland faster than greased lightning. So you take heed of my words. I have friends who owe me many favors. I find out you've been letting Smythe know about us being here, I'll have one of my friends pay you a visit, an unhealthy one. Then they'll visit your sister. Are you clear on this?"

"Yes." Gaines did little to mask his fear.

"We're going to take what money you've got and tie you up," Stallard said. "You can tell them all you were robbed."

Prescott tied Gaines's hands and feet, then gagged him. Stallard turned down the light, and they gathered their belongings and moved out the door.

Stallard stopped before leaving. "Two more things," he said. "Don't raise a fuss until the morning, and be of good cheer. If Smythe has a bad time of it, your sister will be a very rich woman, and she'll need a brother to help her run the business."

And with that, he was gone.

Chapter Thirty-Three

Present Day
August 3

"Frankly, we don't know what to call it—a professional hit, a carjacking attempt, a robbery and murder." Griffin sounded frustrated on the phone to Sparks. "There were valuables taken from the body, but he was shot through the driver's side window and the car was just the right distance from the stop sign that another car appears to have been in front.

"The door had been opened and the car put in Park and shut off. Even with his lack of field experience, I'm sure he wouldn't have let someone walk up to his car on an empty street in the middle of the night—unless he was distracted."

"The chance of something like this happening right now, you know, is pretty long." Sparks was standing next to his car at the Gettysburg National Military Park Visitors' Center. Coulthard had gone on ahead to the restroom, and Sparks had told her he needed to check in with Griffin. "My gut says it had to be Richardson."

"My men on Richardson didn't report any unusual activity or calls. No mention of Goldberg by name or inference."

"He's still the prime, though."

"We'll be on it," Griffin said.

"There's another reason I called. The park ranger believes she found the third letter."

Griffin paused. "Is she sure?"

"Sounded so. I'm about to see for myself. I need what backup you can muster from Philly here by this afternoon. If this is the real thing, I want to set up an exchange for Jennifer as soon as possible."

"I'll have a team there in less than five hours. Call me back on my cell phone with the location. I'll be en route."

"You up to it physically?" Sparks asked.

"This is Jennifer we're talking about."

Jennifer finished eating her breakfast brought in by the man whom she only knew as her abductor and who was responsible for the death of her lover, but who had then come to save her life when she was about to be raped. The whole situation was emotionally draining.

He was talking less now that they were out of the house. He was on edge and was making notations between trips outside to use a cell phone. He was planning something, but he was careful to keep her out of it.

She didn't mind, for despite the sleep, fatigue was with her always now. The clear, regular cycle of days was blurred behind the opaqueness of captivity. She knew not how many days she had been held—the experience would be remembered collectively, as if it had happened in one long day.

He was sitting in the corner making notes into a book, a baseball cap pushed back to reveal more of the blond hair. He had not spoken for an hour and a half. She could tell because she had watched an entire talk show and half of another. Today's topics had been married women confessing lesbian affairs and hot fashions for the fall.

"How long are we going to stay here?" she asked.

He finished writing for a minute and looked up. "You'll be back with your father by the end of today." His voice was calm but there was an emotion she could not read behind it. "I have decided to cut my losses and move on. This was a bad concept with bad decision-making."

"I don't know what to think. I don't believe you would walk away without being paid. You've seemed very clear on that. I also know you're saying that just to keep my cooperation."

"You're logical for a young woman, if I may hedge into sexist territory." He smiled. It carried no warmth from behind the dark glasses. "Without an extended explanation—I have been making some calls to people I know, and I've found out my employer intends to not fulfill his part of our agreement."

"I don't understand."

"He intends to kill me after he has acquired the gold."

"Oh."

"Unfortunately, it happens in my line of work. That's why you double-check with whom you deal."

"Why not just leave me somewhere and then call my father with where I am?"

"There's something I need to tell your father face-to-face. And I want to make sure you get into his hands safely. My employer will be a dangerous man for as long as he's alive."

Jennifer's heart fluttered, and she felt cold.

"You're going to kill him yourself," she said.

"'Mine honor is my life; both grow in one, take honor from me and my life is done,'" he said. "Richard the Third . . . no, Second."

"There's no honor in murder."

"Ah, . . . 'an honorable murderer, if you will, for naught I did in hate, but all in honor.'"

"And what tragedy was that from?"

"*Othello.*"

"You can recite Shakespeare all you want, it doesn't change the fact that there's no honor in murder."

"Men and women murder during times of war. Governments execute people for crimes," he said. "Are these more honorable because they're official actions?"

She didn't respond.

"Keep those beliefs close to your heart, Miss Sparks," he added. "The world needs more people like you, not less. Another reason to take you back to your father."

"Let the authorities bring your employer to justice."

"Justice belongs to those who hold the power."

"Where was that from?"

"Myself . . . though I suppose someone once said it more eloquently than I."

She managed a smile. "No matter, you should just leave. You can relay the message through me."

"Some things must be done directly."

"What do you have to say to my father?"

"I'll apologize."

Sparks and Coulthard met with Munson in a conference room located within the Cyclorama Center, the building just a few hundred feet away from the copse of trees that marked the high-water mark of the Confederacy.

The building, aside from administrative offices, housed the Gettysburg Cyclorama with *The Battle of Gettysburg*, a 360-degree painting by nineteenth-century French artist Paul Philippoteaux that depicted a view of Pickett's Charge.

Sparks and Coulthard had arrived at the visitors' center nearby and had been informed as to where to meet Munson. She had kept them waiting for forty-five minutes, and Sparks was agitated by the time she appeared.

"We were growing concerned about the delay," he said.

"I couldn't take the letter out without written permission from the superintendent, and he's away. I could get in trouble, even if you're with the FBI," Munson said apologetically. "I can't even bring it out of the storage room officially, and I can't make copies—same rule—so I transcribed it all and made copies. I'll be able to show you the original by tomorrow. I hope this is OK."

"You were able to read the handwriting?" Coulthard asked.

"Yes. It looked like the handwriting on the copy of the letter you left with me, though I'm not an expert," Munson said.

"For now, I guess that will do." Sparks gestured his reluctant acceptance. "Did you copy everything down on the letter, left nothing out?"

"Absolutely everything."

"Let's see what Stallard wrote," Sparks said.

June 28, 1863

Cassias,

Circumstances have grown desperate. We have brought the shipment to within a day's train ride from Philadelphia, but we have suffered injury. Now comes word, as I am sure you have read, that General Lee has brought his army into the north. I would imagine General Hooker will be coming to meet him somewhere in Pennsylvania.

I believe the time is at hand for providence's decision. This coming battle will decide the war. I feel compelled to join with my brothers, if they will allow. If fate is to decide against me, then you and Lawrence together will find good use for the fruits of our family's labors.

I have sent Lawrence one letter and a second to my law firm in Boston with instructions it is to be delivered to my brother upon the end of the war. When you receive this letter, guard it well, for the information herein, along with the information I have sent to Lawrence, will reveal to you the hiding place.

What you seek can be found where the owner of the Den lives. His house is strong, as is any house that is built with love and strength—for the foundation can withstand any hatred and bitterness.

God bless you, sir.

Parker

"This is it?" Coulthard asked with disappointment. "There's nothing specific here to tell us anything."

"It has to be the correct letter. The odds are immense. I mean, look at the name and the date. It fits perfectly," Munson stressed.

"It does fit, and I know you're correct about the house, Brenda," Sparks said.

"What house? How does this tie into the house we stopped at outside of town?" Coulthard was more hopeful now.

"You have to remember what puzzle pieces we already have. We have the first letter that gave us Gettysburg and the biblical phrase, 'He showed unto him all the kingdoms of the world in a moment of time.' The devil tempting Jesus. The Devil's Den is one of the most prominent locations on this battlefield. It's too much to be a coincidence."

"But you said the name wasn't given to the area until after the battle." Coulthard looked at Munson.

"It's disputed when and where the name came about," Munson said, "but there's some evidence the area had the name beforehand. It's possible the locals, or at least some of them, called it by that name."

"All right, then how does this letter tie in with the location?" Coulthard asked.

"Look at the last paragraph—'what you seek can be found where the owner of the Den lives.' I think he's talking about the person who owned Devil's Den at the time," Sparks said.

Munson nodded. "The land that encompassed what we know as Devil's Den was a tract owned by a man named John Houck. The ridge above the Den is known as Houck's Ridge. They were a prominent family in Gettysburg at the time. I'd have to check, but I think the family lived on Baltimore Street. Anyway, the family, or one of his children, was building that house out off the Emmittsburg Pike when the battle occurred. The Park Service has been in possession of it for a number of years, even though there wasn't any fighting directly on the grounds."

"Why was the Park Service interested in it?" Coulthard asked.

"Because the land around it was used as a staging area for the Confederate activities on the first day," Munson said. "I think there was even some evidence that Lee himself stopped briefly at the house before moving farther up the road toward the town. The Park Service has been researching the house's history in hopes of adding it permanently to the park. When I told Agent Sparks here what the letter said, he asked me straight off who the owner of the Devil's Den land was in 1863, where he lived, and if the house was still standing."

"She was aware of the house, so she mentioned it to me on the phone," Sparks said. "That's why we made the quick drive out there while she was double-checking."

"Could it have been in the house downtown?" Coulthard asked.

"That house is gone, so if the gold had been hidden inside that house, it's long gone," Munson said.

"So the house outside of town could be it," Coulthard said.

Sparks agreed. "The house was under construction at the time. Stallard must have been acquainted with the Houck family. Why he hid it there we may never know. All I do know is that our best chance now is at that house—our best chance to save Jennifer."

"So, we go search the grounds and the house?" Coulthard asked.

"No, we start in the basement of the house," Sparks said.

"Why there?"

"Look at the last line of the letter," Sparks said. "'His house is strong, as is any house that is built with love and strength—for the foundation can withstand any hatred and bitterness.' The foundation, I'll bet, is where we'll find what we're looking for."

Chapter Thirty-Four

Through the glasses, the house and barn were a pile of cinders, charred by intense heat. There was no smoke, and the land appeared untouched by flames.

The land had been spared—there were young crops peeking out from under the topsoil on the east forty acres—but there was nothing left of the farm itself. Stallard dropped the glasses and rested his forehead on the eyepiece.

"We're too late," he said.

They were lying on a ridge a half mile southwest of the farm. They had come along the lake road and backtracked west of the farm. They had encountered no one other than an occasional farmer or traveler.

There had been no quick glance of recognition, no quick movement for a pistol—their way had been clear. But now the reason why lay before them in the small valley. Smythe and his men had found the farm, and Prescott knew that for the rest of his life, he would remember this day.

"I don't see any activity around the farm—it looks empty." Prescott had taken the glasses away for himself. "I hope to God they took Andrew and Abby with them and didn't . . ."

"Damn them to hell for this." Stallard got to his feet. "Someone in the town will know. A fire large enough to burn the house and barn would have been seen for some distance. Let's look at the grounds first, and then we'll move into town."

The house and barn were burned to charcoal and ash. Even the brick chimney had been reduced to rubble, a loose grouping of individual bricks spread about the grass. The day was overcast, gray with the threat of rain. Normally one could smell the prospects, but not here, where the odor of burnt wood hung in the nostrils.

In the past months, Prescott had seen the ghastly work of war, the horrible mixture of results from shot and mini ball. When a battle began, the land took on a persona unique to its own birthright, its own version of hell.

For his regiment at Antietam, it had been a field of corn on an open ridge of land above a town. For others that day, it had been a sunken road just south of that field. For others, it had been attempting to cross a bridge in the face of a hail of fire from above. Each piece of land would carry its own memories for the men who were there. That was why the land would never be the same for those who followed. Would they look over the field of corn and not hear the cries?

Would it be the same for this land they stood on now? Prescott wondered this as he walked the grounds. He concluded that someday a house would be rebuilt on this land—a barn, too. Life would continue, and the land would eventually hide this small event.

"Jackson!"

Prescott ran around to the back side of the foundation, over by a stand of trees. Stallard stood among them with his head down, and as he approached, Prescott could see what had drawn the southerner's cry. Four fresh graves were laid out in a row with simple headstones of wood. They bore the names of the family that had lived in the house—the husband, his wife, and the two children.

The anguish rose from Prescott's chest, and he leaned against a tree. Stallard said nothing, but he lowered himself to one knee and soft words of prayer drifted up on the wind through the trees. A few minutes passed before either spoke—then it was Stallard.

"There was no reason for this. They were nothing to him—no value. They weren't part of this business."

"You know Smythe . . . but this is cold-blooded even for him," Prescott said. "Do you suppose they have Brison and Abby?"

"There's nothing here to tell," Stallard replied.

"Then we go to town and find out if the neighbors heard or saw what happened." Prescott had turned to walk back to their horses when he caught sight of a lone rider coming from a back road. From the manner of the rider and the horse's color, he knew who it was.

"They came in the night, as you would expect," Brison said with bitterness. "Earlier in the day, I was riding along the main road just outside of town, and I saw the lot of them at the general store. There were about ten of them, I believe, but I never got a right count."

They were standing again in the trees by the graves—a flask of whiskey from Stallard's saddlebag was being passed around. The first question out of Prescott had been about Abby's safety, and Brison had smiled and nodded.

"What happened here?" Stallard asked.

"I made it back here and hitched up the teams for the wagons," Brison said. "Before Abby and I left, I instructed the Andersons to tell them that we had left two days before, headed for the east, and that we had said something about New York. Abby and I took the wagons to that old farm on Styler Pike, the one that heads directly for Cleveland. The house and barn are empty, and you can't see the barn from the road. It was a chance, but we would not be able to outrun them. I made sure things were right there, and then I rode back to the Andersons. My God, Jackson, I was too late when I returned. It was a dark night, no moon, had to make my way slow through the thickets. I saw them fixin' to ride out, and I could see the bodies in the light from the fires."

"He's gone insane," Stallard said.

"Which way did they head out?" Prescott asked.

"They took the main road heading to Cleveland," Brison said. "They never gave the farm Abby was at a look."

"They'll know after a while that the trail is cold," Stallard said. "He perhaps will leave a man behind here to cover all possibilities. I would be much obliged if there would be suggestions forthcoming."

"We move, take a wide berth to the south, and take back roads east in Pennsylvania. He may split men up, but he cannot cover every pike between here and Philadelphia." Brison looked at Prescott, his eyes a flash of consternation.

Prescott nodded slightly. "I agree. The main roads to Cleveland and out of the city to the east will be too dangerous. We move south and east. It will take more time, but we'll still arrive in Philadelphia by the end of the month."

Stallard was silent for a time, and the other two let him be.

"I agree with you gentlemen. I have contacts with the railroads, but Smythe'll have spies along the main lines," Stallard said. "We'll take the gold into Philadelphia ourselves as we had planned, we'll just take a more southerly route."

"There's something I must do first," Prescott said. "And then I'll meet up with you all along the way."

May 4, 1863

They stood away from the crowd in a small room off the main station area. Abby's arms were around him, holding on as if the pressure would take them away in a stolen breath. He felt her body shake from crying, but there was no sound for the commotion. He was sending her back to New England until this business, and perhaps the war, was over.

She had protested with loud words and had even struck him in the face for his arrogance at telling her she had no choice. Stallard and Brison had kept their distance, creating work that took them away. After a time, she had given in with bitterness, and while the other two took the wagons on a road directly south into the interior of Ohio, he had taken her into the city where they had stayed a night at a hotel.

"Is last night the final time we'll ever be together?" Her question surprised him, for she was talking of the passion of the night before. It had been deliberate and savoring.

"I can lie and say for certain it was not," he said, holding her chin in his hand, "but I owe you the world, and until I can give it to you, I'll give you only what I have—the truth. I don't know what the days ahead hold. With God's grace, I'll survive the war, and we can begin our lives together. That's what I'm hopeful for."

She began to speak, but thought better and remained looking at him.

"And I have a very resourceful man with me," he continued. "I have seen his quality in few other men. They're men of valor and honor, and they have a most peculiar way of staying alive. It's the damnedest thing, if you'll pardon my words."

She smiled at him through her tears. "He saved my life at the farm, and he helped save me at the foundry."

"Darling, he has saved my life in such numbers it's becoming near embarrassing. I do hope I'm afforded the opportunity to respond in kind."

A laugh came to both of them, and it eased the burden in their hearts.

A whistle blew from the engine up the line, and the shouting surrounding them reached a new crescendo. Prescott moved her to the platform and near the car's steps. When he looked again into her face, he saw that it had changed. Gone were the tears, and she looked at him with the determination he had grown to love. It comforted him to see her strength return.

"You listen to me well, Jackson Prescott," she said. "I have never given a man my heart as I have you. I have designs that you would be my husband, and I charge you with bringing yourself back to New England when this is done. I'll wait for you to come walking up the path to my doorstep so we can walk on the beach, and I'll be full of anger with you if you don't. You have a debt to pay to me, and that debt is for me to see you as an old man on my front porch." She paused. "I love you."

He kissed her. "And I love you."

May 7, 1863

Prescott's return to his comrades passed without incident, except for the newspaper reports he learned of on his way. Stallard would welcome the news and would want to press on, of that Prescott was sure, for a battle had been fought near Fredericksburg in Virginia and again Lee had prevailed.

It was late in the afternoon when Prescott rode into the small camp east of Columbus, and Brison and Stallard greeted him with a meal of beans and dried beef. Before he even sat down, Prescott handed the newspapers over to Stallard.

"Conclusions are hard to come by when working with Yankee papers, I have found," Stallard finally said.

"Seems clear enough to me." Prescott spoke with a large mouthful of beans. "Hooker got tired of waiting around across the Rappahannock and swung around to the west to flank Lee."

"A sound enough strategy," Brison interjected.

"But then your General Lee turned around and did likewise to old 'Fightin' Joe,'" Prescott said. "The papers say the two armies are still engaged and there might be more of a scrap. Of course, the last story there was written a day ago or so. The last heavy fighting, it says, was four days ago. Don't know what has happened since."

"Lee commanded the field after the third. My God, gentlemen, the papers here are howling and all wrathy with themselves over Hooker's bungling." Stallard sat himself down without letting his eyes leave the papers. "General Lee will not be defeated! That man is some general, of most strong convictions. A great strategist."

Brison caught Prescott's eye. "I would believe his men had something to do with it."

"This is disconcerting news." Stallard's enthusiasm lessened. "There's a report here that General Jackson was wounded. That's troubling. I do hope he's not seriously injured. But what this means, gentlemen, is that the superiority of the Southern soldier is clear. I do believe this summer we'll see General Lee take it to the Federals . . . with all due respect, Jackson."

"Can't say I can argue the point based on what has happened," Prescott agreed. "Though he was well-bloodied at Sharpsburg. I was there, Parker, remember. We near enough had him in a fix there. I thought now since Hooker was taking over he would move swiftly, and he did, but I expected better results. Lincoln, no doubt, is beside himself now."

"The opportunity is nearing for us to exert political pressure." Stallard let his excitement splash forth like fast water over rocks. "With another victory, and our first payment in hand, England will begin to make demonstrations, and they will be howling in the streets of New York, Boston, and Philadelphia. Lincoln will be forced to pursue a political solution. The Confederacy will gain legitimacy with the rest of the world."

"Not as long as slavery is her mother," Brison chided.

"Coming from a mercenary, a moral rebuke is highly inappropriate, sir," Stallard retorted, but with a smile. "I'm counting that you're incorrect."

"Would not be my first error," Brison said.

"I'm concerned about us even reaching Philadelphia, let alone getting the shipment across the Atlantic." Prescott finished his first helping of beans. "There are three of us, and ten or so of Smythe's men."

"That's another of our reasons for taking a more southerly route to the east," Stallard said. "We'll head east to Pittsburgh, then on to Harrisburg and then to Philadelphia. I have business associates in Columbus—men like yourself, Brison, perhaps not as accomplished, but men who will do dangerous work for a price. And I'll make sure they're handy with a pistol."

"Would they be from this group that their actor Booth mentioned?" Prescott asked.

"That they would."

"Can we trust them?" Prescott retrieved another plate of beans, knowing he would pay in the morning, but preferring to have a full belly now.

"For the cause, they will help us."

"For our lives, I hope you're correct." Brison pulled out his pouch of rags and made ready to clean his rifle.

May 17, 1863

The road leading into Pittsburgh was rough and made travel difficult for the two drummer's wagons, each pulled by a four-horse team, with Prescott driving one and Stallard the other. Brison stayed away, never close to the teams for very long during the days. He was scouting ahead, to either side, and from behind, with skilled precision. But he was not alone. Three men rode with him.

Prescott didn't know their full names, only the names given by their fathers—Calvin, Billy, and John. All were in their twenties. The first was a clerk in a dry goods store, the second was a simple laborer who said he found regular work, and the third was a butcher by trade who doubled as the snow warden during the winter months.

Stallard had ridden into Columbus armed with knowledge given to him by the actor Booth. Two days later, he had returned with the three men. They openly professed to being members of their own group loosely connected to the Knights of the Golden Circle and were eager to help with the transfer of the wagons to Philadelphia. Stallard had impressed upon them the urgency of the matter for the Confederacy and offered to pay them five hundred dollars apiece in gold upon completion of the journey.

They also were aware of Smythe, his men, and the danger ahead. Prescott looked to them for any sign of interest in what was so valuable in the wagons, but the three showed a singular lack of concern other than that they were helping the Confederacy.

The sun was approaching the tree line when Stallard pulled the team off the main road and into an open area that led up to the edge of some woods. He motioned to Prescott and yelled instructions that they would make camp. Within a half hour, Brison rode up, and when he reported no sign of Smythe's group, they unhitched the teams and led them to a small stream that ran through the trees.

As the light faded from the day, their fire cooking a pair of chickens purchased the day before from a farmer, the five rested from the hard day's ride.

"We won't be heading into Pittsburgh proper. It will be too dangerous." Stallard turned the chickens on a makeshift spit. "I figure Smythe will keep watch on the rail lines between here and Harrisburg. We'll definitely get to Harrisburg, but we'll go along the roundabout way."

"You didn't tell us what was in these wagons that this here fellow, Smythe, is all fired up about." The one called Calvin put his finger to the seared, browning meat over the fire. "What's the big fuss?"

"His desire is to see us stopped from getting these wagons to Philadelphia and on to England," Stallard said. "Plain and simple. President Davis desires these wagons to get through. It is utmost for the Confederacy that we succeed."

"Gold, I expect." Calvin smiled. He always seemed to talk for the three.

"We make it through, and old Jeff will see to it you boys will be heroes in the South. I expect there will be parades and such. And the women will be mighty impressed."

That notion brought smiles from the three, and they elbowed each other with delight. Prescott rose from his place at the fire and walked over to a rock where Brison was yet again cleaning his rifle in what light reached him. Behind Prescott, Stallard began a tale to entertain the three.

"How were they today?" Prescott asked, keeping his voice low.

"About what you'd expect." Brison worked a rag along the barrel of the carbine. "They're all in a fuss about being part of the war, no matter they aren't in uniform. They see glory ahead."

"Do they seem the type to take advantage of equal numbers?"

"Greed is always a strong drink, Jackson. Many who don't seem the type will kill for wealth, but these three are more interested in the South winning the war—hell, two of them were born in Virginia and North Carolina. I expect Parker will have great stories all evening about the Carolinas."

"How far do you expect we can get before we scrap with Smythe?"

"Before we get to Harrisburg. He'll have men on the main roads leading into the city, but I expect if they see us, they'll hit us as far away from any towns as possible. It will be rough on you two, that's why, beginning in the morning, we'll leave an extra man with each wagon while the third rides with me. Two men out on the move will still be useful, I think."

"When we get to Harrisburg, I'll wire Washington," Prescott said. "We should know the shipping date by then."

"Jackson." Stallard was waving Prescott back to the fire. "The meal is ready."

Brison closed the carbine's lever and walked with Prescott to the fire.

"These chickens will be some mighty fine eatin'," Calvin said.

Before Prescott and Brison reached the fire, Stallard put his arms out to stop them and led them a few steps away. "I need to ride into Pittsburgh tomorrow. I'll take Calvin, there. We need to pick up a few supplies, and I need to send a letter to Fitzroy."

"Should we continue on?" Brison asked.

"We need to keep moving, but we need all six of us here in case Smythe comes calling," Stallard replied.

"These trees and this ridge provide good protection," Prescott said. "We can hide the wagons back in here. They'll never see us from the road."

"I'll ride up at first light and be back by the afternoon," Stallard said. "And maybe we can get some miles in before sundown tomorrow. Now, let us eat before those three leave us nothing for our trouble."

May 22, 1863

The sun rode unusually high and hot on the wagons and the road was dry, but there was little wind, so the only dust in the air came from the wheels. Their pace was slow, as Prescott, in the lead, was careful to avoid any irregularities in the road that would tax the suspension. Stallard had made his trip up and back from Pittsburgh four days ago, and he had returned with correspondence from Fitzroy. The plan called for the group to stop in Harrisburg at a place just on the outskirts of the city and then contact Fitzroy so they could coordinate the shipment's arrival in Philadelphia with the departure of a ship bound for England. The letter had been dated May 6.

The traveling had been difficult, the road rutted from the spring rains gone dry. The land was ridge-filled, with streams, some with bridges, but they often had to not use them for fear of collapse. Each wagon was loaded near enough to three tons, with the gold ingots hidden beneath a false floor and the drummer's wares placed in prominence for any wandering eye.

It was well into the fourth day, and still there was no sign of Smythe or his men. Prescott estimated they were just six miles west of a town called Chambersburg, deep in the Cumberland Valley, still in Pennsylvania, but close to the Maryland border. His map lacked details, but the names of the towns along the way had been accurate and the country was beginning to flatten out. Brison's flanking duty took on greater urgency, and there had been few cheerful words in the evenings. They had been eating mostly cold smoked beef and some bread. They refrained from building a fire for fear of drawing attention.

It was just past noon and Prescott had been mulling the idea of stopping for a meal when he saw four riders on a stretch of road visible from a half mile away. They were moving at a moderate pace, not pressing hard. Prescott exchanged places with Calvin—the three had decided he was the smartest of the Columbus trio—the signal went out, and Stallard handed over the reins to Billy.

John was riding with Brison, and they were to the west of the two wagons. This Prescott knew because the pair had come into view not twenty minutes before, working their way over a ridge to the north, but heading west. Prescott swore softly to himself and issued a quick prayer that Brison had not wandered too far to be of any help.

The riders appeared out of a dip in the road just a few hundred yards in front. Their manner had not changed, except they had slowed to a canter. There were four, riding in two pairs on the left side of the road as Prescott peered from a gap under the seat. He had a pair of revolvers with him, and Calvin had his own tucked under his right leg, handle side out. He would only need to raise his leg a bit. Prescott knew Stallard would be in a similar position but also mindful of what was behind them on the road.

As they approached, now just a hundred feet away, the four riders split off and were riding four abreast across the road. Calvin pulled the team to a stop, and the riders settled in forty feet in front, blocking the road. Prescott didn't recognize any of the four. They were all armed with revolvers and carbines.

"We're all blessed with a fine day to travel." The rider second from the right moved his mount slightly ahead of the others. "Where are you all headed with all these wares?"

"We've been restin' a bit at a few towns," Calvin said cautiously, his hand next to his right leg on the seat. "What's up ahead?"

"If you go up a ways, you'll run into Chambersburg, then Cashtown a ways beyond that. What sort of wares do you all have? We might be in need of some. We have farms outside of Chambersburg."

"Well, won't likely want to take everything out here, but we'll stay around the town for a spell if you want to see what we have to sell," Calvin said. His hand was now just under his leg. Prescott could not see, but he heard the movement of horses approaching either side of the wagon from the front.

"We would just as soon see what you're carrying now," the leader said. The sound of a hammer moving into place was audible even from inside the wagon.

Not yet, Calvin. Not until the others have reached the back of the first wagon. Not yet. Prescott crouched in the middle of the bed, ready to go either way. The back entry was latched from the inside but would not last more than two or three good ax blows. And they could always just fire bullets into the wagon's brightly colored sides— the wood didn't afford much protection. He had to hope Stallard and Billy would take care of those circling behind him. He had to look to supporting Calvin.

The sounds came simultaneously—the report from a pistol and the muffled *thud* as the bullet hit. Calvin exhaled with a grunt and his arms fell to his side as he leaned back against the seat. His weight was going to take him back into the small opening behind him, but Prescott could not, dare not, pay attention.

He was already aiming his Colt from underneath the seat. He was still above the level of the horses, but his view gave him a clear shot only at the second rider, who had stayed in front with the leader. The Colt exploded in his hand and shook him, the report coming in such an enclosed place, but his aim was true, for the second rider disappeared from view.

The spring countryside became chaotic—the horses fought the harnesses and whinnied, gunfire roared from behind the wagon, men shouted. A horse and rider fell hard against the wagon, but Prescott didn't notice, his attention purely on the second man in front. As he rose through the opening, revolver in front of him, the wood to his right splintered. The leader was fighting his horse, but gaining control, reins in his left hand. Prescott fired at the leader, but missed high, his aim negated by the jerking wagon.

Cursing under his breath, he re-cocked the hammer, moving still more into the open, past Calvin, and stood up to steady himself. They were thirty feet apart when they fired together. This time the burning came to his left side and made him turn his body to the left. The leader took Prescott's bullet high in the chest or neck and fell without bracing from his mount.

Feeling his side, Prescott realized that he had been grazed by a shot. His flesh burned, but it was just on the outside of his side, below the ribs. The shooting ended abruptly, and he peered around the wagon's left side. His eyes found Stallard bending over a body in the road. With no threat there, Prescott jumped down and moved cautiously in front of his team.

The leader was clearly dead from the wound at the base of his throat. The first rider he had shot was lying in the dirt, rocking from side to side, muttering sounds. Prescott moved to him, but as he approached, the man's rocking slowed and then stopped, his eyes already vacant.

He picked up their pistols and headed back to the left side of the wagon.

"Did you get both of those two in back of here?" Prescott asked.

"Billy got one, I got the other. Billy's dead. Took one near the heart."

"That's all of them, then," Prescott said. "I didn't recognize any of them. They might not even be Smythe's men. Could have just been highwaymen. Damn, Calvin was hit, too."

They moved to the front and found Calvin lying on his right side on the seat. He was breathing, but it was fast and shallow.

"How far are we from the next town?" Prescott asked.

"Chambersburg is a few miles east of here if you want to believe the map and the word of a murderer." Stallard jumped down and motioned for Prescott to follow. When he spoke again, it was softly. "He'll not survive the trip there, I think."

"We still have to try."

They both turned at the sound of horses approaching. It was Brison and John at full gallop on the road from the west. They pulled up abruptly and then let the horses walk the final yards alongside the wagons.

"Sorry we weren't here for all the goings-on—" Brison's grin vanished in pain as he was spun out of his saddle by a rifle blast from close range. He hadn't hit the ground when John, the last of the Columbus Copperheads, took a bullet in the back as he watched in surprise as Brison was hit. Stallard and Prescott were rigid as the words came to them not as a shout, but in a conversational tone.

"I would be much obliged if you two would drop your guns and step back from them," the voice said. "You'll be dead if you don't."

In the confusion, they hadn't stopped to think if the four had been riding alone. It should have been obvious—always be wary of a flanking maneuver. Prescott was bitter with self-consternation. It was his fault—he should have recognized the danger. More so, he realized that it was his fault that Brison lay in the road.

The two dropped their revolvers at their feet and took two steps back.

"My fault," Prescott said.

"No, Jackson, it is mine."

There was a chuckle from behind them and a large figure stepped from behind the wagon, carbine leveled on the pair. He was covered in a thick layer of dust and his beard and sideburns were gray as a result. They turned to face the figure, and they both recognized him from the foundry. It was the one called Joshua.

"You two are the most difficult men I've ever had to deal with," he said. "I was pondering whether we'd ever be able to come up against you again so I could repay you for the hole in my arm. I had a wager of a few silver pieces against a new Colt that we would find you. I was beginning to fuss about losing this fine piece." He patted the revolver in his side holster.

"Where's Smythe?" Stallard asked bitterly.

"We'll meet up with him by and by," Joshua said. A second gunman came from the bushes on the road's far side. His features were softened by the same layer of dirt, but his manner was hard. Joshua motioned with his carbine. "Take a look to make sure the wagons have what we want. Be quick about it. This road gets travel, I expect, and more bodies would just spoil the fixings. Move over there." The last words were for Stallard and Prescott as he set aside his carbine, pulled out his Colt, and pushed them to the side of the road opposite the lead team.

Prescott peered down from the road's edge. There was a steep grade down through the brush for about eighty feet. The ravine was obscured from the road. It would take more than a casual look for anyone to find someone down there. He looked over and his eyes met Stallard's, each knowing they would be dead in a few minutes. Prescott's mind tried to fight the panic and come up with a plan. They both had knifes on their person, but Joshua was making sure to stay more than a lunge distance away—and his eyes had left them only twice since they had dropped their guns.

He stood between them and the front of the wagon, his back to the wagon's seat. The other gunman was finished checking the first wagon and was moving to the second. Prescott was thinking their only chance was to rush Joshua at the same time. One would die, but the other might be able to use his knife and then have a chance against the other behind the second wagon. He turned to Stallard to see if they were again thinking alike, but instead the southerner was looking at Joshua.

"It's Joshua, isn't it?" Stallard asked.

"It is."

"You know you have an opportunity here. There's enough gold here for us to make a barter. We'll give you a certain amount and you let us go. If you kill us and take the gold back to him, your, shall I say, compensation would be far less than what I can offer you."

"I could just kill you and take the gold for myself . . . leave Smythe out of it."

"But you know how he is," Stallard pressed on. Prescott knew enough about Smythe's men that bribery was useless, and this one was his first lieutenant. Stallard was wasting breath. But then something caught Prescott's attention. He looked down at his boots as if in dejection. He could not let Joshua see what Stallard had and why he was trying to carry on a conversation.

While Stallard continued on, Calvin, still alive, was trying to bring his pistol to bear on Joshua's back. There was blood near Calvin's mouth, and his manner was of a man with clouded sight, but he was almost upright, and agonizingly he pulled the weight up with both hands.

Prescott brought his eyes on Joshua. *Almost there—oh, God, he isn't going to make it! Yes! Pull the trigger!* Every muscle in his body tensed and for a fleeting moment he thought Joshua could see him preparing to launch himself across the score of feet between them, but Joshua was still listening with forced interest to Stallard's rambling.

In the next few moments, three things happened. The sound of Calvin's hammer clicking into place caused Joshua to spin, looking for the fresh menace, his pistol swinging in front of him.

Prescott and Stallard both threw themselves across the road as Joshua turned his back on them . . . as he moved, Prescott brought up his knife from behind his back. The third event was the double explosion of pistols from in front of them as Calvin and Joshua both fired. Stallard's bad leg limited his quickness, and Prescott was the first to reach Joshua as the big man exclaimed, grabbing his left arm with his gun hand.

Joshua was already bringing his gun hand around and turning back to Prescott when the Union lieutenant hit him with his shoulder, right on the arm where the bullet had just entered. The force threw them both against a horse as the team struggled but, amazingly, didn't bolt. The pistol didn't fall, and Prescott grabbed for Joshua's wrist. Smythe's man had been stunned by the shot and Prescott's weight against him, but he regained his balance and roared with anger. It would only be a second before he could turn the pistol into Prescott's face and fire.

With all the strength he had, Prescott plunged the knife into Joshua's side. He felt the knife meet resistance of bone, and so didn't reach the hilt. Another cry came from Joshua as the gun fell from his hand, and the two staggered apart as Prescott pulled the knife out and withdrew.

With distance between them, Prescott looked for Stallard, and what he saw disheartened him. The southerner had tried to reach the pistols where they had dropped in the road, but had not. Instead, he was standing with his arms up while the other gunman stood by the second wagon, carbine at the shoulder and ready. They were already beaten.

Joshua cussed a vile string of words together and surveyed the damage before pulling a hunting knife from down by one of his boots. He ignored the gun and his wounds, and instead moved toward Prescott as the latter retreated, backing across the road.

"You're a bastard that's going to die slow," Joshua growled deep.

Even relatively uninjured, Prescott knew he was overmatched. He hoped the arm and side wounds would draw enough blood to weaken Joshua.

Joshua yelled and charged like a bear. No dance of slashing blades here, he came at Prescott with his knife above his head, preparing to bring it down. Prescott was quicker and threw himself out of the way as the big man brushed by him. They were both at the ravine's edge now, and Joshua recovered with another string of foul words. Now he moved closer, holding the knife in front. His next lunge would come from a shorter distance.

Prescott didn't know why, but at that moment, the cornfield above Sharpsburg flashed into his mind. The roar of explosions as canisters hurled death—the screams of men killing with raw ugliness—and the hundreds of individual battles fought with musket, or pistol, or bayonet. Hell on earth, it was.

From far away, generals must have seen great blue and gray figures slamming into each other with a muffled moan. There, victory was calculated by movement laid before them. But in the cornfield, killing was an individual affair.

As it was now.

Joshua lunged again, and Prescott threw his left hand up and latched on to the other man's wrist while his own knife arm was turned away by the other. The two men pressed together, each trying to gain an advantage with their own knife, willing their blade closer to their opponent.

Prescott's arms burned with the effort, and then, almost imperceptibly, he felt Joshua's grip weaken against his knife. Blood was saturating his shirt, and sweat flew off their faces as they staggered together. Prescott could see Joshua focusing on fighting off the blade as he voiced another growl, inhuman in its tone. The time was now.

With quickness and strength, he snapped his free hand from Joshua's wrist and grabbed the man's arm higher, at the same instant pulling the knife hand away, twisting it against the other man's weaker left side. He then threw his knee into Joshua's side where the knife had hit. Another animal howl came forth, but Prescott didn't wait. As Joshua bent over from the pain, Prescott drove his knee up into the man's face.

The sound of a bone cracking was sharp, and Prescott brought the knife up and prepared to drive it home to the heart from behind. But again he underestimated Joshua's strength. With his shoulder down, Joshua drove hard into Prescott and pushed him, backpedaling, into a tree at the ravine's edge. The shock stole Prescott's breath—pain exploded up his left side. The blow took much from Joshua, who moved a few steps back.

Prescott gasped, breath hard in coming. He braced for another blow. He looked into a face he would never forget. A battle's blood lust had swept over Joshua. He threw down his knife and moved to put Prescott between him and the ravine. It all seemed to happen slowly, for Prescott knew what the madman wanted now. With the face of the devil himself, Joshua came at him.

He moved high with all his weight, and Prescott ducked at the last instant, throwing the man's weight on his back while at the same time jamming the knife up and into the stomach. The momentum carried the two of them over the edge, and Prescott felt himself without the ground for a moment, then came a terrible crashing against rock and tree as they tumbled down. He heard Joshua shriek as they broke free of each other, and then the fight was just to slow his fall. Over and over he went until, near the bottom, he was thrown up against a large oak and caught it squarely.

Joshua's scream was the last sound he heard.

Chapter Thirty-Five

Present Day
August 3

The one-hundred-fifty-year-old stairs creaked with all the satisfaction one would expect from a structure of its age. The handrail against the stone wall was recent and provided stability to the three persons moving down into the cellar of the stone- and wood-framed house. The moisture-laden air clung to the skin and seemed to bring in the walls. With each breath came the feeling that one was taking in decades of stagnant air, untouched by the outside.

It had been only thirty minutes since they had seen Munson's re-creation of the letter, and the anticipation had been enveloping Sparks. At the bottom of the stairs, Munson reached up to one of two bare light bulbs. Even as she turned on the second, the light was feeble against the cellar's darkness. There were no windows, and the corners and details in the stone and brick walls were lost in shadows.

The cellar was not empty: it had numerous boxes that, with a quick glance, could be seen to hold household items left by the previous owners. Munson handed out flashlights, and the three of them started examining the walls, beginning with the wall closest to the stairs.

"I hate places like this." Coulthard shivered. "It's too creepy."

"Definitely the stuff of horror movies," Munson agreed.

"Do you know much about this house?" Sparks ran his fingers along the irregular stone.

"I did some checking and made a phone call before the two of you came over," Munson said. "John Houck was something like seventy-five or seventy-six years old, and he owned land in and around the town, including the land down south where Devil's Den is located. He had a son named David and a daughter named Jane. The records aren't clear, but the family owned this property, and this house was built in the summer of '63.

"Where they were in the construction at the time of the battle, we don't know, but the house was completed in the summer of '64. I would expect, with the large wounded population that stayed on here for months, that construction was delayed. But the house stayed in the family for fifty years or so and then was sold a couple of times before the most recent owner purchased it back in the fifties. He then sold it a few years ago to the park service. We've been working on a proposal to restore the house and grounds."

Sparks worked his way down the length of the cellar until he got to the wall farthest from the stairs. "The stones have had mortar put in between them over the years, but it doesn't look like the foundation has been disturbed since the house was built."

He continued with his survey of the walls, making his way around the perimeter five times over the next fifteen minutes without a word. Munson left for a few minutes and went outside to check the exterior walls between the ground and the house's wood frame. She returned with a shrug of her shoulders. "The frame of the structure has been worked on over the years, but I don't believe anything was done with the foundation up above, either," she said.

"I think we've run into a dead end," Coulthard said, moving under the light to look again at the transcribed letter. "I think we should look at the house the family owned in town."

"The gold had to have been placed somewhere that hasn't been disturbed, and this house fits the scenario perfectly . . ." Munson stopped as Sparks murmured something under his breath and moved to the stairs.

"We need the stepladder I saw outside, and do you have a measuring tape?" he asked.

"Yes, but why?"

Sparks ignored questions from both women and disappeared upstairs. They followed him outside, and Munson went to the truck she had followed them in to retrieve the tape. They both watched in confusion as he walked back and forth along the outside.

"Can you let us in on what's clicking in that mind of yours?" Coulthard asked.

"Help me measure on the outside here," he said. "We start here. You agree this is close to where the stairs are to the cellar and the wall they're against?"

They measured, holding the tape out and counting off out loud. When they reached near the end of the house, they had reached fifty-four feet.

"OK, this is where the far wall should begin, right? About here?" Sparks asked.

"Sure," Munson said. "Fifty-four feet—kind of a rough estimate."

Sparks grabbed the ladder, and they went back down into the cellar.

"You've lost me, Jason," Coulthard implored.

"I think I know where he's headed with this," Munson said, then to Sparks, "The distance doesn't match?"

"Let's see," he said.

They measured beginning at the wall next to the stairs and repeated the process outside. When they reached the far wall, Sparks looked at Coulthard.

"Forty-seven feet," he said.

"A seven-foot difference," Munson said.

"Even allowing for some error, that still leaves a big space," Sparks said. He set the ladder against the wall and moved up until he could shine his flashlight on the upper corner between the wall and the ceiling. After a moment, he worked his hand up around the top edge of the wall. "There's no pressure on the top." He moved the ladder down five feet and repeated the process, his movements gathering excitement. "No pressure is being brought to bear on this wall at all."

"What does it *mean*?" Coulthard said impatiently.

"It's a false wall—it's not part of the foundation," Munson said.

"Some of the houses in this part of the country had hiding places in them"—Sparks was off the ladder now and running his flashlight along the bottom third of the wall—"the Underground Railroad and all."

"It's certainly possible." Munson joined Sparks in looking over the wall.

Sparks focused his interest on a large stone near the left corner and began running his hand along it. "Would the park service mind if we knocked down a wall?" he said.

"I would lose my job," Munson said. "We're making a large assumption here, and we're doing it without permission."

"Maybe we won't have to knock it down," Sparks said. "See, the mortar work around this stone isn't very extensive. It seems kind of shoddy when you compare it to the other work on the foundation." He picked up a hammer from a nearby crate and began to dig at the loose mortar around the stone with its claw. Within a few minutes, he had cleared the debris from around the stone. "This feels good." Sparks couldn't hide his excitement. "This stone can be moved. Look, someone even chiseled holds on the sides! You can't see them if you step back, but feel here!"

Both women exclaimed as they felt on either side of the stone. Sparks told them to step back, and he knelt before the stone and pulled on either side. On his first attempt, the stone moved slightly, but rocked back into place. Again he pulled on it, this time crying out—a weight lifter straining against the load. The stone moved out from the wall a few inches. Sparks paused and again pulled on the stone, this time moving it six inches more. On his fifth try, with better leverage, the stone moved clear of the wall.

"That thing's got to weigh two hundred and fifty pounds," he said. "My back's never going to be the same." He took the flashlight and peered into the black hole. "There's an open space in here."

"What can you see?" Coulthard tried to peer over his shoulder.

Sparks moved his whole upper body into the hole for a few seconds, then, without warning, he was all the way through.

"Jason, be careful," Coulthard said.

"We don't know anything about this. It could be dangerous," Munson added.

They both looked in to see the lower legs of Sparks standing in front of the gap. And then he was out of sight.

"Do you see anything?" Munson asked, but there was no response. Then the two women could hear movements from inside, and then a single muffled exclamation. Suddenly, Sparks was back at the opening, telling them to step back. He climbed through and rose to one knee.

"Is there anything in there?" Coulthard asked.

"I would say so," Sparks said. He reached back into the hole and pulled out an object heavy in his hand. He turned the flashlight on it.

The light reflected with a golden hue against their faces.

Munson and Sparks were sitting on boxes in the barren front parlor room after Coulthard had excused herself to use the bathroom and call her office. Sparks pushed the button to end the call on his phone and smiled thinly at Munson.

"Your work is done here, Brenda," he said. "You need to head on back to the visitors' center. I've kept you from your work for long enough."

"That's it? There's nothing more I can do? What's going to happen now?"

He raised his hand to slow her questions. "You did a miraculous job. Now it gets dirty, and I want you out of the way. One final thing: I need you to convince your boss to keep park personnel away from this house for the next few days. I don't know how this will end, but I don't want construction workers or rangers stumbling in on something and getting hurt."

"I hope your daughter comes home safe . . . Jason."

"With what you've given me," he said, "we've got a chance."

It was approaching 1 p.m. as Coulthard and Sparks said their good-byes to Munson and drove back to their hotel. They were climbing out of the car when Sparks's cell phone rang. The number was a new one, and the kidnapper's voice greeted him.

"You and I need to meet face-to-face tonight," the voice said.

"I want to talk to my daughter," Sparks responded.

"Not possible, but she's safe."

"Why do we need to meet?"

"Circumstances have changed. We'll meet tonight at the Twentieth Maine monument on Little Round Top at eight forty-five. Come alone."

"There's something you should know. We just came from a house west and north of the town. We found the gold."

There was a moment before the voice responded. "You've performed well under great pressure. You're to be commended. But my desire for a meeting is unchanged."

"I'll be there." Sparks ended the call on his cell phone and looked across at Coulthard, who had been watching from across the car roof. "This all ends tonight," he said.

Chapter Thirty-Six

May 22, 1863

Prescott heard his name first. Before he could focus on the image in front of him, he could hear and understand the voice. Stallard's southerner accent brought Prescott from the darkness. Then his memory flooded in, and he began to try to bring himself to his feet in desperation against the attack he knew would come.

"Whoa, Jack! Too early for you to be jumpin' up and taking on the world again," Stallard said. "You'll look like you're laying out a Virginia fence. Best you take a few moments to knock away the fog in front of your eyes."

"Joshua?"

"He's as dead as any man can be. Broken neck, back maybe as well. He's all twisted up at the bottom of the ravine. You're lucky to have hit this tree square."

"God almighty, I feel terrible," Prescott moaned.

"You look worse." Stallard laughed.

"I don't believe anything is broken." Prescott tenderly moved his body to test his limits.

"Nothing obvious, except you're going to be the most black-and-blue-colored man I've ever laid eyes on," Stallard said.

Prescott noticed the blood that had saturated Stallard's shirt from mid-rib down, and he remembered the scene above him. "What happened?"

"Got this when all the shooting started. Just a graze. Chopped up the skin a bit, bled some."

"Brison?"

"That's a bit more of a dilemma. He took a bullet through the shoulder and hurt the other shoulder when he fell from the horse. He's got more grit than any man I've ever met, though. He got the other rider just as you and Joshua decided to take a tumble down here. I packed his wound as best I could before checking on you, but I don't know how he'll take to a wagon ride. The bullet went through, didn't hit bone, but there's no telling how much damage was done, and how much mending he's going to take."

"We need to get moving, don't we?" Prescott struggled to his feet, holding on to the tree to steady himself.

"I knew that Harvard education of yours would benefit us eventually." Stallard began to pull his companion up the slope.

Brison was almost unconscious when they reached him, but the dressing job Stallard had done was holding well. They gently moved him to the back of the first wagon and left the rear door open to provide air. They then took the bodies of Smythe's men and rolled them down the stretch of slope Joshua had fallen down. The three Columbus men were wrapped in cloth shrouds and put in the back of the second wagon—it was clear neither Prescott nor Stallard had the strength to dig three graves.

Chambersburg was only a few miles ahead, but the road's roughness and Brison's condition put them into town in the early evening. It was past 11 p.m. when the pair settled into a boarding room after securing feed for the horses and taking Brison to a doctor. While he was attended to, Stallard and Prescott themselves were looked over and also given a thorough questioning by a town official who doubled as a law officer. He seemed glad when they mentioned that the robbers had taken off in a westerly direction—better to have trouble heading away.

Prescott struggled to remove his boots, already eyeing the bed. There was a soft knock, and Stallard opened the door to their adjoining rooms. He shuffled over to a chair and slowly, to avoid brushing his dressings against the chair's arms, lowered himself.

"There's an item of note I must convey to you," he said wearily. "I owe you and your friend Brison a great debt of gratitude. I . . . never meant for this adventure to turn this way. I made a great error in bargaining with Smythe. He's a man driven by greed . . . and now revenge. We'll not make it to Philadelphia—not without the loss of more life. My decision is thus. We'll wait for a short time here and see how Brison is mending, then we'll go on to a town just a ways southeast of here called Gettysburg. It's the county seat, and there's a college there . . . Pennsylvania College . . . and also a Lutheran seminary. Nice little town."

Prescott had let Stallard go on, his eyes closed. "What is there for us?"

"I know a gentleman, a family, who lives there." Stallard leaned back gingerly. "He owes me a small sum of money, but he'll help us also out of friendship. His family owns a good measure of property in the area. We're going to hide the gold until the threat of Smythe is eliminated."

"Hide it? Where?"

"We'll scout the area and see what's available."

"And how are we going to rid ourselves of Smythe? We don't know how many men he has on the roads to Philadelphia, and you can be certain he'll have the railroads watched. We can't even ask the militia for protection. If you have forgotten, this is Pennsylvania."

"I don't know. I'm tired."

"What of the man in Washington you have?" Prescott asked. "Is there any service he could render us?"

"He's of great importance, but I don't think it would be wise to contact him." Stallard's voice had not a hint of suspicion. Prescott thought his fatigue was overwhelming. But then he was leaning forward as if he was about to begin a new thought, then moving slowly to his feet and walking to the door. "Tired men make unwise decisions and say unwise words. Our first priority is sleep."

And then he was gone and the door closed.

Prescott managed to sit up and begin to remove his clothing. As Stallard had joked, he was, indeed, covered with bruises on his upper arms and torso. Each new one surveyed, Prescott drew in a breath. It would take time for him to heal, and he needed time to decide what to do.

He fell back onto the bed, not even bothering to turn down the lamp. He was asleep in a moment.

May 28, 1863

The days since the trouble on the road west of Chambersburg filled themselves with anxiety. Brison languished in fever for a time, then would rally and awaken, only to slip into a haze of mumbled words and night sweats. Prescott spent much of every afternoon and evening in the doctor's office, where a sickroom had been set aside. His own aches lessened to become minor annoyances by week's end.

Stallard's wounds were ugly but were healing, with little infection showing. He spent the days arranging for the wagons to be stored in the back of the livery stable, hoping to draw little attention to them, lest some enterprising thief stumble upon a lifetime's chance. They kept themselves out of sight as much as possible, concerned over an appearance from Smythe's agents.

The newspapers brought in from other towns were screaming the news of a nation in conflict. The Conscription Act was criticized in one paper and lauded in another, and Stallard wondered with much humor if he would have to be spending three hundred dollars of his own money for his name having been selected in Philadelphia. The war talk was mostly of the news in the west, with Ulysses S. Grant laying siege to Vicksburg on the Mississippi. Stallard was disheartened by the increasingly desperate news, especially of General Jackson's death following Chancellorsville.

It was late in the afternoon when a boy messenger from the doctor came to get Prescott, who hurried along, fearing the worst. Instead, he was greeted by a smiling Brison, who was sitting up in bed without fever, taking soup from a neighbor's wife.

"I don't know why I was ever worried sick about you." Prescott shook Brison's hand on his good side. "Should know better than to think a single bullet could ever kill you."

"The doc here was kind enough to regale me on the goings-on up the road." Brison's voice was weak, but his color had much improved and his eyes were clear.

Prescott asked the doctor to leave them alone for a spell, and he proceeded to give Brison the details of the attack and the days since. Brison listened with impressive concentration and asked a few pointed questions. When Prescott finished, Brison nodded as if seeing the conclusion.

"Smythe must be taken down like you would a rabid dog," Brison said. "So, Stallard wants to hide the gold until it's safe? That will at least lessen the possibility of losing it before we reach Philadelphia."

"And I'm convinced we'll come into contact with his counterpart in Washington," Prescott said urgently. "The odds are good upon it. But before all of that, I've got to remedy our problem here."

"You mean me." Brison's tone reflected his knowledge of what was coming next.

"You're not fit for duty, and you know it. I've got bruises and sores in places a gentleman doesn't discuss in fair company, but I can still fight, and most importantly, I can still move." Prescott moved around the room. "You cannot, and despite the number of times you've saved my life, saved Abby's life, and kept our assignment alive with your skills—despite all that—now you would be a hindrance." He turned to face Brison. "I can't afford to have you with us."

"Seein' as I cannot climb out of this bed and come at you full chisel, I expect the decision is all yours." Brison's words were tinged with bitterness. "Can't say I blame you. I would make the same decision. Perhaps I'll be stronger soon and be of some help."

"I'll remain hopeful. The question still hangs with us, what will we try to do with Smythe? Parker has something he's stirring up, but he doesn't confide in me as before. I fear he may be wary."

Brison shook his head. "He has taken much in the way of setbacks. The toll of human life on his excursion has been high. Innocents have suffered. I expect this is why his mood suffers."

"I still must be alert."

There was a knock, and Stallard swept into the room. "I received word just now at the stable." He smiled. "Thank God Almighty you're getting stronger. You had me worried for a time."

"I was telling him what happened after he took the mini ball back on the road," Prescott said.

"Brison, you would have been proud of Mr. Prescott here." Stallard pulled up a chair and turned it around, resting his arms on the back. "He alone took on that Joshua while I stupidly went for the guns and came to grief with the other gunman. You do remember saving my life?"

Brison nodded. "It was my last memory before today."

"It seems both of us owe you our lives," Stallard said.

"You returned the favor by bringing me here." Brison shifted in the bed and grimaced in discomfort. "Just where is here? It's the one thing Jackson here didn't speak of."

"Charming little town called Chambersburg. We're west and north of Cashtown and then the county seat of Adams County: a town called Gettysburg. That will be our next stop, and we must, indeed, hurry there. Could you make the trip now?" Stallard asked.

"Still rather poorly, I'm afraid," Brison replied with a weak smile. "Maybe tomorrow. Jackson told me of your plan to hide the gold. A well-thought-out idea, but have you given thought to how the two of you will, shall I say, eliminate Smythe as a problem?"

For the first time in days, Prescott saw Stallard smile. "Actually, I have a notion, and if I'm right, we won't have to worry about dealing with him alone." Brison and Prescott looked at each other with bewilderment, and Stallard chuckled. "It is simply astonishing what can be done when farmers and store clerks get their dander up." When the other two faces became even more perplexed, Stallard laughed out loud and thumped his cane on the floor.

June 1, 1863

The afternoon sun had given way to a high overcast blanket as the two drummer's wagons pulled to the side of the road, the monotonous barrage of creaking wood, banging pots, and jarring movement giving way to a welcome silence. Prescott set the brake and looked back in the second wagon upon the figure of one miserable Andrew Brison, who had not barked once about the rough treatment his body had been subjected to through the day. He had sat with his Spencer across his lap, grinding hard on a wad of tobacco. He looked up at Prescott with a hopeful expression, and Prescott knew what he wanted.

"I can see Gettysburg laid out before us," Prescott said. "We're just a mile or so outside of town. Parker has stopped us outside an establishment—it's called Herr's Tavern. We've been going by some farms recently here, just saw a schoolhouse a few hundred yards back. Parker says this town is like the hub of a wheel, with the spokes being roads leaving in every direction. A good centralized place. There's even a railroad spar that leads from the town northeast, so that has possibilities. For now, Parker's thoughts are on a bit of drink to soothe ourselves from the road."

"I'd be much obliged if you would bring something out to me," Brison said.

Prescott looked for Stallard near the first wagon, but the southerner was not there. As Prescott approached the tavern, he met Stallard coming out of a side door, prodding along a youth in his late teens. "Remember what I said: go first to fetch Josiah Arnold, then let John Houck know that Parker Stallard is in town and would like to see him. Don't talk to anyone else, and don't let the family run you along. You speak to the old man yourself, you hear?"

"Yes, sir!" The youth went to the side, took his mount, and headed down the pike to the town as Stallard grabbed Prescott's arm, leading him into the tavern.

Windows were open for airing purposes, no doubt, so there was a lighter feel to the establishment, which was empty of customers. The owner gruffly acknowledged their presence, and Stallard ordered two beers before he was corrected by Prescott, and when the drinks arrived, Prescott took one out to Brison, who accepted it with enthusiasm. Prescott rejoined Stallard, and they drank in relative silence for a time before a second round came to the table.

"Who are the people you sent the boy to fetch?" Prescott asked.

"Arnold is going on seventeen now. He and his father work a brickyard just north of town—at least, they did the last time I was through here, a year or so ago." Stallard wiped some excess from his chin, relishing the lager. "The old man Houck is a prominent man in town—a farmer, I expect, but he owns a great deal of land and maybe a building or two. I'm hopeful for his discreet knowledge of a place we may use."

"Is he a trustworthy sort?" Prescott asked.

"With these riches, I trust no man."

"So you won't reveal to him your intentions or what we're transporting?"

"I'll only ask him to use an available hiding place on his land." Stallard took another drink. "The rest will be up to the two of us."

"And what of Smythe?" Prescott insisted. "How do you intend to solve the problem? And what about Brison out there? We need to move him out of harm's way. He's done enough for us. I think we should pay him his worth and move him along. We could sorely need him to cover our backs, but not without tearing himself up inside. I'll grant a man a chance to die on his own feet, fighting for his beliefs or for his reward, but I'll not be a party to a man dying when he cannot defend himself proper."

Prescott could not read the look Stallard gave him. It was hard for a moment, but then softened. "I agree. We'll take him up to Harrisburg. I know a lady—"

"'I know a lady . . .'" Prescott rolled his eyes. "Do you have designs on most all the women in the North? For a man who takes to the Bible, you sure are well acquainted with breaking a few of its commandments. I find the notion that you're not married to be a minor excuse, if you please."

Stallard smiled. "I'm no doubt a sinner, Jackson. But I believe God will forgive me my faults. I have never harmed an innocent, and as far as the ladies of the North, I have found them to be both generous and beautiful of heart. I just do the best that's possible for this soul, I expect. What about you there, young Lieutenant Prescott? A man without a country?"

"I expect I'll be needing another name to avoid the thunder of justice. I'm hopeful Abby and I will be able to live away from what the war's conclusion will bring." Prescott finished his second beer. "I left the army because I was through with the slaughter—I traded it in for just more killing."

"You can't be putting the blame on yourself for recent events, Jack," Stallard said. "Smythe is the devil in this play. We could have completed our transaction with him and been on our way, but instead, greed brought him against us."

A young man in his late teens peered in the door and scanned the room, quickly setting his gaze upon the lone two men. He was a good-sized youth with disheveled hair and a flannel shirt with overalls. He was covered in dirt from his brown hair down to his brogans, but he carried himself with confidence. He caught sight of Stallard and a luminescent smile spilled forth.

"Mr. Stallard!" The boy grabbed Stallard's hand with a strong shake. "I was told you were here. My father and the boss man gave me a bit of a Jesse, but they allowed me a short time to see what you were wanting. It's good to see you. What has you back in Gettysburg?"

"Business as usual, Josiah," Stallard said. "The war hasn't stopped business here in the North. This is Mr. Jackson. This here's Josiah Arnold—the smartest young man in Pennsylvania, he is. Knows everyone in town, just about, and he's aware of most of the town gossip, I expect."

"You make me sound like Miss Gentry's collection of gabbers," Arnold said.

"Untrue, untrue, but you do know all the goings-on?"

"I suppose."

"Well, sit for a moment and enlighten us." Stallard slapped the boy's shoulder, sending dust about the table.

The last trace of light glowed from the west as the two wagons made their way down the pike toward the town. Stallard took the second wagon, with Brison in the back, while Prescott took the lead with the Arnold boy sitting by his side, giving an impromptu tour of the town's notable landmarks and any gossip he thought would interest him. The boy was doing his finest to display the knowledge Stallard had boasted about.

Though fatigued, Prescott was intrigued with this town. It could have been anywhere in the North. From New Jersey to Massachusetts to stretches of Ohio and Indiana, you could have placed this town there, and it would have settled nicely. The war would be entering its third summer in three weeks and this land was still unscarred—unlike Maryland to the south and the Confederacy's glorious Virginia just below her. Pennsylvania and her brethren had been spared until now, at least on the surface.

Arnold was saying something about a Lutheran seminary, and Prescott looked over his right shoulder to see a large building rising above the land. It was an impressive structure, Prescott thought—not in a city like Washington or Philadelphia, but here it held a regal stand, with its four stories and a white cupola perched high in the evening glow. Then the boy pointed to the left at an even more impressive structure looming over the tree line on a hill north of the town.

"That there's the college," he said. "I've been helping my father at the brickyard, but he's been talking up a storm about me getting an education, becoming a college man. But I won't be no student heading to the seminary—no, by thunder, I will not."

"I'm sure he just desires you to better yourself," Prescott said. "Many a man never receives a chance of such worth."

"You been to college?"

"Yes."

"Was it worth the book readin' and writin'?"

"Not for everyone, I expect, but it was the right path for myself." Prescott smiled.

"We're turning onto Chambersburg Street now, and we'll be coming up on the Diamond in just a short ways."

"The Diamond?"

"The main square. The big attraction would be the McClellan House—it will be on the left. Then there's two dry goods stores—

Spangler's and Schick's—but I guess you won't be needing anything from them, since you all have your own goods right here." Arnold tipped his head back to the opening behind them.

"Of course. Where are we headed? Did Mr. Stallard say we'd be trying to stay at the hotel there on the square?"

"Mr. Stallard said he wanted you all to be put up in the same place he stayed when he was here last. Not the best hotel in town, but if you're heading south, there's not a faster way out of town. We'll be turning up here at the Diamond onto Baltimore Street. Mind the folks out walking—they tend to get a bit absentminded."

As it was near candle lighting on a Monday, the square had little traffic, and the lights from the buildings spilled onto the street. They turned between the two dry goods buildings. One was a fine three-story brick, the first Prescott had seen aside from the two educational institutions. They moved south on what the boy had called Baltimore Street, moving down an incline before making their way back up a hill. After a time, they came upon a place where the street wish-boned, with the left spur continuing to move up the hill and the right extending into the darkness on a flat course.

Arnold pointed to a box-like building standing in the fork's middle. "That'll be the Wagon Hotel. The road there to the left becomes the Baltimore Pike and that one there's the Emmitsburg Road. Mr. Stallard said you would be staying a short time and then would be heading perhaps to Harrisburg. You just go back up Baltimore Street here through town and then the Harrisburg Road takes off to the northeast. The brickyard where I work is up that way."

The boy bade farewell to Stallard from a distance and untied his horse. Explaining he was going to catch hell from his mother for being late for supper, he took the horse at a quick canter back up the street. While Prescott helped Brison from the back of the wagon, Stallard went inside to procure rooms. An hour later, the wagons and horses were bedded down, and Stallard had managed to convince the innkeeper to fetch a doctor from just up the street to take a look at Brison before they turned in.

The doctor arrived, and without much inquiry, cleaned and put fresh bandages on Brison's shoulder. There was little sign of infection, but the doctor became testy when he learned of the wagon ride from Chambersburg and insisted that Stallard and Prescott promise to, as he said, "refrain from punishing this man along the roads." Just as the doctor was leaving, the young man Stallard had originally sent along from the tavern arrived with a message. Stallard read it and nodded.

"John Houck will see me tomorrow morning. For now, it's best if we get some sleep. I'm going to check on the wagons one last time. The chains and locked-down wheels should be enough, but I always like to check to be certain."

"I'll go with you," Prescott said, noting with a nod that Brison was already asleep.

The two men walked down to the nearby barn and were satisfied the wagons were locked down, then returned to the hotel and sat on the second-floor balcony for a smoke. The air was still and warm, and they savored Stallard's special cigars.

"You and I will hide the gold alone," Stallard said with authority. "The fewer who know, the better, and Brison is no good to us, as far as using his back is concerned. We'll take him to Harrisburg, and we'll wait for Smythe to come."

"Two of us against a group of eight or so?"

"You think I'm a fool for going after him?"

"Have you thought on this matter these last days? You've been skeery-like with your words on this." Prescott clamped down on the cigar. "I thought this would be a task we would coordinate together."

"And so you shall. My idea is not all that difficult. It will require playing two halves against themselves. It should be a fine time."

Prescott detected a smile from Stallard and raised his own eyebrows in wonder. "You, sir, are acquiring an ornery habit of being less than forthcoming."

Stallard laughed quietly. "First, we'll secure the gold in a place of safety. Then we shall discuss Smythe and all my awful secrecy."

"That brings me to another point. How are the two of us going to hide nine thousand pounds of ingots? It will take us hours—more than we can do in a day. Or are we hiding the whole lot, wagons and all?"

"No, we need the wagons to draw Smythe and his men out, and yes, it will have to be just the two of us. However, we'll try to do it over time, so as to ease the burden. Neither of us is ready for a spree, mind you. My side is aching like a cold day in February, and I have a fair suspicion there isn't a muscle in you without the purple right now. Still, we need to do this alone."

"You've been in this town before," Prescott said. "Any notions of where?"

"Actually, I do. But it depends . . ."

"On what?"

"On John Houck. The land I'm looking at, I believe, belongs to him. It's south a ways, just off this road here. 'Tis a desolate sort of place, full of boulders and rocks, not fit for farming, if I remember. I took a young lady on a picnic there once."

"And you can show your face in this town again?"

"I was with her siblings," Stallard replied. "Very proper and all."

"Of course."

"It's rough land, so I expect we might find a suitable spot."

Chapter Thirty-Seven

Present Day
August 3

Sparks waited for the lone car coming in the opposite direction to pass him on the Emmitsburg Road, now known as Business Route 15, before turning left onto what the map said was South Confederate Avenue.

The gate set a short distance from the intersection was still locked in the open position, as it was 8:30, still a few minutes before sunset and an hour and a half before the park would be officially closed. He continued down the avenue, the same way he had come earlier with Munson and Coulthard when they had toured Devil's Den.

Now the sun was well gone from the sky, leaving a brilliant dark blue edging to black. The trees along the gentle sloping fields to his left were already losing their definition to the night, but he could see Big and Little Round Tops, the two hills at the southern end of the battlefield. They sat against the sky, as dominant now as they had been all those years ago on a blistering July afternoon when the Confederates swept through this area on their way to immortality.

The avenue's right side was lined with monuments and markers to Southern units placed in this area. Sparks gave them a passing glance, but his attention was focused on those two hills. Just off the summit of the smaller of those two would be the 20th Maine monument and the site of his meeting with Richardson's man. Perhaps, as he had said to Munson earlier in the day, tonight would be when everything was finished.

The road turned in a slow curve to the east, and he followed it, still looking ahead to any glimpse he could have of Little Round Top. All that could be done was done. The preparations had been made—the house would be the setting, and Griffin and his men would be there when the moment arrived. And as an added precaution, there was Sam. Munson was safely removed from the situation, back at her job, and Coulthard was at the hotel, angrily restricted. She had put up a fierce objection to his demands, but he had stood firm. She would answer questions in the future.

As he approached the parking area near the summit of Little Round Top, deep in the trees, Sparks noticed that there were still two cars in the small lot. He continued as the avenue descended into the saddle between the two hills. He remembered what Munson had said about how sometimes people would hang around after dark a few hundred yards to the west, in the Devil's Den area, waiting for a paranormal visit. Ghosts. It was a stupid notion, Sparks thought, hoping there would be none of those people hanging around in the dark.

He reached the bottom of the saddle and crossed a road called Warren Avenue, named for the commander credited with saving the Union's left flank on Little Round Top. The woods above and to his right-front was where the monument was placed, up in the trees, where the men of the 20th Maine had fought off members of the 15th Alabama regiment.

There was a small grouping of cars on the crest of the road, just off the summit, and Sparks could see some tourists standing up by the small tower where the Union breastworks had once stood. He pulled over to the right side, ahead of the last car on the right, and stepped out. The gloom smothered itself upon the ground. The last light stretched from the west horizon, but here the blackness was rushing in, just minutes away.

It was 8:30 p.m.

Jon Samuel Anderson was not satisfied. Dressed in black, his two men appeared from the dark with their equipment. He knew everything was in place and had been tested, but still he swore to himself. Sparks would be taking a huge chance with this one, and for the first time in years, Anderson let doubt wedge its way in.

The house was surrounded by woods on three sides, with the south side facing an open field. The ground to the north and west sloped up a ridge to a height of forty or fifty feet above the house, then it fell away to the dirt road where Anderson's two SUVs were parked.

"We're set," the first of the two men said.

"We proceed as planned," Anderson said. "Cooper, you take the west Alpha position that's elevated." He then looked at the second figure, just arrived. "Loring, you take the east Bravo position in the tree. Remember, we're the last safeguard. This scenario can plot out a number of different ways. I'll be in position Charlie, just south of Alpha. You both will be hooked up, so we stay put unless I OK a move. We have minutes now . . . into position."

Sparks walked down the path leading into the woods. At the entrance was a sign for the 20th Maine monument and a marker with a description of the regiments that had held this position. There was a couple peering at the marker, holding jackets with cameras over their shoulders—a brunette and her baseball-capped companion.

Sparks continued deeper into the woods until he reached a small breastwork of stones where the 20th Maine had been placed, with the 83rd Pennsylvania, 44th New York, and 16th Michigan to its right. Looking down through the trees, he could see the road he had just taken through the saddle between the two Round Tops.

The 20th Maine had refused its line to the south at an angle during the battle, and it was while looking down this line that Sparks saw a small monument. There was a figure next to it, and a small, flickering light appeared. The man was lighting a pipe. Sparks made his way down the slope, very aware of the Glock in the back of his waistband under his untucked shirt and the .22 Beretta strapped to his right ankle underneath the jeans. Even though a humid night approached and perspiration stuck his shirt to his back, he felt cold and naked.

"Hallowed ground we're standing on here." The voice was the same as in Boston, but the appearance was changed. Gone were the mustache and goatee, and the hair was lighter. He was wearing a Boston Red Sox cap pushed back slightly on his head. He was dressed in a black shirt and jeans. The dark glasses were the only constant.

"I want to see my daughter before I take you to the gold," Sparks demanded.

"A moment. You know Chamberlain and the Twentieth charged down through these woods here, some of them with empty muskets. It is truly astonishing what men will do when they're led properly. They will throw down their lives for something as simple as an idea. Rare was the war before this one that could claim that, I would say."

"Fine words coming from a man who has killed and kidnapped for monetary gain."

"For this particular time and this particular assignment . . ." Streeter let the words fade. He pulled a gun casually from behind the monument but didn't point it in Sparks's direction. "I assume you're armed. Where?"

"Back waistband."

"Just keep the hands clear of your back."

"What is this about? I expected to be taking you to the gold, and it doesn't appear you have the manpower with you to make the move," Sparks said. "Four to five tons of gold will require a vehicle or two, at least."

"That's all unimportant, and it's not the reason I chose this meeting."

"Then why?"

"I'm a professional, and I like all the elements of a job to be neat and well planned. When this contract began, it was a simple retrieval of lost merchandise. A bit unusual, I admit, but barely illegal. A bit of pressure here, some research there, and my employer would walk away with millions in untraceable wealth. I was to have a sizable fee. I don't expect you to understand or care about my reasoning, but I have concluded that the risk to my person outweighs the benefits. And, not in any lascivious way, I have grown fond of your daughter. You should be proud of her and never let her lack knowledge of your love for her."

"She knows."

"Does she truly? I'll not criticize. In my discussions with her, I found her both singularly brave and focused. She'll do well with her life, I think. It's true I put her through an ordeal no woman should have to endure. For this I will, with sincerity, apologize to you. I have already to her. The action was not entirely my decision, but I could have stopped it. And at some base level, it was the correct choice. You did find the gold."

"It's getting dark, and I want to get this over with . . . My daughter."

"There's a tree about a football field's length on a line that way," Streeter said, pointing around the back side of Little Round Top. "She's tied to a tree and gagged, because, though I had her word, I feared enthusiasm would get the best of her. You'll go to her, and I'll take my leave."

"Just like that? What about the gold, the reason we've gone through this hell?"

"As I stipulated, the situation has changed," Streeter said. "My employer made it clear that the two of you were to die when this was done. You're a professional in these sorts of things, you understand. But your Jennifer . . . well, it would have too great a loss for the legal profession."

Sparks thought better of asking, but the desire to know was too strong. "What about the boy she was with?"

"Regrettably, he was killed by one of my former associates who had, I should say . . . designs on your daughter. I did save her life on that occasion. She will, no doubt, give you the details."

"What about your employer . . . Richardson?"

"So, you have been busy." Streeter nodded again in understanding. "But you took an incredible risk that Richardson would move on sealing off links to himself."

"I had to know who I was dealing with. Did he have Goldberg killed?"

"The assistant director at the FBI? Was that the contact inside?" Streeter was genuinely surprised.

"You didn't know about him?"

"I only knew there was someone feeding him information. I would never have authorized that action."

"Why cut your losses now and walk?" Sparks asked.

"I accept failure in this respect—I didn't realize Jonathan Richardson would choose to eliminate me. My sources tell me he's taken a contract out on me."

"So you choose to disappear."

"If one has the resources, it can still be done, even in the era of Homeland Security."

"I already know the answer, but I'll ask anyway. Anything you can give us on Richardson?"

Streeter shook his head. "I have a reputation to maintain. He'll pay, nonetheless."

Sparks knew what the man across from him meant. A professional would not leave betrayal unpunished, but not by turning state's evidence. "And if we're unable to bring him to justice with what we have at the Bureau?"

"The world is a dangerous place, and life has a way of balancing things out," Streeter said.

"What name does Richardson know you by?" Sparks asked. "Just a point of reference."

"Streeter. But that is, of course, an alias."

"Naturally."

"Go to your daughter. And once she's safe, don't come after me. You would be dead long before you thought you were close."

Streeter waved the gun up the slope, and Sparks moved up at a quick pace. The FBI agent turned back after a few moments and saw Streeter already hurrying back up the path around the ridge and back to the road. Now at a jog, Sparks called out Jennifer's name. It was dark enough now that the trees were only black sentries. After another minute, he heard her muffled cry to his right, farther down the slope to the east side of Little Round Top. With a last exclamation of her name, he was next to her and wrapping his arms around her.

Tears, for the first time since the ordeal began, came to him and to her, as well.

"Dad." It was all she managed to say after he removed the gag and was untying her, but when he was finished, she clung to him as a small child does, and her words came rapid-fire. "I love you, Dad. I thought they were going to kill me, I really did. They killed Bret, did you know that? But the man who brought me here . . . he saved me and let me go. Did you see him? Did you talk to him?"

"Yes, I saw him. Jen, thank God you're all right!" Sparks allowed himself to hug her again. "We need to go, now. I want to get you to the Bureau and protective custody. I also need to give you something."

They made their way in roughly the same direction he had come from the monument, but actually came into an area just north of the marker and found the path leading back to the road. Logic said that Streeter had been telling the truth—there was nothing to gain by deception—but Sparks still had his gun in his right hand and his left wrapped around Jennifer's shoulder.

As they approached the markers at the woods' entrance, he noticed that the couple was gone and the minivan that had been parked closest to the entrance was, as well. There were still some people on Little Round Top's summit across the road, their silhouettes framed against the day's last light. Sparks's car and two others remained.

"Did you come this way before, when you arrived with him?" Sparks asked.

"No, we were on a different road, I think, but I don't know which direction it was from." Jennifer's reply was edged with concern. "What's wrong?"

Three shadows separated themselves, one on either side of them and the third slightly ahead and next to the road. "Not a word, Sparks, and keep your daughter quiet. Place the gun on the ground and step back four paces. Now, or your daughter takes a bullet in the leg."

Sparks surveyed his position and knew it was pointless to resist. He laid his Glock in the dirt and moved back with his arm around Jennifer. The man nearest the road approached and pocketed the gun. He was small in stature, and when he spoke, it was with a strong Massachusetts accent.

He raised his arm and spoke into a phone. "We have them."

A vehicle approached up the road from the saddle. A paneled van glided to a stop near them, and the man closest to them motioned for Sparks and Jennifer to move toward it.

"Don't attempt anything," the man said. "We don't want no unpleasantness, you understand?"

"Leave the girl be," Sparks almost ordered. "She doesn't know anything and can't identify anyone."

"Not possible. Move now."

The van's side door slid open and another figure stepped out.

"Dad?" Jennifer kept her panic suppressed.

"Nothing we can do now," Sparks whispered. "Stay focused."

They moved to the van, and the man patted down Sparks, took his car keys, and roughly pushed them into the back. The keys were passed out to the short man, two of the others jumped inside, and the door was closed as the van moved off. The short man went to Sparks's rental car and followed along behind the van. Inside, Sparks and Jennifer had their wrists bound. The back was empty except for a dark, long-haired wig, a couple of jackets, a baseball cap, and the huddled figure of Streeter, lying in an uncomfortable position.

"Dead?" Sparks asked to no one in particular.

"Just gave him a tap on the head," one of them said. "He'll come around soon enough."

The men made no attempt to hide their faces or blindfold their captives. They knew there was no need. What scenarios were left open to Sparks swept through his mind as the van moved west on Wheatfield Road and toward Business 15, the Emmitsburg Road. Their lives now depended on others, and for one not accustomed to relying on others, it was disconcerting.

The van slowed to the side of the road, and when it stopped, Sparks was positioned so he was next to the sliding door. Momentarily, it was opened, and he faced a large SUV with tinted windows. The driver opened the rear door and out stepped a man in a dark suit, with white hair and a mustache. He used a cane to step the short distance between them, but that didn't detract from his physical presence. Here was a man who was always center stage.

"Agent Sparks. It is providence that brings us together at last," he said.

"Jonathan Richardson," Sparks said in a flat tone.

The Boston financier tilted his head to the side, letting the light from inside the van carry to his face. "Almost a century and a half ago, a South Carolinian buried a shipment of gold ingots somewhere in this town, and through an act of God or ill-luck or whatever, it was never recovered. It remained lost . . . until now. I find it inspiring. But I've never been one to let idle diversions sway me from my objective. You'll direct us to the gold's location now."

"Let my daughter go, and I'll take you there."

"Alas, that's the one condition I cannot grant, for now," Richardson said, "but you take us to the location, and after we have recovered the shipment, I'll consider granting you that request—provided there are no agents in the area ready to apprehend us."

"I have contacted no one."

"That's not the information I have. You just called me by a name."

"Your point man, Streeter in there, gave me your name."

Richardson allowed a look of slight surprise. "I'll have to discuss with him the matter of privacy—you know, management-employee relations and all. But I doubt he was your initial source. You were in contact with the Bureau, weren't you?"

"Only for routine contacts, for appearances," Sparks said. "I was supposed to be looking for the gold. It was my assignment."

"Perhaps, but my source believes you made some calls of quite a mysterious nature, and so I have to believe you had the Bureau trying to find my identity. You know what the penalty for this action was going in, did you not?"

"Don't fuck with me. Who was your source?" Sparks demanded, standing up from the edge of the van.

"Let's keep this civil. Don't you agents take classes in public relations? My dear, would you step from the car, please?"

Movement came from inside the car, then a pair of blue-jeaned legs. Tracy Stallard carried a look of forced confidence.

"Tracy?" Sparks knew Richardson would read his reaction.

"I'm sorry Jennifer was brought into this, Jason, I really am," she said. "This whole mess was supposed to involve just you."

"You've been working for him all this time?" He stepped forward but was stopped by his tied hands being jerked back. "You bitch! You strung me along until I found the gold. Even after you knew they had taken Jennifer!" Sparks was thrown back against the van.

"My dear, I do believe he would harm you right here if he was free to do so," Richardson mused. "Get back in the car. Your presence is apparently disruptive."

"What do you need us for, Richardson?" Sparks barked. "She was there. She saw the gold we found in the farmhouse's foundation. You don't need us."

"Under normal circumstances, that would be true. But in telling me the tale of how you two and the park ranger broke through the foundation and found the lost shipment, she mentioned something I feel warrants you taking us there."

"What is that?"

"She said you brought out a single ingot from behind the wall, but she mentioned she never saw the entire shipment. Only you went behind the wall. I believe you should stay with us until I see the entire shipment for myself."

"Who knows what's behind the wall, right?"

Richardson allowed himself a grin. "We do think alike. You would have done well in the private sector." He motioned to the men beside Sparks. "Put him in the van. We'll go to the house now."

Secured in the van, Sparks saw Streeter massaging the back of his head. He swore bitterly to himself and looked up to greet Sparks's gaze. "A less-than-fortuitous turn of events."

"It appears, as you feared, that you have fallen from grace," Sparks said.

"Such are the fortunes of my line of work. Was that Richardson's voice I heard just now?"

"Yes, he took time to meet me . . . and to let me in on his secret mole."

"Secret . . ."

"Coulthard."

"Oh, I neglected to mention her. My oversight . . . I apologize."

"What did you offer her and how long was she working for you?" Sparks asked.

"A percentage of the profits, and I recruited her at the beginning, when you went down to Jacksonville."

"That seems a lifetime ago." Sparks looked out through the windshield and the passenger side window at the broad expanse of darkness to the right of the Emmitsburg Road they were taking into town. They were passing across the land Pickett's men had crossed on their way to The Angle, crossing against the fury of shell and bullet, yet compelled to continue on, driven beyond the threshold of self-preservation.

Even now, sitting in the back of the van with strangers holding weapons against him and his daughter, Sparks still thought of those men who had met along a line a few hundred feet into the darkness . . . and wondered how they had summoned the courage.

And as he sat there, the van continued on what was once the Emmitsburg Road, but now was Route 15—past the Visitors' Center of the Military Park, the restaurants, motels, and businesses, across the intersection of Washington Street and onto the intersection with Baltimore Street, where they were stopped by the traffic light. They would turn left in a moment, but for now they sat just twenty paces from where the Wagon Hotel had once stood.

Chapter Thirty-Eight

June 4, 1863

For two days, they had bided their time in the small Pennsylvania town of two thousand five hundred people. Prescott had kept a low profile at the Wagon Hotel out of necessity, as he worried that a stray Wanted poster from eight months ago might draw recognition.

Stallard had met with the businessman, John Houck, for the better part of a day and seemed quite satisfied with the meeting. He had spent the previous day away from the hotel, leaving Prescott to grow impatient while he watched over the also growingly impatient Andrew Brison.

The doctor from up the street had stopped by in the early evening each day to check on the wound in Brison's shoulder. The colonel was gaining strength, and it was matched by his orneriness. He was taking walks around the hotel and one occasion went up the neighboring street to a cemetery. The walk had proved to him that exertion would come hard to him for a while, and the realization brought disappointment.

So it was with some relief for Prescott when, in the late afternoon, Stallard announced that the two of them were going to look at a piece of land he had selected. They took two of the better animals in their teams and headed south on the Emmitsburg Road. The land was open here, sloping down from their left at the Evergreen Cemetery to the south and west. Abundant land dotted with farms and woods—good land on which a man could build a home, grow an orchard, raise crops, build a life. Prescott found himself envious. "What county is this?" he asked.

"Adams County."

"Good land here," Prescott offered. "These people seem untouched by the war. I suppose it's this way in much of the north. Most of the suffering has been south and west of here."

"General Lee will be back up this way again—got to take it to Hooker, now that Vicksburg is under siege. He'll probably meet up with Hooker somewhere in Maryland, just south of here. Then he'll destroy the Army of the Potomac and move on Washington. Then, with political or material force from England, the Union will be forced into settling the issue and a new nation will join the world. I can see it as clear as that farmhouse there in the distance . . . the edges a tad ragged but with a majestic look that could use but a bit of polishing." A sudden breath of wind whipped up dirt from the road and brought a cough from Stallard. "Did you ever see my family's place near Charleston?"

"Never visited."

"Magnificent plantation. Servants' quarters were as impressive as these here farmhouses. Ah, it was a splendid time—lazy, hot summers growing up, coming to realize the importance and beauty of the South's ladies, parties on the grounds, horse races in the late afternoon, and the evening's dances. It was a grand time. And one we'll have again when this war is over."

"You're an optimist, sir." Prescott shook his head. "There's still much in front of us that can prevent it."

"You're always so gloomy, Jack! You'll see your Abigail again." Stallard reached over and thumped Prescott on the shoulder. "Here's our turn up ahead."

They passed a dark, brick farmhouse with its companion barn adjacent to the road. To the left stood trees in rows of definition stretching away to the east. A peach orchard it was, and Prescott found himself struggling briefly with a desire to climb over the fence in search of a treat. They approached another house, and Stallard led them to the left, up a gentle rise through the orchard and then out into more open ground. After a short distance, they came upon a set of woods on the left and a large wheat field on the right.

To their right were a pair of prominent hills. The northernmost of the two was the smaller one, cleared of trees and filled with large boulders. The larger, southern hill was lush with trees and stood out against the horizon. They came to a stream running across the road, and there was another road that wandered off to the south. Stallard pulled his horse to a stop.

"A fair change in scenery, wouldn't you say?" Stallard asked. Prescott could see what he meant. The land sweeping before them contrasted with the rolling fields of wheat and corn. Here, nature had tossed boulders of every size loosely upon the ground leading up to the smaller of the two hills before them.

Interspersed were small bushes or trees, sparse in nature. The ridge crossed into a small valley and back up to a smaller ridge to their right as they faced south. The area was singularly void of any apparent use, though Prescott did see a few cattle grazing in one corner on what grass could be found.

"Inhospitable, ungodly land, isn't it?" Stallard smiled at Prescott's raised eyebrows. "Land not fit for much except a little lumbering and letting cattle free for a spell. This piece of land here between Little Round Top there and this ridge to our right belongs to John Houck, the fellow I told you about. He's leasing the land to someone, but he saw fit to let us on without being disturbed."

"There isn't much to it besides the rocks."

"Wait till you see a little south of here." They followed a small road along the stream, but then Stallard led them off as it turned west. They picked their way among the boulders, which led them to travel in a roundabout fashion along the base of the ridge. They quickly came upon a mass of boulders larger than anything else in the area, and their appearance left Prescott stupefied in the saddle.

He estimated their weight in the many tons. They were stacked on top of each other in a jumble of sheer immenseness. The men dismounted and picked their way below the massive rocks. Prescott put his hand upon the face of one and felt the boulder's coolness, and he looked straight up the face as it disappeared somewhere above his head.

"Impressive things," Stallard said. "I spent the good part of yesterday and earlier today walking among these rocks. The folks in town sometimes come out here for picnics and such, Sunday outings, to climb around. There's a hole in the rocks just a little ways over here that carries a local legend with it."

"A legend?"

"Seems the citizens in this area tried to clean out a mess of snakes years ago and had trouble with this one particular rascal who eluded them." Stallard continued around the boulders, picking his way for good footing. Prescott followed. "So they continued to kill off the lot, except this one they couldn't get rid of. The story goes they called him 'The Devil,' for obvious reasons."

"Well deserved."

"He disappeared eventually, and the story goes that he died in this here place, his den." Stallard pointed at an opening in the rocks through which a spring came forth. "So it goes by the name 'Devil's Den.' A charming little story for a desolate sort of place?"

"I wouldn't bring my true love here for an outing."

"But the folks around here do just that," Stallard said.

Away from the massive boulders, Prescott looked over a jumble of smaller rocks littered about the ground leading to where the tree line began, carrying on up to the large hill in front of him.

Stallard saw his gaze. "That hill there is called Big Round Top."

"Unusual ground."

"More than you know from appearances," Stallard said. "Some of the locals say there was once a large battle between Indian tribes near here. Hundreds of warriors. Don't know what they were fighting for or about, but the folks around here have found arrowheads and trinkets of other kinds. No bones that I've heard of, but there are whispers of strange noises coming from this land during the lonely hours of night."

"Now it's ghost stories." Prescott chuckled. "Why are we out here, Parker? You plan to hide the gold out here?"

"Absolutely, sir!" he said with enthusiasm.

"What, here in this Devil's Den? Someone could come along and just carry it out of this cave, with a fair amount of trouble, I venture, but it wouldn't take more than a couple of boys out in search of adventure to run across it."

"You're correct, of course, but I hadn't planned on hiding it amongst the rocks here." Stallard smiled at the bewildered Prescott. "We're going to hide it under the rocks." And as the notion came to Prescott, Stallard exploded with a laugh and headed back to where the horses were tethered.

June 9, 1863

The hotel maid poured the last bucket of hot water into the tub and mumbled a goodbye. As soon as she closed the door, Prescott eased himself into the water. His muscles barked at him still, even though it had been four days since he and Stallard had finished placing the gold for safekeeping. It had taken the two of them the better part of three days to complete the job, and Prescott still found himself awed by their ability to complete it.

Stallard, for his part, thoroughly enjoyed watching Prescott come to the realization that they were going to be successful. Then again, Stallard's resolve had long ago failed to surprise the lieutenant. Brison had been left out, for his wounds still kept him from lifting, but Stallard had used that to keep the gold's location between himself and Prescott.

There was a quick knock and Stallard strode in.

"Caught you and your regiment in a poor position, Lieutenant." Stallard laughed. "The Rebels would pick you off at will while you're all stuck in the water there. Still, it's a good idea to wash God's good earth from your body when you can."

"You did enough to dirty a man up, you did," Prescott chided.

"Ah, but the task is completed and now that the goods are stored, shall we say, and with the thankful cooperation of Mr. Smythe leaving us the hell alone, we can now turn our attention to him."

"What's been rumbling around up in that head of yours? You've been going out about town for days, talking to people at all hours. I expect you have a plan."

"I do, indeed, sir."

"You planning on telling me, or you just sort of figuring I'll come by it naturally when Smythe puts a bullet in me?"

Stallard smiled. "I can't imagine you without worrying yourself and getting in a fuss. I know you've been pacing about in this stable for some time, and I appreciate you not jumping at me, but there has been a reason for it all. By the by, have you been hearing the rumors? There are reports General Lee and his army are going to be here any day. Think of that! I suppose we could forget about England and just hand the whole lot right over to Bobby Lee and be done with it, ha!"

"I suppose we could, at that, but might there be a few unpleasant men in Parliament when your gold fails to appear?"

"Yes, yes, there's that. Just a thought, I suppose, but it would be glorious to see the look on Bobby Lee's face," Stallard said. "Of course, these rumors probably have nothing behind them. The folks around here are a bit jittery after the fighting came north in the fall. Still, the rumoring does help our cause."

"Shouldn't we get some help from your man in Washington?" Prescott inquired again. "Does he have resources to help us?"

"I don't have direct contact with him. There are rules. His position is one of importance, and I should not risk compromising him. The information he's providing to the Confederacy is more valuable than our task here," Stallard said. "My contact was intentionally meant to be limited. I'm to make Richmond aware of our progress when the gold is on its way to England. Then, Richmond will advise her gentlemen in London. Of course, Fitzroy will be traveling with the shipment to England. But, first, we must eliminate the threat from Smythe. We head up to Harrisburg with the wagons, and we let Smythe make the move on us."

Finished with the bath, Prescott climbed out and sat on a chair, drying himself. "Are you intending to have General Lee lend you a regiment to have lurking in the bushes?"

"You aren't very far off." Stallard grinned. "Just the wrong side of the war."

June 18, 1863

This time, when they came, it was at a full gallop down the road from the north. When Prescott saw them, they were coming down the slope of a field in a jerky motion like skipping children, their heads bobbing about. Prescott recognized them for what they were and reined in his team as Stallard did the same behind him.

They were fortunate in that the area was wide and there were no fences to restrict their ability to reverse the wagons. Still, the horses weren't well trained in backing up with a load, so both men went to their leaders and swung the teams round smartly. They had but a few minutes before the group would be on them.

Stallard yelled encouragement up to Prescott, who again had the lead team, and they charged off down the Harrisburg Road, kicking up a trail of dust that immediately obscured the pursuers already a scant half mile behind them. Prescott had a clear view of the land ahead—scarce were the towns or farms here, and there was little traffic, save a single runabout they had passed not ten minutes before. They were approaching quickly, and the driver, notified by the uproar from behind, was pulling off with haste.

Prescott had never broken a horse before, though he had seen men in his regiment do so to appropriated stock, but he figured he was experiencing the same now. Even with the heavy suspension, the drummer's wagon tossed him about in a chaotic dance with the road. The hanging pots and other implements clanged with a shattering din.

The driver of the runabout shook his fist as the wagons rumbled by, and Prescott tried to look around behind him on the left and only glimpsed for a moment Stallard's team. The dust had lessened, and Stallard had moved his team to the road's left side to clear his way. They were coming up on a majestic oak that Prescott remembered from their trip up. They were still two miles away, he estimated, and

Smythe's men would be upon them before then. A sharp jolt sent Prescott into the roof.

He was fast getting into an ornery mood with the pounding, and he found himself, even with concentrating on the road, thinking of the physical brutality he had been through since sitting in the president's office—from the iron bar to the head, the climb above the alleyway from the burning building, the fall over a cliff and through a fir tree, the fight and fall with Joshua, and then the work of hiding the gold.

Those kinds of efforts upon the body tend to pile on and stir up the anger. Often the hero on the battlefield was not the bravest, but just the one who was wrathful enough to not care about anything except changing the situation. And that was how Prescott felt when, to his left, he noticed a man at full gallop, with pistol drawn, pointing it at him and shouting a command over the explosion of noise.

Prescott gasped for breath, but his body wouldn't respond, the muscles contracting against the blow from Smythe. He had lost count of how many there had been, and they had not all been to his gut, but to his jaw.

As his breath finally returned, he moved his tongue along the loose teeth and tasted the blood from within. Smythe stood back and crossed over to where his men also held Stallard, who, from Prescott's estimation, was holding up in far better shape.

Stallard struggled against the men and spit at Smythe's feet as the foundry owner grew close. Shirt off, Smythe had worked himself up a good sweat over the past half hour. Some of his men were beginning to look up and down the road with discomfort, no doubt assessing how much longer this scene could unfold without detection. But Smythe's attention was equally divided between the two prisoners before him.

"Answers are what I need, Stallard," he said. "The wagons are empty. Where did you hide the gold? Or is it already on a train to

Philadelphia? I can beat you until you'll beg me for death, you bastard!"

"Again—and for the fifth time, I believe, and even your dullminded self should be able to grasp this idea—you can go to hell." Stallard tried to stand himself up straight.

Smythe measured up the target and threw his right hand into Stallard's gut. The southerner coughed and bent over. This time, the two men let him fall to his knees in the dirt. Prescott swore and spit a tooth he had worked free, bringing Smythe's attention.

"Parker, we would have had a profitable venture, but I always saw you had a flaw in your character that jeopardized your plans. It started when you brought this one into it. You didn't listen to me when I warned you about him. Your faith in him was misplaced, and worse still, you refused to alter your view when presented with the truth."

"Enough of your lies," Stallard said from his knees. "Jackson has saved my life more than once. We would never have gone this far without him."

"He's still a Union deserter." Smythe poked at Prescott's shoulder. "Or is he? You continue on with your faith in him like a stupid dog following his master." He looked over at Stallard. "You truly are a fool." Smythe walked over to his horse and pulled a pistol from a holster draped over the saddle horn and walked over to Prescott. The barrel came to eye level and the hammer was pulled back. "I should have handled you myself months ago."

"No, Smythe! There's no reason!" Stallard cried.

"There's every reason! This man cost me men and material, my foundry, and my left eye, and he made me a cripple for the rest of my days. You both no doubt killed Joshua and his men. You have cost me more than any man ever has. There's every reason!" He forced the barrel into the side of Prescott's head, as the men on either side flinched.

"I'll tell you where the gold is," Stallard said.

"Yes, you will. But I don't need this one because I have you."

"Let that hammer go, and you'll never see the gold." Stallard pulled his still-mending arm to his side in pain. "I'll make sure you never see it. It will be lost until some lucky fool comes upon it years from now. And it will not be you!"

"I suppose you mean as God is your witness," Smythe scoffed.

"Absolutely."

Smythe grunted and pulled the pistol back, uncocking the hammer with his thumb. The group's attention suddenly swung in the direction of the road to the south as a pair of wagons came over a rise a half mile away.

"Witnesses. They do tend to complicate matters," Stallard mused.

"Put them in the first wagon," Smythe ordered, then put his face close to Stallard's. "We'll take you to Gettysburg, and you'll take us to where the gold is hidden—before the day is over. If I don't see the gold by sunset, I'll slit his gizzard like the dog he is. Then I'll set about working on you."

The wagons and horses were keeping just under a trot, for Smythe didn't want to arouse the attention of other travelers. He remained on horseback, to the left of the lead wagon. He had two men in front and one to the other side while Stallard and Prescott rode on the wagon's seat. Prescott had the reins.

The other four men were driving the second wagon just behind. Smythe and the other man riding to the side of the first wagon rode with their guns drawn—the implication being that a move of any sort to change the situation would be met with a bullet.

The road dipped between two rises and on the right was a stone rather than a wooden fence. It was built unusually high for the farmland of this area, but it afforded excellent protection and concealment. Prescott thought to say something to Smythe, a final chance for a condemned man, but the words failed to come forth. He turned and looked at the battered face of his companion and nodded. Prescott pulled on the reins and brought the wagons to a halt.

"What the hell are you stopping for, Prescott?" Smythe held his pistol up at eye level, apparently aware of the danger.

From behind the stone wall came a barked order, and a company of men stood in unison with a second group rising just head-high above the wall's edge. A uniformed officer with a sword outstretched stood prominently to the side. "By the command of the Twentieth Pennsylvania Militia, you are ordered to drop your weapons!"

In the following moments, a number of events happened simultaneously: Smythe fired up at the entrenched militia and spun his horse to cut behind the wagon as Stallard tried to leap to bring him down, failing and falling to the road. Prescott dove inside the wagon to the base of the bed. Fire erupted from the stone wall, and Smythe's men were torn from their saddles as the horses panicked and men screamed from the road. Two of Smythe's men managed to return fire, but were cut down from a second volley. The order to cease fire came from the officer as Smythe spurred his horse north on the road.

There was now only the commotion of the militiamen hollering congratulations to each other amid yells of "Dirty Rebs." Stallard stepped from behind the wagon and yelled up to the officer, who stepped quickly down to the road, followed by four of his men.

"Captain, your men performed admirably," Stallard said. "These Confederate spies will not bring any more harm upon Pennsylvania. Please, sir, my companion and I are on strict orders from General Hooker. We must go after their leader. Have your men take these Rebs for burial and move our wagons back into Gettysburg."

"It was an honor to serve Mr. Lincoln and General Hooker on this duty, sir." The major threw his shoulders back and saluted. "The boys, I'm sure, will have much to tell their folks."

"Ah, remember, Captain: we must have secrecy, especially if the rumors are true of the Reb army coming north. Go, now."

As the militiamen came down the slope, Stallard and Prescott recovered their pistols and carbines and mounted their horses in pursuit of Smythe. They galloped off, following him north on the Harrisburg Road, but within a few hundred yards, they saw him turn off on a road heading east and could see they weren't gaining any distinct advantage, for Smythe was a good horseman. He disappeared around a corner as the road wandered up the slope of a ridge near a tree line, and Stallard and Prescott pushed their mounts to maintain their pace up the rise.

They had not said a word since the shooting had begun, and now they rode in silence, accompanied only by the horses' labored breathing. They came around the bend and found an empty road framed by dense woods that canopied before them. The scene reminded Prescott of the road many miles away that had been covered by snow, and he was overwhelmed by fear. The road was empty, save Smythe's horse, which stood alone tethered to a tree.

As they pulled back their mounts, a shot cracked and echoed around them. Prescott found himself on the ground with his shoulder on fire, stunned into inaction. He saw Stallard, off his horse and moving toward him. Stallard froze at the sound of Smythe's voice.

"Don't move, Stallard! Or you'll take one in the back!" Smythe's voice came from just a few feet away. "Hands away from your weapons." Smythe stepped forward from behind a boulder and swung his carbine stock-first into the back of Stallard's head. Within a minute, he had tied the South Carolinian's hands and was standing over Prescott.

"He never saw you for what you are, did he?" Smythe said, his voice almost quiet.

"No, I don't suppose he did."

"What was this whole business about? Just rooting out a few Copperheads for the sake of the papers? Doesn't matter to me, for I have only one charge and that's the gold back in Gettysburg, and then restoring my business so I can continue to help with the war. It is highly profitable."

Blood seeped between the fingers of Prescott's left hand as he tried to stem the blood flow from his opposite shoulder. He never thought his death would come on an empty road in the heat of Pennsylvania, but here he was looking into a killer's eyes.

A killer who had kidnapped Abby, had tried to have himself and Parker eliminated, had butchered a family in Ohio for no reason other than to inflict pain. Unlike in battle, where death comes arbitrarily and doesn't choose by rank or station, death was here and preparing to take him alone.

And then he saw a shadow.

"Smythe, my name is Lieutenant Jackson Prescott of the Twelfth Massachusetts Regiment, on assignment by order of the president of the United States. You should drop your weapon so I can place you under arrest by order of the same."

Smythe pulled back on his pistol's hammer. "I'll see you in hell—"

His neck exploded, splattering Prescott with blood as another shot echoed through the trees.

June 19, 1863

The hotel they had chosen was simple, yet clean and away from the main traffic of Pennsylvania's state capital. They had arrived late in the day before and, with a few extra coins, got themselves rooms in the back, away from the lobby.

Prescott's wound had been attended to by a doctor called near 10 p.m., and the news had been good—the shot had been as well placed for a man as possible in such matters. It had traveled below the collarbone and through soft muscle, avoiding bone and vessels. There had been some bleeding, but the doctor pronounced Prescott a lucky man and packed off the injury, telling him to rest for two weeks before trying to get himself killed all over again. Stallard had been more of a concern at first, for he had not come around for an hour or so after being hit with the rifle butt. For the ride north, he had spoken little and had held his head, often gingerly running his fingers along the back.

By early afternoon of the next day, Stallard and Prescott were propped up with pillows in the same room, Prescott on the bed and Stallard on a sofa dragged in from the hallway. They had both slept until noon and were rested, but suffering. They still wore a badge of embarrassment to the figure leaning on his good shoulder against the window, his attention on the activity outside.

"I would be less of a man if I didn't thank you for saving our lives," Stallard said.

"Yes, we would be remiss in our manners," Prescott added.

Stallard continued, "As has been shown before, it was wise for you to remain separate from the militia. I know we argued about this for a time, and I had been on the side of you staying in town, considering your injuries. But you again proved to be correct on a matter of strategy."

"The two of you charging up that road into a natural breastworks with a killer ahead of you who was handy with a rifle and pistol . . ." Brison smiled slightly and raised his eyebrows. "I would venture you realize how lacking in prudence that action was? Whatever. It did accomplish one task: it made the two of you look sorrier than I do, and that, I might add, takes a bit of doing."

"It's one thing to be gracious in accepting thanks, Brison, the least you could do would be to refrain from spiking my rum with vinegar. I'm ashamed for my stupidity," Stallard said.

Brison laughed. "I meant no disrespect—I was only trying to give you a laugh. You both look so forlorn!"

Stallard and Prescott smiled in unison and put their heads back. There was quiet briefly, and then Prescott brought himself forward again. "How many more times are you going to save my life, Andrew? I thought I would be dead in a moment, and instead it was Smythe. As I have seen before, you're a hell of a shot. Any sharpshooter regiment would be happy to have you counted among its ranks."

"You two haven't given me the particulars," Stallard said. "It seems I missed the entire scene with my face in the dirt."

"Smythe was preparing to execute me," Prescott said, "but Brison threw a shot at him in time."

"And right difficult it was, what with my arm still in a sling." Brison moved to the lone chair near the door. "I almost didn't get the Spencer up in time. I might not have had a second chance."

"I'm indebted to you, and you'll be rewarded with a handsome compensation deposited in any bank on the East Coast you wish. Now, with the threat of Smythe eliminated, we can turn our thoughts back to completing our task. I've been thinking, there's a railroad line that runs out of Gettysburg, and I can arrange to have the shipment taken directly to Philadelphia."

"Do you plan on hiring help to move it from your hiding place?" Prescott asked. "None of the three of us are in a condition to be hauling the gold back onto the wagons and then into crates for shipping by rail. And that's how you would have to accomplish it. Disguising it will be imperative. If you're concerned about safety, contact your friend Booth there, or someone else."

"We shall do it ourselves after we spend some time healing up," Stallard said. "It's going on late June, and I expect time is, indeed, growing short. Lee will be looking for a fight soon enough, and we need to have our political votes in place. Fitzroy's deal called for a significant military success in the East. When it comes, our gold must be at least on the way and confirmed by Fitzroy's counterpart from England."

"You rely on faith more than you should," Brison said.

"'Tis a fault. I bow to your observation." Stallard smiled.

"Still, I expect the worst is over for us," Prescott said.

Brison carried a worried look still, but he replied, "It would appear so."

Chapter Thirty-Nine

Present Day
August 3

"Does the house have security monitoring?" Richardson asked, directing the question to Coulthard as they all stood at the front door.

"The park guide just unlocked the door with a key. No alarm. She mentioned they don't even patrol out here yet—at least, not regularly."

Richardson nodded to Stubbs, who then produced a crowbar and wedged it between the door and frame. In thirty seconds, they were inside. Richardson instructed three of the men to remain outside—two in front and a third to walk the grounds. Stubbs and a second man led the hostages from the living room to the cellar stairs. When the group had settled into the basement, Richardson had Stubbs stand away so as to be able to survey the room and its occupants with the large-caliber pistol in his left hand.

"Behind the wall?" Richardson looked at Coulthard.

"The large stone there can slide out," she said.

Richardson pointed his cane at Sparks and told Coulthard to untie him. While she worked, Richardson stepped over to Streeter. "You would not be in this situation if you had only followed my instructions. Your work was professional. It makes it all the more shocking to me that I've had to take these measures." He waited for a response, but Streeter only looked impassively at his former boss. "No clever repartee?"

"I must admit, words fail me," Streeter said flatly.

"Can't blame you a bit on that one." Richardson smiled.

Stubbs tossed a pickaxe to Sparks, keeping his gun steady. "Open up a larger hole."

Sparks wordlessly glanced at Richardson, who motioned to the wall.

The two men left out front might have considered themselves professionals, but their actions belied amateurs. They immediately pulled out cigarettes and lit them while cradling their weapons. In the dark, he couldn't tell what they were—Stens, AK47s, or Colt AR-15s.

Anderson had heard that a small shipment of those had been stolen in Massachusetts just six months ago. He watched as the two men stood to the side of the front door in the glow of the light from inside.

He was shocked, and fought to sort out what he was seeing in front of him. The hostages and the suspects were inside, save the guards, but the expected FBI team was not in place. Instead of a sufficient force working themselves into position in standard procedure, he was watching a team of three moving in. If this was Griffin's group, then something was very wrong.

"J.A. . . . J.A.!" Loring's hushed whisper was urgent. "Subject on the east side just took out the rover and is moving back into the tree line."

"They're moving into position to take the front two," Cooper added. "Orders?"

"We stay put and let it play out," Anderson said. "Keep listening in on what's being said inside."

The two guards flicked ashes from their cigarettes and continued talking. There was a slight breeze through the trees, and Anderson was too far away to make out the conversation, but one of the guards was making hand gestures while no doubt telling a story. The other one listened for a few moments, then began to look to either side in anticipation of seeing the rover come from around the corner. With each passing moment, his body movement showed concern.

He was just beginning to move to the east side with his story-teller in tow when he suddenly jerked, then slowly slid to the ground. The second guard stood over him for an instant, recognition coming far too late, and then he, too, silently slipped to the ground. Anderson observed that in five minutes, Griffin's team—if it was, indeed, them—had neutralized half of Richardson's men.

Sparks had managed to pull out the stone he had moved before, along with hacking away at some stones and mortar placed around it. The gap was larger, but not yet large enough to easily gain access to the space behind. Sparks paused to catch his breath.

"You have miscalculated tremendously if you believe you can get away with this. Murder numerous times over, millions in gold ingots. You really think the government is going to stop looking for you . . . ever?"

"Continue on," Richardson said. "I don't need to disappear forever. I only need fifteen or twenty years or so, and with the money I have, if the government comes calling, I'll be gone and well insulated. While Mr. Streeter here was handling the recovery of the gold, with you as the point, of course, I was working to finalize my plans elsewhere. Everything is in place."

"You're assuming you'll make it out of Gettysburg with the gold."

"There will be no rescue by your Bureau. My source inside tells me your operation was, indeed, known only to yourself, your director, and the deputy director."

"Who, conveniently, is dead."

"I had nothing to do with that," Richardson insisted. "Just a helpful coincidence. Keep digging."

The opening was almost large enough to allow a man in if he stooped. Sparks worked at a final stone, knowing Richardson would then want to see the gold behind the wall. Sparks straddled the wall, trying to work the large stone free, using the ax on the side out of view.

A voice came from the upstairs, followed by the sound of something falling onto the floor above. There was a cry of pain and a string of obscenities. Everyone except the short one, who kept his eye on everyone from the corner, turned to look at the stairs. The voice from above yelled something about breaking his knee, and the guard closest to the stairs looked at Richardson.

"Go see what the moron did to himself," Richardson said.

The second man went up the stairs, and Sparks continued to hack away at the stone, trying to make as much noise as possible, grunting with the effort, still checking for the positioning of the people left in the room. Stubbs remained in the corner, his attention squarely on Sparks and Streeter. Richardson turned back to Sparks and banged his cane on the planks of the wooden floor.

"Can you pull a box out on your own?" Richardson asked.

"No, I'll need help in a minute."

Footsteps could be heard at the top of the stairs, and a set of legs with dark pants and black, soft-soled shoes appeared, coming down. They were the same as what Richardson's men were wearing, and Sparks saw everyone, including Richardson's keen-eyed observer, look over at the stairs. Without changing his position, Sparks moved his obscured left hand up to a small ledge. With a sudden movement, the figure on the stairs swung into a crouched position.

"No one move! FBI!" Grimes moved his gun toward the one figure who was armed. But Stubbs had only to swing his pistol arm, and he moved a fraction of a second faster than Grimes. The sound of two shots, fired in rapid succession, exploded in the confined space. Stubbs collapsed to the floor, the gun falling from his lifeless hand.

With matched precision, everyone's attention swung over to the entrance at the stone wall. Sparks, crouched in the opening, held a still-smoking gun. The room was silent, shock numbing reactions. Grimes spat out a command, and a second figure, Wallace, came down the stairs and brought a gun to bear.

"It's over, Richardson," Sparks said. "It ends here."

The Boston financier swung around in panic and found three guns trained on him. A look of resignation grew and his eyes blackened with hatred.

Another set of steps came, less determined than the first two, a slower pace. "We're secure," Grimes said. Sparks saw that it was Griffin, and he lowered his gun and moved to put his arms around Jennifer. He gave her a hug and smiled at Griffin as the director reached the floor.

"You were beginning to worry me," Sparks said as he moved over to check on the dead man. "Thank God you all moved in. Everything secure upstairs?"

"Yes. So, you're Jonathan Richardson," Griffin said. "You have put a lot of people through a lot of trouble. I expect the Federal charges against you would take up a dozen pages."

"I . . . I don't understand." Richardson turned to Sparks. "My source told me you were going to get help, but I thought my early intervention here would . . ." He let the words trail off.

Sparks stuck his gun into his waistband behind his back. "We knew about Goldberg, and you, Tracy, from early on. Goldberg let slip he knew about Gettysburg when there were only three people in the world who knew about it—myself, the lab tech, Baker, who I would trust with my life, and you. So I used you to string Streeter and Richardson along, though I didn't expect they would go after Jen. That's where it became ugly, Richardson, and why you'll get life without parole—maybe even the needle. I can't imagine the government not going full bore on this."

"I demand to see my lawyer immediately!" Richardson had regained his balance and was blustery. "I'll not say another word until my demand is met!"

"Fine with me," Sparks said, "but we'll be able to link you to Goldberg's death. We'll get the link, and with that and kidnapping, it's a lock."

Richardson drew himself up and turned to Griffin. "I was only after the gold. I never agreed to the use of these kinds of measures. I'm innocent of all matters with violence here. I demand to see my lawyer. I want him waiting for me when we get back to your offices!"

"That won't be necessary." Griffin raised his arm where a silenced Mauser had appeared. There was a muted cough and a red blossom appeared between and just above Richardson's eyes. His surprised look remained as he slipped to the floor.

"Clark!" Sparks shouted, but he was abruptly stopped by the barrel of the Mauser, now swung in squarely at him. His mouth hung open in horror, his mind stunned to inaction.

"'Win us with honest trifles, to betray us in deepest consequence,'" Streeter said, then to Sparks, "You never saw this coming, did you?"

"I do this with regret, Jason, but I must see this through," Griffin said. "I need the two of you to keep digging. We need access to that space."

"In cold blood, Clark! Have you lost your mind?" Sparks asked. Grimes took his gun from him.

"Perhaps. Reality is really just an absolute from your own perspective. My reality changed when I saw the results of a CAT scan. Priorities change, relationships begin to soften, fade under the weight of a thousand memories soon to be lost. Then, the realization of what I could accomplish with the untold millions—my family taken care of for generations, free to follow their dreams without the worry of financial realities.

"I watched to see if the gold was, indeed, here. And so, we have moved in at the appropriate moment. As for Richardson, I've done the prosecutors a favor. He was as dirty as most. You don't become as powerful as he is without ruining many lives along the way. That's how corporate America works."

"You don't believe that . . . you can't," Sparks said quietly.

"Not for all, but in his case . . . it was his way," Griffin said. "Both of you, continue digging and if there's another weapon behind the wall, tell me now. If I find one behind there . . ."

Sparks and Streeter moved to the opening and began to work on the stones. "You had Goldberg killed?" Sparks asked Griffin.

"Yes."

"But why? It was dangerous to eliminate him before you had the gold. You didn't know how Richardson would react. He might have shut everything down."

"That was exactly what I was worried about." Griffin turned to Wallace and sent him to check the perimeter outside. "Goldberg was panicking. He had found out somehow that I was working on something outside. He was partially correct that I was in contact with you, after I had stipulated to him that he was to be your contact. Again, he was only partially correct."

"He assumed you were trying to help me locate Jennifer."

"Grimes and Wallace here *were* trying to locate the safehouse where she was," Griffin said. "There was just more to the mission than that. I wanted to isolate Jennifer so she could be factored out completely."

"You didn't want her here," Sparks said.

"No, Jason, I didn't. Anything but that. You understand?"

"Yes."

"You can blame Streeter there. If he hadn't removed her from the safehouse . . ."

"Uncle Clark." Jennifer stepped forward on the verge of tears. "He might be guilty of many things, but Mr. Streeter saved my life, and he was decent. I can't believe you would do all this. *Please*, stop this now!"

Griffin began to say something twice, but stopped himself.

"The CAT scan . . . a tumor?" Sparks asked.

Griffin nodded. "Inoperable. But I'll have enough time to set the funds up overseas. The accounts are ready, and I even have a ship leaving Philadelphia in a month that will move the gold to a foreign site where it will be melted down and reintroduced into the market slowly."

There were more questions Sparks wanted to ask, but he was only delaying the events to follow. He stopped swinging the ax and put his hand on Streeter's shoulder to stop him. Wallace returned and said the area outside was secure, no activity. Sparks put down the ax.

"Why have you stopped?" Griffin asked.

"We might as well stop now. The gold isn't here," Sparks said.

Griffin's face flushed, and he touched the side of his head. "What are you saying?"

"The third letter the park ranger showed to myself and Mrs. Coulthard was fake," Sparks said.

"What we read wasn't in the letter?" Coulthard asked.

"You remember that Munson said she couldn't take the document out of the archives, but that she transcribed the text for us," Sparks said. "She altered the gold's location."

Griffin motioned Sparks and Streeter away from the opening. He tossed a flashlight to Grimes. "Check it out."

Within a few seconds, Grimes was back out. "Just debris, no boxes."

"But I saw you go in and bring out a bar of gold." Coulthard was incredulous.

"Did you use a touchstone on it?" Streeter asked.

"A what?"

"A touchstone. A stone, kin to flint, used in the past to test the purity of gold. You struck the stone using the gold and the tell-tale streak would help gauge the quality of what you have." Streeter looked at Sparks. "What was it?"

"Actually, it was a gold ingot, but not from the original shipment back in 1863," Sparks said. "I owe a certain Steve McPherson of Gettysburg a letter of thanks—a friend of Munson's who lent us the ingot."

"Where's the gold?" Griffin hissed, his eyes wild with anger. "Did you ever actually find it?"

"Yes, but it's not here. It's at Devil's Den itself."

"On the battlefield! Impossible!"

"The actual text of the third letter is under the driver's seat of my car," Sparks said. "It gives precise directions to a large boulder under which the gold was hidden, northeast of the Den area."

"Wouldn't the points of reference have changed over the course of time?" Streeter asked.

"Normally, yes," Sparks said. "But the one key reference in the text remains as it did a century and a half ago. It hasn't changed at all. It's a large flat boulder, and by its description, it has to be the Table Rock—perhaps the most recognizable diabase boulder in the entire area. It points the line we must travel. The distance is marked off.

Then a boulder itself has Parker Stallard's initials chiseled on the west base of the stone. The gold is underneath." Sparks looked at Griffin. "More problematic, isn't it? Broad daylight for the work, a national park with hundreds of visitors a day, curious onlookers all."

"We need to talk about this," Grimes said to Griffin.

"No, there's a way, there's a way," Griffin replied. "We have access to the equipment needed. We'll go now. After, Jason, you give a call to the park director and have that part of the park closed off. We'll begin work in the morning and work until it's done."

They went up the stairs, with Grimes first making sure the group was alone, then covering Sparks and Streeter, who came next, followed by Coulthard and then Wallace. Griffin brought up the rear with Jennifer. She continued to talk to him in low whispers until he finally squeezed her arm and coldly told her to be quiet.

The group reached the inside foyer, the design of which seemed out of place with the original architecture. Grimes stood with his back to the door and waited, his gun trained on Sparks while Wallace covered Streeter.

"We'll take Richardson's van." Griffin tossed the keys to Grimes. "Secure them in the van, and Wallace and I will take the SUV and the other car. I don't want them left here. Then you'll need to return and take care of the bodies."

"Just what are you planning to do?" Sparks asked. "Even if we locate the gold, it will take machinery and hours to get the gold loaded into trucks. I say 'trucks' because it will overload that van quickly."

"We're prepared. We have a safehouse set up, and we'll find the gold first, then return to recover it." Griffin flipped his Mauser. "Move out."

Grimes opened the door and the group began to make their way out in the same fashion as they had before. As they reached the door, Sparks leaned slightly to Streeter and whispered, "Down." The only light filtered outside from a single source inside the house, and Griffin was leaving it on. Sparks knew why. Darkness would be dangerous with unrestrained captives, and Griffin was not foolish. But it didn't matter, not now.

Grimes and Wallace were just ahead of Sparks, Coulthard, and Streeter, with Griffin and Jennifer just at the door, when the entire front of the house exploded in blinding light. Everyone threw up their hands in an involuntary reaction and closed their eyes. All except Sparks, who shoved Coulthard, knocking her off her feet as he yelled "Now!" to Streeter, who dove to the ground.

He heard a double *thud* and both Grimes and Wallace coughed as their legs buckled. They were dead before reaching the gravel. Sparks turned in desperation back to the front door. Jen had not been part of the equation, and he prayed Anderson and his men were flawless. But they didn't have a chance. Griffin had been delayed coming out of the door, and his reactions were quick. They were back inside and gone, the door slammed shut.

"He's got Jennifer!" Sparks yelled in the direction of the lights. "I need you down here, now!" He covered the few steps to the door and slammed his shoulder into it, but gasped at the resistance. The door flexed with his weight, but something was propped against the brass work. He continued to throw himself against the door, frustration manifesting into panic. Then he felt a presence beside him . . . Anderson.

"You heard everything?" Sparks asked.

"Yes."

"He's got her in there. No way to know how he'll react. Keep one man here, send another around to the side in the woods. Which way did they come from?"

"Southeast."

"Then that's where he'll try to get to . . . maybe."

Sparks stepped back and yelled at the house. "Clark! Talk to me. It's over. You don't want to hurt Jen. You know that!" There was no response. Sparks felt Anderson grab his hand and slip something familiar into it. Sparks knew instantly it was the gun he had used in the cellar.

"Remember, you're down one unless you want something else," Anderson said.

"I won't need it." Sparks moved off to work his way along the wall to the left side of the house. Anderson followed, speaking softly into his mouthpiece. They moved along until they reached the west corner and then they were on the west side, moving to the back.

Sparks didn't know what rooms were where, and he chastised himself for not memorizing the layout when he was there before. One thing he did know was that there was a door in the back, leading onto a patio. The question was whether Griffin had already gone out the back. They had their answer in seconds—the door was open.

"Front is still secure, and Loring is working his way around the other side," Anderson said.

"They're already out and into the woods," Sparks said. "Tell Loring to go back and work his way to the southeast and look for their vehicle, but tell him to watch for them coming through the woods."

They reached the back door, and Sparks glanced inside and saw nothing, even though light from the house's front was filtering down the hall. He was just about to begin his move to the tree line when there were shouts and a scream. Sparks tore through the house, bumping into a wall and slamming his head against it. He shouted back at Anderson, but his man wasn't there. Just a few seconds more.

He got his bearings and reached the front of the house. The door was open, and he stepped into the light and immediately realized his sheer stupidity—he was exposed, and the light kept him from seeing beyond the first twenty feet. Wood splintered next to his head, and he jumped back inside the door.

A car engine turned over, and gravel rumbled as the tires spun loose rocks against the car frame. Sparks darted out in time to see his own rental sliding sideways briefly, but then straightening itself out and disappearing down the driveway and on out past the tree line.

"Jason!" It was Coulthard, and she was kneeling over a figure lying on the ground. Sparks reached them just as Anderson did. It was Anderson's other man, and he was in a bad way, shot through the side and bleeding heavily, his breathing labored.

"Take care of your man, call an ambulance," Sparks said. "I'm going after them." He sprinted over to the bodies of Grimes and Wallace, finding a set of keys to Richardson's SUV, then was back past the three of them as Loring made his way back to the group. "When you make the call, give them a description of the car and tell them to shut down Routes 15, 134, and 97 south of town and pray he's headed back to Washington."

"They won't get the roadblocks up in time," Coulthard said. "He could go anywhere."

Sparks didn't answer—he was already accelerating out of the parking lot and onto the dirt road, swinging around to the west and heading away, the engine screaming in protest.

"They'll never get roadblocks up in time," Coulthard repeated to Anderson, who had just finished giving instructions to the rescue squad.

"They will if they listened to him properly earlier today," Anderson said.

"What do you mean, if they listened to him earlier?"

"We sort of asked the locals to keep a few patrol cars out on the roads leading out of town," he said, "just in case it was necessary." Anderson worked a compress onto the wound. "What happened out here?"

"He came out the front door and shot this man here, then tried for Streeter, but missed, and then he dragged Jennifer out and to the car."

Anderson looked around and motioned to Loring, who moved off.

"Where's he going?" Coulthard asked.

Anderson answered with annoyance. "Do you see Streeter around anywhere?"

Chapter Forty

"God created the earth in six days, Jackson, and it has taken Bobby Lee just those same six days to put absolute fear into the hearts of every Yankee in Pennsylvania." Stallard pushed up his chest as he looked out from the second-floor window of the hotel. "Look at them run about like chickens with a fox at the gate." Below him, on the street, the leisurely pace of a summer Sunday had been replaced by a desperate crowd's panic.

Horses bayed and reared up among shouts and curses as men forgot their manners and women gave away decorum. For days, the newspapers had been reporting rumors of the Rebel army approaching from the south, preparing to strike at this city on the Susquehanna. With Hooker's Army of the Potomac absent, the state capital was in turmoil. "Lee is up here, I can feel it." Stallard turned from the window. "Lee is going to draw Hooker out and defeat him. A move on Washington will follow."

"There's no doubt a fight is coming," Prescott whispered from his bed. He tried to sit up but, as he had for the past several days, found the effort difficult. An infection had set in on his shoulder wound, and he had suffered through alternate fever and chills for the past two days. He was able to keep food down, but the doctor was checking on him every day, barely keeping his anger down that they continued to refuse that Prescott be taken to a hospital. Stallard's conciliatory words had worked at first, but yesterday the doctor had threatened to bring in his own orderlies and have Prescott physically removed.

Brison had stepped in, taken the doctor outside, and somehow managed to placate him. Today, Prescott's fever was gone and the wound infection was drying up. It appeared the worst was past, though there would be some permanent loss of muscle, and it would be difficult for him to raise his right arm above his shoulder.

What was clear was that he would be of no use in helping to get the shipment to Philadelphia in time for the transatlantic voyage. Prescott knew Stallard would want to go ahead without him and in haste. He was clearing his throat in preparation to speak when Brison walked in.

"A bit nasty out there," he said, taking off his hat and slapping it against his leg before shutting the door. "The locals are panicking . . . thinking Lee is about to come up and shell the town."

"What's the latest word on the street?" Prescott said.

"It's not official, but a newspaperman arrived in town and informed a group of us that it's the Second Corps under Lieutenant General Ewell—Richard Ewell, I believe."

"Ewell—he's here? Just across the river?" Stallard asked.

"So I'm told," Brison said.

"I know him!" Stallard spoke now with an absence of focus. His gaze had returned to the chaotic street below. "Before the war, at an officer's party . . ."

"He's from South Carolina?"

"No, no, from Virginia—oh, around Washington itself. I was there on business and was invited. Some sort of official function. But he liked my stories. Curious sort . . . spoke ill of women, looks like a big old buzzard or some such. Well-pronounced nose, balding head. He would remember me."

"What are you thinking about, Parker?" Prescott asked.

The corner of Stallard's mouth upturned. "I have some business to attend to, and then we must talk. I've made some plans, at least in my head. You should be concentrating solely on improving your position. You still look like hell."

"I'll kindly thank you to keep your opinion of my appearance out of the conversation," Prescott mused, his voice pushed to cracking.

"Ease up there, Jack," Brison said.

"Listen to your friend. I won't be long. I have correspondence to write and deliver to the wonderful Yankee postal service." Stallard smiled.

There was a knock at the door, and Brison answered. It was a runner with a message and a package for Stallard, who dispatched the boy with a kind word and a coin. He read the note and laughed wholeheartedly as he opened the package. "One door has been closed for me, gentlemen." He reached in and retrieved a silver eagle's head. It was the one given to Gray Bear on that cold night in Minnesota. Stallard removed the simple wooden piece he had been using and replaced it with the cane's rightful head. "This completes my family's obligation."

Prescott's eyes met Brison's. "Parker, I know I'm no good to you for the remainder of this effort, but I could go stay with Fitzroy while you and Brison take the gold to the ship," Prescott said. "Perhaps we could even have a meeting of your . . . our group in Philadelphia. We could plan contingencies—you could bring in your man in Washington. If the gold does do your bidding in London, then we must plan, and perhaps even bring in President Davis on the designs."

"Perhaps . . ." Stallard was again distant, but then he returned his attention to them. "I do thank you both for your efforts these past months. I owe you more than I could ever repay. I must go attend to my business. One thing you need to know, the first opportunity to secure a ship to England comes on July 7. Fitzroy wrote me with the ship name, which escapes me at the moment, and the building, the Trenton Warehouse, where we can store the shipment if there's a brief delay. Time is growing very short. Brison, make sure our patient keeps his horse's ass in that bed. And no ladies for him, neither. I would not want the guilt of one Abigail Stinson on my conscience."

"A noble cause, indeed," Brison went along.

"You both deserve a taste of the leather for how you're treating a wounded man," Prescott groused.

And with that, Stallard was gone through the door. Brison listened as the steps faded down the hallway. He walked over to the window and watched the street. "His words were most peculiar, wouldn't you say?"

"I don't know. He does seem compelled toward some purpose as the Rebs close in here," Prescott said. "Do you think they will attack here in Harrisburg?"

"It may be just the action and not results that Lee seeks."

"Hooker away from Washington?"

"We can only deduce from what we have read in the newspapers, and you know how reliable they are." Brison saw Stallard cross the street against the maelstrom of horse and buggy. "You prodded him with another question about the operative in Washington, and I do believe that for the first time, he actually considered your point."

"He did, at that."

"But we cannot let the shipment reach that ship. He said July 7 for the shipping date. We need to message the president so we can seize the gold at the warehouse."

"But the president specifically instructed us that we were to find out who in his government had ties to Stallard and Fitzroy's group," Prescott stressed. "He felt that threat was great."

"And rightly so, but he didn't foresee a fortune in gold being shipped secretly out of a northern port."

"Or being handed over to the Army of Northern Virginia directly."

"You believe he'll try to get a detail from Lee to recover the gold?" Brison stepped from the window.

"We must consider it. Something has changed in his thinking. My long convalescences could affect his plans. I'm no good to him now, at least as a physical asset."

"If Hooker does move out to meet Lee, the war could be over within a month," Brison said. "Perhaps he sees the gold going for Philadelphia, or it could be . . ."

"He sees it staying right where it is." Prescott's voice cracked.

Brison put down his money and accepted a receipt from the telegraph operator. He then stepped outside and glanced a final time at the wire he had just sent to Washington.

To: Office of the President

Executive Mansion

Washington, D.C.

June 28

North to Trenton troops not constant lines information intervene shipment in for black rounders notice early July day available put ice just all should warehouse arrive star Adam Liberty sailing one requested to orange swim in JP prior seven July shipment.

The coded message was based on a route cipher Brison had arranged with Lincoln's code staff before he had left to follow Prescott. The code word was north, and it signaled Brison's using a six-by-six block with a person deciphering the message going down the first column, up the third, down the fifth, up the second, down the fourth, and up the sixth. A handful of key words were substituted, and Brison was sure one of the three young code experts in Washington would decipher it in good order. When the message was handed to the president, it would read:

Urgent. Shipment to arrive in Philadelphia early July. Trenton Warehouse. Shipment sailing July 7. Troops should intervene one day prior. Not all information requested available. JP.

It was late in the day, near dusk, when Brison returned to the hotel after checking on their horses and wagons. His shoulder was healing nicely, but the amount of time he had spent on his feet had fatigued him, and he wanted to have a good sleep.

He ate a quick meal of beef with boiled potatoes, then ordered an extra serving to take up to Prescott. Upon arriving at the room, he found Prescott asleep—a heavy sleep, he gathered, because of the lieutenant's snoring. Stallard was not there, and there was no sign that he had ever returned after leaving to attend to his business. Brison, tired and sore, took to the cot next to the window and was asleep within minutes.

June 29, 1863

Prescott was first aware of the noise from the street below as his head cleared of sleep. He immediately realized that the sounds seemed unhurried . . . routine in nature. He moved himself into a sitting position, aware of Brison stirring on the cot. Prescott's fever was gone, his stomach rumbled with hunger, and his head was clear for the first time in days. He swung his legs off the bed and attempted to sit upright.

With that mastered, he tried to stand up and was surprised to find his legs strong enough to support his weight, but he was certain much more than a short walk would be difficult. He sat back down, and it was then he noticed the folded paper as it slipped to the floor. With a little awkwardness, he retrieved it. The handwriting he recognized as Stallard's.

My friend,

I regret not being able to give my regards in person. Events require me to take action. By the time you read this, I will be across the Susquehanna and will have met up with General Ewell.

There is little doubt, as I see events, that General Lee will engage the Federals somewhere south of here, perhaps in Maryland. I believe a good fight now could end the war and perhaps our gold will not be needed in England.

The efforts of Brison and yourself have been incalculable. I bestow on you my most heartfelt gratitude. I have instructed the First Harrisburg Bank to compensate you in a method of your choice. I am sure the amounts will be satisfactory, certainly more than you both will receive in pension from the United States Government . . .

"Damn! Andrew . . . Andrew!" Prescott exclaimed.

"What's the shouting about? I'm already awake."

"Damn it to hell! He knew all along!"

"What are you talking about?"

"Stallard," Prescott said bitterly. "He had us all along. There's more . . ."

The gold's original purpose may have been intended for those who would bring pressure to bear on your president, but now the purpose will be to the betterment of my family. I do not judge your motives, for there is no higher calling than in the service of your country. I have come to know this through my association with you and Brison.

To that end, I am hopeful General Ewell will accept me into a South Carolina regiment, should he have one under his command. If not, I hope somewhere in the Army of Northern Virginia there is a place for a humble South Carolinian to fight with his countrymen, despite a lame leg.

I accept your belief that your cause is just, but I believe God's providence will shine on the Confederacy in the coming months, and I pray it does with as little bloodshed as possible. There has already been so much. You and I fought side by side these last months, and I have come to look upon you as a brother, for you are, in many ways, much like my brother, Charles.

You are a restless soul, as he was, but you have not found your way free. Perhaps it awaits you in New England with Abby, a woman of whose love, I shall dare say, any man would find himself blessed to be the recipient. I write this with the deepest respect. She is a remarkable woman.

When the war is over and we are blessed to meet again, I hope you will take my hand.

Your obedient servant,

Parker Stallard

Prescott handed over the note to Brison, and while the latter read, he struggled to put on his clothes, the room's only sound coming from the street below.

"He's abandoning the effort with England," Brison said upon finishing, "but he still has countless charges to face, as well as Fitzroy. They still committed crimes against the Union, conspiracy in the least."

"He'll not leave the gold there for after the war. He'll try to retrieve it for General Lee."

"I don't understand. How do you decipher that from these words?" Brison held out the note for display.

"You've been with him almost as long as I have these last months," Prescott said. "His words about joining up with Lee may be true, but I doubt it. What are the two qualities you see in that man? He'll change his mind on the method when it needs changing, but he never alters from his task. The gold going to his family? I think not. He's going to get the gold to Lee. If Ewell is at the Susquehanna, then Lee has had to have moved north into the Union."

"We talked about this, yes, but he's alone. The wagons are here, not in Gettysburg."

"Then instead of taking the gold to Lee, he'll take Lee to the gold." Prescott was becoming more agitated. "He used me like a fool, then when the time was right . . ."

"He could have done us harm while we slept, Jackson," Brison said. "I believe this last part of his letter is true. He's quite fond of you."

"We must get to Gettysburg. He'll get Ewell to swing down or, if Lee is closer, he'll go directly to him."

"Perhaps they will think of him only as a southerner caught up in the fight. Perhaps he'll not get to Lee quickly." Brison's words were tinged with hope.

"His family is well known in South Carolina, especially his father. All there needs to be is a courier or wire to Richmond. In the absence of that, Parker is persuasive. He'll acquire a meeting with Lee, and if the army is close, then three million dollars in gold that can be obtained with honor, not stolen as spoils of war, will be pursued faster than greased lightning." Prescott had finished dressing and tested his legs again. His mind stayed clear, but his shoulder still flickered with fire. He knew he was in for a rough time on the ride to Gettysburg.

"We go after him?" Brison brought his Spencer carbine from the closet, along with his ammunition pouch.

"No, we go straight to Gettysburg and contact the local militia—move the gold east by rail out of town. Then we wait for Parker to come calling with his help."

"Unless he brings the whole damn Reb army," Brison lamented.

Walking just ahead of Stallard was the captain, whose name he had already forgotten, and to either side were soldiers of undistinguished rank, probably privates, who didn't hold his arms, but paced themselves next to him as they walked to the half-open tent by the tree line. The captain saluted a colonel and voiced the intentions of their party, only to have a figure step from behind the tent flap on crutches as they exchanged words. "What the hell . . . what would be the business with this man?" he asked.

Stallard could see Ewell was looking at his face, the bald head thick with perspiration and his pronounced eyes narrowed, searching for a place to put Stallard's face.

"General, I am Parker Stallard, from South Carolina, sir," he interrupted the captain. "We met at a social function a few years ago. You were still in the Federal Army, home in Washington for a furlough. I regaled you with stories of some of the more . . . shall I say . . . less proper attributes of the ladies I had met in travels."

"Your face is familiar . . . yes, I do remember the function you speak of. Your family is prominent in Charleston, isn't it?"

"Yes, sir, my father is friends with President Davis and his own business dealings work well for the Confederacy. Sir, I have come here because I have urgent news for you and General Lee, if he's near."

With the mention of Lee, Ewell's eyes became more expansive, and he nodded to his aide. The captain made a face of disapproval and gave a sort of grunt. Ewell moved back to allow Stallard entrance to the expansive tent, and it was then Stallard noticed that the general had lost a leg.

"I was not aware of your injury, sir. The Yankee papers I've read made no mention of it," Stallard said.

"Lost it at Groveton, near ten months ago . . . actually, ten months ago yesterday. Just returned to duty last month." Ewell motioned for Stallard to sit down in the only chair besides the cot, which was propped up by two barrels so it was easier to climb into and out of. Ewell took to leaning against it. "So we're up here to take it to the Yankees, and not ten minutes ago, I received word to turn my troops away from Harrisburg and move south. Then, a man I hardly know, but do remember as coming from fine South Carolina stock, comes charging into my camp with urgent news. I suppose you have the position and strength of the Federal Army and want to do your duty for the Confederacy."

"I know nothing of the Federals, General, and I know you must guard against spies and those who would mislead you. But you must believe me. I've been working with like-minded men in the north and we have procured a large sum of gold with which we had intended to gain the support of certain members of the English Parliament. But my route out of the country has been compromised. My best alternative now is to get the gold to General Lee, and he can secure it to Richmond or points south. The gold is in a town, Gettysburg, just south of here near the Maryland border."

Ewell tilted his head to the side in response. "The stars are aligned for you. It seems we're headed in that direction. General Lee is bringing us together. We're headed in that general vicinity—Cashtown or Gettysburg, I mean. It seems I've been given the choice of which is best. A choice for which I have no information. I find myself in a damnable position."

"It's fortuitous, sir, that you're heading your army south, but if General Lee is closer, I must get to him and retrieve the gold with haste. There are others who have knowledge of this and will work to recover the gold before us."

"Your story has the color of a fairy tale, Mr. Stallard," Ewell gruffed. "It's not the information a man stakes his reputation on . . . is it?"

Stallard felt desperation rising within him—time could not be wasted. The presence of the army heading south on the roads to Gettysburg would block Prescott and Brison—they would have to swing around a different way, or Ewell could send out pickets to the west and south and watch for two men with wagons—or would they bother with the wagons? Would they travel with horses alone and get the help of the town's citizens? All that was necessary were a few militiamen and a train car headed east out of the station. "General, it will be my reputation and my family's to be questioned. Once the box lid is opened, I'll be vindicated."

Ewell raised his eyebrows, drawing lines in his forehead that swept farther because of his hairless crown. His eyes flashed with a coldness that Stallard just now remembered from before, and when he spoke this time, there was not a trace of his prominent lisp. "Finding a touchstone for a man's word is a hard road . . . but it is one that always has a conclusion."

There were few times in his life when Stallard had lacked the confidence to know his way. He was in one of those times now, standing outside another tent, this one near Cashtown. His future was in doubt.

The day had been spent on a ride under escort from Ewell's corps along the back roads south and west to where they had run straight into a huge column of Confederate troops, a separate body from the one they had left behind just south of Harrisburg.

Stallard's escort had left him under guard in the shade of a tree alongside the road, and he watched as an endless stream of men, horses, and artillery paraded by him. This was the best his home had to offer, and they were in great spirits, many of them singing songs as they came by—other times the melodies of home would drift on the wind from a band somewhere near. It was all almost enough to quell the anxiousness within him.

Ewell had been glad to have his leave of Stallard, dismissing his claims to a point, but then offered to send him along, with an escort, south to find the most advanced body of the Army of Northern Virginia. It was clear to Stallard as he rode away that Ewell's strategy was simple—pass the problem to someone else, but retain the ability to take credit should something come of it.

Stallard had also come to learn that the corps of troops marching by him as he sat under his tree, eating blueberries picked by the soldiers, was A.P. Hill's 3rd Corps. They would be followed tomorrow by James Longstreet's 1st Corps. The entire body of General Lee's army was converging just to the east of where he sat. Not a word had been spoken to him as to where they expected Hooker and the Federals to be coming later on this week.

Finally, as dusk came, the escorts returned and said he was to be taken to see Hill, whom Stallard had never heard of, but who was the commander of the units closest to Gettysburg. As they rode along the road, still choked with the elements of war, Stallard ran through in his mind what he would say to Hill when given his audience.

For a time, he thought he would press to be allowed to see Lee, but realized that it would take longer. The opportunity had to be taken now to recover the gold. The escorts told Stallard that Hill was an aggressive commander—it was his men who had arrived at the critical moment to save Lee at Sharpsburg nine months ago. That information buoyed Stallard's hopes that his words would be taken as an opportunity.

They arrived at the bivouac east of Cashtown and west of Gettysburg. Because of the darkness, Stallard was unable to see familiar ridges or turns in the road, but he knew this was the same road he and the two Federal officers had traveled just weeks before. They were just a short ride from the town. Stallard was led through the camp of Hill's staff, still under armed guard, until they approached a tent set aside.

There was a good-sized fire attended by two men cooking a small side of beef or perhaps a side of pig. Stallard's belly rumbled to the smell coming from the flames, and he suddenly realized how hungry and tired he was, for the berries had long since worn off. There was a sharp reply from inside, and the tent flap was pushed aside. He was ushered in and left standing alone in the light of three candles. Ambrose Hill was standing with his back turned.

"So, you're Parker Stallard." His voice cracked with the strain of speaking, and he turned to face his guest. Hill wore only his shirt and trousers—his boots were next to the cot. His dark hair, parted on the right, was set back a bit and slicked down as if he had just taken a bath.

His heavy beard and mustache hid his mouth, but the prominent bridge of his nose carried above the growth and led one's gaze to his eyes. Stallard could not tell their color, for the light reflecting off the canvas was yellow, but they were penetrating. "This message from General Ewell mentions you have a large amount of gold placed in Gettysburg?"

"Near Gettysburg, sir. Through the efforts of men like myself, working as we can north of the border to help President Davis's government." Stallard remembered the words from the escorts along the road. As he continued, he heard rain beginning to splatter against the tent. "General, I understand General Ewell's reluctance to give my words merit to General Lee, but he did send me along to you, as your corps is the closest to the town. I came down this road not a few weeks ago after a long travel from Chicago. I intended to ship the gold to England, where persons I'm in agreement with would use it for leverage within Parliament."

"A bold plan," Hill interjected. He moved to his cot and lowered himself with some difficulty. "Continue."

"My plans were compromised on two fronts that I don't have time to explain, nor do you care for the details of such trifles, so I felt compelled to offer the opportunity to General Lee to take custody of the shipment."

"How much gold are we conversing over?"

"Near five tons, sir, fairly high quality. It has been processed at a foundry in Chicago."

Hill put his hands to his face and rubbed his eyes, then took to running his fingers through his beard. "Your story is you have taken five tons of gold across Indiana and Ohio and half of Pennsylvania without detection from authorities, and all we need to do is take a detail to Gettysburg and retrieve it?"

"Yes, sir. It has been intimated to me that you're known as an aggressive commander, sir. The Confederacy owes you a debt for helping turn the battle at Sharpsburg. This is neither as grand an endeavor, nor as dangerous, but will land the government of your army much needed funds."

"There's a fight coming sometime soon here," Hill said. "We might not need those funds for fighting materials. The war could be over in days or weeks, should we prevail. Still, I see no reason not to go out and bring it back in . . . should your words be true. I still find your story too much like one a man would tell after a night of spreeing."

"Sir."

Hill held up his hand to stop Stallard. "I'll have my adjutant procure you a tent. Tomorrow, we'll see about taking a brigade into the town and securing your gold."

"But sir, there's more you need to know. There are Federal agents on their way to Gettysburg—they may have gotten there tonight."

"Agents?"

"And there's a rail head out of Gettysburg," Stallard stressed.

"Would they be able to move the gold out of the town tonight?"

"No, sir, that would not be likely," Stallard admitted. "But there's the militia. There are elements of militia in the area. I actually came in contact with them. I'm well known in the town as a businessman."

Hill took a rag and dipped it in a small bucket next to his cot and pressed it against his forehead. He was silent briefly before he mumbled some words and shook his head. "The best I can do for you is to have you move out with Heth's brigade. Word has come to me that he's heard a rumor of a large quantity of shoes being avail-able in the town and is going to investigate."

Stallard was disappointed, but he understood about moving men at night in enemy territory. He understood more when Hill spoke again.

"You'll remain with my corps, regardless, until this matter is settled," Hill said. "Can't have you wandering off with details of our whereabouts."

Stallard smiled. "I'm not offended, General. I'm not a Federal spy—I'm a true patriot of South Carolina. But caution should rule the night, I understand."

"The Federal Army is on the move." Hill hadn't seemed to hear Stallard. "Hooker has been replaced—George Meade is in command now. But he is well down in Maryland, surely. We should be able to eventually move into the town. The general will want us there. Roads lead in many directions, like the spokes on a wheel."

"General?"

"My apologies, sir. I fear I'm coming down with a sickness of some kind. My mind tends to wander a bit. My aide will see to getting a tent for you with General Heth's division. I'll send a message along concerning the situation, but I'll be intentionally vague. Best to keep the true nature of your appearance between you, myself, and General Heth."

"I agree, sir. You have my sincere thanks."

"Your country will be in debt to you when we recover the gold." Hill stood and moved to shake Stallard's hand. "Let us hope it will be used not for more war materials, but to help rebuild our new nation."

June 30, 1863

Prescott and Brison rode into town along what they came to realize was the York Pike, bringing them in from the northeast. Dawn's first light was coming over their left shoulders as their horses walked down the road with the town just a mile away. The day and night had been difficult—Prescott's injury mandated a methodical pace, and they were forced to stop on numerous occasions to let him rest. He didn't say a word for the near twenty hours, trying his best to hide his agony.

More than once Brison had leaned over from his mount and grabbed Prescott to keep him from falling, and the wound itself had started to bleed again, both front and back of where the bullet had assaulted. Prescott could see Brison wincing from his own wound. It was well along in the healing, but he was in far from good health—certainly not well enough to be in a fight—and a fight was coming, provided the Federal Army was coming up to meet the Rebels, for the Army of Northern Virginia was here and in great numbers.

And that was the second reason for Brison and Prescott's trials. The roads leading south from Harrisburg were choked with men and materials of war, and they forced the pair to swing through the countryside in a wide arc to the east. And still they ran into small pockets of Rebs, all turned in some fashion and heading south.

Brison told Prescott he had been traveling attached to a brigade in John Pope's army in August of last year when the Federals had had their noses bloodied a second time at Manassas. There, the fight had come quickly—Jackson's boys had appeared out of nowhere. Brison said he had an uneasy feeling about today. He could sense the battle approaching—a colossus. It would dwarf all that came before.

During quiet moments since that cold night when he saved Prescott from the fire, they had talked of the war and the experience. Prescott's memories had come forth a little at a time until one night they flooded out, and he told Brison of Antietam. Of walking through the mist of a cool September dawn only to submit to hell in a cornfield: a hell of cornstalks and bodies, blood and mangled flesh, the earth's bounty in chaos with the corruption of man in death.

And there had been epic chaos since then, at Fredericksburg and Chancellorsville, and the papers told of a siege at Vicksburg in Mississippi—when that city fell, the river would be open to New Orleans. Yet it seemed to Prescott, as he fought exhaustion in the pale light that brought definition to the trees, that Lee was the force Washington had to subdue. And that task now belonged to another new general, George Meade—so the papers had said yesterday.

"Too many generals," Brison had said. Lincoln shuffled them "like pies at a county fair, presenting the one that looked best according to the person's tastes standing before the table." Now another new general was taking command hours before a fight. Brison seemed melancholy at the thought. The fight was approaching—it was only a matter of where and how soon.

As they turned onto York Street and moved toward the Diamond, there were people moving about on their early Tuesday morning chores. Brison led Prescott's horse, and he noticed that the lieutenant was almost asleep in his saddle as they turned south onto Baltimore Street.

Within a few minutes, they were at the Wagon Hotel, and Brison moved Prescott into the bedroom still reserved from four days ago. A few quick questions, and Brison learned Stallard had not returned yet. The clerk asked if a doctor was needed, but Brison begged off for the present and helped Prescott up the stairs and into the room. Prescott was asleep shortly, beginning to mumble with restlessness and fever.

Brison went downstairs and sent word along for the doctor who had treated him to come by and see Prescott. The messenger boy said the Rebels were coming down from Cashtown and the Gettysburg folks were in an uproar. The doctor arrived after an hour. It was near noon when he came out of the room.

"He had a rough time of it," the doctor said. "You said you both rode down from Harrisburg yesterday and through the night?"

"We had no choice," Brison admitted.

"There are always different choices when a man's life is at stake." A tinge of rebuke.

"Not in times of war, sir." Brison was stern. "Do you think he'll survive?"

"Well, if you can and be on your feet as you are now, then I'd say anyone has a chance with a serious shoulder wound, but a fever has set in. You'll need to keep the cold cloths on him. It's entirely up to him whether he survives."

The doctor offered no other comfort and left.

Brison had just reached the balcony of the hotel when he heard the thunder of approaching cavalry and walked around the corner in time to see half a regiment sweep past the hotel and turn up Baltimore Street and the center of town. Brison recognized the regimental flag as being the 17th Pennsylvania, belonging to a brigade in the 1st Division. Brison didn't know the brigade commander, but he knew the commanding general. They had been good friends before the war.

John Buford was here.

"You have but a few minutes, Andrew," Buford said. He ran his hand through his hair and dropped his hat onto the bench just outside the Lutheran Seminary. He appeared fatigued, a look that stayed with a soldier for long stretches when the sleep attained is never enough. "There's going to be a hell of a fight here tomorrow, and the rest of the army isn't up yet."

They were seated near the main entrance to the seminary with much activity about them, and while Brison spoke, they were interrupted four times by couriers, and Buford was forced to have Brison pause while writing a response. He had a dark complexion with a hint of gray in his mustache, as there was in his eyes. There was a heavy crease lining each side of his nose, and his overall appearance carried the mantle of a beaten-down but still persistent fighter. He completed his message and let Brison continue.

Brison passed over the details of the trip west and Chicago, but concentrated only on the importance of keeping the Rebels out of the town and, particularly, south of it. He detailed the gold shipment and that Stallard was probably attached to a Rebel unit as they spoke. He finished by stressing to the general the importance of secrecy, as that was what the president had wanted.

Buford listened with patience, but when he responded, his words carried the note of finality.

"You say the gold is well hidden, but you yourself don't know its location?" he said. "And of the only two men alive who know the location, one is unconscious with a fever here in town and the other is sitting a couple of miles up the road there." He pointed north and west. "Andrew, there's more at stake here than the prospect of keeping funds from Jeff Davis. And I cannot allow myself to be concerned with that issue. I can only, and must only, concern myself with what is coming tomorrow. We're standing here because we'll have the good ground. I cannot dictate strategy on information I cannot confirm."

"This issue is of the utmost importance to the president, John," Brison pleaded.

"I dare say the president should be more concerned that his army is not destroyed as it comes up," Buford snapped back. He paused, stood, and paced a few steps in two directions and then stopped. "Tomorrow morning, just a few hours from now, I believe Lee's main body will be coming down that road over there. I've got my men lined up along a creek, backed up by a pair of ridges. We have to hold here while the rest of the army comes up from Frederick. I have no time for this. When the fight is over and opportunity arrives, I'll relay your needs to General Meade. We'll secure the gold, and you can ride on the train with it all the way to hell as far as I'm concerned. I suggest you take your sick friend and stay indoors, or, better, move him to the east. There's going to be a damnable fight here."

Stallard rode behind the two Confederate escorts, who in turn were trailing behind the commander of the 2nd Division, Major General Henry Heth, and his 1st Brigade commander, J. Johnston Pettigrew. They were traveling through the army on their way to see A.P. Hill, and it was Stallard's hope that they would convince him to allow a press into Gettysburg.

It had been a day of frustration for Stallard. Hill had sent him along to Heth's camp, and he had slept but a scant three hours before he was roused. With no details of his reason for being with the brigade, Heth had sent him, with his two escorts, along the Chambersburg Pike with Pettigrew, ostensibly to look for a storage barn with shoes they had learned was in town. Stallard had no knowledge of a business that would have this size of footwear in storage, but in his own best interests, he thought better of adding his opinion.

They had proceeded and approached Gettysburg, only to find troops along a creek bank west of the town. Much to Stallard's consternation, Pettigrew decided to turn his brigade around and move away from the resistance. Pressed for a reason by Stallard, Pettigrew indignantly told him that the orders from General Lee were to avoid conflict with the enemy until the entire army was together, and he, Pettigrew, didn't know what was in front of him.

The news brought great concern to Stallard. If there were Federal troops in Gettysburg, then Prescott and Brison would have the manpower to move the gold out by train. It would be lost.

They arrived at Hill's headquarters and immediately were before the 3rd Corps' commander. It was the three of them—Hill, Heth, and Pettigrew, with Stallard standing off to the side.

Heth was agitated, stressing to Hill that his division needed the shoes General Early had not confiscated a few days earlier upon going through the town. Upon Heth's insistence, Pettigrew repeated what his brigade had encountered west of Gettysburg.

"I'm of the opinion, General, that those may have been cavalry troopers, but it's possible infantry may have been there, as well, coming up, and since General Lee's desire was to avoid a direct engagement, I thought it was prudent to withdraw," Pettigrew said.

"General, some of our men are walking without shoes and feeling mighty poorly about it," Heth stressed. "When the fight comes, they will be in fine spirits if they have leather on their feet. Those shoes are there for us to acquire with ease. Those troops could only be perhaps a patrol of cavalry or militia. We can sweep them aside and go about our business."

Both men waited for a response. Hill was standing with his hands behind his back, looking more piqued. He glanced over at Stallard, who at first looked questioningly at Hill, but then realized that the general was looking for a sign from him, and so he nodded once. Hill nodded in response and then declared, "The only force at Gettysburg is cavalry, probably a detachment of observation. The

Federals are most likely still down in Maryland and haven't struck their tents."

"If there's no objection, General," Heth interjected quickly, "I'll take my division tomorrow, go to Gettysburg, and get those shoes."

Said Hill, "None in the world."

Chapter Forty-One

Present Day
August 3

The SUV fishtailed, the dirt road wash-boarded in places, and Sparks fought the vehicle's desire to slide off into the field on either side. The exertion back at the house had left him sweating, and drops were falling off his brow. He wiped his eyes with his shoulder, one at a time. He was just seconds from the main road, and he looked to see what traffic was around.

The dust from his own rental, with Griffin and Jennifer inside, still remained at the intersection, and Sparks could see the sedan off to the left, accelerating down the ridge. Sparks slid the SUV to the left and hit the pavement as quickly as he dared while still keeping control.

The jolt bounced his head against the headrest and elicited an unexpected expletive from the back seat. Sparks gained control and slammed the accelerator, then brought his gun up with his left hand. Even in the darkness, he could make out Streeter's face. "What the hell are you doing here?" Sparks yelled.

Streeter put his hands up in mock surrender. "I thought you might need some assistance, plus there was a lot of shooting going on back there, and I thought it might be best for old Streeter to get away. Too many bullets flying around."

"Bullshit." Sparks dropped the gun into his lap and put both hands on the wheel. "I don't give a damn about you for the moment."

Sparks was having a difficult time closing in on Griffin's car. They moved past two other cars heading, like them, into town. Even after 10 p.m., the narrow streets would be filled with traffic, and some would have cars parked on either side—not an easy area to elude a pursuing car. Griffin couldn't be trying to get lost in town. Then, Sparks knew what Griffin would do.

"He'll turn off here soon," Sparks said, not realizing that Streeter had crawled over into the front seat. They were coming down the Chambersburg Pike—Griffin's car was slowed by oncoming traffic, and he couldn't get around cars in front of him. Sparks was just two hundred feet behind Griffin when a van pulled in front of him from the right. Sparks braked hard and swung the SUV onto the shoulder, but there was too steep a ditch to the right. He brought the SUV back onto the road and tried to pass, but he was thwarted by the same line of oncoming traffic.

"Too much traffic," Streeter said. "Where will he go?"

"He wants to get south of town and head for the interstate heading back into Washington. I don't know what he's thinking, and that's what scares me to hell. He's not rational—he spent too many years doing good work to destroy it."

"He said something about a tumor?"

"Possibility," Sparks said, then he pointed to the right. "That's it!"

"What?"

"He's going to go through the park and bypass the town."

Griffin's car crossed over a sidewalk and grass and cut the corner, turning right and moving quickly past yet more traffic. Seconds later, Sparks made the same move, though having to swerve around an additional pickup truck. They had turned onto Seminary Avenue and were now passing by what was once the Lutheran Seminary on their right, its white cupola visible, illuminated from the lights below.

July 1, 1863

Brison stood off to the side from where General Buford watched through glasses at the battle, now in full fight, spread out before them to the west and north of town. The *boom* of cannon fire and the crackling spit of rifles created staccatos through the air.

The morning had begun with a light rain, but the clouds had given way to an oppressive sun, burning off the mist hanging in the shallow depressions of earth laid out before Brison and Buford, standing as they were in the cupola of the Lutheran Seminary. It provided a perfect view of the battlefield before them. Brison could not tell whether either side had an advantage, but Buford's manner reeked of anxiousness.

"Where the devil is Reynolds?" Buford said quietly. He turned to look east at the town and beyond. It was near enough 8:30 a.m., and the fighting had gone on for three hours. Buford received a message from a soldier who had climbed up the ladder into the cupola.

Brison had already decided he was going to check on Prescott and move him east or south of town, out of the way of the fighting, when Buford issued an emphatic, "Damn! Everyone down," as he climbed down the ladder.

Brison followed, and as he reached the ladder's base, he heard a voice from below.

"What's the matter, John?" It was a sharp-looking officer on a fine horse. His presence was immediately felt by the soldiers next to Brison. He heard one of them whisper that it was General Reynolds.

"The devil's to pay," Buford replied, taking his hat off and wiping his forehead.

"Do you mean that you cannot hold the town?" Reynolds asked.

"I reckon I can." Buford's face had lightened, and he continued down to meet up with the commander of the 1st Corps.

Brison touched Buford on the shoulder. "General, with your permission, I'll see to the lieutenant I'm traveling with," Brison said.

Buford only nodded and kept going.

They reached outside the building on the main grounds. As Brison went to his horse, he heard Reynolds give a message to an aide intended for General Meade. "Tell him the enemy are advancing in strong force, and I fear they will get to the heights beyond the town before I can. fight them inch by inch, and if driven into the town, barricade the streets and hold them back as long as possible. Go, man, as fast as your horse will take you."

The words from Reynolds galvanized Brison, and he charged off on his own horse, heading for the Wagon Hotel at the south end of Baltimore Street.

In just minutes, he was there. The streets were empty of civilians, the sound of battle driving them inside.

Brison reached the hotel's entrance and ran into Prescott coming out the door, adjusting his sidearm. "Jesus, Jack! What are you doing?"

"What's the word from the field?" Prescott nodded toward the battle sounds.

"Our cavalry has been holding west of town, and there's infantry coming up from the south." Brison pointed up the Baltimore Pike as the lead men coming at double quick chose that moment to charge down the hill. "There's going to be a hell of a fight here. I've got to get you out of town."

"He'll do one of two things, Andrew," Prescott said. "He'll stay with the lead brigades and push through the town—"

"What'll he do if the whole Union Army ends up sitting along this ridge and the town?" Brison interrupted.

"—or he'll figure the army is coming up from Maryland and his best chance of getting the gold would be to get it himself, and he'll do it himself before the army entrenches itself along the line."

"Now? Won't he wait for the fight to die down? Will he have time to load it?"

"He's practical, but not so much so. He knows this fight just might be the last one. In either outcome, it would benefit him and the Confederacy if he had the gold in hand. The fight sounds like it's west and north of town. We'll take hold of the town now and hold it with our backs against this good, high ground here. The fight should stay out there. That means troops will be feeding along these main roads, but the area with the gold might be overlooked."

"Jack, I was on my back. You've never told me exactly where the gold is hidden."

"A mile and a half down that way." Prescott pointed south, but left of the Emmitsburg Road. "We have got to get there now."

Brison grabbed Prescott's arm. "Neither you nor I are in shape for a fight. My shoulder is burning to beat all hell, and I imagine your arm and shoulder are in the same shape. Plus, you've had a fever, which I suspect is still with you. I talked with General Buford. He knows me, and he believed my story, but he rightly made the decision not to concern himself with an unconfirmed report. He had to fight what was in front of him. Stallard is out there sitting with the whole Army of Northern Virginia. He'll let them do his work, and he'll clean up after this is all over."

Prescott said, "He knows we're over here."

Brison looked to the ground as he thought. "He'll go for it now, won't he?"

"As soon as he realizes the Rebels aren't just facing local militia. He has to. He has no other choice."

"Then neither do we."

Present Day
August 3

Griffin's car accelerated through the intersection with Route 116, the Hagerstown Road, and moved onto West Confederate Avenue, the lane traveling down Seminary Ridge to the south and west—what was once the Rebels' battle line. Sparks hit his brakes and slid through the same intersection to avoid crossing traffic, regained control, and accelerated his SUV onto the unlit road.

"He can't believe he can slip past an alert, does he?" Streeter asked, looking around for a seat belt.

Focused on the road and the taillights a hundred yards ahead, Sparks didn't respond.

"Do you have a plan? Is your backup at the house calling in the troops?"

"Yes, but I left the location of roadblocks to the locals," Sparks said. "Where they'll be posted is a guess. All I can hope is that Clark realizes he can only go so far, even with Jennifer. God, I can't believe he would harm her."

The pursuit continued down the avenue, a tree-lined, narrow road with numerous monuments and display markers. Sparks glanced down at the speedometer. It said seventy-five miles an hour, but with the darkness and the trees on either side, it felt like they were going well over a hundred.

Griffin's taillights disappeared as the road took a left bend. Seconds later, Sparks took the same bend and got the lights again. He was closing slightly, hands wet on the wheel. They sped past an observation tower and onto a long straightaway.

"I've been here, just a few days ago," Sparks exclaimed. "The Emmitsburg Road is coming up. He'll turn right onto it—that's Route 15, and it will take him south down to the interstate."

Sparks was now within two hundred feet again, closing the distance.

Griffin's lights flashed and the sedan fishtailed right, then left, then right again before settling on a straight line, and Sparks could see why. A quartet of police cruisers blocked the route south at the intersection of West Confederate and the state road. Sparks slammed his foot onto the brake pedal to avoid rear-ending Griffin, and Streeter yelled "Watch it!", throwing his hand onto the dashboard even though he had found the belt.

The right front tire of Sparks's vehicle dropped off the pavement, and he fought to keep control as he decelerated, but Griffin was already pulling away as he charged through the intersection and swerved around the lone fifth cruiser that blocked the continuation of Confederate Avenue.

"The gate!" Sparks cried. But Griffin had seen the single, steel-bar gate and steered around it through the heavy grass on the side, returning to the road on the other side. Again, Sparks put the pedal on the floor and repeated what Griffin had just done. The SUV went airborne for an instant as they returned to the road.

"Jesus! I should have stayed back at the house," Streeter barked. "We're headed back to Little Round Top."

"He'll have to slow down. It's too dangerous on these curves. He's running out of options."

"He can turn right between the hills and cut over to a main road to the east," Streeter said.

"How do you know that?"

"I scouted it before I set up the meeting with you tonight."

"Or he could turn left or head straight," Sparks lamented. "He could weave himself all over these park roads."

"There are many ways this can end badly." Streeter's voice was so soft Sparks didn't hear it over the wind.

July 1, 1863

Prescott and Brison didn't bother taking the Emmitsburg Road and instead took the Baltimore Pike, cutting against the horde of troops trying to move up to the fight. Prescott winced as they varied between a canter and a gallop through the Federal troops. Many asked what was up ahead, and Brison replied often that it was going to be a hell of a fight. He was without a uniform, but he still commanded a presence in the saddle. The men held their faces up, looking up at him into the morning sun, and asked the question time and again. Prescott wondered how many of these men would be dead at day's end—and then his thoughts returned to Antietam.

After a while, they turned off the pike and headed across land, picking their way through the fields and tree groves, crossing the Taneytown Road at one point. Prescott told Brison they would be coming in from the northeast of the hiding spot. Brison had loaded his Spencer and readied his ammunition pouch. Their plan was simple: they would get near the hiding place and wait for a Federal officer of high rank who would assign a detail to take the gold, or they would stop Stallard themselves. They came upon the east side of a small hill, just to the north of a more prominent hill.

"We're almost to Little Round Top," Prescott said. "We're near the gold. If he's bringing wagons to try to slip in and out without detection, he'll have to pick his way along some bad ground."

They slowed to a walk, picking their way through the woods on the east side of Little Round Top. Prescott was holding his bad shoulder lower, appearing ready to fall from the saddle. They approached the top of the hill, where the tree line stopped. Brison was about to say something when Prescott held up his good arm and grabbed for him.

"He's already here," Prescott said.

Brison could see that across a small valley to the west of their position was a large grouping of huge boulders. The remaining ground was littered with rocks of all sizes, tossed about the ground like a child's spilled marble bag. He let his breath escape through his lips. He could see two wagons with five men visible sitting atop the seats. They were moving slowly, finding places to negotiate the terrain.

"Terrible ground," Brison said. "I'm glad the fight is up north."

Prescott didn't respond for a minute. Finally, he turned to Brison. "This is what we need to do."

Present Day
August 3

Anxiety churned Sparks's stomach as he tried to keep pace with Griffin's car. It would only be seconds before they reached the next intersection, in the saddle between Big and Little Round Tops. These roads were designed for tourists to drive at slow speeds in daylight, not for a chase in the dark, and Sparks could tell that Griffin was having difficulty controlling the car, dropping wheels onto the dirt shoulders and weaving to regain control on the surface. Sparks ached with what Jennifer must be going through, pleading with Griffin to stop the madness.

Griffin's car slowed at a sharp left turn, descending into the small notch between the two hills. Sparks, trailing, lost sight for a second, then hit his brakes hard as Griffin's car came into view at the intersection.

"He's turning!" Streeter said.

Griffin slid the car into the turn and went sideways onto Warren Avenue, which extended through the southern portion of the

Valley of Death and met up with Crawford Avenue, which swung through Devil's Den. In the valley, Griffin accelerated yet again. To avoid losing the SUV in a ditch, Sparks slowed considerably and lost distance.

"He can't keep up those speeds. Too many sharp turns around," Sparks said.

"He's going to lose it!" Streeter yelled.

Sparks muttered an "Oh, God" as he watched Griffin's car swerve first to the right, then cut sharply to the left onto Crawford Avenue, and then lose control. The car slid sideways, kicking up dirt and scraping one of the Den's boulders before spinning around and slamming into a tree in the small parking area. They knew they would be approaching Griffin's car in seconds, but already Sparks saw the FBI director pulling Jennifer from the car and leading her across the road and into the rocks of Devil's Den.

July 1, 1863

Stallard had been given four soldiers by A.P. Hill, and they were pulled from Heth's division. The four—three privates and a captain—were furious at being taken from duty as the corps went into battle, especially as the morning unfolded and it was clear they were facing regular Federal troops. Stallard's decision had been quick—time was valuable, and he needed to risk an attempt.

With two wagons, they had swung southwest of the Emmitsburg Road as the fighting continued to the north. Federal troops were visible along the ridge to the east, flooding north to the town and beyond. The four had tried to procure the equipment they would need and clothes that would allow them to pass as local farmers should they run into Federals.

The area was filled with Union troops—they could see activity north of them as they picked their way through the south rocks of Devil's Den. Stallard lined himself up with the large flat boulder with a prominent apex and led the two wagons with teams up the little road he had come down with Prescott just days ago. They had just started across the marshy field next to a stream when they heard orders barked from just behind them and to the right.

"Parker! Halt the teams!"

Stallard knew the voice and pulled his wagon to a stop, turning in his seat. Prescott stood next to the boulder he had risen from, a cavalry carbine awkwardly held to his good shoulder. Stallard could see the stance and aim weren't steady.

"This isn't going to happen," Prescott continued. "God knows I wish it could be different. A man should be allowed to reap the rewards of his labors, and what lies here belongs to your family. But you aren't trying to take it to them, are you?"

"You know what I'm about, Jack," Stallard said. "I can assume Brison has his Spencer on us?"

"You can."

Stallard looked around for a moment, only making half an effort. "The fight up there's what's going to determine the future, not you or I. We worked hard, risked our lives . . . killed some men over what's here. A lot of blood and sorrow to waste and end up in Abe's coffers." There was an increase in cannon fire from the north—the battle was fully joined. "In the end, I owe my brother, Charles, for his efforts in the territories."

Prescott shifted his weight, the gun becoming heavy, and his eyes finding it hard to focus. He felt unbearably hot with the morning sun fully on his back. "That's not all there is to our story," Prescott said. "The name of the spy in the Federal government. Your contact with Washington, Parker."

"The gold was always secondary." Stallard nodded. "Of course." He paused for a moment. "I regret your efforts will be in vain."

"You'll stand trial."

"I'll not betray Richmond."

The captain next to Stallard swung around and fired his pistol in the same motion as Stallard cried out for him to stop. There was a double report as two weapons fired together and the captain toppled from his seat. The three soldiers in the second wagon turned to see a man standing on the other side, swinging his carbine around to them.

The first private tried to bring up his pistol from beside him, but failed as Brison's second shot caught him in the chest. His two companions saved their lives by jumping down and crouching behind the wagon. Brison turned his attention back to Stallard, but the southerner was gone.

"Stallard!" Brison slipped behind the boulder. "I have a better position, and I can wait you out all day. You'll never get the gold, and the entire Federal army will be camping out around here in a few hours. Your chance is gone."

An answer came in the form of a bullet hitting a boulder to his side—more of an angry response than a threat. Brison could not tell if Prescott had been hit, but there was no fire coming from the valley.

The battle continued with its noise unabated, and so Brison began to work his way around, hoping to come in at Stallard from the front. When he could see the wagons clearly again, the lead one was moving as someone was guiding the team, shielded by the animals. Appearing from behind the rocks, Brison jumped down and fired at the feet of the animals, hoping to get them to run. He fired the first shot and was locking another cartridge home when a voice snapped his spine.

"Drop your rifle!" Stallard ordered.

Brison realized that as he had worked his way around to the north, Stallard, instead of trying to escape, had taken an aggressive move and circled around behind him. The Union colonel was tired and hurting, and he knew he had made a mistake. And soldiers rarely got a second chance.

Present Day
August 3

The headlights from Griffin's car cast a ghostly pall over the huge boulders, shadows cutting into the recesses. The trees, driven by a breeze, moved their arms as if beckoning Sparks and Streeter as they slid their car into the parking area and skidded to a stop. With the engine off, they were greeted by only the wind through the leaves and a single exclamation from Jennifer that came from somewhere above them in the rocks.

"Clark . . . let her go," Sparks shouted. He looked at Streeter standing by the car, reloading a clip into the pistol. "I'd rather you stay out of this."

"No chance. I told your daughter I would deliver her out of this, and I always keep my word," Streeter said. "You know this area?"

"Devil's Den. I was here just days ago. That path swings up and around."

"He'll be on top."

"I'll take the main path—you follow the road, swing around, and come up from the back," Sparks said.

Streeter nodded and was gone, moving along the base of the boulders.

Remembering his walk around the Den, Sparks knew it would take Streeter a few minutes to be in position, but he couldn't wait any longer. He crouched as he ran up to the base of the boulders, next to the flat sentry with its apex pointed to the northeast, across the Valley of Death—as if pointing in the direction the Rebels had been headed as they swept into the valley.

He began his climb, feeling the stone's coolness as he braced himself, shifting his eyes, looking for any movement. The wind was a blessing and a curse—he couldn't hear any movement from ahead, but Griffin wouldn't be able to hear him, either. Keeping low and on the balls of his feet, Sparks moved along until he reached the crest of the rocks. This was the south end of Houck's Ridge. The light from the car spilled up from below, but Sparks's visibility remained poor. He could only continue to pick his way along until he got close.

July 1, 1863

"Drop the rifle, then the cartridge belt," Stallard said coldly. "Then lay down on the ground away from the rifle."

Brison turned slightly so that he could see Stallard. He was just twenty feet away. Brison kept hold of the rifle in his right hand and bent his knees to place it on the ground, buying more time to keep it in his hand. He would have to try it. There was no choice, and though he was a better marksman than Stallard, he knew his chance was feeble. Just as he was about to swing around and try to get a shot off, a cry came from the valley.

"Parker!"

The South Carolinian would not have been human had he not turned his head to the sound of Prescott's voice, and that was the split second Brison needed. He spun on his heel, and without aiming or even bringing his left hand to the stock, he fired, knocking Stallard off his feet, then continued on until he leveled the rifle on the Confederate privates with the first wagon.

"Just bide your time right there," he said.

The privates, not knowing what to do, nodded and slumped to the ground next to the wagon, apparently satisfied with their safe capture. Brison looked to Prescott, but only saw his partner lying facedown in the grass. He hurried over into the field and bent over the lieutenant, who was bubbling blood from his mouth—the Rebel captain's quick shot had caught Prescott in the lung.

"Hold on, Jack, I'll get you to a corps doctor straightaway," Brison said.

Prescott was calm, but he grabbed the collar of Brison's jacket. He struggled to speak. "Tell . . . Abby . . . I'm sorry . . . and tell her to walk on the beach for me."

"I'll tell her myself, Jack. You have my word."

Prescott smiled for a moment, and squeezed Brison's arm, and then he was gone.

Brison put him back in the grass and leaned back on his knees, trying to calm himself. In a minute, he walked back to where Stallard lay and knelt by him. His shot had gotten Stallard clean in the heart—the southerner was dead before he had fallen to the ground.

Present Day
August 3

Sparks was naked unto the night, and Griffin would be able to gun him down. The irony was poignant. His life was in the hands of a man clearly sent to the brink, while his deliverance was in the hands of a hired assassin. Sparks moved along the path, crouched for any margin of advantage he could garner. He searched the darkness for Streeter as much as for Griffin, and he would later admit to a feeling of hope that Streeter would take a bullet first and give him a chance to take Griffin down.

From just off to the right, he was shocked frozen by the sound of Jennifer's voice crying out, followed by the report of three shots grouped together, just like he had taught her on the range. He flinched with the reports, as if the bullets had struck him. And then he was running into the dark, away from the light, and into his past, looking for his future.

He found her kneeling over Griffin's body, sobbing. She clung to him when he reached her, and the tears poured unabated. He took the gun from her hand. It was the small-caliber Beretta he had slipped to her from his ankle holster a few hundred yards away and a lifetime ago.

Epilogue

August 20, 1863

They sat in the dark, outside of the main residence. The president was eating an apple, and his companion, with permission, was smoking a cigar—not to celebrate anything, but only to pass the time. The words spoken carried no rebuke.

"Your story is quite remarkable. One would do well, I think, to show confidence in our intelligence efforts," Lincoln took off his suit jacket and laid it across the railing. The yellowish light from inside the mansion gave his face deeper creases. Brison saw how much the president had aged in the eleven months since their last meeting.

"Mr. President, I appreciate your kind words . . . but Lieutenant Prescott and I failed," Brison said. "The conspiracy didn't succeed, yes, but the gold itself is missing these seven weeks, and Stallard and Prescott—the two men alone who knew the gold's location—died within minutes of each other. Fitzroy has made no suspicious movements since the battle, and we're no closer to finding out whom Stallard was in contact with here in Washington."

"You sound like myself when one of my generals misses an opportunity," Lincoln mused. "The victory becomes impossible when you miss that first chance. If the conspirators had been able to ship that gold to England, the influence could have tied up the political situation. The riots in New York are an example of how we wrestle with this conflict. Gettysburg was a great victory, and Vicksburg's falling was supremely important, but your work was, indeed, important—not for what occurred, but for what you prevented from occurring. The fight is often won by this caveat."

"But what of the traitor in your administration?" Brison almost whispered.

"That's why our efforts will need to be directed down a different path. And that's why we haven't arrested Cassias Fitzroy. He'll be watched, but I cannot afford the scandal an official inquiry, arrest, and trial would bring upon my administration. I had hoped we could have captured the conspirators and extracted the information, then shown them all to the people. The sting of political retribution would have been eased. There's an election next fall."

"And what of Jackson Prescott? Must he be remembered as a traitor?"

"For now, I'm saddened to say yes."

"For the same reasons you just spoke?"

"Those are the issues we face."

"And what of the gold?" Brison asked. "I have a general idea of its location. We have searched, but it was also the site of some of the battle's most intense fighting. We have searched nearby houses, barns, and sheds. We should continue the search . . ."

"Perhaps it was already moved?"

"This Stallard could have contacted others, sympathizers in the North, this Knights of the Golden Circle group."

"I'll accept that risk. You mentioned in your report that Stallard's body was lost during the battle, when the town was taken by General Lee's forces."

"My responsibility, sir. I had taken it, along with two Rebel prisoners and Lieutenant Prescott's body, into town, when I met our corps coming back at me through the town. The fighting was difficult, and men were stumbling through closed-in alleys and such. A surly scrap, sir. I had put the wagon in an alley briefly, but had to scramble for my life with the rest. I spent the next two days of the battle in our lines, with General Meade's permission, and upon our retaking the town when the Rebels pulled back, I couldn't locate them. Nor were they marked on any official lists. Many of the dead were buried without their identities, sir. I fear that's what happened to them."

"Unfortunate."

"Another of my errors in judgment, sir. It's why I'll be asking for a transfer. I have a desire to join a fighting unit. My work here has been less than exemplary."

Lincoln gazed at the flowered tree next to the porch, then reached out for a bloom. Brison felt the president was considering his request. "Your decisions were shaped by the latitude I presented Lieutenant Prescott. By your own account, you saved his life on three occasions. You have proved invaluable, and I'll have other assignments for you. I need men like you who can move outside the regular military and political arenas, and I promise you, I'll bring you back to Gettysburg to complete your task. Just not now."

"Yes, sir," Brison said and paused before continuing. "I do have an additional request. I would like to take a few days to notify someone of the lieutenant's death. Privately . . . and I can assure you of her silence."

"A relative?"

"If time had allowed."

Present Day
August 5

A thunderstorm had swept through during the night and a comfortable morning was greeting Sparks and Anderson as they stood in the valley between Little Round Top and Devil's Den. The sun was not yet above the trees to the east, but the crew was already working on clearing a century of dirt and growth from around one particular diabase boulder.

There were no tourists, as the park was, strangely, closed on what would normally be a busy August day. Sparks surveyed the line from Table Top Rock, the boulder that sits atop what was known as the Den. A sharp corner of it pointed to the northeast, through the

Valley of Death, and across to a point just northwest of Little Round Top's summit. There, on the north side, they dug. The letter from Stallard to Fitzroy had said only that Lawrence Stallard would be coming north after the war . . .

Lawrence has the town and the land where the shipment can be found. You have the location: On the land owned by Houck, take the rock that points northeast and forge a line through the valley five hundred and forty-five paces to a rock on the north side of the next hill. You will find my initials on the southern side, below the earth line. Use a team to pull the rock back, and you will find what you will find. God bless you both.

Parker

"I wonder if Stallard ever knew that the land he chose would become hallowed ground," Sparks commented. "The most hallowed ground of the war."

"We'll know as soon as they pull back that boulder. It must be three, four tons," Anderson said. "Did you talk to Jen?"

"She's at the hospital, sedated to let her sleep. I spoke to her before, and she was pretty shaken. She's been through more than anyone should have to be."

"Any problem with the locals?"

"There'll be no charges," Sparks said. "She acted to save a life."

"The press is going to run with this when they get it. You going to insulate her?"

"As best I can . . ."

"And the story will be . . ."

"That FBI director Clark Griffin, taking personal charge of the investigation into the kidnapping of an agent's daughter, was tragically killed, as were other special agents, in a shootout with criminal elements tied to Boston financier Jonathan Richardson."

"And that will fly?" Anderson raised his eyebrows.

"I have a team cleaning up the details. Clark's family deserves his honor intact—and his pension."

They walked over to where the crew was strapping grappling hooks over the top and to the base of the boulder, now uncovered thirty inches below the soil level. The letters *P* and *S* were clearly chiseled into the rock on the side facing south. Sparks and Anderson moved so they were on the hill above the boulder.

"And what happened to Streeter?" Anderson asked.

"As I was leading Jen away, he appeared, running up from where I had sent him. He was going to be there for us. He saw that Jen was safe, and then disappeared."

"You let him go."

"He saved Jen's life twice. For a father, that can absolve many sins."

"No trouble by my account."

Sparks's cell phone beeped. He expected the voice on the other end.

"I trust your daughter is safe and you have found the gold." It was Streeter.

"Yes on the first—we're about to find out on the second in a moment. They're pulling back the boulder the gold is supposed to be under."

"Keep me on the line, would you? I would like to live vicariously . . ."

The heavy earth-mover pulled against the chains, and the boulder eased out of its home with surprising ease. Sparks and Anderson were peering down into the hole as Munson approached from the summit and moved to stand next to them.

Underneath the great boulder was a row of rotten wooden boxes. When the boulder was safely out of position, Sparks stepped down and pulled the remnants of a top off the nearest box. Inside were neatly placed golden bars. He held one up to Anderson and Munson. "Parker Stallard's shipment," he said simply.

"Where will it go and who does it belong to?" Munson said.

"I'm afraid the lawyers will have to decide that one," Sparks said. "Tracy Coulthard will have her attorneys filing motions before the day is over."

"A lot of people died for this," Anderson said.

"Greed leads the way," Sparks said. He made to speak into the cell phone, but Streeter was gone. *So be it—don't ever cross my path again.*

August 9

Jennifer held on to her father's arm as they stood near the observation tower on Little Round Top. Their view was across the Valley of Death and to the west as the sun set, nestled in with the clouds, casting a brilliant red and orange hue on the battlefield. They were nearly alone, save a few tourists milling about taking photographs. Jennifer put her head on his shoulder and squeezed his arm.

"You feeling better tonight?" he asked. "I was surprised you wanted to come by here before we left."

"I believe in facing your fears."

Sparks smiled. "That's my girl." He let the moment continue for a time before he spoke again. "When is the service?"

"It's Friday afternoon," she said. "I owe it to Bret and his family."

"I'm sorry I never got to meet him."

"Me, too."

"Would you mind terribly if your dad came along with you? I want to meet his family."

"Absolutely." She squeezed his arm again, and he responded by putting his arm around her shoulder. "I love you, Dad."

"I love you, Jen. In triplicate."

September 17, 1863

The air carried a cool, salty taste—a welcome change from the hot summer of the war, now so far away. Then again, Brison realized, he himself had brought it to this Massachusetts beach. Stinson was quietly crying into his shoulder, her face buried while the wind swept her hair around his face. He had dreaded this day coming, had tried to practice what words would comfort.

Yet it was unnecessary, for when she saw him approach on the beach, she had known his reason for coming.

Brison thought of his own wife and three children and how they might be had someone walked into their world to tell them he was gone. The emptiness he felt was like gasping the frigid air for breath on a winter morning. After a time, Stinson separated from him and wiped away her tears. She composed herself and calmly asked the questions that needed asking.

"His name back—he must receive his name, his honor back," she said after a time.

"I implored Mr. Lincoln to do just that, but we must wait until the war is over and politics allows."

"They took his life—must they also take his honor? It's the only thing a man has in death."

"I know. But it would be enough for Jackson that if he had nothing else, he had your love. And since he knew, he had enough at the end."

"Were you with him?" she asked.

"He said to tell you he was sorry for not coming back to you. And"—Brison looked up along the shore—"he said to take a walk on the beach for him."

"I'll travel to Washington and see Mr. Lincoln. I'll demand he clear Jackson's name."

"I know."

"He'll not be forgotten."

"Let's take that walk for him."

She nodded and took his arm. Brison felt her exhale as if to clear away the sorrow from within, and he knew he had to do the same. He would go and see his family, hold them in his arms, and steel himself for the time in the near future when he would face the war again. But for right now, on this day, he would help begin mending one broken soul.

And so she let him lead her north along the beach as September's wind brought foam as bright as snow onto the sand.

Afterword

This story came about after what could be called a very unconventional journey. The idea came about while sitting at a card table in a very Cuban household in the Miami suburb of Westchester in 1998. Inspiration came from a humid July day among giant diabase boulders in Gettysburg, Pennsylvania, then became an outline while sitting on a back-porch picnic table in Jericho, Vermont. It grew into a rough draft that was shelved, brought back, and shelved again numerous times over the next ten years back in Miami, just in a different suburb.

Then came the economic downturn, more free time, and a writing partner who kept saying, "Just finish the damn thing." So I did. But even then it wasn't a full-time gig, this searching for representation. A regular job had to be found and there was already a new story flying into the laptop.

And then, by chance, after five months, someone saw the story posted on a Web site and expressed interest. And so, a story that percolated from the idea that events from the distant past can affect events now was able to find an audience.

I want to thank Jason Aydelotte of Grey Gecko Press for mining the back streets of the Internet and giving new authors a chance, particularly one middle-aged journalist, and also for his work coordinating the effort after the words were handed in. A thank you goes out to Staci Reed and Nathan Morimitsu for their design work on the cover.

A special thank you goes out to Joyce Sweeney, Christy Phillippe, and Hilary Comfort for their editing skill and encouraging words through the process. No matter how good the writer is, an editor provides the ingredient every writer must have . . . perspective. We see the world through our view, and it's not a clear lens, but a prism of our influences.

Also, a note of thanks to Susana Betancourt for her expertise and counseling.

Next, a preemptive apology. Whenever you have fictional characters intermingling with real historical people, the timeline is always in danger of contamination. At least, that's what all good science fiction tells us. *Beneath Hallowed Ground*'s characters encounter some famous people, and I have tried to accurately blend them in. John Wilkes Booth really was in Chicago in the winter of 1862-63. John Buford was there in Gettysburg on June 30, to set his dismounted cavalry to delay the Confederates moving through the town before the Union's main body moved up the next day. But as with any endeavor, there is a possibility of error, and while I have worked very hard for accuracy, when known history meets fiction, no one is infallible.

Finally, a word of thanks to my parents and grandparents for filling my early years with books.

Steven P. Locklin
January, 2013

About the Author

Steven P. Locklin is presently a freelance editor after having worked as a writer and editor for twenty-eight years with six newspapers in five states—West Virginia, Illinois, Tennessee, Vermont, and Florida. He spent most of his youth growing up in New England—where his family history dates back ten generations—reading every Alistair MacLean, Robert Ludlum, and Clive Cussler novel he could.

For his own adventure novel, he chose the Civil War as the backdrop. An avid history researcher, he is particularly fascinated by the war and the family members who fought in the conflict.

He is presently working on his second novel, a story of redemption for the father of a baseball talent whose career is ended by one ill-fated pitch. A sequel to *Beneath Hallowed Ground* is also in development.

He lives in South Florida with his wife and two sons, four cats, and a dog.

Connect with Steven

Email:	splocklin@gmail.com
Web:	www.greygeckopress.com
Twitter:	@StevenPLocklin
Facebook:	www.facebook.com/StevenPLocklin

Grey Gecko Press

Thank you for purchasing this book from Grey Gecko Press, an independent publishing company that focuses on new and emerging authors, bringing readers the best in fiction and non-fiction at reasonable prices in all formats.

With books in nearly every genre of fiction and non-fiction, there's something for everyone, and you can be sure that buying books from us leads directly to the support of independent authors like Steven Locklin. Grey Gecko pays our authors some of the highest royalty rates in the business and strives to produce only high-quality books.

Visit our website to purchase our titles, pre-order upcoming books at a discount, sign up for our free monthly newsletter, and find out about two great ways to get free books, the Slushpile Reader Program and the Advance Reader Program.

And don't forget: all our print editions come with the ebook absolutely free!

Authors First!

www.greygeckopress.com

store.greygeckopress.com

9 781938 821189